★ ★ ★ FIRE by NIGHT

This book belongs to

Patricia Stebelton

Fire by Night

★ ★ ★

LYNN AUSTIN

BETHANYHOUSE
MINNEAPOLIS MINNESOTA

Cover design by UDG DesignWorks

Published by Bethany House Publishers
11400 Hampshire Avenue South
Bloomington, Minnesota 55438

Bethany House Publishers is a division of
Baker Publishing Group, Grand Rapids, Michigan.

Printed in the United States of America

Library of Congress Cataloging-in-Publication Data

Austin, Lynn N.
Fire by night / by Lynn Austin.
p.cm. — (Refiner's fire)
ISBN 1-55661-443-8 (pbk.)
1. United States—History—Civil War, 1861–1865—Fiction. 2. Passing (Identity)—Fiction. 3. Female friendship—Fiction. 4. Women soldiers—Fiction. 5. Young women—Fiction. 6. Nurses—Fiction. I. Title II. Series: Austin, Lynn N. Refiner's fire.
PS3551.U839F57 2003
813'.54—dc22 2003014248

To Ken
for your encouragement,
support, and love.

Books by

Lynn Austin

FROM BETHANY HOUSE PUBLISHERS

All She Ever Wanted

Eve's Daughters

Hidden Places

Wings of Refuge

REFINER'S FIRE

Candle in the Darkness

Fire by Night

A Light to My Path

CHRONICLES OF THE KINGS

Gods and Kings

Song of Redemption

www.lynnaustin.org

05C

LYNN AUSTIN is the 2002 Christy Award winner for her historical novel *Hidden Places,* and the 2003 Christy Award for *Candle in the Darkness.* In addition to writing, Lynn is a popular speaker at conferences, retreats, and various church and school events. She and her husband have three children and make their home in Illinois.

PART ONE

By day the Lord went ahead of them in a pillar of cloud to guide them on their way and by night in a pillar of fire to give them light. . . .

Exodus 13:21 NIV

Jesus said, "I am the light of the world. Whoever follows me will never walk in darkness, but will have the light of life."

John 8:12 NIV

Chapter One

Bull Run, Virginia
July 21, 1861

The rippling cry split the air like torn cloth. It shivered down Julia Hoffman's spine, making the hair on her neck stand on end. "What was that?" she murmured.

"The Rebels," Uncle Joseph said. "God help us . . . they're attacking." He passed his binoculars up to Reverend Nathaniel Greene, seated in the carriage across from Julia. "Here, Reverend. Just look at them all!"

Julia leaned forward, watching the young minister's face as he pressed the field glasses to his eyes and surveyed the distant battlefield. When Nathaniel spoke, his voice was hushed with awe or maybe fear. "Where did they all come from?"

"What's happening?" Julia asked. "Tell me what's going on."

"Confederate reinforcements have arrived," Uncle Joseph said. "Looks like thousands of them. Is our line going to hold, Reverend?"

"I can't tell." Nathaniel offered the binoculars to Congressman Rhodes, seated beside him. The portly congressman shook his head, rubbing his eyes with the heels of his hands.

"I've gotten sweat in my eyes. Burns like the devil. This blasted heat is too much." He slouched on the seat beside Nathaniel, looking very much like a lump of lard slowly melting in a frying pan.

Empty champagne bottles clinked at his feet.

Julia turned to her uncle, who stood in the dusty road beside the carriage wringing his hands. "I thought you told me we were winning this battle," she said.

"Well . . . we were. But now . . . I don't know where all these Rebels are coming from."

The carriage horses suddenly tensed. They lifted their heads in unison and stared in the direction of the fighting. They had grazed sluggishly along the roadside all afternoon while Julia and the others had watched the battle, but now the pair stopped eating. The hair along the big gelding's spine rose in a ridge, and he whinnied softly, a sound like a shiver.

Julia stood and took the binoculars from Nathaniel. They gave her an excellent view of the two armies fighting in the distance and the battered farmhouse that stood between them. But what she'd thought were stones scattered across the field were clearly fallen soldiers. Dead soldiers. She quickly looked away from them, pointing the glasses toward the horizon. A solid mass of gray marched forward into the clearing, bayonets glinting, crimson flags visible in the wavy heat. Then the binoculars slipped when the carriage lurched, and Julia fell backward against her seat.

"Are you all right?" Uncle Joseph asked her.

"I think so. Here, you can have these glasses back. What's wrong with the horses? Why are they acting this way?" They had grown increasingly restless, capering nervously in place, rocking the carriage. The Negro coachman pulled hard on the reins to hold them steady.

"Sorry, miss," he said. "Must be some horses out there been hurt. Making these ones upset."

Julia had encountered few Negroes during her nineteen years, and most of those had been viewed from a distance—former slaves who'd spoken at the abolition meetings she'd attended with Reverend Greene. There weren't any Negroes back home in her wealthy Philadelphia neighborhood, and she'd certainly never observed one as closely as this coachman. His skin was very black. Glistening with sweat, it reminded her of black satin.

"Yes . . . I can see some fallen horses," Uncle Joseph said, looking through the binoculars again. "A cavalry unit is fighting near Sudley Road."

The carriage rocked as Nathaniel jumped down from it. He was tall and lanky, with the ruddy, freckled look of an overgrown schoolboy in a clerical collar. Julia climbed down to stand beside him. She wished he would take her hand and offer her comfort and reassurance, but he took no notice of her. She watched the steadily mounting activity on the distant battlefield, feeling as uneasy as the horses.

They'd all been here since noon—four hours—and Julia had quickly grown restless. Like the congressman, she hated the sticky Virginia heat that pressed against her like too many sweaty bodies in a crowded bed. Beneath her bonnet, Julia's golden brown hair had escaped from its hairpins, curling damply around her face. But after pleading to come along in the congressman's elegant landau to watch the battle, she hadn't dared complain when she'd grown hot and bored with the distant skirmish. She had tried to engage Nathaniel Greene in conversation—the minister was the real reason she had begged to join the group—but he seemed more interested in talking politics with the men than in conversing with her.

As the hours passed they'd eaten crab cakes and ripe peaches from the picnic basket. The two older men had drunk champagne, cheering with hundreds of other spectators as the Union army slowly pushed the Rebels across the battlefield. "This should teach them a lesson or two," the congressman had said. "Now we'll see how eager they are for war."

"I daresay it will all be over with after today," Uncle Joseph had predicted.

But now the tide of battle had clearly changed. The men appeared worried and no longer confident as they stood silently beside Julia, watching. The intermittent pop and rattle of gunfire grew to a steady clamor, like a storm of hailstones. The smell of sulfur and gunpowder drifted across the field in a haze of smoke. Julia's cousin Robert was fighting out there. Uncle Joseph was surely thinking of his son.

"Do you think we should leave, Joseph?" the congressman asked from his seat in the carriage. "Your niece . . ."

"I'm not afraid," Julia said, even though her legs felt strangely limp and she had to lean against the carriage for support. No one spoke as they watched for another half hour, the flash of exploding rifle fire visible through the smoke. Shouts, screams, and the blare of bugles filled the stagnant air with noise.

The thrill of fear that tingled through Julia was both dreadful and exhilarating. She'd been jealous of her cousin Robert—now Lieutenant Robert Hoffman, a newly commissioned graduate of West Point—as he'd prepared to invade Virginia with the Union Army. She'd pleaded for permission to travel with her aunt and uncle to Washington by train to see him, especially after she'd learned that Reverend Greene would be joining their party. Her cousin and his company of ninety-day volunteers had been certain that the rebellion would end quickly. None of them had wanted to miss out on the excitement—and neither had Julia.

But that excitement now turned to apprehension as she watched the Rebels slowly force the Union army to retreat the entire distance they had advanced. The ground shook with the rumble of booming cannon.

"This is not going well," her uncle murmured.

"Hold your line!" the congressman shouted to the distant troops. "Don't let them push you back!" But the blue-coated line gradually splintered and broke apart before the onslaught of gray. Union soldiers scattered as the field dissolved into chaos.

"Dear God, our men are retreating," Uncle Joseph moaned.

"That's not an orderly retreat," Nathaniel said. "It's a rout."

Julia clutched her uncle's sleeve. "They're coming this way!"

"Stop, confound you! Stop!" the congressman yelled. "Stand and fight!"

Then, above the din of clattering gunfire, an eerie whistling sound sliced the air. A roar like a burst of thunder crashed nearby, followed by another, then another.

"They're shelling us!" Congressman Rhodes cried out.

Nathaniel gripped Julia's arm. "Everyone into the carriage. Quickly!" He propelled her up onto the seat, then helped her uncle.

The congressman's face was pale behind a sheen of sweat. "Driver, let's go! Make haste!" he said. For a long moment the coachman didn't move, his eyes wide and very white against his dark face. "Hurry! Move!" the congressman shouted. "What are you waiting for?"

The coachman finally turned around and snapped the reins. The horses, more than eager to run, lurched forward, throwing Julia backward against the seat. The carriage started down the rutted turnpike toward safety. But dozens of other carriages, coupes, and landaus bearing fleeing spectators already mobbed the road, slowing their progress. Julia turned around to watch the battle as the sounds of warfare grew unmistakably louder: exploding cannon, volleys of gunfire, and the eerie, inhuman scream of the Rebel yell.

Congressman Rhodes suddenly stood, swaying in the jolting carriage, waving an empty champagne bottle at the retreating soldiers. "Stop! Go back! Stand and fight, you cowards!" His orders were lost in the tumult as troops sprinted across the fields toward the river, their panic made worse by the mad flight of everyone around them.

"Please, sir. You'd better sit down," Nathaniel urged as the cannonading grew louder. "Those shells are falling much too close."

"The Rebels are probably trying to destroy the bridge across Bull Run," Uncle Joseph said. "Can't you go any faster, driver?"

"I sure would like to do that, sir, but they all backed up ahead. Everybody try and get across that bridge, same as us."

Julia saw a long line of army wagons with white canvas covers clogging the road ahead. Her carriage made very little progress, then, a few minutes later, stopped altogether. The excitement she'd felt earlier vanished, replaced by horror as fleeing soldiers staggered past, dazed and bleeding, their lips blackened from tearing open their powder cartridges. Sweat and dirt and fear covered their faces. Their abandoned knapsacks and bedrolls littered the road.

"Let us through!" someone shouted. "Please! This man needs help!" Two soldiers hurried past the stalled carriage, supporting a third man, whose bloodied foot dangled from his leg. Julia quickly looked away.

A hundred feet ahead, a tangle of vehicles and pushing, shoving men jammed the bridge. Dozens more men plunged headlong into the river in their haste to retreat. Then Julia heard the eerie whistling sound again, tearing the sky apart, roaring toward her like thunder.

Her heart seemed to stand still. She was going to die.

The shell slammed into the ground nearby, the powerful blast pulsing through her body and hurling her to the floor of the carriage. Julia felt the explosion at the same moment that she heard it. Her nerve endings prickled from the concussion as dirt and grass and tattered cloth rained down on her. Everything vanished from sight in a blinding cloud of smoke and dust.

Above the ringing in her ears, she heard the terrible screams and moans of the wounded and the driver's frantic shouts as he fought to restrain the rearing horses. She was still alive.

"Are you all right?" Uncle Joseph asked as he lifted her onto the seat. He sounded far away even though he sat right beside her. Julia nodded and realized she was weeping. Dirt filled her mouth and coated her tongue. Grit stung her eyes. The front of her new blue dress had turned gray with dust.

"Hurry, driver!" the congressman pleaded. "Get us across that bridge before they reload their artillery!"

Julia felt the carriage jolt forward again. Through a blur of tears and dense smoke she saw that the Confederate shell had missed the bridge by only a few hundred feet. A jumble of blue-coated bodies littered the roadside where the missile had struck.

"Help me! Please!" a soldier begged. He lay beside the road, both of his legs missing below his knees. A man lay dead beside him, still gripping his gun, the top of his head blown off.

"Driver, stop," Nathaniel said. "We have to take some of these wounded men on board."

"No, don't!" Julia cried, hugging herself in terror. "Don't stop. Please don't stop! We have to get out of here!"

Nathaniel stared at her, shocked. "Julia! These men need our help."

"I don't care! I don't want them near me! Keep going. Please, keep going!"

Then, unable to stop herself, she leaned over the side of the carriage and vomited her lunch. Her entire body shook. Bile burned her throat, humiliation seared her cheeks. She reached for the handkerchief Uncle Joseph offered, her movements clumsy with fear. She couldn't control her arms and legs. They seemed to belong to someone else.

"Please, we must help these wounded men," Nathaniel begged.

"No! *No!*" Julia was terrified that another bomb would explode, that a shell would destroy the bridge and they'd be trapped, that the carriage would become an enemy target if they took soldiers on board. And she could no longer bear to see the blood and muscle and glistening bone of the soldiers' wounds.

"Don't force her, Reverend," Uncle Joseph said. "She's very upset. I'm responsible for her, and I don't want her hysterical."

"Help me . . . please!" One voice carried above the moans and cries of a dozen others. Nathaniel stood and leaped off the moving landau as it finally reached the bridge.

"What are you doing, Reverend? Come back!" the congressman yelled.

"We can't wait for you," Uncle Joseph pleaded. "Come on. Get in, get in!"

"No, go on without me. I'm staying to help."

"We can't leave you here."

"Go on," Nathaniel called. "I'll find another way back."

"Please, get me out of here!" Julia begged. "I don't want to die!" She covered her face with her hands as the horses clattered across the stone bridge and plowed through the crush of stampeding soldiers on the other side. The horses gradually picked up speed as they finally pulled ahead of the troops, leaving the cries of the wounded far behind. Only then did Julia dare to open her eyes.

"What should we do about Reverend Greene?" the congressman asked. Dirt and sweat turned his handkerchief black as he mopped his face. "We can't leave him here. He's in danger."

"It was his choice to stay," Uncle Joseph mumbled. He looked pale and badly shaken. The layer of dust on his hair and mustache aged him ten years. "Look, I have my niece to consider. Let's get her back to town, then we can decide what to do about Greene."

The ride back to Washington seemed very long. Though the sounds of battle gradually faded in the distance, the thunder of artillery and the screams of the wounded continued to echo in Julia's mind. At dusk, Washington's church steeples finally appeared on the horizon beneath lowering clouds. The carriage reached the safety of Congressman Rhodes' home moments before the rain was unleashed.

"I'm so sorry, my dear, for putting you through that," Uncle Joseph said before a servant helped Julia upstairs to bed. "I should have known better than to let you come with us."

"It wasn't your fault," she murmured. Her hands still shook as she accepted the laudanum pill and glass of water her aunt offered her.

Julia held back her tears as the maid helped her undress and turned down the bedcovers so she could crawl in. Then, alone in the darkened room, with rain hammering on the roof above her, she finally allowed herself to cry. She wanted to die of shame. It was bad enough that she had proven a coward, fleeing in fear and leaving Nathaniel stranded. But refusing to help the injured men had been unforgivable. Worse, she had disgraced herself in Nathaniel's eyes. If she was ashamed of herself, what must he think of her? Julia wept until the laudanum took effect, then fell into a nightmare-filled sleep.

"Has there been any word of Reverend Greene?" Julia asked one of the maids when she awoke the next morning.

"He arrived a few minutes ago, miss."

Julia sat up in bed. The sun, streaming through the cracks around her curtains, looked high in the sky. "What time is it?" she asked.

"Nearly half past eleven. You had yourself a good sleep, then, didn't you?" The servant's cheerfulness seemed wrong to Julia, as if the entire world should still be mourning over what had happened yesterday.

"How did it get to be so late?" Julia murmured. "Open the curtains, please."

"No, Mrs. Rhodes said to keep the room dark and let you rest, seeing as you had such a terrible time of it yesterday. I never did see anyone shake the way you was shaking last night. Had yourself a terrible scare, didn't you?"

Julia felt a wash of shame all over again at her cowardice. To let Nathaniel think she was bedridden from the experience would only add to it.

"I want the windows open, Bridgett. Hurry." Hot, humid air poured into the room along with the sunshine as the servant reluctantly tugged open the draperies and opened the windows. Julia untangled the sheets from around her legs and climbed out of bed. "Help me get dressed."

"But Mrs. Rhodes says you ought to stay in bed for the day, Miss Julia."

"I'm not staying in bed. Come here and help me." Julia reached behind her back, trying in vain to pull her loosened corset laces tight by herself while the young servant gnawed her fingers as if unsure whom to obey. "Bridgett! Are you going to help me with these corset laces or must I ring for another servant? Where's my dress?"

"The blue one? We're still trying to clean it, Miss Julia. It was nearly ruined, you know, especially all that lovely lace. Just covered with dirt, like you been rolling around on the ground, wrestling or something."

Julia's skin tingled as she remembered the force of the blast, the blinding cloud of debris. "Then I'll just have to wear my evening dress. Come on, then. Help me with it. Hurry." She drew a deep breath as Bridgett yanked the corset laces. "Pull tighter!" Julia wanted her figure to appear as dainty and frail as possible. "Where is Reverend Greene at the moment?" she asked, carefully exhaling when the ordeal was over.

"In the study with Mr. Rhodes. That reverend's looking all tuckered out, like something the cat dragged in. I heard Mrs. Rhodes telling them to fix his bath."

"Is my uncle with him?"

The maid stood on a stool, lifting Julia's hoops and layers of petticoats over her head one by one. "No, miss. He left for the railway office to buy tickets to take you all back to Philadelphia."

"Did he say when we were leaving?"

"Tomorrow, I think."

"Do you know if Reverend Greene is going home with us?"

"I don't think so, miss. I heard him talking about staying to help the wounded soldiers."

Julia wanted to weep. She had hoped to finally win Nathaniel's affection on this trip as they spent time traveling together. Instead, she was further from her goal than ever before, having disgraced herself in his eyes yesterday.

"Hurry," she begged. "I must speak to him before he retires to his bath." With her dress finally in order, Julia sat down in front of the mirror and dabbed a little color onto her cheeks and lips while the maid tried to tame her wild hair with a brush. Julia didn't want to look like a painted woman, but she had to do something to disguise the pallor of her face, still ghostly from yesterday's ordeal. When the maid finished brushing her hair, parting it in the middle, and pinning it back, Julia thought it looked much too severe. She pulled a few curls loose to soften her face. Then, satisfied with the way she looked, she splashed on some perfume, shoved her feet into her shoes, and hurried downstairs.

The door to the congressman's dark-paneled study stood open. Julia stayed outside in the hallway for a moment, waiting to catch his eye and be invited inside. Nathaniel's impassioned voice drifted out along with the congressman's cigar smoke.

"But the Rebels should be the least of your concerns, sir," he said. "The government simply must find accommodations for all of the wounded men. There aren't enough hospital beds for them all, and they're being forced to wander the city, looking for medical care."

"What good are hospitals if our city is virtually undefended?" Rhodes said. "There's nothing to stop the Rebels from crossing the Potomac and attacking Washington!"

"I don't think you'll have to worry about that. The heavy rains have turned all the roads to mud. Believe me—the enemy will have as hard a time getting here as I did."

"General McDowell ought to be fired for being so ill-prepared. We made a terrible spectacle of ourselves yesterday. I expect Jeff Davis is having a good laugh at us right about now, and—Julia! My dear! Come in, come in. I didn't expect to see you today. Are you all right? Have you recovered?"

"I'm quite well, thank you," she said, sweeping into the room. "When I heard that Reverend Greene had returned, I simply had to see him and assure myself that he was all in one piece." She turned to him, looking him over with what she hoped was an affectionate gaze. "Are you all right, Reverend? I've been praying for your safety all night."

"I'm fine, thank you."

"Thank heaven. I want to apologize for my appalling behavior yesterday. I've never had such a terrible shock before, and I simply wasn't myself. Will you ever forgive me?"

"Of course," he said after a moment. But Nathaniel's cold, sullen expression didn't change. She waited for her apology to soften his features into his boyish smile, but it didn't. An ugly silence fell, made worse by the room's gloomy atmosphere. The study was filled with dark heavy furniture and papered with drab wallpaper. The liver-colored drapes on the windows had been pulled half closed, adding to the melancholy. Julia wanted to say something to dispel the dismal silence, but she didn't know what.

"Were you able to help those poor, suffering men, Reverend?" she finally asked.

"Some of them."

"Goodness, you must be exhausted. I know all of us were by the time we returned home, weren't we, Congressman?"

He nodded vacantly. Julia remembered the quantities of champagne he'd drunk and how he'd managed to fall asleep on the bone-rattling ride back to Washington. She wondered just how much he remembered from yesterday.

"Our government was disgracefully unprepared for so many casualties," Nathaniel said, ignoring Julia. "You must publish a report on it, Congressman. The wounded had no transportation, too few physicians, inadequate field hospitals. . . . Our fighting men deserve better."

"Yes, I expect Congress will be busy for some time debating this appalling disaster." As Rhodes began fussing with his cigar, trying to relight it, Nathaniel turned to stare out the window. Julia followed his gaze and saw the unfinished dome of the Capitol building in the distance, covered with scaffolding. She had offered her apologies.

Neither man seemed to want her here. The polite thing to do would be to leave.

"Well, then . . ." She smiled uncertainly at the minister's rudely turned back. "I'll leave you gentlemen to your discussion. I thank God you're all right, Nathaniel." Julia never used his first name and didn't know what had prompted her to use it now. His coldness made her feel like a scolded child, but she held her head high as she left the room in a swirl of hoops and petticoats. She got as far as the first stair landing before remembering that she was going home tomorrow. She'd forgotten to ask Nathaniel if he planned to go home, too.

She hurried back to the study and saw that Congressman Rhodes had moved to stand beside Nathaniel at the window. They couldn't see Julia in the doorway, but their voices carried out to her quite clearly.

"She's sweet on you, Reverend," the congressman said.

"Miss Hoffman, you mean?"

"Yes. I may be old and gray, but I can still recognize the signs. She's a lovely young woman from a very fine family. Quite pretty, too. You're a lucky man to have caught her eye."

Julia smiled at the compliment and moved away slightly so she could listen without being seen.

"I do believe you're blushing, young man," the congressman said, chuckling. "Have I touched a nerve?"

"Truth be told, I find Miss Hoffman's attentions toward me embarrassing. But I'm afraid I haven't found the necessary . . . words . . . to discourage her."

"Why on earth would you wish to discourage her? Don't you find her pretty?"

"I really couldn't say if she's pretty or not. As the Scriptures say, I made a covenant with my eyes not to look upon a girl in that way."

"You're much too serious, Reverend. You needn't call it a sin to say a girl is pretty. How old are you . . . twenty-four, twenty-five?"

"Twenty-nine, sir."

"You look much younger. Listen, how do you expect to find a

wife if you never look at a woman? Don't you plan to marry someday?"

"I wish very much to marry, God willing."

"Then, as I say, you would do well not to ignore Julia Hoffman's attention. In fact, I'd advise you to encourage it. Aside from her physical loveliness, she is purehearted, comes from a sterling family—and she tells me she's involved in your abolitionist causes, too."

"Well, yes . . . I suppose she is. . . ."

"Then what's the problem, my good fellow? I understand from her uncle that she can have her pick of eligible suitors back home and that her father is quite eager to see her well married and settled down, especially with the Union in an uproar."

Nathaniel heaved a sigh that Julia could hear even outside the door. This conversation was making her more and more uneasy, and she wasn't sure she wanted to hear Nathaniel's answer.

"To be perfectly honest," he finally replied, "Miss Hoffman is not at all what I'm looking for in a wife. I find her shallow, spoiled, and unbearably self-absorbed."

Julia slumped against the wall as if he'd struck her. Shock left her momentarily numb; then the pain of his cruel words slowly grabbed hold of her.

Apparently he'd stunned the congressman, as well. "My dear fellow!" he said.

"Forgive me for being so blunt, but I find it to be a true assessment of most of the young ladies in Miss Hoffman's social position. They can't—or won't—do a thing for themselves, whether it's combing their own hair or fixing a cup of tea. And their works of charity are always about themselves, done for selfish motives, not from true Christian love and compassion. Outward beauty rarely lasts a lifetime, Congressman, and then what would I be left with once it fades? A whining, nagging wife wrapped up in her own needs, whose only passions are spending money and spreading gossip? I need a devout wife, one who spends her time in the Scriptures and in prayer, one who is devoted to meeting the needs of others, whose lifelong passion, like mine, is to spread the Gospel."

Julia hated him. She longed to stalk into the room and strike back at him for insulting her. But to be caught eavesdropping would further disgrace her in his sight—and in her host's. Every part of her seemed to ache as she slowly backed away from the door. She didn't want to hear another painful word, but she couldn't stop herself from listening.

"Don't you think you're being a bit hard on young Julia?" Rhodes asked.

"Frankly, no. I don't. You saw her lack of compassion for those wounded men yesterday."

"I saw a frightened young lady who has never been exposed to such gruesome sights before. Neither have I, as a matter of fact. The battlefield is no place for a woman."

"I disagree. I've been reading the accounts of Florence Nightingale and the work she and her band of nurses did during the war in Crimea. The 'Nightingales' displayed remarkable courage and saved many lives on the battlefield."

"Ah, yes. I've read about them, too. Extraordinary. We could use a few Nightingales in our own war."

"Even when Miss Hoffman has attended abolition meetings with me, she seemed more interested in flirting and being noticed by everyone than in what the guest speakers had to say. I realized that she had aimed her sights on me some time ago. But the more I've tried to discourage her, the more she has leeched onto me. I seem to be a prize she has set for herself, and the more coldly I treat her, the more determined she has become to win me over. Forgive me for sounding harsh, Congressman, but I'm very frustrated. I don't quite know how to get rid of her."

"Would you like me to have a word with her uncle or her father?"

Julia knew she would curl up and die if Congressman Rhodes ever repeated Nathaniel's words to her father. The mere thought of it made her shrivel inside herself in shame. She considered storming into the room and telling Nathaniel that he needn't think she would ever bother him again, when she heard his answer.

"No. . . . Thank you for offering, but I think I'd better learn to handle her advances myself."

"All right. But be careful, Reverend. Judge Hoffman wields a great deal of power in Philadelphia, and he's a generous contributor to your church. If you insult him or his daughter, I guarantee you'll be looking for a new position."

Julia finally turned away and hurried up the stairs as her tears began to fall. That's what she would do—have Nathaniel fired as soon as she returned to Philadelphia. She knew her father had the power to do it and that he would gladly do it after she told him how Nathaniel had insulted all the women who did charity work for the church. She couldn't remember ever feeling so angry. How dare he speak of her that way? She'd had dozens of worthy suitors, but she had loved only him, pursuing him alone for more than three years. Well, no more! She felt nothing but loathing for Reverend Nathaniel Greene.

Julia cried for a good long while, comforting herself with images of Nathaniel being drummed out of the church, out of Philadelphia, out of the ministry. Then a better idea came to her. Rather than having him leave with such a low opinion of her, she would first prove to him that she wasn't shallow and self-absorbed. Once he was sorry for everything he'd said, *then* she'd have her father get rid of him.

She pressed her handkerchief to her eyes to stop her tears and sat down in front of the looking glass to repair her face. Julia knew she was pretty, even with red, swollen eyes and blotchy cheeks. Other men considered her a prize; why didn't Nathaniel Greene?

But the more she thought about his words and how she had reacted yesterday to those pleading, wounded men, the more clearly Julia began to see herself—clearer than any mirror might have shown. She saw her reflection, not in glass but in the words of the man she loved, a man who didn't return her love, a man who didn't look at her face but at her soul. There were things she could do to dress up the outside of herself. But all the lace and silk and rouge in the world couldn't camouflage her heart. Nathaniel had called her "shallow" and "spoiled" and "unbearably self-absorbed."

Julia Hoffman looked beyond the mirror and knew his words were true.

Chapter Two

Western Virginia
September 1861

Phoebe Bigelow was as homely and horsefaced as a hound dog—and she knew it. She was nineteen years old, old enough to get married, but there probably wasn't a man in Bone Hollow who'd be willing to marry her, except maybe Rufus Shook—and most folks agreed that he was a little "tetched" in the head. She was much too tall, for one thing—nearly six foot, just like her three older brothers. And she was built like them, too—big-boned, with square shoulders and a sturdy trunk, and wiry yellow hair. She flatly refused to shape her figure into womanly curves with a corset, so there wasn't a single thing feminine about her except her name. And for reasons that Phoebe never quite understood, her brothers had even changed that to "Ike."

As she'd watched the three of them—Junior, Willard, and Jack—getting ready to march off to war, she considered it the worst misfortune of her life that she had been born a girl. She was just as patriotic as they were, wasn't she? She wanted to see the Rebels stopped from seceding just as badly as they did. Maybe she had been born and raised right here in western Virginia, but like all the rest of the folks in Bone Hollow, she wanted her state to stay in the United States, thank you very much, not join some crazy Confederacy. That's why her brothers were fixing to go up to Cincinnati to sign on with the Yankees. Problem was, they were fixing to leave Phoebe behind.

"Come on, Ike. Will you hurry up in there?" Willard yelled from outside the cabin door. "Gonna be past noon before we get to town at the rate you're moving."

"The whole dumb war's gonna be over at the rate she's moving," Jack added, making sure he spoke loud enough for her to hear. She surveyed her family's cabin one last time, memorizing every inch of it—ash dust, cobwebs, and all—then stuck Pa's old slouch hat on her head and hefted her burlap sack of belongings onto her shoulder. As she emerged through the door, dragging her heels, Junior took one look at her and leaped off the wagon.

"Hang it all, Phoebe. Didn't I tell you to put on a skirt? You can't be working in Miz Haggerty's store and minding her young ones dressed like a man."

"Told you. Don't want to mind her store or her snotty-nosed brats. Why can't I stay right here on our own land—where I belong?"

"We been over this a hundred times. The farm's leased to Jeb White 'til we get back from the war. You gotta move to town where you'll be taken care of."

"Don't need no one to take care of me. Ain't I been taking care of myself just fine 'til now?"

"Jeb's new wife don't want you here. You're gonna earn your room and board with the Haggertys."

The thought of prune-faced Mrs. Haggerty bossing her around all day made Phoebe feel desperate. She grabbed Junior's arm to plead with him one last time. "Let me go with you, Junior. *Please!* Ain't nobody but you gonna know I ain't your brother. And you know I can shoot twice as good as you can. That means I can kill twice as many Rebels as you."

"You're a *girl,* Ike." He made it sound like a worse fate than being born a rattlesnake. "Girls don't fight in wars, no matter how good they can shoot. Now put your blasted skirt on, or I'll hog-tie you and put it on you myself." Junior was bigger than she was, the biggest one of the lot. He'd sat on her plenty of times in the past when she'd gotten him riled, so she knew he could easily do it again.

Jack and Willard would gladly join in, too.

She dragged herself back up the cabin steps and went inside to put on the hated skirt, mumbling under her breath about that no-good busybody, Mrs. Garlock. It was all her fault that Phoebe had a skirt to put on in the first place. She had always worn her brothers' hand-me-down shirts and overalls until Widow Garlock told Pa it was a disgrace to her mother's memory for Phoebe to show up for school in Bone Hollow dressed like a boy. The widow had given Phoebe a calico skirt, muslin bloomers and petticoat, and a threadbare shirtwaist that had belonged to Mrs. Garlock's sister who'd died of pneumonia earlier that year. Phoebe's own mama had died when she was barely out of diapers, which is why no one had ever taught her how to act like a girl. She wished Pa was still alive. If he hadn't took sick and died a year ago, she never would have had to leave home and go work for Mrs. Haggerty.

Phoebe had no choice but to change her clothes. She barely got the blasted skirt closed around her waist. And she'd grown bigger on top, too, so the shirtwaist gaped open between each of the buttons. It would serve Mrs. Garlock and Mrs. Haggerty right if the buttons popped clear off right in front of Mr. Haggerty, that leering old coot. Phoebe folded up her shirt, overalls, and union suit, stuffed them into the burlap sack with the rest of her things, and said goodbye to the cabin a second time.

"About time," Willard mumbled as she emerged through the door. When Jack gave a wolf whistle, Phoebe punched him in the arm. He punched her back, so she socked him again, harder.

"Quit your fighting," Junior ordered. "Save it for Johnny Reb."

Phoebe hopped onto the back of the wagon as it started forward and sat with her legs dangling over the edge. From the way her brothers yammered on and on about the things they were gonna do and the sights they were gonna see, no one would ever guess that not a one of them had ever traveled more than twenty miles from home before. Phoebe hadn't, either, but the difference was that now they were finally gonna get a chance to see the world—and she wasn't. It made her mad enough to spit nails. As they drove down the narrow dirt road into town, she wished a band of wild-eyed Rebels would come flying out of the woods and carry her off as booty. It couldn't possibly be a worse fate than working in the Haggertys' store.

"Hey, Ike, you gonna write to us once in a while?" Willard asked. "Tell us what-all's going on back home?"

"Only if you write first," she said sullenly.

"You know I ain't no good at writing. Can't spell worth a hoot, neither."

"Then don't expect to hear from me."

"Why're you being so ornery?" Jack asked.

"You'd be ornery, too, if you had to wear petticoats and a dress and work for Miz Haggerty. You know she's just about the meanest woman in town. How'd you all like to live with her?"

"You forgetting that she's gonna pay you every week?" Junior asked. "Plus give you room and board? Save up that money and you could be rich by the time this war is over."

"Ha! Why don't you put on a skirt and go work for her, then, and I'll go fight in your place."

For Phoebe, the worst part would be living in town. She hated town, preferring to work in the fields alongside her brothers all day or to roam the hollows and hills around the farm, shooting rabbits and squirrels for supper. Junior was going to loan the wagon and team of horses to Jeb White, so once Jeb and his bride drove out of town with it, Phoebe would be trapped.

The wagon sank axle deep in mud in a couple of spots, but with all of her brothers pushing, they didn't stay bogged down very long. They reached town shortly after noon and pulled to a stop in the narrow, littered alley behind the general store. They may as well have dropped Phoebe off at the jail—it felt no different to her. The ramshackle building looked as though it had been built with leftover packing crates—and probably had been. The Haggertys lived above the store on the second floor; they'd promised Phoebe a bed in the attic. It would be hotter than blazes up there in summer, and she'd probably get frostbite in winter.

"You better behave yourself for Miz Haggerty," Junior warned, "and do what she says. You can't lip off to her like you always done at home, or she'll smack you right on the mouth."

Phoebe stayed rooted in place in the back of the wagon, feeling too sick to move or speak.

"Well, what're you waiting for?" Willard asked. "Get off, already! We ain't got all day." He shoved her from behind until she slid off the rear of the wagon. Her knees felt so weak when her feet hit the ground that she had to grab onto the wagon bed to keep from falling.

"So long, Ike," Junior called. "See you after the war." He started to give the reins a shake and drive away, when the Haggertys' back door flew open and a horde of children poured through it, swarming around the wagon like flies around a carcass.

"How many blasted kids do they have, anyhow?" Willard murmured.

The kids remained in constant motion—poking, punching, tussling with each other—so that Phoebe couldn't even begin to count them all. The biggest girl, who looked to be about nine or ten, was the only one who stood still. She planted herself squarely in front of Phoebe, holding a squalling baby out in front of her as if waiting for Phoebe to take him. Phoebe retrieved her sack of belongings from the wagon and clutched it tightly to her chest in self-defense.

"Go on! Y'all get out of the way now," Junior yelled, "or I'll run you over!" The wagon began moving slowly forward, and the flood of children parted like the waters of the Red Sea.

"Hey, Ike," Jack called, "if you find yourself in church on a Sunday, say a little prayer for us, okay?"

Phoebe was too dazed to reply. She stared at the retreating wagon until it rolled around the corner, out of sight. This wasn't happening to her. Her brothers should have tied her up in a sack and thrown her into Bone Creek like a litter of kittens if they didn't want her—it would have been kinder than this.

As the dust settled, the stream of swirling children surrounded Phoebe, propelling her forward through the back door and into the lean-to that served as the kitchen. The top of her head grazed the roof beams, where bunches of dried herbs were hanging. It took a long moment for her eyes to adjust to the scant light that seeped through the grimy window. The air was so greasy with the smell of bacon that it seemed to Phoebe that she could just scoop out a handful and grease wagon axles with it.

"About time you got here," Mrs. Haggerty said in greeting. She stood at the table with her hands in a pan of gray dishwater, scrubbing a frying pan. "They told me you was planning on getting here before lunch—so's you could help me feed this brood. Now lunch is over and the dishes are done and here you are just showing up. What took you so long?" She slammed the frying pan down on the table.

"Sorry, ma'am. We—"

Mrs. Haggerty didn't wait for an explanation. She lifted the dishpan with both hands, kicked the back door open, and slung the dirty water outside without bothering to look where it landed. Phoebe decided she'd better not stand around by the back door after meals.

"Noon's always the busiest time in the store," Mrs. Haggerty said as the door slammed shut again. "That's why I need you. My, you sure are a big gal, ain't you? Built like a brick wall. No wonder you ain't married. How old are you?"

"Nineteen, ma'am."

"Don't know who sewed your clothes, but you're busting clear out of them. Never mind, you can sew yourself some new ones at night when the kids are asleep and your chores are all done. I'll take the thread and cloth out of your pay."

"Oh no, ma'am. These clothes are fine," Phoebe said as she saw her meager earnings going up in smoke—and for a hated dress, no less. "I don't need—"

"You take over with these kids now so's I can get back to work. Store closes at six-thirty, and Mr. Haggerty and me are gonna want our dinner about then. Your brother says you can cook." She removed her filthy kitchen apron as she talked and put on a slightly cleaner shop apron in its place. Before Phoebe had a chance to ask what she was expected to fix for dinner, Mrs. Haggerty disappeared through the door that led into the store.

"Here, take him." The oldest girl had planted herself in front of Phoebe again, only this time she dangled the squirming baby by his arms, ready to drop him on the floor if Phoebe didn't catch him in time. "He's poo-ey," the girl said. "Change him." Her voice was every bit as bossy and insistent as her mother's.

A smell like rotting cabbage drifted up to Phoebe's nose. She had no choice except to set down her bag and grab the baby before he dropped to the floor with a *splat.* Mrs. Haggerty would likely subtract the price of mending his cracked skull from her pay, too.

Phoebe's burlap sack had barely hit the floor before half a dozen Haggertys pounced on it like catfish going after breadcrumbs. "Touch that bag and I'll skin every last one of you like you was raccoons," Phoebe said. The swirling bodies froze for a moment, their dirty faces upturned as if trying to measure her meanness. She narrowed her eyes, trying to look ornery enough to scare a nest of rattlesnakes. She felt ornery, too, as something warm and wet oozed from the baby's diaper and ran down her arm.

"You're ugly," one of the bigger boys said.

"Oh yeah? Well, you'd better get yourselves outside before I count three, or your sorry little faces will wind up even uglier than mine. One . . . two . . ." The back door slammed shut on the last of them before she got to three.

That night Phoebe's attic room proved hotter than she'd imagined—plus it had bats. She'd been standing across the alley at dusk, trying to herd all the Haggertys home, when she'd seen the bats streaming out of her window. She'd counted thirteen of them—which seemed unlucky. Phoebe still hadn't counted all the Haggertys. Every time she thought she had their number, one or two would wander off somewhere and three or four new ones would wander home from who-knows-where, and then she'd have to start all over again. She had tried to wipe one boy's bloody nose after he'd gotten himself punched, and he'd squirmed away from her, saying, "I ain't no Haggerty! Leave me alone!" That had thrown her count way off. Who knew how many of them she'd already counted who weren't Haggertys at all?

She wondered if Mr. and Mrs. Haggerty themselves had any idea how many there were, seeing as nobody but the two of them ever bothered to sit down to eat. And how could anyone keep track of their kin when they were all called Bubba or Sissy?

From the moment her brother Willard had shoved her off the back of the wagon, Phoebe had seen nothing but kids, chaos, and chores. The worst part was never having a moment to herself from the time she'd arrived until she'd climbed the ladder to the airless attic—and now she was too tired to enjoy the fact that she was alone. Phoebe lay down on her scratchy corncob mattress, feeling wretched enough to hang herself from one of the spidery rafters above her head. Not only was the bed so short her feet hung off the end, but she was wringing wet with sweat after only five minutes, even stripped down to her chemise and bloomers. She could probably wring a cupful of water from her hair.

"Ain't no way I can stand living here," she mumbled aloud.

When the war had begun last April, everybody said it wouldn't last more than ninety days. Now here it was six months later, and the Rebels showed no signs of backing down. In fact, they were cockier than ever after whipping the Yanks at Bull Run. Who knew how long the fighting would drag on, how long she'd be sentenced to this Haggerty hell?

Somewhere in a room below, the baby began to cry. It was the last straw. Better to die with a Rebel bullet between her eyes than get worked to death by these blasted Haggertys.

Phoebe stood, careful not to crack her head on the rafters, and dug in her bag for her beloved overalls and shirt. She tore a long, wide strip of muslin from her bloomers and tied it around her bosom to flatten herself, then put on her one-piece union suit. She had to admit as she changed her clothes that girls' underthings were a whole lot cooler than men's, but that was about all that could be said for women's clothes. When she was finished, she laid the chemise, petticoat, skirt, and bodice neatly on the bed so that it looked as though she'd simply shriveled up and vanished, leaving her clothes behind. Then, carrying her shoes and burlap sack, Phoebe descended the ladder and crept down the stairs to the kitchen.

She found a sewing box on the kitchen mantel and dug through it for scissors. Grabbing handfuls of her hair, Phoebe chopped it short without even bothering to look in a mirror and threw it into the fireplace by the fistful. The embers sparked and sizzled when her damp hair hit them, but Phoebe poked and fanned until it finally burned. The smell made her gag nearly as badly as the baby's messy diaper had.

She took a heel of bread left over from supper and a cold baked potato from the larder, figuring she was owed at least that much for a day's work. Then Phoebe Bigelow ducked through the back door to freedom, disappearing into the night.

Chapter Three

Philadelphia
October 1861

"Julia Anne Hoffman! Whatever is the matter with you?" Julia's mother stood in the bedroom doorway, kid gloves on her hands, hands on her hips.

"Go without me," Julia mumbled. "I don't feel like going." She stared at the top of her vanity, avoiding her mother's reflection—and her own—in the mirror.

"Why not? And don't try telling me it's 'the curse of womanhood' again. You used that for an excuse last week. And the week before, if I'm not mistaken."

Julia didn't reply. Her silence seemed to make her mother angrier. The older woman stormed into the room, hoops swaying like an unanchored skiff, her Richmond accent growing more pronounced with every word.

"Look at you. Why, your hair isn't even fixed. Inga!" she said, turning to shout at Julia's maid. "Why are you standing around like a dolt? We are supposed to be taking afternoon tea at the Blairs', and we are already late."

"If you please, ma'am . . . Miss Julia wouldn't let me comb it."

"Julia, I want this silly business of brushing your own hair stopped immediately. Do you hear me?" She picked up the brush with an angry swipe and shoved it into Inga's hand. The maid carefully began brushing, as if she expected Julia's hair to fall out in clumps.

Mrs. Hoffman's hands returned to her hips as she stood beside the dressing table. "You've been moping around for nearly three months—ever since you returned from Washington. I've tried very hard to be patient with you because of the shock you received at that battlefield, but honestly, I am all out of patience. I'm absolutely exasperated with you. Your behavior has been downright rude—refusing dinner invitations from perfectly fine gentlemen, walking out on your social obligations. And that insulting remark you made to Mrs. Reed about not fixing the tea herself. I was positively mortified."

"But she doesn't fix it herself, Mother. Neither do I . . . and neither do you."

"Well, of course we don't. Why should we? That's what servants are for. Will you *please* hurry, Inga."

"Yes, ma'am. . . . One more pin, ma'am."

Julia reached up to feel the knot of hair coiled at the nape of her neck and fought back tears as she remembered Reverend Greene's condemning words: *They can't—or won't—do a thing for themselves, whether it's combing their own hair or fixing a cup of tea.*

"Inga has made it much too loose," Julia said. "It will be falling down in half an hour."

"Well, it's your own fault if it does," her mother replied. "We are leaving this instant. No, put down that brush, Inga. It's too late to fix it. Fetch Julia's cloak. And her shoes. She doesn't even have her shoes on yet. Where's her bonnet?"

The maid skittered around like a colt on ice, as if unsure what to do first. "I can fetch my own shoes," Julia said, rising to cross the room.

"I don't know what to do with you," her mother said with a sigh. "Your father thinks we should send for the doctor."

"I don't need a doctor," Julia said as she bent to put on her shoes.

"Then why are you behaving this way?"

"Because I'm sick of it all, Mother. My life is boring and meaningless. We make social rounds and call on people, then they call on us. It's absurd. In the evenings we go to endless dinner parties, theater engagements, and boring lectures that put everyone to sleep. Oh yes, we do our part for charity, but you know as well as I do that most of our charity work is really about maintaining the fine Hoffman family name and being noticed and supporting the right causes. It's not about being charitable."

"I know nothing of the sort."

"Here's your cloak, Miss Julia." The maid inched toward her like a child approaching a barking dog. "Shall I help you put it on?"

"I can do it myself, thank you."

"*You* are being absurd!" her mother said with a huff. "I'm fetching the doctor, first thing tomorrow morning."

Julia followed her mother downstairs and outside to the waiting carriage. It was a chilly day for late October, and her mother rolled the shade on her side of the carriage closed against the wind. Julia rolled hers all the way open, gazing out at the nearly bare tree branches that arched above the avenue. Brown and gold leaves lay strewn along the cobbled street, and against her will Julia recalled the blue-clad bodies sprawled beside the road like scattered stones. She remembered the soldier being carried by his friends, his foot dangling like a dried leaf, ready for the wind to blow it free. Her life felt as worthless as the dying leaves. What was the meaning of it all? Was her only purpose to look beautiful for a time, then die?

"That's too much air, Julia," her mother said. "Close it before you catch a chill."

Julia ignored her, letting the breeze wash over her face as the carriage picked up speed. She felt feverish with pent-up energy and restless at the prospect of sitting demurely in the Blairs' drawing room all afternoon, sipping the tea their maids had brewed. The urge to get out of the carriage and run, to escape her "respectable" life, was suddenly so strong that she had to cross her legs to keep from doing it. Unconsciously, she began kicking the carriage seat across from her.

"Stop that," her mother said, putting her hand on Julia's knee. "You'll ruin your shoes. And you know better than to cross your legs like a man, much less kick your foot that way."

"I wish I *were* a man."

"Julia! Don't say such a thing in public." Mrs. Hoffman kept her voice just above a whisper.

"We're not in public, we're inside a carriage," Julia said loudly. "Who's going to hear me, the coachman?"

"Yes, as a matter of fact," her mother replied, still whispering. "Our servants talk to other people's servants, you know. That's how gossip spreads."

"Of course it's the servants," Julia said acidly. "Respectable people like us never gossip."

"Shh! It's bad enough that Inga and the other maids think you've lost your mind, would you like our coachman to confirm their opinion?"

Julia stuck her head through the open window and shouted, "I don't care!" as loudly as she could. When she drew her head inside again, her mother slapped her.

"There! If you're going to act like a spoiled child I shall have to treat you like one."

Julia stared at her mother for a long, shocked moment, then slumped against her and wept. "That's what he said, Mother. He said I was spoiled . . . and . . . and self-absorbed."

"Who did?"

"But he's right. I am. And I don't know what to do about it. I want my life to matter. I don't want to grow old and die with nothing to show for it."

"Listen to me." Julia's mother took her by the shoulders and made her sit up so they could face each other. "What you need to do is get married and—"

"No, that won't help!" She wanted to wail like a child.

"Oh yes, it will. It's time for you to grow up, Julia. Your father's right; we have spoiled you for much too long. You say you want your life to matter? Good. That's what marriage is for. What you need is a husband to care for and children to raise and a household to run. There is no greater purpose in life for a woman."

Before the Battle of Bull Run, Julia would have agreed. She had directed all of her energy into looking pretty enough to attract Nathaniel Greene, believing that her life would be complete once she married him. But the conversation she'd overheard had revealed to her how shallow her life was—and it made her long for something more. *"I need a devout wife,"* Nathaniel had said, *"one who is devoted to meeting the needs of others, whose lifelong passion, like mine, is to spread the Gospel."*

"Now, I know for a fact that Mrs. Blair's son Haywood is quite interested in you," Mrs. Hoffman continued. "So are young Ralph Woolsey and David Jennison and Arthur Hoyt. But you've given all of them the brush-off."

"I went to the church social with David Jennison last August, and he bored me to tears," Julia said. But she knew that the only reason she'd gone with him was because of Nathaniel. He had just returned from Washington, and she'd wanted to make him jealous. But why had she wanted to make him jealous if she hated him so much? She'd never felt so confused in her life.

"You haven't given David Jennison or anyone else a chance. I'm not blind, Julia. I know you've been sweet on Reverend Greene for some time. I don't know what happened between the two of you down in Washington, but—"

"The war happened," she mumbled. *And he broke my heart.*

"Indeed . . . Well, I'm glad that your infatuation with him is finished. I didn't want to say anything for fear you would dig in your heels, but he really isn't up to our social standards. His family are a bunch of preachers—nobodies, really—and he barely makes enough money to keep you in ball gowns. Then there are all those radical ideas of his. He filled your head and your poor cousin Caroline's head with his nonsense. It simply won't do for a Hoffman to marry a fanatic."

For the first time in months, Julia thought of her cousin Caroline in Richmond. Her letters had stopped arriving after the war began, but before then, every line Caroline had written reverberated with love for Charles St. John. Julia was certain that if she had turned off the gaslights Caroline's letters would have glowed in the dark. Julia had once felt that same breathless, shimmering joy whenever she was around Nathaniel. Now she wondered if she would ever feel anything like it again.

"Your sister, Rosalie, did so well for herself with her husband,"

Mother continued. "You could do just as well if you'd make an effort."

Julia nearly groaned aloud. She didn't want a life—or a husband—like her sister's. The last time she had visited Rosalie, the emptiness of her life had frightened Julia so badly she had canceled her theater date that evening with Ralph Woolsey because he reminded her of her sister's bland, unemotional husband. Rosalie was Louis' possession, swallowed up in his shadow and resolved to do his bidding. Like an actress on stage, she played the part of wife and mother fastidiously—and joylessly. Rosalie was not a happy woman.

"Do you love Louis?" Julia had asked her sister.

"Of course I love him," Rosalie had snapped at her. Not a very convincing performance. Nor did her life seem to have any more meaning now than it had before marriage.

"Yes, a husband and children will give your life a purpose," Mother said now, plodding forward as energetically as the carriage horses. "That's why women get married. And speaking of Louis, I understand that his cousin Martin is interested in courting you."

"Rosalie's husband is a conceited bore. So is his cousin Martin."

"I simply won't tolerate this behavior for another day, Julia. Our servants have better manners than you do. Now you listen to me. This is no time to be particular about who you marry. The war is changing everything. Half of the eligible men are taking commissions and enlisting, and the other half are eager to settle down as soon as they possibly can. You're going to dillydally too long and lose out. Do you want to end up an old maid like your aunt Eunice? She was too picky, you know, and the boat sailed without her."

The thought of spending her life alone disturbed Julia, but so did the idea of spending it in a loveless marriage with a man who bored her to tears. She'd been terrified at Bull Run when she'd come face-to-face with death, but she had also felt truly alive for the first time in her life. She wanted that kind of passion in her life and in her would-be suitors. She wanted adventure, excitement, fireworks in her relationships. Nathaniel had the kind of passion she longed for—if not for her, at least for his causes and in his sermons.

That's why she had fallen in love with him. And it was why no other man could compare with him.

"If you don't snap out of this pretty soon," Mother continued, "we will simply have to arrange a suitable marriage for you. . . . Julia! Are you even listening to me?"

"Yes, Mother," she said dully. "I heard every word you said."

They were the last ones to arrive at the Blairs' for tea. As they entered the parlor, the conversation stopped so abruptly that Julia was certain the women had been discussing her. Strangely, she found she didn't care. All her life she had flattered and flirted, craving the admiration of her social circle. Now, after seeing herself and her peers through Nathaniel's eyes, their opinion no longer mattered to her. She felt so detached from the other women as she listened to them talking that she may as well have been standing outside, looking in through the window.

"Harriet was wearing one of those new Garibaldi blouses."

"Yes, I saw those in *Godey's Lady's Book*."

"I hear they are all the rage."

"I'm having my seamstress make one."

Julia used to prattle on and on about such silly things, too. Now she simply sipped her tea, feeling numb. Eventually the conversation shifted from fashion to courtship. Everyone, it seemed, was racing to pair off with an eligible gentleman. The girls her age discussed the scramble as if it were another California Gold Rush—hurry up and stake your claim or you'll lose out.

"Wouldn't you just die if you were left with the second helpings?" Olivia Blair asked her.

"No, Olivia," Julia replied coolly. "If I loved a man, I wouldn't care if he was rich or poor, handsome or ugly. I wouldn't even care if . . . if he was a penniless immigrant."

The room fell silent for a long, awkward moment.

When the discussion resumed, Olivia and the others carefully ignored Julia—which suited her just fine. She barely uttered another word all afternoon until one of the women said, "Have you heard about the Fitzhughs' son? He went to London to study medicine last year and returned with a wife. It seems he's fallen for a woman who was a Nightingale."

"Excuse me," Julia said, remembering what Nathaniel had said. "Do you know anything about the Nightingales?"

"I read an article about them in the *Illustrated News,*" Mrs. Blair replied. "They're nurses, named after Florence Nightingale. She went to the Crimea during the war and organized the hospitals over there. They were dreadful places, it seems, filled with injured, dying soldiers. After she and her little band of nurses cleaned them up and began caring for the men, fewer of them died. She has become quite famous and is widely admired for her work."

"I saw wounded soldiers at Bull Run," Julia said. "One of them had both of his legs blown off."

Silence dropped again, like a stage curtain.

"Julia, dear," her mother said in a tight voice, "kindly change the subject."

"No, Mother, don't you see? If I knew how to be a Nightingale, I could have helped those soldiers."

The very scandal of Julia's suggestion made the topic irresistible to the older women. "Why on earth would you want to do that, dear?"

"Don't you think that sort of work is beneath someone from your station in life?"

"Do you want to end up like that poor Dorothea Dix?"

"Who's she?" Julia asked.

"Miss Dix had her name in all the papers for a while, clamoring for improved health care for paupers, prison inmates, the mentally ill—*those* types of people. Disgusting work!"

"Yes, but she had nothing to lose," another woman added. "Her family were nobodies. She didn't have the opportunities Julia has to marry quality."

"Isn't Dorothea Dix the one who's involved with the Sanitary Commission?" someone asked. "I thought I read somewhere that she's training nurses for the war now."

"One and the same. But you'll notice that the men still aren't lining up to marry her. She'll die an old maid."

"Maybe it was Miss Dix's choice not to marry," Julia said stubbornly. "Maybe she'd rather do something important with her life."

"No woman ever *chooses* not to marry," Mrs. Blair said. The other ladies murmured in agreement. "Besides, you can have a husband and still do respectable charity work."

"Charity work isn't enough," Julia replied. "I would still like to become a nurse."

If the matrons were shocked, the girls Julia's own age seemed gleeful. In the race for an eligible husband, one of their prettiest, wealthiest rivals was eliminating herself from the competition with such outrageous ideas.

The ladies soon tired of that topic and went on to discuss other things. To Julia, it seemed as though the afternoon would never end. She longed to excuse herself and go home, but she knew that as soon as she did the whispering would resume.

". . . Have you noticed how oddly Julia Hoffman has been acting since she returned from Washington?"

"Her poor mother doesn't know what to do with her. . . ."

Julia wanted to weep at the prospect of facing a lifetime of these afternoon teas. Her mother and Rosalie were content with this life; why wasn't she? Was it only because of Nathaniel's words? Julia closed her eyes to shut out the gossiping women and wished with all her heart that she had never eavesdropped on his conversation.

For most of the ride home, Julia's mother remained stiff and silent on the seat beside her. But as their carriage labored up the last hill, she finally spoke. "If you were trying to embarrass me today, Julia, you did a splendid job of it. I'm sending for Dr. Lowe first thing tomorrow."

Julia didn't reply. Maybe there really was something wrong with her.

"And I plan to tell the doctor— Oh dear," her mother said suddenly. "That's your father's carriage. Why on earth is he home so early? Driver, let us off in front, please." Mrs. Hoffman opened the carriage door almost before the wheels stopped rolling and stepped down without waiting for the coachman to help her. Julia hurried to the front door behind her.

"Philip. . . ?" her mother called from the foyer. "Philip, are you home?"

Julia's father emerged from the library. "There you are, at last," he said. "I was about to send for you."

"Send for me? Why? What's wrong? Why are you home so early?"

Ordinarily, nothing ever ruffled Judge Hoffman's calm dignity. But for the first time in Julia's life, she saw that something had. His jacket and waistcoat lay carelessly tossed aside, and his hair was mussed as if he'd been running his hands through it. The drink he carried shook in his hand. "Come in and sit down, Martha," he said, taking his wife's arm.

"I don't want to sit down. I want you to tell me what's wrong."

He led her to a chair in the library in spite of her protests, and Julia followed, both women still wearing their cloaks.

"My brother received a wire from Washington a few hours ago," the judge began.

Mother drew a quick breath. "Oh no! Not Robert."

"I'm afraid so. There's been a battle . . . another terrible disaster for the Union. Robert is missing."

The news of her cousin's disappearance stunned Julia. She sank down on the arm of her mother's chair as she tried to comprehend her father's words. She'd grown up with Robert, lived on the same street with him, and had been conscious of his annoying presence for as long as she could remember. She'd made fun of him for his clumsiness and for his silly preoccupation with soldiers and battles. But even when he'd donned a uniform and marched off to war she'd taken it for granted that he'd always be hanging around in the background of her life somewhere, making a nuisance of himself. But now he wouldn't be. He was missing.

"Oh, Daddy . . . not Robert. . . ." she pleaded.

Her mother gave a little cry. "But . . . they'll find him, won't they? He'll be all right."

"We don't know for sure, we can only hope. They believe he's been taken prisoner, and if so, we should hear in a few days. In the meantime, his parents are quite distraught."

"I can well imagine!"

"Robert's mother fell into a swoon when we told her the news, and we had to use smelling salts to revive her. They've sent for the doctor, but if you could go to her, Martha . . . In fact, I think we should all go over there."

"Of course," Julia's mother said. "Right away. Just give me a moment to collect myself."

Julia knew that her mother was more than capable of handling a situation such as this. Once her initial shock passed, she would become the pillar they would all lean on in the next few days. Julia saw the relief on her father's face, his calm returning now that his wife was home, and it surprised her to see how much her father depended on her. Maybe her mother was more than just an ornament on his arm.

"What a day this has been," he said with a sigh. "Joseph received the telegram around noon, and I've been trying to get more information about the battle ever since."

"What happened, Daddy?" Julia asked. "You said it was a Union disaster?"

"This isn't the time, Julia," her mother said.

"No, it's all right," her father said. "I think I can talk about it now . . . I think maybe I should." He closed his eyes for a long moment, then drew a breath. "I have a friend in the news office at the *Enquirer*. He found out some of the details for me. It was supposed to be a simple reconnaissance mission. A small Union force crossed the Potomac at a place called Ball's Bluff to check out the Confederate defenses. There was a skirmish. The Rebels sent for reinforcements, but we didn't have enough boats to get our own reinforcements across the river in time. Our only choice was to retreat—but there weren't enough boats for that, either. The men were trapped on the riverbank beneath the bluff, with nowhere to go for cover. It was a shooting gallery. When some of the men tried to swim, the Rebels shot them all to pieces in the water. A couple of boatloads of men who'd been wounded in the earlier skirmish got swamped as desperate soldiers tried to climb aboard . . . and they all sank."

He paused for a long moment, then drew another deep breath. "The officers, including Robert, waited to cross the river last, allowing their men to get to safety first. They evidently fought valiantly, but there were too many Rebels and no cover . . . they had their backs to the water. So, rather than see all of their remaining men slaughtered, they surrendered. More than five hundred were taken prisoner, hundreds more were killed in action or drowned, and nearly two hundred were wounded. Altogether, we lost nearly half of the force we started out with."

Having seen Bull Run, Julia could easily imagine the scene—the panicked retreat beneath a hail of gunfire, the blinding cloud of sulfur and smoke, the screams of dying men and flying shells. The earth beneath Robert's feet would have been peppered with enemy bullets as he'd waited for the boats, but he'd stood his ground in the midst of chaos and death to let his men cross the river first. His courage had gotten him captured. Julia's cowardice as she'd panicked and run had cost her Nathaniel's respect—and her own.

"Poor Robert," her mother murmured as she stood, ready now to go console Robert's parents. Julia stood, too. Her father rested a comforting hand on her shoulder as she wiped her tears.

"He'll pull through, Julia. The boy is strong. He has what it takes."

But Julia's tears were more for herself than for Robert. He had always known what he'd wanted—to be an army officer. Now he was following his dream. She'd had no dream except to marry Nathaniel Greene, and he'd made it clear that he could never love her the way she was. This afternoon Julia had recognized herself in the other young girls, interested only in fashion and flirting—and she'd hated what she'd seen. She longed to be different, to be brave and self-sacrificing like her cousin, to be the kind of woman Nathaniel would love and respect. But as she hurried down the street to her cousin's house that cool October evening, she had no idea how to change.

Chapter Four

Western Pennsylvania
October 1861

One week after leaving the Haggertys' store in Bone Hollow, Phoebe Bigelow stood in line at a U.S. Army enlistment office in western Pennsylvania. She'd wrangled rides in several farmers' wagons, a couple of nights' sleep in their haylofts, and even a few free meals at their tables after she'd told them she was fixing to enlist. They'd sent her off with their blessings, stuffing her pockets with apples and buttermilk biscuits. But now she thought she just might faint from the heat as she waited in line in the overcrowded storefront office with dozens of young men eager to enlist.

Phoebe was so tall she could see clear over the head of the man in line in front of her. And she couldn't help overhearing the enlisting officer as he bellowed at him. "I have to write you up as '4-F'! That means you're missing your four front teeth!

"What's that you say?" the man shouted in return. Seemed the poor fellow was not only toothless but deaf to boot.

"You can't fight. I can't enlist you."

"I can't fight?"

"No."

"Hang it all—why not?"

"No teeth," the officer shouted, pointing to his own. "You need teeth."

"Since when does a fella need teeth to fight Rebels? I ain't gonna bite into them, am I? Just give me a gun and let me shoot them."

"You can't tear open the gunpowder cartridges if you don't have your teeth."

"What?"

"I said you need your teeth to open . . . Oh, what's the use. Corporal, get him out of here."

He signaled to a uniformed man standing nearby, and before Phoebe could blink, the corporal whisked the toothless man away and she stood before the officer's table. The wide strip of muslin she'd wrapped around her bosom was drenched with sweat. She wondered what would happen to her if the U.S. Army discovered she was a girl. Would they throw her in jail for lying? She decided she'd better play her part well so they wouldn't find out.

"Come on, come on. Who's next? Step forward and tell me your name, son."

"Um . . . Ike Bigelow." Phoebe had spent the past few days rehearsing her lies so she wouldn't get tangled up in them. But she was broiling hot, her nerves were buzzing like flies, and her voice came out higher pitched than she'd intended. She repeated her name in a deeper voice. "Ike Bigelow."

The man stopped writing and looked up, his brow wrinkling as he studied her. "How old are you, boy?"

"I turned nineteen last June." At least that much was the truth.

His frown deepened. "Then how come all you got is peach fuzz on your cheeks?"

"Begging your pardon, sir, but ain't none of my brothers or me ever been able to grow a beard worth a hoot. Our pa, neither. Ma says it's the Injun blood in us."

"Indian blood? With all that yellow hair?"

"The yellow's on Ma's side. Pa's family—"

"Where're you from?"

"Kentucky, sir. Across the river from Cincinnati." She hadn't dared say Virginia for fear she'd be taken for a Rebel spy. What little geography Phoebe knew had come from her few years of schooling in Bone Hollow and from listening to her brothers plan their own trip. She'd deliberately traveled in the opposite direction from them for the last week and ended up in Pennsylvania.

"Why'd you come all the way over here to enlist?"

"Well, sir. There's four of us brothers in the family, and Ma made us all sign up in different states so's we wouldn't end up all getting kilt in the same battle. I picked Pennsylvania 'cause Jack and Willard already picked Ohio and Indiana. Junior joined up back home in Kentucky."

"Are you sure it's not because you're underage?"

"Oh no, sir. You bring me a Bible and I'll swear on it that I just turned nineteen on the eleventh of June."

"That won't be necessary," he said with a sigh. "Let's see your teeth. You got all your front ones?"

"Yes, sir." Phoebe grinned widely, displaying them. "And I can shoot like nobody's business. Better than any of my brothers. Go on and set an empty bottle on that barrel out front, and I'll bet I can knock it clear off from across the street in a single shot."

"Empty bottles don't shoot back," the officer said sternly. "And they don't come running at you screaming like banshees, either, like the Confederates do. You ready for that?"

"Yes, sir, I'm ready to do my part."

"All right, then. These are your enlistment papers. Once you sign them you're obligated to serve in the United States Army for a period of three years. Your pay will be thirteen dollars a month. Can you read and write, son?"

Phoebe nodded.

"Read this carefully, then, and sign right here."

She quickly scanned the words, too excited to make sense of them. Her sweaty hand made the ink run as she signed her name, *Ike Bigelow,* in neat letters.

"Good. Who's next?" the officer asked. Phoebe didn't move.

"Wait a minute. Ain't you forgetting to give me a rifle?"

"You'll get one when you get to Washington. Next?"

"Washington! Ain't no Rebels in Washington. I signed on to fight—not visit Abe Lincoln."

"First you have to learn to march. After that you'll get your rifle—and your fair share of fighting, believe me."

"But any old fool knows how to put one foot in front of the other. Pa says I been marching all around the farm since I was a year old. And I know how to shoot, too. Give me a rifle and I'll prove it to you."

"There will be plenty of time to show what you can do, son. Go on in the back now, and get yourself a uniform from the quartermaster." He pointed with his thumb to a doorway behind him.

"Thought sure they'd at least give me a gun," Phoebe muttered as she ducked through the door. She found herself in a large, crowded storeroom that was even hotter than the storefront had been. It smelled of leather and warm bodies and kerosene from the lanterns that lit the windowless room. A soldier stood near the door doling out Yankee uniform jackets, shirts, and pants from the large piles beside him. About a dozen other men milled around inside the room, laughing and joking as they stripped off their overalls and work shirts and put on their new blue uniforms.

Phoebe hesitated, wondering what she had gotten herself into. Then she remembered that her only other choice was to wear a dress and work for the Haggertys, and her doubts faded. Seeing men in their underwear was nothing new. Neither was a lack of privacy. After all, she'd grown up in a one-room cabin with three brothers. She took the heap of scratchy wool clothing the quartermaster handed her at the door and found a space for herself in a dim back corner.

The trousers stopped two inches above her ankles—but then, Phoebe was taller than most of the other soldiers by four or five inches. The shirt was too short to tuck into the pants, but she could have fit two heads through the neck hole. "Guess they figure I might grow another head," she said to herself. The material was coarse and itchy, and if she didn't get out of this stifling room pretty soon she would die of the heat. She slid her arms into the dark blue uniform jacket and tried to button the long row of shiny brass buttons, but it fit so snugly across her shoulders and chest that she felt like a snake about to burst out of its skin. The only thing that fit halfway decent was the forage cap.

"Hey, there," a voice beside her said. "Want to trade jackets?"

Phoebe looked down, then smiled. The little fellow standing alongside her wore a coat that was so huge he looked like a tiny little pea in a big blue pod.

"Sure," she said. "Guess it can't hurt to try." Phoebe unfastened the long row of buttons and traded jackets. The other fellow's coat fit her a little better, but not by much. "Must have been a sale on all these brass buttons," she said as she fastened them again. "Can't see why else we'd need so many."

"We have to keep them all shiny-looking, too," the little fellow said. "My uncle joined up a few months back, and he says we have to polish the brass with emery paper every night or we'll get into trouble."

"Seems like a waste of time, don't it?" Phoebe said. "I joined up to fight a war, not polish buttons."

"Hey, you aren't from around here, are you?" the little stranger asked. He had an eager, friendly voice that dipped from high-pitched to low and back again when he talked, like a wagon wheel sliding in and out of a rut.

"No, I crossed over from Kentucky to enlist," Phoebe replied.

"What's your name?"

"Ike . . . Ike Bigelow."

"Nice to meet you, Ike," he said, extending his hand. It was soft, with no calluses, a city boy's hand. "I'm Theodore Wilson. Folks call me Ted."

The top of Ted's curly brown head barely reached Phoebe's chin. He had a wiry build that made him look as though he'd be quick as a deer if he decided to run. His smooth, tanned skin and wide brown eyes gave him the innocent, trusting look of a child. Then he smiled, revealing a pair of oversized front teeth, and he reminded Phoebe for all the world of a squirrel.

"I don't mean to insult you," she said, "but you hardly look old enough to enlist."

"I'm nineteen," Ted told her. "I live around here, so folks know I'm old enough. Hey, did you get all your other gear yet?"

Phoebe shook her head. "They only give me this uniform. The man said I wouldn't get me a gun until I get to Washington. If I'd a known that, I'd have brought a gun from home."

"You have your own gun? You know how to shoot already?" Ted was practically dancing.

"Sure. I been shooting since I could walk and talk. I hardly ever miss, either."

"Will you teach me how?" His voice squeaked with excitement.

"I reckon so," she said, hiding a smile.

"Great. Thanks. Hey, we get our knapsacks and stuff in that line over there. Come on."

Phoebe followed her new friend to the supply line, enjoying the fact that Ted already looked up to her in more ways than one. As the youngest and smallest sibling back home, Phoebe had always been picked on by her brothers and had to fight for the right to do all the things they did. Her brother Jack, especially, took great delight in reminding her that she was a girl.

"You got a girl, Ike?" Ted flung out the word *girl* so suddenly that it threw Phoebe off balance. It took her a moment to realize that he wasn't accusing her of being one but was asking her if she had one.

"Huh? No . . . no, I never had a gal or nothing."

"Me, either, but I sure would like one, wouldn't you? Some of the other fellows carry pictures of their girlfriends. They were showing them all around a while ago and bragging about which one was the prettiest. Sure wish I had a pretty girl's picture to carry with me. . . . But, hey, I kissed a girl once."

"You did?" Phoebe looked at Ted's lips—soft and full, like a baby's—and tried to imagine them pressed against her own. She couldn't recall ever being kissed, not even by her ma or pa, much less a beau.

"Yeah, I kissed Maggie Fisk in the schoolyard one day. Just on the cheek, though. Gosh, she smelled good. Like something you'd eat for dessert."

They finally reached the front of the line. The supply sergeant began piling items into Phoebe's outstretched arms: a haversack for her provisions, a woolen blanket and waterproof sheet, a cartridge box and belt, a bayonet, a tin drinking cup, a canteen, and a knapsack to carry all her personal belongings. The supply sergeant glanced down at her feet, then set a pair of square-toed brogans on top of the pile. Phoebe had never owned a brand-new pair of shoes in her life; she'd either worn her brothers' hand-me-downs or gone barefoot, which she preferred.

"How do you know them are gonna fit me?" she asked the soldier doling out the shoes.

His look told her that asking questions was the wrong thing to do. "We only have three sizes left," he finally said. "Since your feet are the biggest ones I've seen all morning, I gave you the biggest pair I got. Move along now. Gotta keep this line moving."

Phoebe sighed in resignation and followed her new friend through the back door and into a vacant lot behind the building where the other recruits were gathering. The fresh autumn air felt good. Ted flopped down in a small patch of shade to try on his new shoes; Phoebe did the same. The leather was very stiff, and they made her feet feel squished, even before she laced them up. She decided she'd better keep her old, worn-out shoes for now and stuffed them into her new knapsack along with her blanket, rubber sheet, and the possessions from her burlap bag. The knapsack was crammed full to the top, and she was still left with a tangle of straps, sacks, and all the other contraptions they'd just given her.

"What're we supposed to do with all of this?" she wondered aloud.

"My uncle showed me how to carry everything," Ted told her. "Watch." Following his lead, she soon had her cartridge box, belt, bayonet, and haversack fastened properly, her canteen and tin cup hung where they'd be handy, and her bedding rolled up and fastened to her knapsack, ready to carry. She hefted the pack onto her shoulders with a grunt.

"I sure hope they don't expect us to carry this stuff very far," she said. "Feels like somebody's hanging onto the back of my pack, trying to pull me over backward."

She looked down at Ted and saw that the little fellow was bent nearly double beneath his load. She'd watched him pack a lot of extra stuff from home into his knapsack—three books, four extra pairs of socks, two flannel shirts, two spare suits of underwear, a sewing kit, a mirror and shaving items, a jar of homemade preserves, paper and writing utensils, and a bottle of Dr. Barker's Blood Tonic.

"I . . . um . . . hope you don't take offense, Ted, but you better get rid of some of that extra gear you're carrying or you'll be a hunchback by the time the war ends."

"I'm fine," he said, puffing slightly. "Hey, I think we're supposed to go on over to the train depot when we're done changing. You know where that is?"

Phoebe shook her head.

"Come on, I'll show you." She set off down the lane beside Ted, both bearing their loads like pack mules. Phoebe's shoes squeaked and groaned. When she and Ted walked side by side, their tin cups, canteens, and other equipment jangled and clanked and rattled so noisily they sounded like a tinker's wagon going down a bumpy road.

"I think I know why the Union ain't won very many battles," Phoebe said.

"Why's that?" Ted asked, panting.

"I reckon them Rebels can hear us coming for miles."

The army fed them supper in the town's only hotel, then billeted them there for the night, cramming as many recruits into each room as they possibly could. When the train arrived before breakfast the next morning, it seemed to Phoebe that the entire town turned out to see their boys off. The ladies boohooed, waved their handkerchiefs, and threw flowers as mothers and sisters and sweethearts said farewell to their loved ones. With no one to see her off, Phoebe was the first one to board the train, and she took a seat by a window. She'd never been on a train before—had never even been this close to one—and she didn't know if the tremor that rumbled through her was from the huge steam locomotive or from her own excitement and fear.

Outside on the platform, a woman who had to be Ted's mother cried a cloudburst of tears and gripped him in her arms as if she had no intention of ever letting go. She was small and squirrel-like, too, with the same tanned skin and curly brown hair that Ted had.

"Teddy! Oh, my Teddy! Don't leave me. Don't go," she cried in such a heartbroken voice that tears filled Phoebe's eyes. She sometimes dreamed of someone holding her that way, rocking her, loving her, but as far as she knew they were only dreams, not memories. She slouched down on the stiff bench seat, pulling her forage cap over her face and closing her eyes to block out the sight of hugs and kisses and expressions of love beyond her reach. She didn't open her eyes again until the train whistle shrieked, nearly startling her out of her seat.

"Hey," Ted said a moment later. "Mind if I sit here?"

"Go ahead. It ain't my train." She tried to sound indifferent and gruff, but she was secretly pleased to see him. They'd only met yesterday, but she'd already taken a liking to the little fellow. She moved over to make room for him.

Ted perched on the edge of the seat, shrugging off the straps of his bulging backpack so he could set it on the floor. He balanced a huge parcel wrapped in brown paper on his lap.

"Confounded woman got me all wet," he mumbled, wiping his face against his shoulder. "Did your mama bawl and carry on like that when you left home?"

Phoebe glanced at him, then quickly looked away. The tears Ted was trying to wipe away were his own. "My ma died when I was pretty young," she told him.

"Oh. Sorry."

"That's okay. I don't remember her at all, so I can't really miss her."

That much was true. But Phoebe did miss knowing what a mother's love was like. She'd seen mothers like Mrs. Haggerty who yelled all the time and went after their kids with a hickory switch when they didn't mind. But she'd also seen mothers back in Bone Hollow who looked at their kids like they were made of gold or something. Those mothers couldn't stop touching their kids' cheeks or ruffling their hair all the time. She was willing to bet that Ted's mother was the second kind—the kind Phoebe dreamed of.

The whistle screamed again, drowning out the last good-byes and cries of farewell from the platform. The train gave a huge lurch, nearly pitching Phoebe out of her seat. It began rolling forward, hissing steam and huffing like a tired horse plodding uphill. She gripped the armrest, excited and scared at the same time.

"Guess your ma was sorry to see you go, huh?" she asked, trying to push away her fear as the locomotive picked up speed.

"Yeah, I'm all she has now that my sisters are all married and my father's passed on." Ted's voice sounded even shakier than usual. "She didn't want me to go to war at all. Begged me and begged me not to enlist. But I had to get away, you know? See new things, meet new people. I'll have to send my paycheck home every month so she'll have something to live on."

He unwrapped the parcel while he talked, and Phoebe saw that it contained food—fried chicken, a square of johnnycake, several dill pickles, a couple of turnovers, a jar of plum jelly. It also contained a small frypan, a pair of homemade mittens, a pocket-sized Bible, and three more bottles of Dr. Barker's Blood Tonic.

"What're you fixing to do with all that stuff?" Phoebe asked. "Your knapsack's gonna burst at the seams if you try and put anything else in it."

"Hey, I'll make you a deal. If you help me carry some of this, I'll share my food with you."

Phoebe reached for one of the turnovers. "It's a deal."

Outside her train window, the rolling Pennsylvania countryside flew past faster than a whole team of horses could have carried her. She was on her way to an exciting new adventure, with good food in her stomach, new shoes on her feet, and a new friend by her side. Nobody knew that she was a girl. Phoebe Bigelow had never felt happier in her life.

Later that day they arrived in Harrisburg, and Phoebe's happiness quickly began to fade. She and the other recruits were thrown together with greenhorns from other small towns across southern Pennsylvania, and army life truly began. She had her first taste of U.S. Army rations—stringy beef, overboiled potatoes, and bitter coffee. She spent her first night in a Sibley tent, a round, pointy-topped contraption where eighteen recruits slept spoon-style, their feet pointing toward the middle. And she met her new drill sergeant.

Phoebe was barely off the train, her head still spinning and her knees all wobbly, when Sergeant Anderson herded all the new recruits together and began to yell at them. He was almost as short as Ted but very broad across the chest, and he wore a look on his face like he was about to pick a fight with someone. He turned red all over when he yelled, and his neck swelled up and his eyes popped until he reminded Phoebe of a bullfrog.

Sergeant Anderson ranted on and on about how he was going to turn this trainload of pantywaists and mama's boys into real men, how he'd better not hear any bellyaching from anybody or they'd find out what hell on earth was really like. He screamed for the longest time, until Phoebe was not only getting a headache but was also starting to worry that the man would maim his vocal cords if he kept on that way. When she couldn't stand any more, Phoebe took a step forward, raising her hand politely like she'd learned to do in school.

"Excuse me, mister, but I don't reckon you have to yell like that. I can't speak for everyone, but I can hear you just fine. Besides, I saw a man who was hard of hearing trying to enlist, and they wouldn't let him."

She heard ripples of nervous laughter behind her. Sergeant Anderson bellowed a word that might have been *"Quiet!"* but he was so angry, Phoebe couldn't tell. She'd never seen a face as mean as his in her life. He stuck it right up close to hers and roared so loudly and for such a long time that her ears rang and she started to see spots. He scared her so badly she didn't catch most of what he said, but she did understand that she had to report to his tent after all the others were dismissed.

"Good-bye, Ike. It's been nice knowing you," Ted whispered when the time came. She could tell he was trying to make a joke of it, but his boyish face looked paler than usual.

"Aw, I'll be fine," she replied, trying to believe that she would be. "I reckon he can't shoot me—that's Johnny Reb's job. I just hope he don't start hollering in my face again."

When she first arrived at Sergeant Anderson's tent, Phoebe did have to listen to him yell for a while. He carried on about military discipline and how she needed to learn to hold her tongue and to show respect for officers, but he'd clearly run out of steam after screaming at all the other recruits for the past two hours. She supposed that even a rattlesnake had to slither off and make some new venom after biting two or three people, and she felt a little sorry for Anderson.

Her punishment was to clean up after him—tidy up his tent, wash his clothes, clean his lanterns, scrub the mud and manure off his shoes, shine all his uniform buttons. It was women's work and probably would have been very demeaning if it weren't for the fact that she was a woman. True, she had joined the army to get away from cleaning and scrubbing and things like that, but her brothers had left much bigger messes for Phoebe to clean up than Sergeant Anderson had.

"Can you clean and oil a rifle?" he asked when she was finished with everything else. His voice was softer this time, and truth be told, he sounded a little hoarse.

"I ain't never had a rifle," Phoebe replied, "but my pa taught me to clean his shotgun as soon as I was old enough to hold one."

"Let's see how you do with this." He handed her a brand-new Springfield rifle, and it was the most beautiful gun she had ever seen, with a smooth walnut stock and shiny metal bore. She lifted it to her shoulder, sighting down its length.

"My, oh my . . . I bet I could hit a fly off a fence post with this," she murmured.

"Are you a pretty good shot, Bigelow?"

"I'm a crackerjack shot! I been trying to tell the army how I hardly ever miss, but they ain't seen fit to let me show 'em what I can do."

He studied her for a moment through squinted eyes. She could tell he was trying to look mean, but she thought he was probably a little curious, too. "How about if I take you out tomorrow afternoon, Bigelow, and you can put your money where your mouth is."

His words baffled Phoebe. "Put my money. . . ? No, sir. I ain't got any money, but if I did, I don't think I'd want any of it in my mouth."

Sergeant Anderson started to laugh, and he laughed so hard he began to cough and had to sit down for a minute on his campstool. "You're something else, Bigelow," he said when he caught his breath again. "No, what I meant was, how would you like to show me what you can do with a rifle?"

"I'd like that real fine!"

While Phoebe lovingly cleaned Sergeant Anderson's rifle, they talked about different kinds of guns and how they both liked to go deer hunting. By the time she returned to her own tent, Sergeant Anderson didn't seem quite so mean anymore.

He sent for her the next afternoon, as he'd promised, and they walked out to the edge of camp with his Springfield rifle. For the next hour, Phoebe hit every target he gave her, big and small, until they ran out of old tins and bottles to shoot at.

"I've never seen anyone who could shoot as good as you, Bigelow," the sergeant said as they walked back to camp. "I should put your name in for a sharpshooter."

"That'd be just fine with me." Phoebe ran her hand over the smooth wood one last time before she had to give the rifle back. "I can't wait to get me one of these," she said. "In the meantime, can I ask you a favor?"

"What's that?"

"Will you let me come back tonight and clean it again?"

Anderson snorted. "You're a corker, Bigelow. All right, report to my quarters after dinner and I'll let you clean my rifle."

Phoebe was very disappointed that she didn't get to shoot it again. Her daily routine took on a numbing sameness that bored her to tears. She was awakened at dawn by the off-key squeal of fifes and the clatter of drums and was forced to scramble out to the lane in front of the long row of tents so Sergeant Anderson could call roll. Everyone quickly ate breakfast, then for the next two hours, she and the other recruits learned to march—elbows touching, rows thirteen inches apart—using short lengths of fence rails for rifles. They learned to march in a column, to form a battle line, to march double-quick, to dress the line. They drilled until the noon meal, then drilled for two more hours after that. There was a brief rest period in the afternoon, but they were expected to use that time to clean themselves up and polish their buttons—"I told you so," Ted said with his toothy grin—then get ready for another roll call and inspection. Sergeant Anderson would strut up and down the rows, carefully looking them over from head to toe, and Phoebe could tell he was just itching to find a reason to yell.

After inspection they drilled until dinner, and by that time she and the others had been on their feet for most of the day. She figured they'd probably marched several miles and could have caught up to some Rebels if they'd been allowed to keep going instead of hiking back and forth across the same field all day. Shortly after dark, everyone fell asleep, exhausted, and then woke up at dawn to do it all over again.

Every day was the same, drill and more drill. By the end of the first week Phoebe had finally had enough. Instead of joining the scramble for breakfast after roll call one morning, she went forward to talk to Sergeant Anderson.

"Excuse me, sir, but I don't get the point of all this marching around in circles all day. What does it have to do with shooting Rebels? Seems like we're just wearing out our new shoes for nothing." Anderson's eyes bulged. A scarlet flush began slowly creeping up his neck to his face. "Please don't yell at me," she said quickly, "but I just don't understand what it's all for."

"It's not your job to understand," he said through gritted teeth. "Just do what you're told." He turned to stride away with all the dignity of an officer, but Phoebe easily kept pace beside him. Anderson's legs were so short and her legs so long that it was like a stubby little burro trying to outpace a Thoroughbred.

"It's just that it seems like a mighty big waste of time," she continued, "turning this-a-way and that, coming and going and marching around all day until you end up right back where you started. Don't anybody care that there's a war to fight?"

He halted suddenly, glancing all around as if to make sure no one was listening. "Listen, Bigelow. You're going to get yourself in big trouble if you keep shooting off your mouth like this. I'll tell you the reason why we drill because I like you. But in the future, you have to stop asking so many questions and just do what you're told, okay?"

Phoebe nodded.

"It's my job to get everybody in shape for long marches. If you learn to advance in neat rows, then everybody will keep up and there won't be stragglers. You're also learning how to quickly form a battle line from a marching column. And as ugly as this sounds, I'm teaching you to dress the line so that you'll move together, elbows touching, after the fellow beside you falls. You'll keep on firing and hold your line so it doesn't fall apart. Our troops weren't prepared at Bull Run, and it turned into a shambles. But we have a new commander now, and General McClellan is determined to be ready this time." Anderson finished his speech with a curt nod, his chin jutted forward as if ready to take on the entire Confederate army all by himself. Phoebe would have gladly joined him.

"When do you reckon we'll get to fight?" she asked.

"You're just a foot soldier, kid. You'll be the last person to know what's going on and when it's going to happen. Sometimes your company will go on the march for two or three days, then march back again without ever knowing what it was all about. Usually when the whole army marches, only the generals know where they're going and why. It's better that way, see? If you get captured, you can't tell the enemy our plans. Understand, Bigelow?"

"I guess so . . . sir." She remembered to salute, then watched the sergeant's retreating back as he finally strode away.

Ted sidled up alongside her, chewing a piece of bacon. "Hey, you're awfully brave asking questions like that. What did he say?"

"He says we're gonna keep on marching and drilling until we don't have to think about it anymore, just do it in our sleep."

"Well, next time you talk to him, tell him that I march up and down that blasted field every night in my dreams."

After a month in training camp, the U.S. Army finally loaded Phoebe's company of recruits onto a train bound from Harrisburg to Baltimore. They spent the night in a rest home for soldiers, then boarded another train the next morning and headed south to Washington. Phoebe enjoyed her second train ride much more than her first. In fact, now that she knew how fast a train could go and how many miles it could lick up in a day, the knock-kneed horses and rickety farm wagon back home were going to feel like they were standing still. As more and more army encampments came into view outside her window, she nudged Ted, who was napping on the seat beside her.

"You better wake up. I think we're almost to Washington City."

"How do you know?" he said without opening his eyes. "Ever been there before?" Ted's voice, thick with sleep, made Phoebe smile. But then, lots of things about Ted made her smile.

"No, I ain't ever been there, but it's starting to look like fields of cotton out my window, only it's acres and acres of white tents all lined up in rows. And soldiers everywhere. Like a mess of blue grasshoppers."

Ted finally stirred and sat up. He leaned close to Phoebe, who was near the window, and they gazed at the passing scenery together. "I wonder which of these camps is going to be ours?" he said.

"I hope it's none of them. You see what all them soldiers are doing?"

Ted watched for a moment, then shrugged. "What?"

"I been watching for a few minutes now, and most of the ones we passed looked like they was doing exactly what we just spent the last month doing—drilling."

"Maybe the soldiers you saw were greenhorns, like we were back in Harrisburg. Some of them are doing some real soldiering, aren't they?"

"I seen some armed men guarding a bridge back there and a couple more peeking out from behind a cannon—but look at the rest of them, Ted. I swear they're just marching back and forth in rows just like we done, going nowhere."

Ted flopped back against his seat as the train slowed to a crawl. "I've had it up to here with drilling," he said, slicing the air above his head with his hand.

"Me too. I'd just as soon go on home than waste any more time. I sure do hope we finally get to fighting."

"Oh, I expect we will," he replied. "I read in the paper the other day that President Lincoln ordered a unified aggressive action against the Rebels. I think he means business."

It took Phoebe a minute to figure out Ted's ten-dollar words. He had to be one of the smartest people she'd ever met—working as a clerk in his uncle's factory and all, counting money and keeping his books. She decided that what he'd just said meant that Mr. Lincoln was finally going to let her fight.

"When I signed up," she said, "they promised we'd get ourselves some real guns once we got to Washington City."

"I sure hope so. Hey, Ike, don't forget—you promised to teach me how to shoot."

"I won't forget," she said, smiling at his eagerness. Ted had his hat off, and she had to resist the urge to ruffle his curly brown hair the way you would a child's.

They quickly left the outlying encampments behind and entered the city itself. Phoebe's first glimpse of her nation's capital left her disappointed. There were some bigger buildings that looked brand-new, but the city didn't look nearly as nice as Baltimore or even Harrisburg. And most of the streets weren't even paved. She hoped they didn't stay here too long.

When the train finally pulled into the station, Phoebe and Ted shouldered their gear and stood in the aisle with all the others. Soldiers crammed the platform outside, and Phoebe worried that little Ted would get lost in the sea of blue uniforms.

"Grab onto my belt," she told him. "I'll keep an eye on Sergeant Anderson."

"Lucky for me you're so tall," he said as he slipped his hand around her canteen strap.

Together they followed the sergeant through the station and outside into the street. The air was smoky from hundreds of campfires, and Phoebe thought she also smelled the damp, fishy scent of a nearby river. A military band played a rousing march to welcome them, and the lively sound of bugles and drums seemed to make her blood pump twice as fast through her veins. She could lick a whole gang of Rebels if they kept on playing music like that. It even made her want to march—which was a lucky thing, because the sergeant told them to fall into formation. He ordered a roll call, and when everyone was in place, they began to march down the street through ankle-deep mud. If Phoebe's new shoes hadn't been a size too small they would have been sucked right off her feet. She wondered if the army had planned it that way.

Except for some of the newer buildings, Phoebe thought most of Washington City was pretty ugly. The streets around the government buildings were nice and wide, and the Capitol building looked like it was going to be fancy once they got that dome-thing finished. And Mr. Lincoln had himself a pretty nice place, too, even if there were a bunch of soldiers lined up outside in his yard. But the streets were mired in so much mud the people could have used boats to get around instead of wagons. There were so many soldiers marching and horses trotting and mules pulling long trains of white-roofed army supply wagons that they kept the mud all churned up and soggy.

Phoebe had never seen so many Negroes in one place before, either. Everywhere she looked she saw dark faces—and all of them wearing rags. Folks back home in Bone Hollow didn't have much, and Phoebe had never worn brand-new clothes or a pair of new shoes until she'd joined the army. But these folks were so pitiful-poor they brought tears to her eyes, especially when she saw little children begging.

The march to their new camp near the river was the longest one Phoebe's company had ever taken in a straight line. She had helped carry some of Ted's supplies in her own pack, but even so, he looked done in by the time they arrived.

"You better throw out some of that extra gear you're toting," she told him as they ate supper that evening, "or it's gonna weigh you down so deep in all this mud it'll take a team of mules to pull you out."

"I know, I know," he said, yawning. "I'll sort everything out first thing tomorrow."

Ted crawled into the Sibley tent they would share with a dozen other men and fell sound asleep before Phoebe even got her shoes off.

As the sky was growing light the next morning, Phoebe was awakened by the telltale cramping she'd grown to dread. She couldn't believe her rotten luck. *Oh no. Not the curse. Not now.* She had no privacy here, crammed together as she was with dozens of men day and night. This would give her secret away for sure.

She crawled out from under her blanket as quietly as she could, retrieved her knapsack, and carefully stepped over her sprawled, snoring tentmates. As she made her way to the latrine area in the damp, cold air, longing for the warmth of her blanket, she wished with all her heart that God hadn't seen fit to make her a girl.

Phoebe found a private place behind some bushes and knelt on the ground. She was still digging through her pack when a voice startled her.

"What are you doing, Ike?"

She yelped with fright. "Oh, Ted! You scared me half to death!" She pressed her hand to her chest and felt her heart racing like it was trying to run for cover. "Why did you sneak up on me like that?"

"I saw you get up and leave . . . and you had your pack with you. I was afraid you were going home or something."

"Why would I do a fool thing like that?"

"I don't know. You said you were sick of drilling. I was afraid . . . They shoot deserters, you know, and I didn't want anything to happen to you."

Phoebe couldn't reply. She was surprised—and touched—to find out that he cared. "Naw, I'm just using the latrine," she said after a moment. "I think . . . um . . . I got the trots. You know?"

"Yeah . . . everybody's got them."

"Anyhow, I promise you, the last thing I plan on doing is running off. We got a war to fight, remember? Go on back to bed. I'll be there in a minute."

Ted nodded and made his way back through the bushes.

Alone again, Phoebe was dumbfounded to feel tears filling her eyes. She wondered why. Part of the reason, she decided, was because having a friend like Ted was such an amazing new feeling. Nobody had ever cared where she went or what happened to her before. Back home, she had once gotten herself lost in the woods for two days and her pa had never even thought to look for her. Her own brothers had traded her to Mrs. Haggerty like a bushel of corn when they had no more use for her.

But the other reason for Phoebe's tears was fear. She liked her new life as a soldier, in spite of all the drilling. And she was scared to death that she would lose it all if they found out she was a girl. For the next week or so she would have to get up early every morning to make sure she had privacy. But as Ted had just proved, sneaking around in the dark was risky, too. What if someone else followed her? Or what if she forgot the password one morning and a nervous sentry shot her for a Rebel spy?

If only they would hurry up and start fighting. Then everybody would be too busy to notice that she was a girl. Like she had just told Ted, there was a war to fight, and Phoebe Bigelow was determined to be part of it.

Chapter Five

Philadelphia
December 1861

"Are you going to work in this boring booth all night, Julia? Will I never get to spend a moment with you?"

Julia looked up from the pile of hand-rolled bandages she'd been counting. Arthur Hoyt, her escort for the evening, leaned against the trestle table with his arms crossed, as if commanding her to leap over and join him on the other side. His voice had the demanding tone of a spoiled child.

"I'm chairman of the organizing committee, Arthur. I'm sure I explained to you that I'd have to work tonight."

"But surely not all evening . . . and not three times harder than everyone else."

It had been Julia's idea to organize this Christmas bazaar to raise funds for the United States Christian Commission. She had convinced some of her friends to help her, and they'd spent the past few weeks begging merchants for donations to award as game prizes, asking churches and charity groups to contribute items for the soldiers' care packages, and decorating the hall and the booths. The hard work had eased Julia's conscience and helped release some of the aching restlessness that had drummed through her ever since Bull Run. It had also earned the gratitude of Reverend Nathaniel

Greene, cofounder of the Christian Commission's Philadelphia branch.

"You could help me with these bandages, Arthur," Julia said with a smile she didn't feel. "Then I'd be finished sooner."

His expression told her how ridiculous the suggestion was. He grabbed her hands so she couldn't continue her work. "Enough. You're my date for the evening, and I claim you. Now."

"But I can't leave the booth."

"Nonsense." He released her hands and strode over to speak to Nathaniel, who was working at a table piled with hand-knitted items for the soldiers. "Excuse me, Reverend Greene. You need to find someone to take Julia's place. I'm laying claim to her." Arthur was all smiles, his attitude jovial and good-natured, but something about the way he commanded everyone irritated Julia. Who did he think he was?

"Certainly," the minister replied. "Miss Hoffman has worked very hard this evening. She deserves to have a bit of fun." Reverend Greene followed Arthur back to Julia's table and took her place himself.

"Now, let's get some refreshments," Arthur said, taking her arm.

"I'm really not hungry."

"Well, I am." He led her to the food booth and heaped a plate with an assortment of snacks and pastries. He left a generous donation, then sat down across from Julia at a small table for two, placing the plate between them. "That's better," he said, propping his chin on his hand to gaze at her. "I'm tired of looking at you from all the way across the room. And I'm very tired of sharing you with everyone else."

"But I warned you that I would have to work tonight, and you agreed—"

"I know, I know. I'm very selfish for wanting the most beautiful woman in the room all to myself."

The compliment would have thrilled Julia six months ago; now she wanted to leap up and return to work, proving that there was more to her than outward beauty. She tried to smile, to be gracious to Arthur, tried desperately to like him for her father's sake. *"If I was the sort of father who arranged his daughter's marriage,"* Judge Hoffman had told her, *"I'd arrange for you to marry young Arthur Hoyt. There is no finer man in Philadelphia. Give him a chance, Julia, for my sake. That's all I ask."*

She had tried very hard to be a model daughter ever since her cousin Robert had been captured, aware that her parents had enough to worry about without worrying about her. She had attended to her social obligations without sulking or trying to shock anyone. She'd allowed her maids to dress her and fix her hair. And she had dutifully accepted all of Arthur Hoyt's invitations for the past two months. Arthur was good-looking, attentive, and wealthy—everything a woman could want in a man. Julia's friends discussed him as if he were the grand prize in a courting contest and told her how lucky she was to have won his attentions. She had given Arthur a chance, for her father's sake. She had tried very hard to like him. But after all this time, her heart still felt nothing at all toward him except a niggling irritation at the way he bossed her around.

"Eat something, Julia," he said, pushing the plate of sweets toward her. "I bought these to share with you, and you haven't even touched them." She did as she was told and picked up a cookie, but the prickle of irritation was slowly sprouting into a thorn of resentment. They made small talk for a while until Arthur had eaten most of the food. "Let's leave," he said suddenly. "We can go for a carriage ride in Fairmont Park."

"I can't leave yet, Arthur. Reverend Greene is supposed to speak to us about the work the Commission is doing."

He rolled his eyes. "Wonderful. I'm a little short on sleep, and Greene's sermons are always good for a snore or two." Julia opened her mouth to reply, ready to condemn Arthur for his uncharitable remark, but he popped a chocolate into her mouth, cutting off her words. "Oh, don't look so shocked," he said, laughing. "It was a joke. And speak of the devil, I think the good reverend is about to give us his speech right now."

Nathaniel Greene climbed onto the platform as the little band finished a waltz. He held up his hands to quiet the crowd. "I'd like to thank you all for coming tonight," he began, "and for making this fund-raiser for the Christian Commission such a success. I would especially like to thank the bazaar's organizer, Miss Julia Hoffman, for all her hard work."

Julia hadn't expected the hearty round of applause that followed, and it embarrassed her. But she saw a new respect in the minister's eyes as she modestly accepted his thanks and knew that she had won back part of what she'd lost at Bull Run. She hadn't flirted with Nathaniel or pursued him since he'd returned but had quietly kept her distance, talking to him only when necessary. Her desire for revenge had long since faded, and she no longer hated him or wanted to have him fired. Indeed, his simple words of thanks tonight made her feel happier than she had in months.

"There," Arthur whispered, "you've received your recognition and reward. Can we go now?"

Julia's joy dissolved into shame. Arthur Hoyt, of all people, had seen her hard work for what it was—a desire for praise and recognition. If she left now, Nathaniel would see it, too.

"No. It would be rude to leave," she whispered back. "He isn't finished speaking."

"For those of you who don't know," Nathaniel continued, "the United States Christian Commission was founded in New York City a few months ago and has quickly sprouted branches in other cities, including Philadelphia. One of our aims is to supplement the food and clothing provisions our soldiers receive, so the items we've collected tonight will help immensely. A second goal is to offer moral and spiritual relief to our soldiers in the field. Men who are away from their homes and families for the first time will face many new and evil temptations. Our presence in their midst and the Bibles we distribute can provide strength to help defeat Satan's wiles. But our founding goal is to win souls for Christ. Men are never more receptive to the Gospel than when faced with their own mortality on the battlefield. It's the ideal time to tell them of Christ's love and of the eternal home He has prepared for those who are His own.

"I'm very grateful for your generous support tonight in helping us reach that goal. But I'd also like to ask some of you to consider walking the extra mile that Christ spoke of. The Christian Commission is comprised of ordinary men and women who volunteer their time to talk to soldiers, to serve as nurses, to help share the Gospel, and to distribute Bibles. Where there are battlefields there is real suffering. Jesus gave us the example of the Good Samaritan—the one man in three who didn't turn his back on a wounded man but dared to get involved."

Julia felt shame burning her cheeks. She could no longer look at Nathaniel. Even if she organized a hundred bazaars she could never atone for what she'd done at Bull Run. She knew now that she had to go back. She had to return to the battlefield to help the wounded soldiers, not turn her back this time.

"We're commanded to love our neighbor," Nathaniel continued, "and our neighbor is the person in need. Beginning next spring, I'll be taking a leave of absence from the church to offer my services as a Commission chaplain. Please, won't some of you consider joining me? The Commission needs you to go into the field as nurses and aid workers. Can you spare a few weeks, a month perhaps, for this very important work? Don't turn your back on our suffering soldiers. Listen for the voice of God. Perhaps He is calling you tonight. . . . Again, thank you all for making this event a success. Please, enjoy the rest of the evening."

Julia stood, so moved by Nathaniel's words that she was ready to become the first volunteer. But before she could make her way through the crowd that quickly surrounded him on the bandstand, her escort blocked her path. Arthur had risen from the table while Nathaniel had been speaking and had disappeared; now he'd returned carrying Julia's coat. He held it up for her, waiting for her to put it on, a smile barely masking his impatience.

"Come on, Julia, my carriage is out front. It's time to leave."

"But the evening isn't over—and I should stay and help clean up."

"I'll send a dozen servants over in the morning to help. Come on."

There was little she could do but obey. Arthur quickly helped her into her coat and led her outside. She could see her breath in the cold night air. Fresh snow had fallen while they'd been inside, covering the dirty slush and making the city look pretty. Snowflakes sifted gently down as she walked to the carriage, dusting her shoulders like powdered sugar.

Arthur was quiet as they settled inside his enclosed carriage and began to ride. Then he leaned close. "I gave Reverend Greene one hundred dollars tonight for his Christian Commission. Don't you think I deserve a reward?"

"A reward? What do you mean?"

"How about a little kiss? Right here." He pointed to his cheek.

Julia knew that Arthur had only attended the bazaar for her sake. It had been very kind of him to support her cause. She decided to oblige and moved closer to kiss his cheek. But as soon as her lips touched his face, he quickly turned his mouth to hers, kissing her fully on the lips. When she tried to pull away, he held the back of her head so she couldn't escape until he was finished.

"How dare you!" she said when she finally squirmed away. She was afraid she was going to cry. Julia had never been kissed before, although she had long imagined what it would be like, practicing with her pillow in bed at night, pretending it was the man she loved. She had never imagined her first kiss to be stolen from her this way, against her will. She wiped her mouth to rid it of Arthur's touch, feeling as if she'd been robbed. He saw her reaction and frowned.

"I asked nicely, Julia. Besides, one little kiss is the very least you owe me for being patient tonight. Not to mention generous."

"A kiss isn't given in payment for something," she said, her voice shaking. "It's a sign of affection between two people who care for each other."

"I do care for you," he said, taking her hand in both of his. "And I assumed that you cared for me, too, or you wouldn't have allowed me to court you all these weeks."

She pulled her hand away. "Take me home, Arthur."

"Oh, don't be childish! It was just a kiss. Besides, did you think I'd wait forever? I'm hardly a monk like your sainted friend Reverend Greene."

The tears she'd been holding back filled her eyes at the mention of Nathaniel's name. "I'd like to go home," she repeated.

"Fine!" He rapped on the window to give the coachman the order, then slouched against the seat with his arms crossed. Arthur didn't look handsome at all when he was angry. "I was warned that courting you would be a challenge, Julia—like Shakespeare's *Taming of the Shrew*. I usually enjoy a challenge, but tonight I find your attitude ridiculous."

Her tears quickly turned to fury at his words. "Since you consider me such a shrew, I suggest you find someone else to take to the Christmas ball. I no longer care to go with you."

"Oh, no you don't," he said, twisting around to face her. "That ball is next week, and I'm not changing my plans now. I've invested a great deal of my time courting you, and I don't intend to see it all wasted just because I stole a silly kiss. There are plenty of other women who would have been grateful for my company all these weeks—and not nearly as stingy with their affection."

"Then you can just take one of them to the ball."

Arthur looked furious. "You'd better think twice before you cancel a date with me," he said, wagging his finger in her face. "I'll spread the truth about your coldness all over Philadelphia, and you'll be lucky to find yourself with any suitors at all."

Julia knew Arthur could make good on his threat, and probably would, but she didn't care. She grabbed his waving finger and pushed it aside. "Do you really think you can win a woman's heart with threats?"

"I wonder if you even have a heart, Julia. If you do, it's as cold as stone. I respect your father a great deal, which is why I agreed to court you. But I may have to speak with him about your behavior."

Julia closed her eyes, and the tears she'd been holding back began to flow at the thought of disappointing her father. Was it really true that she had a cold heart? Was that the reason she had turned her back on those wounded soldiers?

Neither she nor Arthur spoke again until the carriage came to a halt at last in front of her house. Julia might have relented and given him one more chance if she hadn't opened her eyes in time to see the look of smug satisfaction on his face.

"I'll accept those tears as your apology," he said, taking her chin in his hand, "and I'll pick you up for the ball as planned."

Julia's entire body began to tremble with rage. She pushed his hand away a second time. "I don't care what you tell my father," she said. "I don't care if you're the last bachelor in Philadelphia. I'd sooner die an old maid than spend my life with a man who thinks he can buy a woman's affections—not to mention a man who bullies and bribes and threatens her to get his own way. Good-bye, Arthur. Please don't ever call on me again." She jumped down from the carriage and ran up the walk to the front door, praying he wouldn't follow her.

Julia's father met her in the foyer as she stepped inside. The smile on his face turned to a look of bewilderment as she slammed the door behind her. "Where's Arthur? We were supposed to have a drink together."

"I know you think highly of him . . ." she began, trying to control her tears.

"What's the matter? Did you two have a tiff?"

"I can't stand him, Father! He's arrogant and overbearing, and . . . and he acts as if he owns me!" She could no longer hold back her tears. They seemed to unnerve her father more than her words.

"Oh, good heavens. Where's your mother? Martha . . ."

"No, don't call Mother. I'm all right. I'll stop." Julia quickly pulled herself together. She had tried to make her mother understand how she felt and had gotten nowhere. Her father was her last hope. "I don't want to talk to Mother, I want to talk to you."

"To me?" he said in alarm. "What about?"

Julia felt so desperate to explain her unhappiness to her father that her words came out in a rush. "I can't live this way anymore. I don't want to stay here and court Arthur—or anyone else. I want to go back to Washington or wherever the war is and become a nurse. I want to help soldiers—"

"Absolutely not!"

"Please, Daddy. If I could just—"

"That sort of work is beneath you. You're a young woman of the highest social standing, not a common working girl or servant. Besides, it's highly improper for an unmarried woman to live and work in those army camps amongst such huge masses of men. Do you want to be branded 'immoral'? No one will ever marry you."

"I don't care. I don't want to get married, especially to a man like Arthur, who thinks he owns me."

"Now, Julia—"

"I'm terrified at the thought of being trapped with a man I don't love, the way Rosalie is. And I don't think I could stand living a life like Mother's with nothing to look forward to day after day, year after year but endless teas and boring charity events. I want my life to matter!"

He gripped her shoulders, shaking her slightly. "How dare you insult your mother! Her life isn't worthless—"

"It is compared to Florence Nightingale's life."

"Where are these foolish ideas coming from? Don't tell me you've gotten mixed up in the suffrage movement?"

"I don't want to *vote,* Daddy," she said in exasperation, "I want to be a nurse. Reverend Greene spoke tonight about the need for volunteers to join the Christian Commission. That's what I want to do. I want to join the Commission and go into the field."

"One sermon, Julia, and you're ready to throw away the life you've always known?" His grip tightened, as if he could squeeze such foolish ideas out of her like wringing water from a cloth. "You'd better think this through carefully, because you can't have it both ways. Do you want respectability and a position in society, a decent husband and a civilized life—or do you want to flit around, 'mattering' like some radical suffragette? Those are two opposing things. Now, I won't hear any more of this foolishness," he said, finally releasing her. "And I'm certainly not allowing you to run away just because you've had a spat with your beau."

"You're not listening to me! You're a judge, Daddy. You're supposed to listen to people and be fair and impartial."

"It's impossible to be impartial when I'm responsible for you."

"But you're not responsible for me anymore. I'm an adult now. I can do what I want with my life."

"Don't be absurd. You're a woman, and women need to be protected and shielded all their lives. That's a father's job until a woman finds a husband, then the job becomes his. That's the way civilized societies function."

On some level, Julia had always known that she would go from being under her father's protection and authority to being under her husband's. But hearing the truth put so bluntly made her feel trapped and more desperate than ever to escape. She wanted to scream in frustration, but she knew she'd never change her father's mind by becoming hysterical. The way to win him over was through calm reason and logic—and by letting a man argue her case.

"I'll only ask you for one thing, Daddy," she said, fighting to control her tears. "Come with me and talk to Reverend Greene yourself. Let him explain what the Christian Commission does and tell you about the need for volunteers. Then you can decide whether or not it's proper for me to go with him."

Three days later, Julia and her father sat in the Christian Commission's tiny downtown office with Reverend Greene. The minister spent several minutes enthusiastically explaining the group's goals and principles, probably expecting a sizable donation from Judge Hoffman, who listened in stern silence.

"Any monetary contributions are being spent to purchase Bibles," Greene finished. "We're staffed by volunteers, as you know, who donate a few weeks or months of their time to go into the field with our soldiers. I'll be going as a volunteer myself this spring to distribute the items we collected at the bazaar. By the way, Miss Hoffman," he said, turning to Julia, "I want to thank you again for all your hard work. The event was an enormous success."

"I'm glad." She saw respect in his gray-blue eyes and summoned the courage to plunge ahead, not waiting for her father. "The reason we've come, Reverend, is because I was quite moved by your words on the night of the bazaar. I would like to volunteer my time to work for the Commission."

"Wonderful! We certainly could use your help in organizing more events like the last one. Any funds you raise will be greatly appreciated by—"

"That's not what I mean. I want to go out in the field as a volunteer."

His warm smile faded. He looked from Julia to her father, then back to Julia with an expression of concern. "I'm very sorry if my words were misleading the other night. While it's true that we do need volunteers, I'm afraid that it would be out of the question to accept an unmarried woman as a delegate."

"But . . . but why?" Julia's disappointment was so great the words sprang from her mouth before she could stop them. "That's not fair!"

"I'm sorry . . . but surely you understand, Judge Hoffman. Our volunteers live in tents alongside thousands of soldiers. There are a few female volunteers, but they are all married women."

"Yes, I do understand," Julia's father replied. "I tried to explain this to my daughter, but she wouldn't listen to me. I thought she might accept it better if it came directly from you. Thank you for your time." He stood to go. Julia was unable to move from her chair.

"Please, you said you needed nurses," she begged. "That's what I want to be. Isn't there any way?"

"Women from your station in life simply don't do that sort of work," her father insisted. "Come now. We don't want to take any more of Reverend Greene's time."

"Excuse me, sir," Greene said, "but that's not quite true. Dorothea Dix has been appointed the Director of Nurses in Washington, and I assure you that the women she's training to become nurses have come from the finest of backgrounds, just like your daughter."

"Is that so? Does she accept unmarried women?"

"Well, I'm not sure, but Miss Dix herself is single. And I know that the need for nurses is very great. If Julia is serious about becoming a nurse—"

"I am," she said. "I've given it a great deal of thought, and it's what I want to do."

"Then I suggest you write to Miss Dix for a list of her qualifications," Nathaniel said. "In the meantime, you could gather a few letters of recommendation to accompany your application."

Buoyed by hope, Julia wrote to the Director of Nurses in Washington that same day. The stiff reply she received from Miss Dix's office, outlining the qualifications for army nurses, didn't discourage her in the least:

No young ladies should be sent at all; only mature women who are sober, earnest, self-sacrificing, and self-sustained; who can bear the presence of suffering and exercise entire self-control of speech and manner; who can be calm, gentle, quiet, active, and steadfast in duty. All nurses are required to be plain-looking women. Their dresses must be brown or black, with no bows, no curls, no jewelry, and no hoop skirts.

Julia paid a visit to their family doctor, explaining that she wanted to become an army nurse and asking him for a letter of reference.

"It's no use going to Miss Dix," Dr. Lowe told her. "She will send you right back. You're much too young."

"Will you write the letter anyway?" she pleaded. "I need you to testify to my good character, my upbringing and sincerity. Please, just give me a chance."

When Congressman Rhodes returned to Philadelphia for the holiday break, she asked him the same thing. He stared at her in disbelief.

"Bull Run was a terrible experience for all of us. Why on earth would you want to be exposed to such sights again?"

"I have to go back. I'm so ashamed of my actions that day, and I know that I could do better this time. Please, I want to help."

"The scenes you witnessed on that battlefield won't look any different the second time around," he said.

"The bombs frightened me, falling as close as they did. If I worked in a hospital, I know I could keep my wits about me. I could help those poor wounded men."

"Do you have your father's permission, Julia?" he asked quietly.

"Well, to be honest, he's not at all happy about my decision. But he's allowing me to pursue it. He says that if Miss Dix accepts me, he'll support me. All I need from you, Congressman, is a letter of recommendation."

He sighed and gave her what she'd asked for.

Armed with letters from him, Dr. Lowe, and the retired pastor of her church, Julia went into her father's study one night and begged him to allow her to go to Washington after the first of the year and apply in person to Miss Dix. He looked at her with such distaste, she might just as well have been requesting permission to rob a bank.

"I'm going to ask you one more time, Julia—forget this foolishness and settle down to a respectable life." He sat stiffly behind his desk, appealing to her as a judge might appeal to a criminal to forsake a life of crime. "Why would you want to sacrifice what you have always known, a life that is safe and comfortable and predictable, to venture into the unknown? Don't you realize that if you take such a risk, you might never get this life back again?"

"I don't want this life," she said. But she spoke the words very softly, not sure she believed them. She told herself that it wasn't just a boring, vain existence she was casting aside but the person she feared she would become if she stayed home, the woman Nathaniel had called shallow and spoiled and unbearably self-absorbed.

"In many ways you've been sheltered from the world," her father continued. "And now, for some strange reason, you've analyzed the way you live, the life your mother and I have worked hard to give you, and you've seen only its faults. What I fear is that you will finally come to appreciate what you've been given only after you've seen the ugliness in the world—and by then it might be too late. You might have lost your chances for a decent husband and a respectable life."

Julia couldn't reply. Deep inside she feared the same thing, feared that she was about to make an irreparable mistake. Should she take the risk?

"Surely there is one young man in all of Philadelphia," he said, "who might appeal to you if you gave him a chance?"

She was surprised to find herself thinking of Nathaniel. Even though she knew his low opinion of her, she still dreamed that he would see her in a different light once she became a nurse, that he'd discover she had changed and would fall in love with her at last.

"I'm not ready to settle down," she told her father. "If you force me to marry, I'll be miserable."

"Then why not take a trip abroad—visit London, perhaps, or France?"

"I don't like the ocean. Please, Daddy, let me try my hand at being a nurse for a few months. If you let me go to Washington, I promise I'll take courting seriously when I come home."

He leaned toward her, his eyes soft, as if he'd suddenly stripped off his judge's robes and allowed himself to be her father. "Do I have your word on that, Julia? You will truly settle down if I let you try this?"

She felt a shiver of excitement. He was really going to let her go. "Yes, I promise."

"You do realize that you cannot go without a chaperone." He leaned back in his chair, the analytical judge once again. The tender moment had passed. "And it may be as late as next summer before your mother is free to accompany you."

Julia saw this excuse for what it was—a delaying tactic. Her father hoped she would change her mind before next summer. She knew that she wouldn't. In fact, the delay would only make her more restlessly unhappy than she already was.

"Maybe Aunt Eunice could take me," she said, thinking quickly. Her father's spinster sister adored Julia. She could sweet talk Aunt Eunice into anything.

"You may ask her," he said reluctantly, "but she has social obligations, too. If she agrees to accompany you, I'll agree to let you go. If not . . ."

"Thank you, Daddy! Thank you!" She ran around his desk and surprised him with a hug, then hurried from the room before he changed his mind.

Chapter Six

Washington City
December 1861

Phoebe bent to crawl out of the Sibley tent at morning reveille and came upon a small surprise: three inches of fresh snow had blanketed the frozen ground during the night. A gray, icy haze hung over the camp, and the mess sergeant was chipping through a layer of ice in the frozen water barrel with an ax. Phoebe fastened all the buttons on her new winter overcoat and hunched her shoulders against the cold.

All around her, the other soldiers huddled together in their long overcoats as they tried to shake off their slumber. Some smoked cigarettes, while others cupped their hands and blew on their fingers to warm them. A few stood near the cook's fire, waiting to fill their mugs with hot coffee. The snow crunched beneath their boots, and their breath fogged the air as they waited for morning roll call and breakfast.

The camp was starting to feel like home to Phoebe and to look like it, too. She and the other soldiers had fashioned tables and improvised other furnishings from whatever they could find—logs, empty crates, upturned barrels—to make the camp more comfortable. Near the door of her tent, her brand-new .58-caliber Springfield rifle was stacked teepee-style with five of her tentmates' rifles. The army had finally issued the new weapons, and on this cold

December morning the men were going to drill with them for the first time. Phoebe carefully separated hers from the others and brushed off the snow with her bare fingers, wiping it dry on the sleeve of her coat. She would have kept the gun inside the tent with her last night if she'd known it was going to snow.

When the metal was reasonably dry, she stuck the rifle under her arm and shoved her hands in her pockets to warm them. Ted had gone off toward the latrine earlier, and she gazed in that direction until she saw him striding back. He was easy to spot; the sleeves of his new greatcoat hung below his fingertips and the lower hem reached nearly to his ankles.

"Hey, our rifles aren't going to get rusty sitting out here, are they?" he asked, pushing up his sleeves. "Maybe we should keep them inside with us."

"I was just thinking the same thing." She pulled her hands out of her pockets and helped Ted remove his rifle from the stack. He wiped off the snow, then slung the strap over his shoulder so the gun hung behind his back.

"You know, this blasted thing is heavy," he said. "I'm going to wish I had my fence rail back if they expect us to march with these things all day."

"You don't really wish that," she said, gently poking him in the ribs with her gun barrel. "Can't shoot Rebels with a fence rail, you know." She lifted the gun to her shoulder and sighted down its length, aiming into the distant woods and squeezing the trigger. "I can't wait to try this thing out. How 'bout you?"

"It would be a real treat to shoot it—especially at Johnny Reb. But knowing the army, they're just going to make us march around in circles with it until we're too tired to stand up. I'll bet it'll be months before they even give us any ammunition."

"Boy, I hope you're wrong," she said, lowering the rifle again.

So far, their schedule in this new camp varied only slightly from the one they'd followed in their first training camp in Pennsylvania. Phoebe and Ted drilled endlessly, sometimes eight hours a day. But now their company of recruits was part of a new regiment—which meant hundreds and hundreds of men marching together, with bands playing and drums pounding and regimental flags waving.

Phoebe was starting to hear the tramp of marching feet in her dreams.

Here in their winter quarters in Washington, General McClellan was whipping them into fighting shape. Phoebe often saw him watching their dress parades, riding around on his big black horse or strutting around like he was cock of the roost. The men called him "Little Mac" or "the young Napoleon" because he wasn't a very big fellow. But they loved their commander, and they were ready to follow General McClellan to the ends of the earth.

Phoebe and the others had learned to form a marching column of four men abreast, then change to two tightly packed battle lines on command. The way they all whirled and twirled at the same time, playing follow-the-leader, reminded Phoebe of a row of baby ducklings following the mama duck wherever she went. They had also learned to tell the difference between twenty-two different drum rolls and thirty-four different bugle calls.

"Once the battle starts," their commanding officer had explained, "there'll be so much noise you won't hear me shouting orders anymore. You have to know what each drum roll and bugle call means and be able to respond to it right away."

The new routine also included a daily sick call. Phoebe grew worried when hundreds of her fellow recruits took sick with silly kids' diseases like measles and chicken pox. One of her biggest fears was that she would wind up in the hospital and her secret would get found out, so she kept to herself to make sure she wouldn't catch anything. This morning there were two more suspected cases of measles, including a man from her own tent. Dozens of men were coughing. One recruit, who had a rag tied around his jaw because of a sore tooth, argued loudly with the sergeant who wanted him to report to the regimental physician.

"Nobody's pulling my tooth!" he insisted. "We're starting rifle and bayonet drills today, and I ain't missing out."

Ted was so eager to begin that he wolfed his breakfast, then stood beside Phoebe, nagging her to finish. But when they finally fell into formation and began the drills, Ted's prediction proved all too true. To Phoebe's great disappointment, they weren't given any ammunition. All morning long, as the sun slowly burned away the haze and the blanket of snow melted beneath hundreds of trampling feet, the recruits practiced the nine steps required to load and fire their new weapons—with imaginary ammunition.

"Your goal," Sergeant Anderson told them, "is to load, take aim, and fire three rounds a minute."

By the time Phoebe marched back to camp for the noon meal, her feet were soaked and frozen. "I think the army's trying to kill us off and save Johnny Reb the trouble," she told Ted.

"You know what?" he said wearily. "I wish I'd joined the cavalry or the artillery instead of the infantry. This blasted gun is heavy!"

Sergeant Anderson had warned Phoebe not to ask questions, but when she saw him sitting on a tree stump eating his lunch all alone, she couldn't help wandering over and asking just one more question.

"Sergeant Anderson? Um, I was just wondering . . . Please don't yell, but . . . when are we gonna get us some target practice?"

"When you see the whites of the enemy's eyes," he said without looking up.

Phoebe thought he might be joking, but he wasn't smiling. "Won't that be too late, sir?"

"Nope." He looked up at her. "You'll be motivated not to waste ammunition then, won't you."

"I guess so. But, sir. . . ? What are we waiting for?"

His reply was one word: "Spring."

As the calendar changed to a new year, 1862, Phoebe's regiment crossed the Potomac River into Virginia and pitched their tents on the Rebel General Robert E. Lee's estate in Arlington.

"Hey, let's see how he likes that!" Ted said. "We're camping right on his front lawn."

"Maybe if he comes by to chase us off, the army will finally give us some ammunition," Phoebe said.

In spite of all the waiting and drilling and more waiting, she was certain that life in the army beat chasing kids and slaving in a hot kitchen—even if she was right back home in Virginia again. Besides, the monthly wages the government gave her were a sight better than what Miz Haggerty would have paid her. It was kind of hard, sometimes, explaining why she didn't use the public latrine alongside the others or bathe in the river on mild days, or why she always got up early every morning before anyone else and went off alone. Eventually Ted and her other tentmates got used to the notion that Ike Bigelow was a shy, quiet young fellow who liked his privacy.

In early February, Phoebe's company was given four days' rations of salt beef, hardtack, coffee, and sugar and was ordered out on a probing mission into Rebel-held territory. They filled their cartridge boxes with real live ammunition, too. Phoebe was so excited, it was all she could do to stay in formation and march instead of running on ahead to find some Rebels. But as the day wore on, her rifle grew heavier and heavier, her overcoat hotter and more cumbersome, her feet wetter and colder, and her knapsack and bedroll began to feel like someone had stuffed cannonballs inside when she wasn't looking. What made it even worse, she didn't see a single sign of the enemy all day.

The winter days were short, so the company halted before sunset to pitch camp in a small pine forest. They cut pine boughs for bedding and gathered wood to build a campfire in the middle of the clearing. By the time the fire was kindled and camp was made, everyone was starved. Phoebe sat down on a log beside Ted and watched as he tried to bite off a piece of hardtack.

"How do they expect us to keep all our teeth when they give us rations like these?" He banged the rock-hard cracker against his tin cup for emphasis, then tackled a piece of the tough dried beef, trying in vain to bite off a piece. "Argh! I think they gave us the hide instead of the meat!"

"I guess I'm gonna try cooking mine," Phoebe decided. "Good thing I brought along your frypan."

There had been times today when her pack had felt so heavy she'd wished she could fling the pan into the bushes. Now she was glad she hadn't. She poured a little water into it from her canteen and set it on the coals to heat, then she took out her knife and began slicing her ration of salt beef into the pan. Ted watched her, licking his lips.

"Hey, Ike . ... um, do you think. . . ?"

"Yeah, sure. Throw yours in here, too. It's your frypan." She handed him the knife when she was finished with it. "Here. Go on and slice the beef up in pieces."

She could tell pretty quickly that Ted didn't know what he was doing. When it started to look like he just might slice off one of his fingers, she took the knife back without a word and sliced his beef into the pan herself.

"Thanks," he said sheepishly. "My mother did all the cooking back home. I never went near a kitchen."

The meat began to smell pretty good as it cooked, and soon the other men started crowding around to watch. While Phoebe waited for the beef to get tender, she crumbled a piece of hardtack into powder in the bottom of her cup, then added it to the broth so it would thicken into gravy.

"I was thinking," she told Ted, "maybe if we poured the gravy overtop the hardtack, like it was a biscuit, it might soften up and not taste half bad."

The other men had grown very quiet. Phoebe finally looked up to see why. Every last one of them was watching her and licking his chops. "How'd you learn to cook like that?" one of them asked.

"Well, after my ma and pa died, it was just my three brothers and me. I either had to learn to cook or go hungry. So I learnt."

"Do you suppose you'd be willing to cook my rations like that for me?" someone asked.

The last thing Phoebe wanted to do was slave over a hot fire all night cooking for everybody. That's why she'd left the Haggertys. "Why should I?" she asked.

"I'll pay you two bits."

"Yeah, I'll kick in two bits if you cook mine, too," another soldier said.

Phoebe thought of all the fancy cakes and other sweets the sutlers sold when they drove around to the camps back in Washington. Ted said their fresh oysters were tasty, too. She just might like to try them.

"All right," she said. "Two bits each. And whoever carries the frypan tomorrow gets his grub cooked for free."

They all laughed, and someone gave her a friendly thump on the shoulder. She had let her guard down for once and learned that it was like opening a window just a crack to let in fresh air. By the time they'd eaten their fill, she'd earned everyone's respect—and had gained new friends.

As night fell, they sat on logs around the campfire talking for a while, their faces bright in its glow. Pine needles sent a shower of sparks swirling upward whenever someone tossed in another branch. The freshly cut wood was damp and unseasoned, and Phoebe's eyes stung from the smoky fire. Some of the men whittled, others smoked cigarettes; most of them talked about the wives or girlfriends who were waiting for them back home. Phoebe could only listen in silence, wondering what it would be like to have a sweetheart.

The men were all tired from the long first day's march. After divvying up the sentry duties, everyone turned in for the night. Instead of Sibley tents, each soldier had been given a section of canvas sheeting to use any way he wanted. Some decided to sleep under it like a blanket, others made a lean-to out of it, but most of the men had chosen a partner and fastened two sheets together to make a pup tent.

"Hey, want to hook ours up and make a tent?" Ted had asked Phoebe when they'd set up camp earlier that evening. She had agreed, and together they'd cut two straight tree branches for poles and built a nice-looking little tent. The opening faced the campfire for warmth, and the pine boughs they'd cut made a soft, fragrant bed beneath them.

Now, as she crawled inside the snug little shelter, Phoebe discovered that the cozy space felt very different from sleeping in a big tent full of men. Ted was lying really close beside her, all rolled up tight in his blanket and overcoat. They were alone, just the two of them, and she realized with alarm that her heart was racing like a scared rabbit's. Was something wrong with her? What if her heart wouldn't stop pounding this way, and they had to send her back to Washington to see a doctor? What if her heart worked so hard it got all tuckered out and stopped?

As Phoebe's imagination raced through the terrible possibilities, Ted suddenly gave a contented sigh. She could smell the coffee on his breath and a fresh whiff of pine every time he moved. "Isn't this just the greatest life, Ike? Being out here, chasing Rebels all day?

When I was working as a clerk back home, nothing exciting ever happened. I just sat inside all day, adding numbers." He paused. "You know what? I don't think I'll ever go home."

"Yeah . . . I know what you mean." She felt so strangely breathless she could hardly reply. There was something wonderfully thrilling about the sound of Ted's soft voice murmuring close beside her in the dark. She wanted him to keep talking like this all night.

"Now, if only I had a sweetheart waiting for me back home, my life would be just about perfect." He rolled over onto his side to face her. They were inches apart. "Sometimes I can't help thinking about what it would feel like to hold a pretty girl in my arms, maybe steal a little kiss. Do you ever think about that stuff, Ike?"

Phoebe swallowed. "You sure make it sound nice."

Her heart was going to thump itself to death. For the first time in her life she wanted to be held by a man, to feel his arms around her. She had never wanted to think of herself as a girl before, had always tried to be just like her brothers. But Ted made her feel different—and very much aware that she was a woman. She didn't understand it at all.

"Hey, if we get some time off back in Washington," Ted said, "let's you and me find us some pretty girls, okay?"

"I don't know . . ."

"Why not?"

"I—I don't think anybody could ever fall for someone like me. I'm such a homely cuss."

"That's not true. Whoever said you were homely, Ike?"

"Just about everybody in school back home."

"Aw, don't listen to them." He rolled over again and stared up at the canvas above their heads. "They made fun of me, too."

"Why would they pick on you? You're good-looking."

"No, I'm too short. And I've got beaver teeth. Be glad you're tall. Lots of girls won't fall for a man unless he's taller than they are."

"Well, there's plenty of short girls in the world. One of them's bound to fall for you." She heard a tremor in her voice and wondered what was wrong with her now.

"I've made up my mind to come back from this war a hero," he said, yawning. His voice was growing sluggish with sleep. "All the girls will think differently about me when I come home a hero. You wait and see."

Ted fell asleep first. Phoebe heard his breathing grow slower and deeper. Milky blue moonlight washed through the open end of their tent, and she lay in the dark and watched him. Her heart finally slowed. Outside, the woods were quiet except for the occasional hiss and snap of the dying fire and the soft murmur of the sentries as they changed shifts. She listened to the rustling whispers of the forest, sounds she'd grown up with and loved. They reminded her of home.

But Phoebe didn't want to go home. She didn't have a good friend like Ted back home.

They marched for two days, stopping to camp at night, poking around in the woods during the day as if there might be Confederates nearby. Then, without sighting a single Rebel, they turned around and hiked back to Washington. As Sergeant Anderson had predicted, Phoebe never did find out what it was all about.

"That's okay," Ted said. "We got a taste of what war's going to be like—tramping through the woods, sleeping under the stars at night—and I'm glad I joined up. Aren't you?"

"Yeah," she said, remembering how his face had looked in the moonlight. "Mighty glad."

In the spring, rumors began circulating that General McClellan was going to march his huge army toward the Confederate capital of Richmond soon. Every soldier in Washington grew excited at the prospect. By the time they learned that Union forces had captured Nashville, the men in Phoebe's company were spoiling for a fight. With spring fever in the air and no Rebels to scrap with, the men began scrapping amongst themselves.

Phoebe had gone off by herself for a walk one evening and was just returning to camp when she saw one of the Bailey brothers, the camp bullies, reach into Ted's open knapsack when his back was turned and snatch his bottle of Dr. Barker's Blood Tonic.

"Well, lookee here, Joe," Luke Bailey said to his brother. "The little fella's got some liquor he ain't sharing with us."

"Hey, that's my tonic!" Ted said, making a grab for it. "Give it back!"

The Baileys were a beefy, bullnecked pair with a reputation for fighting dirty. Luke Bailey elbowed Ted in the gut, then pulled the cork out of the bottle. "Smells like booze to me." He took a long swig and let out a hoot. "Tastes like a rusty nail melted down and put in a bottle."

"Does it have a kick to it?" his brother asked.

"Oh yeah! And he's got more of them bottles in his pack."

"Toss me one of them," Joe said. "I'm thinking I could use some medicine."

Luke plugged the cork back in and threw the bottle to Joe. Ted tried to defend his belongings, but he was still winded and hurting from the jab to his stomach. Luke stomped his instep and snatched the knapsack from him.

"Give that back!" Phoebe shouted as she hurried over. The bullies had closed in on Ted so quickly that she felt like she was moving through waist-deep mud as she raced to help him.

"You stay out of this," Luke warned her. "Ain't none of your business."

"And that ain't your bottle or your knapsack. Give them back to him."

"You gonna make me, big fella?" Luke took a threatening step toward Phoebe, his chin lifted in the air. He was shorter than she was but thickset and muscular. She didn't like it that his brawny older brother was behind her, where she couldn't see him.

"Look, I don't want a fight," she said.

"Aw, he don't want a fight," Luke said, mimicking her.

"We're on the same side in this war, remember?"

"What war is that?" Luke said. "You seen a war yet, Joe?" The brothers laughed as if she'd told a hilarious joke.

"It ain't right to go pawing through someone else's things." She wished her voice didn't sound so high-pitched.

"You scared of a fight, big fella?"

"No, but I—"

"Okay, come here and get it, then." Luke slowly backed away from her, taunting her, dangling the pack by its strap.

As she took a step, Phoebe heard Ted shout, "Ike, look out!"

The warning came too late. Joe Bailey tackled her from behind, slamming her to the ground and knocking the wind out of her. She heard both Baileys laughing as Joe rolled off her and sprang to his feet.

"You know what they say, 'The bigger they are, the harder they fall.'"

Phoebe spit dirt from her mouth. Now she was mad. She scrambled up and charged into Luke, butting her head into his ribs like a bull. Surprised, he stumbled backward and fell on his rump, dropping the knapsack. Then she went after Joe with both fists flying. She landed two good blows before taking a punch to her own jaw that made her teeth rattle. That made her furious. If these roughnecks knocked her teeth out she'd be labeled 4-F and she never would get into the war.

Phoebe kept on swinging. She was going to ache all over tomorrow, but she would show these guys. She'd fought against bigger louts—her own brothers. And she'd also taken on all the boys at school who'd called her names and told her she was ugly. After she'd whipped them good they'd grown to fear her.

She gave it back to the Bailey brothers as good as she got it. But she was very surprised when Ted joined in, tackling the younger brother, Luke, slugging and punching him for all he was worth. Phoebe was vaguely aware that a circle of men had gathered around, watching and cheering, glad for a new diversion.

Phoebe heard someone shout, "I'll bet a greenback on the big yellow-haired guy and his friend."

"You mean Ike and the little runt?" someone challenged in disbelief. "Never happen. My money's on the Baileys."

"I'll take that bet."

"Put me down for two bucks on the Bailey brothers."

"Five on Bigelow."

She was tiring, but so was Joe Bailey. They pulled back and circled each other, panting. Phoebe waited until he threw a punch, ducked it, then went in fast and scored two punches to his gut that doubled him over. As he clutched his stomach, groaning, she showed no mercy, hitting him in the jaw as hard as she could.

Phoebe's fists ached. Her knuckles were bleeding from where she'd split them open on Joe's buttons. Her hand would be swollen tomorrow for sure. She charged forward to slug him again, but he'd had enough. He held up his hands in surrender.

She whirled around to look for his brother and saw him locked in a struggle with Ted. She grabbed Luke by the back of his shirt, peeled him off Ted, and wrestled him to the ground. A few minutes later, it was over. Phoebe had Luke facedown in the dirt with her knee in his back, bending his arm behind him the way her brother Junior had always pinned her.

"You gonna mess with other people's things?" she asked, panting for breath.

"I reckon not," he grunted.

She let him up. There was a chorus of groans and cheers from the crowd as money was collected and lost. Phoebe turned to Ted.

"Look at you!" she moaned. The front of his shirt was torn, and blood ran down his chin from a cut in his lip. His right eye was starting to swell, and he would have a shiner tomorrow for sure, but he grinned at Phoebe like he'd just whipped a whole trainload of Rebels. She was relieved to see that his teeth were still all there.

"Hey, that was fun, wasn't it, Ike?" he said, wheezing. "I never won a fight in my whole life. We make a great team, don't we?"

Truth was, the Baileys would have beat the pulp out of Ted if she hadn't helped. But he hadn't turned tail and run. Ted had jumped right into the thick of things, fighting seasoned brawlers who were a lot bigger than he was, so he had a right to be proud.

"Yeah," she said with a smile that hurt her own swollen lip. "We make a great team." Ted looked like he might fall over any minute, so she draped her arm around him to prop him up. They were still congratulating each other when she saw the company captain walking toward them. He was looking right at her.

"Can I talk to you, Bigelow?"

Phoebe suddenly felt more frightened than she had when fighting the Bailey brothers. In defending Ted she had drawn attention to herself—something she'd worked very hard never to do. She stared at the captain, too scared to speak.

"The Baileys started it," Ted said. "We have witnesses."

The captain didn't reply. He motioned for Phoebe to follow him and turned to walk away from all the onlookers. She followed, her knees as weak and wobbly as a newborn calf's. When they'd gone a short way, he stopped.

"I was watching you just now, Bigelow. . . ."

He knows! He knows I'm a girl!

"You did some mighty fine fighting. You ever do any competitive boxing before?"

"You—you mean a *real* match?"

He nodded.

"No, sir. Just messing around with my brothers and the kids at school."

"I'd like you to consider becoming our company champion."

Phoebe was dumbfounded. She had watched some of the boxing matches the different regiments held for entertainment. The men fought with their chests bared, wearing only trousers.

"Our company has never had a decent competitor to sponsor before. But I really think you have the makings of a champion. It would be great for company morale . . . and it might even earn you a promotion."

"I won't run from a fight, sir. But I don't get any fun out of it."

"I can give you a few pointers, help you improve. You're quick on your feet and strong. You don't weigh as much as some of the other boxers, but you're taller and you know how to think on your feet."

"To be honest, sir, I only got into it tonight because they were bullies. They were picking on someone smaller than themselves."

"That's very noble. But wouldn't it be even more rewarding if there was money involved? You could always use some extra money, couldn't you?"

"I don't know. . . . Why don't you ask the Bailey brothers? They *like* to fight."

"The Baileys lost. To you. Will you at least think about it?"

Phoebe didn't know how to say no to her commanding officer without making him mad—but she knew that she had to refuse.

"I'm really sorry, sir. But I don't want to fight fellas that are on my side of the war. I want to save all my fighting for the Rebels."

"All right, Bigelow," he said with a sigh. "But I think it's a shame. I think you could be a first-rate champion."

The ground felt harder and lumpier that night when Phoebe lay in her tent with a bunch of new aches and pains. But whenever she pictured Luke Bailey pawing through Ted's stuff and the helpless look on Ted's face, she knew she would do it all over again in a heartbeat.

She stuck close to Ted after that—not that the Bailey brothers would be fool enough to take her on again. But because . . . well, Phoebe didn't quite understand the reason why. She thought about Ted all through the day and after lights-out at night in their tent full of snoring men. She wanted to eat all her meals with him and march beside him during drill and sit beside the campfire with him at night, listening to him talk about his family back home in Pennsylvania.

But when he asked her to go to Sunday services with him one spring morning, she stopped dead in her tracks. She sure didn't like being away from Ted for very long, but the thought of going to church made Phoebe very uneasy, even if services were held in the open air.

"Some say the reason we lost Bull Run was because we fought on a Sunday," Ted told her. "Now they're giving us a day of rest, setting up chapels and such. Come with me, Ike. Everybody's going."

"Um . . . no thanks." She picked up her tin cup and quickly gulped her coffee.

"Why not? You go to church back home, don't you?"

"Well . . . not too much."

Ted dropped his spoon onto his tin plate. "You're not a believer? You never heard the Gospel?"

"Yeah, I heard it. We had Christmas programs at school with the baby Jesus and all the animals." She quickly forked food into her mouth, hoping Ted would do the same and forget about all this. He didn't.

"What about Easter? We'll be celebrating that pretty soon. You know about Easter, don't you?"

"Of course I know about Easter. I ain't a heathen. It's just . . . I don't know."

"Hey, you *have* to go to church, Ike. It says so in the Bible and everything."

Phoebe stared down at her plate, idly tearing her bread into pieces and feeling just as torn. The last thing in the world she wanted to do was make Ted mad at her. But she had a bad feeling that God was already pretty mad at her, and she didn't want to risk finding out by showing up at His church service. Phoebe knew she wasn't supposed to tell a lie, yet she was lying every day when she pretended to be a man. Even if nobody else guessed her secret, she figured God knew. But how could she explain this to Ted?

"It was a long way into town from our farm," she finally said. "And I never liked to go to church because I'd have to wear a—" Phoebe had almost said *dress* but stopped herself in time. "Uh . . . shoes . . . you know. Can't go to church barefoot, can you? Everybody back home always wore nice Sunday clothes, and I didn't have any."

"You've got yourself a nice uniform and shoes now. Come with me, Ike. Please? Some fellow from the Christian Commission is preaching today, and I hear they're giving out care packages afterward."

Ted kept after her all the way through breakfast, slowly wearing Phoebe down with his nagging until she ran out of excuses. Before she even knew how it had happened, she was walking across the camp with him toward the outdoor chapel. Her uneasiness grew with every step she took.

"Let me ask you something, Ted," she finally said. "You think it's true that God reads folks' minds and knows all their secrets?"

"Sure. And not just their minds, He sees what's in their hearts, too."

Phoebe froze.

"Hey, come on. What are you stopping for?" Ted pulled on her sleeve, tugging her forward. "Don't you want to get a good seat?"

"The preacher back home was always saying 'God told me this

and that.' Do you think it's true? Would God tell the preacher all our secrets?"

Ted punched her arm playfully. "Why? You got a secret you're worried about, Ike?"

Phoebe felt all the blood rush to her face. How had she ever gotten herself into this mess? Now the only way out was to tell more lies. And on a Sunday, no less.

"Naw, I ain't got any secrets. Back home in Bone Hollow, the town was so small that everybody always knew everybody's business. There was no such thing as keeping secrets. But sometimes I wondered if God was in on it. Maybe He was telling the preacher stuff about everybody."

Ted laughed. "You sure get some funny notions. Come on." He prodded her forward again.

Up ahead, Phoebe saw a little brush arbor with a rustic wooden cross and rows of benches. Beside the chapel was a tent with a sign on it—United States Christian Commission. Three men in civilian clothes were helping the preacher set up a pulpit made out of logs. The spring day was cool and breezy, but Phoebe felt trickles of sweat running down her neck. She halted.

"Now what?" Ted asked with a sigh.

"I'm too tall for them benches. Ain't no place for my legs to go, and I just know they're gonna start cramping on me before the time's up. You go on. I'll listen from here."

Ted studied her for a moment. "You're going to sneak on back to our tent when I'm not looking, aren't you?" When she didn't answer he said, "I'm worried about your eternal soul, Ike. You can't go to heaven unless you know Jesus. Don't you want to go to heaven?"

"Not until I'm dead. And I'm planning on staying alive for a while."

Ted's innocent, boyish expression creased into a frown. Phoebe wanted to take his face in her hands and smooth all the lines away and make him smile again. He had such a nice smile.

"I promise I'll stand right here and listen to every single word," she said. But her stomach made a nervous flip as she said it. Ted gave a reluctant nod, and Phoebe watched him saunter forward and sit down. He turned around once to see if she was still there and she gave a little wave.

Phoebe's mind was a thousand miles away as the service started, and in spite of her promise, she didn't hear a word the preacher said. She also didn't notice that one of the men in civilian clothes had ambled up beside her, until he spoke.

"Don't you want to join all the others, son?" Phoebe nearly jumped out of her skin. "I'm sorry," he said quickly. "I didn't mean to startle you."

"That's okay. No, I don't need to sit. I'm fine where I'm at."

"I'm Nathaniel Greene," the stranger said, extending his hand. It had freckles all over it. She looked up at his face and saw freckles there, too. It was a handsome, youthful face—one that every girl back home would probably sigh over. Then she noticed his collar.

"Are you a preacher?"

"I'm an ordained minister, yes."

Phoebe didn't like preachers. The one in Bone Hollow had taken her aside after school one day and hollered at her for getting into fistfights with the boys. She'd tried to tell him all the awful things they'd said to make her mad, but he didn't listen. He'd told her that God had rules she needed to follow, like the rules in school. Then he'd admitted that he was in cahoots with Widow Garlock to get Phoebe out of overalls and into a dress.

Nathaniel Greene must have seen a change in Phoebe's expression because he quickly added, "But I'm not here to preach. I'm here as a volunteer for the Christian Commission. What's your name?"

"Ike Bigelow."

"I just like to talk to people, Ike. Answer any questions they might have about God."

"Well, I have a question." Her heart galloped with fear but she needed to know if this man was going to give her away. "Does God ever tell preachers things—secret things—about us?"

"I'm not sure I understand. But if you mean does God talk to me the way you and I are talking, then no. The only way I can learn people's secrets is if they tell me."

The preacher probably saw her relief and could figure out that she had a real *big* secret, but Phoebe didn't care. At least she could attend services with Ted from now on without worrying too much.

"I don't hear 'confession,'" he continued. "I'm not a priest. But if you need someone to talk to, I'll gladly listen and keep it confidential." When she didn't reply he asked, "Are you Catholic, by any chance? Because there is a priest—"

"I don't belong to any church. I do believe in God, though," she added quickly. "I just feel funny in church, that's all. I don't belong there."

"Where do you like to go to be with God?"

Phoebe looked at him in surprise. His expression was kind, his voice gentle. How had he known that she had a special place?

"Well . . . there was this spot in the woods back home," she said slowly. "I always used to go there when I felt bad. It was so pretty with the trees and the creek and all. And after a while I'd start to feel . . . I don't know . . . like I wasn't all alone. I mean, sure there's animals and bugs and things, but not just them. Someone bigger than them. It was almost like the person who'd made it all was looking at it with me and enjoying all the pretty things He'd made."

Greene smiled. "It was God."

Phoebe shook her head. "Naw, the preacher told me that God lives in a church. That's His house. He said there's rules we need to follow or God gets real mad. But I don't belong in a church. And folks in town didn't much like me being there."

"Jesus came down to earth for all the people who feel like they don't belong anywhere," the preacher said. "In fact, many of the church members of Jesus' day refused to believe in Him. But He came to help all the outcasts."

"How did He help them?"

"He loved them. And He died for them. And His death showed them that God loved them, too."

Phoebe turned away so he wouldn't see the tears that suddenly filled her eyes. The idea of love was still new to her, and she couldn't talk about it, couldn't even think about it. After feeling friendless and unloved for so long, even the feelings she had toward Ted threatened to overwhelm her most of the time.

"You don't have to take my word for it," the preacher said. He took out a pocket-sized Bible and paged through it as he talked. "Here's a story about a man who didn't belong. And Jesus shocked all the religious people by going to his house for dinner." He folded down a corner of the page to mark the place, then handed the book to Phoebe. "You can read it on your own when you have time."

"When do you need this back?"

"It's yours. You may keep it."

"Thanks."

"You're welcome. I enjoyed talking with you, Ike. That's my tent over there. If you have any more questions, you can come see me anytime."

Phoebe watched Nathaniel Greene stride away, then looked down at the Bible in her hand. She couldn't believe he had really given it to her to keep. It was the first book she'd ever owned in her life.

Chapter Seven

Washington City
February 1862

On the morning of her appointment with the director of nurses in Washington, Julia stood before the mirror in her hotel suite and removed her earbobs, rings, and other jewelry. Refusing her maid's help, she pulled her own hair back into a bun, taming the wild, springy curls that everyone said made her look angelic, and pinned it tightly in place without her fancy combs. She scrubbed her face in the porcelain washbasin until it was clean and shiny, then resisted the urge to dab color on her lips and cheeks. By the time she put on the plain brown muslin dress she'd had custom made according to Miss Dix's standards, Julia barely recognized the woman who stared back at her in the mirror. All of the emblems that identified her as a woman of wealth and class had been removed.

Part of her felt stripped down, as coarse and common as her servant, Inga. But another part of Julia felt free, as if she had shed the spoiled, self-absorbed Julia Hoffman whom she'd grown to dislike. She saw a changed person in the mirror—at least on the outside. Perhaps in time she would become a brand-new person on the inside, too, a person Nathaniel would respect.

"Oh, Julia! What a hideous dress," her aunt said when she swept in from her adjoining room. "You can't possibly go out in public in such a thing. It's a disgrace."

"This dress is brand-new, Aunt Eunice. And it's perfectly respectable."

"Not for a woman of your social position. Why on earth would you wear such an outfit? There's no lace, no trimmings, not even a decent tuck or a pleat. There can't be more than five yards of material in that entire dress. And gracious me! No hoops? You look like a common serving girl. People will get the wrong idea about you."

"You carry on as if I'm stark-naked," Julia said irritably. "Besides, this is required clothing for nurses."

"Then I don't understand why on earth you would want to become one."

Julia thought of several replies she could give: that *she* couldn't understand a life like her aunt's; that a nurse's life had meaning and purpose; that she was the same person with or without tucks and pleats and hoops. Instead, she said, "We'd better hurry or we'll be late for our appointment."

The hotel doorman hailed a cab for them, and they splashed across town through the mud-mired streets to the home of Miss Dorothea Dix. The director of nurses was expecting them. She led them into her dark, tiny parlor, asked them to be seated, and told the serving girl to bring tea.

Miss Dix was in her early sixties, a tall, thin woman with the posture of a general. On the surface, her manner seemed stern and brusque, but Julia thought she saw compassion in her gray eyes when she asked Julia why she had come.

"I would like to apply for a position as an army nurse," Julia replied.

"How old are you, Miss Hoffman?"

"Almost twenty. But I've brought letters of recommendation attesting to my maturity and character, if you'd like to see them." She retrieved them from her purse and handed them to the nursing director.

Julia and her aunt sat in silence while Miss Dix read them carefully. As she returned the last letter to its envelope, the serving girl arrived with a tray of tea things. Several long, agonizing minutes passed as Miss Dix filled three cups with tea, passed them around, made sure everyone had cream and sugar, then sat down again. Julia set her cup on an end table, unable to wait another moment.

"I know you'll say I'm too young," she blurted, "but I want to be a nurse more than anything else."

"May I ask why, Miss Hoffman?"

"I was a spectator at the Battle of Bull Run, a guest of Congressman Rhodes. I saw wounded men there who needed help, and I didn't know what to do for them."

Miss Dix nodded slightly, as if encouraging Julia to continue.

"My cousin Robert is a lieutenant in the Union army. We learned last October that he has been taken prisoner. He gave up everything to do his part for his country, and that's what I want to do, too. I want to do something for Robert and for other soldiers like him. Our minister back home started a chapter of the Christian Commission in Philadelphia, and when he told us about the need for nurses I felt compelled to help. . . . It's hard to explain."

Miss Dix took a sip of tea, then said, "Most young women your age are settling down with husbands and starting families. Doesn't that interest you?"

Julia shook her head, suppressing a shudder at the thought of settling down with a man like Arthur Hoyt. "I would like to marry someday," she said, "but not now. I don't want to get tied down when there's work to be done. I want to help our soldiers."

"Nearly all of my nurses are married," Miss Dix said, gazing steadily at Julia. "They volunteer because their husbands are at war and they hope to remain near them. I do accept single women as long as they are over thirty years of age. I've found that the younger, unmarried women who come to me are almost always curiosity seekers. To be blunt, they come to meet men."

"I'm not here to find a husband, Miss Dix. My family is wealthy and very active socially. I've never lacked for suitors, as my aunt can tell you." She turned to her aunt for corroboration and discovered that she had dozed off in her chair. Julia wanted to shout *"Hey! Wake up and help me!"* Instead, she exhaled in frustration and turned back to Miss Dix. "I've read about the work you've done for the underprivileged. How you saw a need and felt compelled to do something about it. Surely you understand how I feel?"

Miss Dix studied her for a long moment. "I believe you are

sincere, Miss Hoffman. These letters attest to your outstanding character. But to accept a nurse as young as you are, especially one who is pretty and unmarried, would go against all the rules I have laid down."

"Please, isn't there any way you can make an exception?"

She shook her head. "No. I can't."

"Please . . . I beg you."

"I'm very sorry."

Julia didn't dare speak for fear she would cry. The room fell silent except for her aunt's gentle snoring and the delicate clink of china as Miss Dix sipped her tea. Julia knew she should leave, but her disappointment so immobilized her that she didn't have the strength to lift her teacup, much less move from her chair.

Miss Dix glanced at Aunt Eunice and smiled slightly. "I know how disappointing it is when things don't go quite the way you hoped," she said. "I've worked so hard to organize a corps of trained army nurses who will work competently and efficiently . . . and do you know that there are hospital physicians who bypass my system all the time? Some doctors seem to hate the thought of having a woman in charge, and they take great delight in overruling all my orders."

Julia looked up. Miss Dix was gazing at her intently, her gray eyes sparking. Julia had the feeling she was trying to tell her something, but she didn't know what.

"How . . . how do these doctors overrule your orders?"

"Well, if an individual physician decides to ignore all my rules, he can hire a woman to work directly with him as a nurse in his hospital—and there is really nothing I can do about it."

"And some doctors do that?"

"Oh yes. All the time. They can ignore my rules and decisions and place anyone they please on record as a regularly enrolled army nurse."

Julia's pulse quickened with hope. She glanced at her aunt again to make sure she was still asleep. "I'm sorry to hear that these doctors hire nurses against your wishes. May I ask, is there any doctor in particular who regularly defies you?"

Miss Dix smiled. "I like you, Julia. You remind me of myself—

only I wasn't half as pretty or as privileged as you are. If I had been, I do believe I would have preferred to marry comfortably and raise a family."

"That might have been nice for you, but it would have been a great loss for our country."

"Thank you, dear." She gently set her cup in the saucer and placed them on the tea tray. Then she scooped the letters from her lap and handed them back to Julia. "You are totally unsuitable, Miss Hoffman. You're young, pretty, and single—everything we do not want in a nurse." She paused, then added, "Dr. James McGrath would like nothing better than to drive me to distraction by hiring you. He's crude, unorthodox, and insufferably rude. Very few of the nurses I've sent to the hospital he runs in the former Fairfield Hotel can stand to work with him for very long—which is probably why he hires his own nurses."

Julia repeated the doctor's name and the name of the hospital to herself, memorizing them.

"More tea?" Miss Dix asked, lifting the teapot. A spoon fell off Julia's saucer and clattered to the floor. Aunt Eunice's eyes flew open. She sat blinking at the two women, as if trying to pretend she hadn't fallen asleep, waiting to slip back into the stream of conversation.

"No more tea for me, thank you," Julia said, placing her cup on the tray. "I know you're busy, Miss Dix, and I'm afraid my aunt and I have already taken up too much of your time."

"Lovely tea," her aunt said groggily. "You've been very kind."

They stood, and much to Julia's surprise, Miss Dix took her arm companionably and walked with her to the front door. As she lifted Julia's bonnet and cloak from the coat-tree and handed them to her she said, "I wish you luck, my dear. I hope you find what you're looking for. And I hope you find contentment with your work."

"Have you found that, Miss Dix?"

"Oh yes. Immeasurably so."

Julia knew her aunt was befuddled as they returned to the waiting carriage. She kept looking awkwardly at Julia as if waiting for her cue, unwilling to admit she didn't know the outcome of their meeting. Julia understood that it was wrong to tell a lie. But she wanted to be a nurse, and the door to accomplishing her goal through honest means had slammed in her face.

"Wasn't that wonderful news?" she asked her aunt, not quite meeting her eyes. "I can't wait to wire home and tell everyone that Miss Dix has accepted me as a nurse."

Aunt Eunice didn't try to disguise her dismay. "Your father won't be pleased. He was quite certain you'd be turned down and that you'd be forced to return home disappointed."

"Well, he was wrong. Listen, let's get an early start tomorrow morning and find a boardinghouse near the hospital."

"Which hospital is that again, dear?"

"It's in the former Fairfield Hotel. They've made it into a hospital." The lies rested so uncomfortably on her tongue that she was afraid to look at her aunt. Julia felt certain that the shame burning her cheeks would give her away. She decided that the sooner she was rid of her aunt, the sooner her conscience would ease.

Julia arose early the next morning and began her quest to find a reputable boardinghouse near Fairfield Hospital. Progress proved frustratingly slow. In fact, she quickly discovered that finding an empty room for rent anywhere in Washington was next to impossible. By the end of a second long, fruitless day she decided to concentrate on finding a room that met her aunt's standards—which meant women boarders only—and never mind what the room looked like or how close it was to the hospital.

They found a vacancy on the third afternoon, but the room was small and depressing. It came furnished with a sagging bed, a dresser with a mismatched washbasin and pitcher, a small fireplace with a watery mirror above it, and a shabby rag rug on the bare wooden floor. The room's only window overlooked the brick wall of the building next door. There was no closet or wardrobe, and the only place she would have to hang her plain brown dress was on a hook on the wall.

"No, no, no. This is dreadful, Julia," Aunt Eunice said, clicking her tongue. "Why, it's no better than a servant's room."

Julia thought of her spacious room at home, with its thick rugs, four-poster bed, and mahogany wardrobe filled with dresses and shoes, and nearly changed her mind.

"Please, dear," her aunt begged, "forget this obsession of yours and come home with me where you belong."

"This room is fine," Julia said. She disguised her doubts behind a smile that she didn't feel. "Why would I need a bigger room? I'll be working at the hospital all day, so I'll only be here at night, anyway. And then I'll be asleep, with my eyes closed."

"But where will you keep all your dresses? And what about your maid? Where will she sleep?"

"Inga is going home with you tomorrow, Aunt Eunice."

"You can't be serious. Who will fix your hair? And help you into your hoops?"

Julia sighed. That was one of Nathaniel's accusations—that she was unable or unwilling to do the simplest tasks for herself. It was why she had started down this long, hard road in the first place. "I can fix my own hair," she said. "Miss Dix's nurses are supposed to look plain. And I won't be wearing any hoops, remember?"

Aunt Eunice's shoulders sagged with fatigue. "This is too much. I need to sit down." But the dismal room didn't have a chair, and Julia knew that her aunt would never commit the impropriety of sitting on someone's bed.

"Let's tell the landlady that I'll take it," Julia said. "Then we can both go back to the hotel and rest."

"You can't live here, Julia. There isn't even a chair."

"I'll ask the landlady for one. Please, Aunt Eunice. You know it's a respectable establishment. It's been highly recommended. And there simply aren't any other rooms for rent. Let me try living here for a few months, and if I'm unhappy I can always return to Philadelphia in April with the congressman and his wife."

Aunt Eunice finally relented, too weary to argue. Julia paid the first month's room and board and told the landlady she would move in tomorrow—right after she sent Aunt Eunice home on the first available train.

Her aunt wept as she said farewell the next day, convinced that Julia was making an enormous mistake for which she would be grievously sorry. "My only consolation," Eunice said, dabbing her eyes as she said good-bye, "is that I'm leaving you in Dorothea Dix's capable hands."

That same afternoon, Julia took a horse-drawn cab to the hospital in the former Fairfield Hotel. The weathered two-story clapboard building looked as though it had been little more than a workingman's hostel at the peak of its career and that now a strong breeze or an errant match would put an end to it. The railing wobbled beneath her hand as she climbed the front steps. The door gave such a weary groan as she pushed it open that she wouldn't have been surprised if it had fallen off its hinges and crashed to the floor.

Inside, the former lobby had been partitioned off, leaving a dark, narrow entryway with little light. But as her eyes adjusted, Julia saw a makeshift office just inside the front door and a hand-lettered sign that read: *Dr. James McGrath—Acting Assistant Surgeon, U.S. Army*. The office door stood open, and the doctor sat behind a littered desk, sifting through a pile of papers.

He was an angry-looking man in his early thirties, with a furrowed brow and dark auburn hair. His short, ginger-colored beard and mustache were neatly trimmed, but they were the only thing, tidy about him. His clothing was disheveled, his hair looked as though he'd been running his hands through it, and his office had a worn, trampled look, as if a Wild West show had recently staged a performance there. The doctor remained seated when Julia entered. In fact, he didn't even look up from his work.

"If you're here to see a patient, don't bother me," he said gruffly. "Talk to the matron."

"I'm not here to see a patient, Dr. McGrath. My name is Julia Hoffman, and I've come from Philadelphia to offer my services as a nurse."

"Go see Dorothea Dix. She's in charge of nurses."

"I have seen Miss Dix."

He stopped writing and finally looked at her, crudely sizing her up with his eyes as if measuring her for a dress. "Let me guess—Miss Dix waltzed you out of the door before you could blink, didn't she? You're too young. Too pretty. Too well endowed." He made a rude gesture with his hands, and Julia gasped. He seemed pleased to have shocked her. "Oh, you won't find 'flat bosom' on 'Dragon'

Dix's official list of qualifications, but that's the way she likes her nurses—flat as dinner plates, just like herself. Good day." He waved her away and returned to his papers.

Miss Dix had warned her that the doctor was a crude man. Julia guessed that the shock and anger she felt were exactly what he'd intended. She determined not to let him get the best of her.

"If I could have a moment of your time, Dr. McGrath, you'll see that I come from a fine, upstanding family. My father is Judge Philip Hoffman, a United States District Court judge, and I have letters of recommendation from Congressman Rhodes of Pennsylvania; Dr. Albert Lowe, one of Philadelphia's foremost physicians; and Reverend Underhill, pastor of—"

"Letters. Big deal," he said, dipping his pen into the inkwell. "You upper-class, high-society folks love your letters of introduction, don't you? I have enough papers cluttering my desk already."

"But if you would read them you would see that I—"

"Have you done any *real* nursing work for any of these people?" he asked, pinning her with his gaze. "Are you trained? Experienced?"

"I—I would like very much to learn."

"I'm a physician, not a teacher," he said, looking away again. "Come back when you've been trained. Good day."

Julia sat down in the chair in front of his desk and removed her bonnet, cloak, and gloves as if he'd invited her to stay. Dr. McGrath ignored her, dipping into the inkwell and scratching his pen across the pages as if she'd gone—although he surely knew she was still there.

She glanced around the untidy office while she waited and spotted a photograph on his desk—a pretty, dark-haired woman holding a small girl on her lap. Julia glanced at the doctor's left hand, holding down the page he was scribbling on, and saw a gold wedding band. She picked up the picture for a closer look. "Is this your wife and child?"

"What a ridiculous question. Why would I have a photo of someone else's wife and child on my desk?"

She bit back an angry reply. "They are both very pretty. What's your daughter's name?"

"Are you trying to annoy me, Miss Hoffman? Because you're doing a first-rate job of it."

"It isn't *Miss* Hoffman," she said, suddenly remembering Miss Dix's words. "It's *Mrs*. Hoffman. I'm married." The lie came remarkably easy to her.

"Is that so?" he said in a disinterested tone.

"Yes. My husband is Lieutenant Robert Hoffman," she said, giving him her cousin's name and rank.

"Does the good lieutenant know that you're away from home, bothering busy doctors when they're trying to work?"

"I haven't heard from Robert since he was captured at the Battle of Ball's Bluff last October. He's in Libby Prison in Richmond."

He glanced up at her again. She hoped his attitude would soften after hearing her tragic story; instead, he said, "And so sweet little Mrs. Hoffman wants to be a nurse."

"Yes, Doctor. Very much so."

He bent over his work again, silently writing for five long minutes. Julia waited until he blotted the ink and moved the paper he'd been working on from one stack to another. Then she said, "All I'm asking is for you to give me a chance, Doctor. I admit I don't know much about nursing, but I'm willing to learn."

He studied her for a long moment, then stood abruptly. "Very well, then. Come with me, Mrs. Hoffman."

Julia's heart soared with happiness as she followed him into the ward in the former hotel's dining room. It had been emptied of tables and jammed full of beds, all filled with ailing men. Some of them talked quietly, many of them were coughing, most simply lay there doing nothing at all and might have been asleep. The doctor stopped beside a small cabinet of medical supplies. The ward matron saw him and hurried over. She was a small, round woman with gray threads in her dark hair. "Is there something I can do for you, Dr. McGrath?"

"No, thank you. Mrs. Hoffman is going to help me change Private Jackson's dressing." Julia saw the matron's carefully neutral expression change to one of concern. "Are you a relative of his?" she asked Julia.

Before she had a chance to reply, Dr. McGrath said, "No, Mrs.

Hoffman is applying for a position as a nurse." He smiled, and Julia had never seen a grin quite as nasty as the one that spread across his face.

The matron's face went rigid. She made no attempt to hide her dislike for the doctor before quickly striding away. Julia's joy began to fade. She was starting to dislike this man, too. He scooped up a pair of scissors, a brown medicine bottle, and a wad of gauze from the supply table, then beckoned for Julia to follow him.

The patient they stopped beside was very pale, his body wasted to skeletal thinness. Dr. McGrath greeted the soldier with genuine warmth, smiling as he met the man's gaze. "How are you doing today, Jackson? The nurses treating you okay? The food all right?"

"I can't complain."

"Good. Good. Listen, I've come to have a look at your leg if you don't mind." He set his supplies on the bedside table and pulled back the covers. Julia braced herself, certain that the soldier's leg would end in a bandaged stump. It did.

"This is Nurse Hoffman," the doctor continued. "She's going to help me remove your dressing so I can have a look."

"How do, ma'am," Jackson said.

"Um . . . very well, thank you."

Dr. McGrath scraped an empty chair across the floor to the bedside and motioned for Julia to sit. He handed her the scissors. She cut through the knot in the gauze dressing and began carefully unwinding the layers. The room fell quiet. Too quiet. She was aware of the patient's whistling breath, rustling like dry leaves.

"Where are you from, Mr. Jackson?" she asked, trying to ease the tension.

"Buffalo, New York, ma'am."

"I've never visited Buffalo, but I hear it's nice. What sort of work do you do there?"

"Well, I worked as a carpenter . . . before the war, that is."

"And do you have a family back home?"

"A wife and three young ones. They—"

It was the last thing Julia heard. When she removed the last layer of gauze, a powerful stench hit her like a fist, knocking the breath right out of her. She tried to stand, to flee from it, but the room tilted crazily, then suddenly went black.

"Mrs. Hoffman . . . Mrs. Hoffman." Julia opened her eyes to Dr. McGrath's smirking face. She lay in a heap on the floor beside the bed and he crouched alongside her, slapping her cheeks.

"Ah, good. There you are. Let's sit you up." Julia's head whirled as he lifted her to a sitting position. The smell that had so overpowered her was everywhere. She quickly covered her mouth, barely managing to choke back her lunch.

"She all right, Doc?" Private Jackson asked.

"She's fine. If you'll excuse us for a moment, Jackson, I'll see that she gets some fresh air. I'll be right back."

Julia felt the strength in Dr. McGrath's arms and shoulders as he hauled her to her feet. The smell that had escaped from beneath Jackson's bandage encircled her like a living thing, pursuing her. There was no escape from it. She wanted to run from the ward before she vomited, but her legs were much too unsteady. As Dr. McGrath propelled her to the front door, she was forced to swallow the bitter mouthful a second time. When he finally flung open the creaking door, Julia desperately gulped the damp February air.

"There you go," the doctor said cheerfully. "A few deep breaths and you'll be on your way home. Today's lesson was on gangrene—you can tell it by the smell. Quite distinctive, wouldn't you say?" She hated his mocking tone. No wonder none of the nurses liked him.

"You may let go of me now," she said, peeling his hands off her waist. "I'm all right."

"Of course you are." He retrieved her bonnet and cloak from his office just a few steps from the door and shoved them into her hands. "Here you go. And now I suggest you return to your mansion in . . . Philadelphia, wasn't it? Wait there for your missing lieutenant."

Julia could barely speak through her anger. "Are you saying I can't work here?"

"I never imagined that you'd still want to."

She drew a shaky breath and exhaled. "Yes. I would very much like to. Now that I know what gangrene smells like I'll be better prepared for it the next time."

"I doubt that," he said. "Listen, I can play this little game for as long as you wish, Mrs. Hoffman."

"I am not playing a game."

He shook his head, his annoying smirk back in place. "I don't believe you. I can't think of a single plausible reason why a wealthy Philadelphia socialite would give up her servants and her diamonds and her ball gowns—and put on a ridiculous dung-colored dress, I might add—unless she was playing *some* sort of game. My guess is you're trying to impress someone."

Julia didn't dare argue with him because he was right. He was trying to make her so angry she would stalk away and never return, but she refused to give him the satisfaction. Besides, she wanted to stay, despite what he'd just put her through. She longed to show him that she was serious, that her compassion was genuine.

"May I ask you something?" she said.

"What?"

"Will Private Jackson live?"

The doctor studied her for a long, uncomfortable moment until she felt herself squirm beneath his gaze. He shook his head. "No. We've sent for his wife. She'd better come right away if she wants to see him alive."

"I'm sorry," Julia said, and she was. "He seems like a nice man." She drew another deep breath. "What time shall I come tomorrow?"

Dr. McGrath hesitated, then said, "I don't have any openings for nurses at the moment, but we need a supervisor for the linen room."

She was sure it was an insult, another one of his games. Julia determined to beat him at it this time. "The linen room will be fine. What time should I come?"

"Six A.M."

"Very well, Doctor. Good day." She turned to go.

"Mrs. Hoffman . . ." he called after her, "be sure to bring your own smelling salts tomorrow. The hospital doesn't stock them, and I'd rather not have to slap your dainty little face again."

Chapter Eight

Fairfield Hospital
February 1862

Dr. McGrath's office was dark, deserted. The coat-tree inside his door stood empty. Julia huffed in frustration. She had risen before the sun, skipped breakfast, and walked two blocks through frozen mud and icy wind to hail a cab in order to get to the hospital by six o'clock—and Dr. McGrath wasn't even here. If his rude behavior yesterday was an indication of his true character, she might have guessed he'd tell her to come early and then be deliberately late himself.

She stood in the hallway for a moment, debating what to do. Except for the distant sound of men coughing in the wards, the hospital was quiet. Since Julia had no idea where the linen room was or what she was supposed to do there once she found it, she decided to take a seat in the doctor's office and wait for him. She had just removed her cloak and hat and hung them on the doctor's coat-tree when the ward matron she'd seen yesterday came into the front hall. She was a plain-looking woman in her forties with thick dark brows and a careworn face.

"Oh . . . hello," the woman said. "I thought I heard the door. I'm Eleanor Fowle. How may I help you?"

"I'm . . . I'm Mrs. Robert Hoffman," she said, deciding to

continue the lie. "But please, call me Julia. I'm looking for Dr. McGrath."

"You were here yesterday, weren't you?"

"Yes, I applied for a position as a nurse. The doctor told me that I could begin working this morning as a supervisor in the linen room."

"The *linen* room? Are you sure?"

"That's what he said. What time does Dr. McGrath usually arrive for his morning rounds?"

Her dark brows creased in a disgusted frown. "It all depends on how drunk he got last night."

Julia was so surprised by the matron's words and the blunt way in which she spoke them that she couldn't reply.

"I've shocked you. I'm sorry," Mrs. Fowle said. "But it's the truth, and you may as well know it. He played a mean trick on you yesterday with Mr. Jackson, and the doctor is even meaner when he has a hangover—which is quite often, I'm sorry to say."

"What about the job he offered me?" Julia asked, hearing the tremor in her voice. "Was that just a mean trick, too?"

"Well, we *are* desperate for help in the linen room, but I don't think it's a job you would be suited for."

Julia felt as though the floor beneath her had given way. This had all been a joke. Dr. McGrath had no intention of hiring her as a nurse. She longed to turn around and march away from this miserable hospital, but where would she go?

"To be honest," Mrs. Fowle continued, "I think the doctor is using the linen room the same way he used poor Mr. Jackson yesterday. He's trying to scare you off."

"But why not just send me away? Why all these games?"

Mrs. Fowle released a long sigh, shaking her head. "Because Dr. James McGrath is a bitter, meanspirited man. He doesn't need any other reason than that. If you're wise, you'll leave before he arrives."

The matron was right—Julia should leave. She should give up the idea of becoming a nurse and go home. It's what everyone had been trying to tell her from the very beginning. But the thought of admitting defeat made her angry. "May I ask, Mrs. Fowle . . . if Dr. McGrath is so horrible, why do you stay here and work with him?"

"Because our soldiers need me," she said without hesitating. "I came to Washington City to take care of my husband after he was wounded at Bull Run. He died from his wounds, but there were so many others who needed my help that I simply couldn't abandon them."

Julia felt her feet touch solid ground again. The soldiers needed her. She'd run away from them once, and she was not going to do it again. "If I did decide to stay," she said, "if I took the job in the linen room, do you think the doctor would eventually allow me to work as a nurse? Because that's what I really want to do—to help wounded soldiers, like you do. I applied to Miss Dix, but she told me I was too young. And in a roundabout way, she suggested that I look for a position here."

"If you're sure that's what you want," Mrs. Fowle said doubtfully. "I'll put in a good word for you when there's an opening. In the meantime, I should warn you that your job in the linen room won't be easy."

"I appreciate the warning, but I would still like to stay."

Mrs. Fowle smiled for the first time. "I believe you've won this round, Julia. Dr. McGrath will certainly be surprised to learn of your decision. Have you eaten?"

"No, there wasn't time. He told me to be here by six."

"Absurd man. Come on," she said, turning toward the ward. "The cooks always feed the nursing staff first—and it's usually ready about now."

Most of the patients appeared to be sleeping as Mrs. Fowle led Julia through the ward and into the hotel kitchen. She smelled bacon and coffee and heard the clatter of dishes even before she passed through the swinging kitchen door. Two other nurses were already seated at a small wooden table, and Mrs. Fowle introduced Julia to Annie Morris and Lucy Nichols, the matrons of two other wards. The women explained to Julia that they were both widows with grown sons or sons-in-law serving in the army. Mrs. Fowle told them Julia's story, and they discussed Dr. McGrath while they ate thick, tasteless flapjacks and bacon.

"There is more than a hint of mystery surrounding that man," Mrs. Morris said. "I understand that he once had a thriving medical practice and was quite well renowned—until he got drunk and killed a wealthy patient he was treating. There are even rumors that he spent time in prison for it."

"He's certainly mean enough to be an ex-convict," Mrs. Fowle said.

"I've never heard anything about prison," Mrs. Nichols said. "I was told that he became a drunk *after* his patient died. And that he's been drinking ever since because of it."

"I don't suppose it matters one way or the other," Mrs. Fowle said, shaking her head. "Regardless of his past, his drunkenness and boorish behavior are inexcusable."

Julia took a bite of bacon. It was as tough as leather and much too salty. "If it's common knowledge that he drinks too much," she said, "why does the army allow him to run a hospital?"

"Oh, he's a very skilled physician when he's sober," Mrs. Nichols said. "After Bull Run they needed every doctor they could get their hands on and weren't about to turn one away. He's a contract surgeon—which means he hasn't actually enlisted in the army."

"And even though he's vulgar to the outside world," Mrs. Morris added, "I must say that he's wonderful with the patients. Very gentle, very kind to them."

"I've been here for almost as long as he has," Mrs. Fowle said, "and I've seen several wonderful nurses leave because they couldn't tolerate his bullying. But at the same time, his hospital has one of the lowest death rates of any in the city."

Julia's curiosity was piqued. She wondered if she could find out the truth about the doctor's past somehow and use it to her advantage. She already considered Dr. McGrath her enemy and would use any ammunition against him that she could in order to secure a job as a nurse. "Where is he from?" she asked.

Mrs. Fowle shrugged. "He won't talk about himself at all—and you'll get your head bitten off if you ask. But I've seen the letters he gets every week from *Mrs.* James McGrath, and the return address is New Haven, Connecticut."

"I saw a picture of his wife and daughter in his office yesterday," Julia said. "She looked like a lovely woman."

"Yes, I've seen it, too," Mrs. Fowle said. "But that's another mystery. For as long as he's been here, he's never once talked about his family or gone home to visit them. The letters arrive every week like clockwork, but wouldn't you think his wife would want to come here to live—or at least visit him? After all, that's why many of us came, to be closer to our husbands."

"No, think about it, Eleanor," Mrs. Morris said. "As horrible as that man is, I'd keep my distance, too, if I were his wife. And I'd be grateful for every mile there was between us."

"You seem like a nice young lady, Julia," Mrs. Nichols said. "Take my advice and look for work someplace else. He only offered you this awful job to try to get rid of you."

"But if you really need someone in the linen room," Julia said, "and if the army is so desperate for nurses, why does Dr. McGrath deliberately drive everyone away?"

Mrs. Fowle spread her hands. "The man is a mystery, I tell you. I don't think he knows the answer to that himself." The other ladies nodded in agreement. "Anyway," she said, pushing back from the table, "it's time we returned to work. I'll show you the linen room, but none of us will blame you if you decide to leave. It's a terrible job. Right now most of our patients are plagued with diarrhea and dysentery. . . . Well, you'll see."

Julia did see. The hotel laundry was a cramped room in the rear of the building with a table, four large wooden tubs, a collection of flatirons, and a stove to heat the water. The shelves where the clean bedding was stored were nearly empty, and the mound of soiled sheets waiting to be washed stood as high as Julia's head. The pile reeked so horribly of sickness and human filth that it made her eyes water. She nearly vomited her breakfast. She pulled a scented handkerchief from her pocket and held it to her nose.

"Am I supposed to scrub all these bed linens myself?" she asked.

"I don't know what to tell you," Mrs. Fowle said. "The army will pay for four laundresses, but they all keep quitting, and no one has time to find replacements. Meanwhile, the laundry keeps piling up. Lena is the only laundress we have left, besides you. With so many patients suffering from diarrhea, we're in an awful mess. Sorry, but I have to get back to my ward now. I'll tell Dr. McGrath you're here when he decides to show up. Oh, and make sure you speak softly to him. He'll probably have a hangover."

The first thing Julia did was open a window to let out the stench. Cold air flooded the room, but she still couldn't keep from gagging. Then she looked around in dismay. Julia had never done laundry in her life and had no idea where or how to begin. Nathaniel's accusation came back to haunt her once again—she was a pampered, spoiled woman.

The stove, she finally decided. She would start by finding some firewood and lighting the stove to heat the wash water. But she had never lit a stove in her life, either, and when the sole laundress finally arrived an hour later, Julia still hadn't managed to kindle a fire.

"You putting too much wood," Lena explained in broken English. "You must to start with small wood, then to put big wood." She soon had the stove blazing.

Lena was fifteen, she told Julia, and needed the job to help support her family, newly arrived from the old country. She had worked in the hospital laundry for two months and knew a lot more about it than Julia did, but Lena was a plump, listless girl who daydreamed a lot. The only way they would ever conquer the mountain of linens was if Julia pitched in and helped.

Together they pumped water and hauled it inside by the bucketful, filling the two copper cauldrons on the stove. "The water must be hot," Lena said. "To kill the louse."

"You mean there are *lice* in this bedding?" Julia cried, dropping the load of sheets she held in her arms.

"Yes, the soldier-men all have the bugs. They hop into the sheets."

Julia found a broom handle and used it to transfer the bedding into the cauldrons. Lena showed her how to shave the soap into the steaming tubs and agitate a load of sheets with the plunger, beating until the soap foamed and her shoulders ached. Any stains—and there were plenty—had to be scrubbed clean by hand on a washboard. Then the sheets were wrung out and transferred to the rinse water to be beaten some more. Julia and Lena each grabbed an end and twisted the sheets to wring out the rinse water, then hung them outside in the frigid air to dry. Julia's hands quickly grew chapped and raw from the combination of hot water, caustic soap, and icy air. She had never done such menial, backbreaking work in her life.

The two women labored all morning scrubbing soiled sheets, but by the time they hung the last one out to dry, the nurses had made their morning rounds through the wards and a new mound of dirty ones had materialized in the laundry room doorway. The only thing that kept Julia from weeping was her fear that Dr. McGrath would arrive and catch her doing it. She remembered his smirking face and scornful words: *"I can play this little game for as long as you wish, Mrs. Hoffman."*

The cooks sent a tray of food out to the laundry after the patients had been fed their noon meal, but the sight and smell of stinking sheets had made Julia too nauseated to eat. Lena devoured both of their portions. Then the girl pointed to the baskets full of dry linens from yesterday's wash. "Those we do now."

"You mean we need to fold them?" Julia asked.

Lena shook her head. "They stiff from hang outside. We must to iron. Making soft."

They took the cauldrons off the stove and began warming the flatirons, then cleared the wooden tubs off the table so they could use it as an ironing board. Lena was adept at juggling several irons on the stovetop at the same time without letting any of them get too hot and scorch the sheets. But Julia's arms and shoulders ached so badly from the work she'd already done that she could barely lift the heavy irons. Twice, she grabbed a handle that was too hot and blistered her palm. When she burned an iron-shaped hole in one sheet she wanted to give up. Her feet ached from standing on them all day. She longed to remove her shoes but feared they would never fit on her swollen feet again if she did.

The work never ended. As fast as the sheets were cleaned and pressed and put on the linen room shelves, more filthy ones arrived. By late afternoon, the shelves were just as empty and the mound of dirty ones just as big as they had been that morning. It was impossible to keep up. When Lena finally announced that it was time to go home, Julia was quite certain it had been the longest, most miserable day of her entire life. She did not wish to ever spend another one like it.

She wanted nothing more than to sneak out and never see any

of these people again, but her coat and bonnet were still in Dr. McGrath's office. Julia would have to go through the ward to retrieve them. She drew a deep breath and opened the wardroom door, looking around for Mrs. Fowle. The least she could do was let the matron know that she would not be returning tomorrow. But when Julia spotted Dr. McGrath bending over one of the patients she changed her mind. He was certain to have a smirk on his face and a sarcastic comment to toss her way, and she didn't trust herself not to burst into tears. Besides, she knew that she looked frightful. Her hair had fallen loose a dozen times, her natural curls frizzing uncontrollably in the steamy room, and she'd hastily pinned it back in place without a mirror. The sleeves of her muslin dress were badly wrinkled from being rolled up all day, and the front of her dress was water-stained and soaked clear through all of her petticoats to her skin. Julia quietly backed away, deciding to use the rear door of the laundry and walk all the way around the building to retrieve her coat.

The late afternoon sky was already turning to night as she stepped outside, and she shivered in the damp, freezing air. She managed to slip through the front door without being seen and quickly grabbed her things from the rack in Dr. McGrath's office. But no sooner had she shoved her arms into her sleeves and yanked open the door when she heard his gruff voice behind her.

"Ah . . . Mrs. Hoffman?"

Julia cringed. She stopped midway through the door but didn't turn around, glancing only briefly at him over her shoulder. "Yes, Doctor?"

"The matron told me you were here today. I meant to come see how you were doing out in the linen room, but we got so busy that I never made it."

"Your presence wasn't necessary," she said coldly. "I'm sure you had better things to do than visit the linen room."

"Yes. Quite true. So . . . should we expect you back tomorrow?"

Julia knew that if she looked at his face he would be grinning, challenging her. She would *not* let him win.

"Of course," she said, then slipped the rest of the way through the door and let it slam shut behind her. But Julia had no intention of ever coming back.

As she emerged into the dark, windy evening, her wet clothing clung to her skin, chilling her with its icy grip. She wondered if she would catch pneumonia. There wasn't an empty cab to be found anywhere near the hospital, and she was forced to wander farther and farther through the dismal streets in search of one. A half hour passed before she finally succeeded. She was about to climb into the carriage and sit down for the first time since lunch, when a ragged little Negro boy no more than five or six years old ran up to her carriage and tugged on her coattails.

"Please, pretty lady, can you give me some money?"

His large dark eyes seemed to fill his face as he gazed up at her. The boy shivered in a thin, ragged jacket several sizes too large for him. He was barefooted—in February. Julia quickly dug in her change purse and gave him a handful. He grinned and ran down the street to intercept the next pedestrian.

"Either you're new in town, miss," the cab driver said, "or else you're from up north."

"I'm both," she said, sinking onto the carriage seat at last.

"Thought so." He snapped the reins and they started forward. "After you've been here a while you'll get used to contrabands. You'll learn not to let them get to you."

"Used to . . . contrabands?" she asked, repeating the unfamiliar word. "What are they?"

"That kid who just duped you is one. They're former slaves from places like Virginia or the Carolinas. Washington is full of them. Most of them ran away and followed our Union soldiers to freedom, but now that they don't have masters to take care of them anymore they don't know how to live. So they send their kids out to beg in the streets. You'll learn to ignore them eventually. Everyone does."

"But what about the Fugitive Slave Law?" she asked, remembering what she'd learned at Nathaniel's abolition lectures. "According to the law, don't all runaway slaves have to be sent back to their owners?"

"Not since the war started, they don't. That's why they're called contrabands. They're spoils of war, the property of the victors, just like land or houses or any other booty that's been won in battle. Except that there aren't any jobs for all these slaves and no place for them to live except in the shantytowns they build. Poor souls have never been free before, and they don't know how to fend for themselves. Now, don't get me wrong, I am sympathetic. But if kind folks like you keep giving them money every time they beg, they never will learn how to earn an honest wage."

"He was just a child," Julia said. "And he was shivering. How could I look the other way?"

"You got Negroes back home where you come from?" he asked. The mention of home unexpectedly brought tears to Julia's eyes. She couldn't reply.

"I figured not. Like I said, you'll get used to seeing them. You'll learn to ignore them."

When they finally reached the boardinghouse, Julia's muscles were so stiff from hard work and so frozen from the cold she could barely climb down from the carriage. She didn't think she would ever be warm again. She pulled open the boardinghouse door and entered the vestibule, grateful for its stingy warmth. Her landlady met her.

"You're too late for supper," the woman said without a word of greeting. "I believe I explained to you when you paid the first month's room and board that we eat promptly at five-thirty, didn't I?"

"Yes, ma'am, you did. But this was my first day of work at the hospital, and I didn't know it would take so long to finish or to find a cab. And there was so much traffic with the streets full of army wagons—"

"Well, a hungry stomach makes an excellent schoolmaster," she said primly. "I trust you'll leave work on time tomorrow." She turned and marched away.

Julia climbed the stairs to her drab little room and found it so cold she could see her breath. She remembered then what else the landlady had told her that first day—she was responsible for her own fire. Shivering, she knelt by the hearth and rekindled the coals the way Lena had taught her, first with "little" wood, then with "big" wood. Her empty stomach rumbled and growled while she worked.

It would be the first time in her life she had ever gone to bed hungry.

When she stood, her hands black with soot, Julia caught a glimpse of herself in the mirror. The bedraggled-looking woman who stared back at her was a pitiful stranger with disheveled hair and a drab, stained dress. The tears Julia had been holding back all day were finally unleashed. She threw herself down on the sagging bed and sobbed. What was she doing here? How had she sunk so low?

If she were home she might be attending a party or a ball tonight, dressed in a gown of silk and lace, with rustling taffeta petticoats and swaying hoops. Her hair would be perfectly curled and trimmed with ribbons and jeweled combs; her grandmother's topaz necklace would sparkle around her graceful neck. She remembered the glorious feeling of entering a room, knowing she was beautiful, and seeing the admiration in every man's eyes, the envy in every woman's. Why had she come here? Why was she doing this to herself?

The life Julia found herself living was not at all what she had pictured. She had given up everything to be a nurse, not a scrubwoman. She was supposed to be saving lives, offering comfort to wounded soldiers, accepting their words of gratitude and blessing—not working for a drunken, abusive doctor, scrubbing human filth from soiled sheets. She wanted to go home.

She had sacrificed her pampered life and had changed completely on the outside. But tonight Julia recognized that she was still the same on the inside—still a spoiled rich girl. No matter how much hard work and suffering she endured, she could never change. And Reverend Nathaniel Greene was never going to love her. Tomorrow she would swallow her pride, admit she was unsuited for nursing, and go home.

Julia awoke to the distant sounds of reveille and drums, coming from one of the hundreds of army encampments surrounding Washington City. The aroma of coffee drifted up the stairs, and she climbed out of bed, shaky with hunger. She quickly splashed water on her face, put on her wrinkled dress, and hurried down to the dining room.

Four other girls already sat around the table, silently eating a breakfast of oatmeal, dry toast, and coffee. They were all plain-looking young women, dressed in the drab clothing of the working class—just like she was. No one greeted her as she slipped into a seat at the table. The serving girl set a bowl of lumpy oatmeal and a plate of toast in front of her.

Back home in Philadelphia, Julia's parents would be eating breakfast in their dining room right now, the table spread with fine china and silver and white linen. Hot food would be waiting on the buffet in silver chargers—soft scrambled eggs, buttered rolls, tender slices of ham, delicately seasoned potatoes. Her father would have his newspaper open in front of him, and he would read a paragraph or two aloud from time to time, as was his habit.

Julia lifted her spoon and swallowed a sticky clump of oatmeal. If she hadn't been famished, she never could have choked it down. By the time she'd finished the last sip of bitter coffee, all her lingering doubts had vanished. She would go home.

Julia nearly raced up the stairs. She changed into her traveling suit, fixed her hair in a flattering style, and packed her plain brown dress and everything else into her trunk. She would hail a cab; she would order the driver to come to the boardinghouse and fetch her trunk; she would go to the train station and purchase a ticket to Philadelphia. Her father would probably be horrified when he found out she had traveled without a chaperone—but then again, maybe he would be so happy that she had finally come to her senses, he wouldn't care.

Outside, the day was bright and clear, the winter sun surprisingly warm, a perfect day to travel. Julia stood in front of the boardinghouse for several minutes, waiting for a carriage. When none drove past she finally decided to walk a few blocks east to one of the main thoroughfares. It was a bustling street with vendors hawking pretzels and fried dough cakes. Uniformed soldiers marched past in tight ranks, their guns and bayonets pointing to the sky. All manner of vehicles clogged the rutted streets, from Conestoga wagons and buckboards to broughams and buggies—everything, it seemed, but a vacant cab. She heard music and followed the sound to find an old Negro man playing his fiddle on a street corner. Passersby tossed coins into his hat. He was crooked and bent with age, his white hair and beard a stark contrast to his dark skin. The tune he played made Julia ache with sorrow. He played as if the fiddle were a fountain that overflowed with memories of all he had endured.

She bent and dropped coins into his hat, then quickly turned away. That's when she saw them—two little Negro girls, no older than three or four years, silently begging with outstretched arms as thin as kindling wood. Unheeding pedestrians hurried past, and Julia remembered the cab driver's certainty that she would learn to ignore the contrabands, too.

Julia slowly walked toward the girls, drawn by pity. The smaller child looked up at her with pleading eyes and said, "I'm hungry." Something inside Julia seemed to break.

She could leave Washington today and return to her elegant life in a warm home with plentiful food, but these two children and dozens of others like them would still be here—shivering, begging, their stomachs as empty every night as hers had been for only one. She would lie down on clean linen sheets in her four-poster bed, leaving suffering soldiers like Private Jackson to die on bare, stained mattresses.

Julia dug two coins from her purse and crouched in front of the girls. "Do you live near here?" she asked.

The older child nodded and pointed vaguely down the street.

"I'll pay you to show me where you live. I'd like to talk to your mama. Will you take me to your house?"

The child took the coins from Julia and nodded again.

Clutching each other's hands, the two girls silently led her down a narrow alleyway off the main street to the shantytown where the contrabands lived. It was stuffed beneath a railroad trestle near the river, a warren of shacks made of packing crates, scraps of wood, old barrels, rags, and jagged pieces of metal. As she picked her way through the debris, following her small guides, Julia could barely distinguish the homes and personal belongings from the scattered piles of trash.

The children led her to a nondescript pile of junk where a

Negro woman sat with a small baby on her lap, poking at the fire she had built in front of the shanty. She watched apprehensively as Julia approached. Julia felt just as nervous.

"Hello . . . I'm Julia Hoffman," she said. A mound of rags behind the woman shifted at the sound of Julia's voice, and a second woman sat up, clutching another infant. There was a strong resemblance between the two women, and Julia guessed that they were sisters. Neither one looked much older than she was.

"I have some work that needs to be done," Julia said, "and I was wondering if you would like to have a job . . . to earn some money?"

The first woman looked at her through narrowed eyes. "What kind of job?"

"I work in an army hospital. I'd like to hire you to scrub laundry. The army will pay you good wages. Have you done that sort of work before?"

"We can wash clothes, sure enough. We used to cook meals, hoe the garden, do all kinds of work."

"Good. Would you like the job? I could use both of you."

The women glanced at each other, communicating silently, then the first one said, "Me and Loretta always willing to work. Lord knows we don't want our girls begging. But who gonna mind these young ones while we work? How these babies gonna eat? Our men working for the army, and ain't nobody to take care these children all day."

It took Julia only a moment to decide. "You may bring the children, too. As long as all the laundry gets done, I don't care if you keep them with you."

The woman gave a quick, hopeful smile as she scrambled to her feet, shifting the baby from her lap to her shoulder. "This hospital very far? Can we be walking there every day?"

Julia hadn't thought about transportation. Fairfield Hospital was too far away for the women to walk, and it would be too expensive for them to hire a carriage every day on laundresses' wages—if they could even find a driver willing to transport Negroes. Yet Julia knew she had to make this idea of hers work. She needed their help, and these women and their children needed hers. As she edged closer to the fire, warming herself, Julia remembered that the hospital used to be a hotel. Surely there were servants' quarters somewhere in the building. And even if there weren't, the laundry room was clean, warm, and dry, a much better alternative than a bed of rags beneath a railway trestle. The only obstacle that she could see was Dr. McGrath. Julia decided she would deal with him when the time came.

"Pack all your things and bring them with you," she said. "I'll let you live at the hospital."

The second woman had crawled out of the shanty and risen to her feet, too. She stared at Julia in astonishment. "That true? We ain't dreaming? You give us a job *and* a place to live?"

"It's true," Julia assured her. "The job is yours if you'd like it."

"I surely would rather work than see my children starve," the first woman said. Tears shone in her eyes as she hugged one of the little girls to her side.

"What's your name?" Julia asked.

"I'm Belle and this here's my sister, Loretta."

"It's nice to meet both of you. Listen, I'm going home to change into work clothes. In the meantime, you can pack all your things. I'll be back in an hour or so with a carriage."

Lena was already at the hospital when they arrived and had just finished building a fire in the stove. She looked completely overwhelmed by the mountain of work she faced and greatly relieved to see help arriving. Belle and Loretta didn't waste a minute. They saw right away what needed to be done and began hauling water, sorting laundry, and setting up the wooden tubs. In no time, they had fearlessly attacked the mound of soiled sheets, working so quickly and efficiently that Lena seemed to be standing still in comparison. The two little girls Julia had found begging now ran errands for their mothers, fetching wood, shaving soap into the tubs, tending the babies when they fussed.

Julia watched in amazement as the women bustled around. It was as though they'd been working here for years. She hardly dared to move, knowing she was probably more of a hindrance than a help. But when the two women began to sing while they labored, Julia was so astounded she couldn't speak.

"My Lord delivered Daniel from the lion's den, Jonah from the belly of the whale . . ."

The joyful sound shivered through Julia, bringing tears to her eyes. She had done the same work they were doing all day yesterday, yet the last thing in the world she had felt like doing was singing. But Belle and Loretta were so grateful for what they had—a warm place to stay, a job that would earn a living for themselves and their children—that they couldn't help bursting into song.

"He delivered the Hebrew children from the fiery furnace, then why not every man?"

The work went smoothly all morning, the little girls helping, the babies napping in empty laundry baskets near the stove. But when the three laundresses went outside to hang the sheets out to dry, one of the babies woke up and began crying loudly for his mother. Julia had no experience with small babies. She picked him up as if he were made of glass and jiggled him in her arms, trying to soothe him.

"Shhh. It's all right. Your mama will be back in a minute. Shhh." He wailed louder still.

Suddenly the laundry room door burst open and Dr. McGrath filled the doorway. "Why do I hear babies crying?" he thundered. "What is going on out here?" His face was so pale and angry-looking that he might have caught Julia giving aid and comfort to a troop of Rebel soldiers instead of tending a helpless baby.

"He belongs to one of my laundresses," she said, trying not to let the doctor see her fear. "He's crying because he wants his lunch."

"Get that thing out of here! Now!" He pointed to the back door as if the baby were a burning stick of dynamite that she needed to toss outside before it exploded. "This is an Army hospital, not a charity."

"I will not," she said bravely. "It's cold outside. Besides, he has no other place to go while his mother works. Do you want your hospital to have clean sheets or don't you?"

"Of course I want clean sheets. And kindly lower your voice. There is no need to shout."

"I'm not the one who is shouting." She gave the baby her knuckle to chew on, and he quieted for a moment. The doctor massaged his temples, looking visibly relieved.

"Now," Julia continued, "I believe you made me supervisor of the linen room, Dr. McGrath, and this is how I've chosen to run it. If you force my laundresses to quit because they can't keep their children with them, then I will be forced to quit, as well."

"Don't tempt me. . . ." he growled. But Julia sensed that he was backing down. She summoned her courage to continue.

"I know how to manage servants, Doctor, and I know from experience that they are most productive when their own needs are adequately met. Since it's impossible to support a family on what the Army pays them, I've told my laundresses they may stay here in the servants' quarters."

"You did *what*?"

"You put me in charge of this laundry room, didn't you?" she asked, sounding braver than she felt. "Look, these are probably the best laundresses the hospital has ever had. Your linen room is running smoothly, and the shelves will soon be filled with plenty of clean sheets. Are you sure you want to fire these hard-working women and let everything go back to the way it was before, just because I'm allowing Belle and Loretta to live in the attic?"

Dr. McGrath glared at her for a long moment, then turned and stomped off. Julia smiled at his retreating back. "I'll take that as a no," she said.

When Julia arrived at the hospital one morning a week later, she was surprised to find Dr. McGrath already at work in his office, seated behind his desk as he had been on the first day they'd met. He had his curtains drawn tightly closed, and he sat in the dark, writing with one hand, supporting his head with the other. His face was pale and pinched with pain. Hangover or not, she had no wish to speak with him and was trying to slip quietly past his office without being seen when he called to her.

"Mrs. Hoffman, would you come here, please?"

She slowly backed up, stopping in his office doorway. If he felt half as ill as he looked, he was certainly suffering.

"Yes, Doctor?"

"Have you ever had the measles?" he asked without looking up.

His question was so unexpected that for a moment she couldn't reply. Julia remembered how she and Rosalie had lain sick in bed together, covered with spots. Dr. Lowe had come twice a day to check on them, while their mother had hovered nearby, wringing her hands and ordering compresses and sponge baths. Julia felt her heart wrench with homesickness the way a stomach twists with hunger, and she suddenly longed for her mother, for her room, and even for her prickly sister.

"Yes," she said, struggling to compose herself. "I had the measles when I was ten years old."

He dipped his pen into the inkwell and continued to write as he talked. There was a trail of ink spots across his blotter from his trembling hand. "Good. Go see the ward matron on the second floor. What's her name? Nicholson. . . ?"

"It's Nichols. Lucy Nichols."

"Whatever. Go see her. Your services are needed as a nurse."

Julia's heart began to race with excitement. She hoped this wasn't another one of the doctor's mean tricks. "Um . . . what about the linen room?" she asked.

He looked up at her, rolling his eyes at her stupidity, then spoke in a slow, condescending tone, as if talking to a simpleton. "Can't they do without you for a few days, Mrs. Hoffman? Are you completely indispensable?"

"Of course not. My new laundresses are excellent workers."

"All right, then. Promote one of them to supervisor and get your dainty little rear end upstairs. We've got a measles epidemic on our hands."

Chapter Nine

Fortress Monroe
March 1862

Phoebe stood at the ship's rail beside Ted, gazing at Virginia's wooded shoreline as they floated downstream. The deck of the river steamer, jam-packed with soldiers, artillery shells, and U.S. Army shipping crates, rose and fell beneath her feet as if it were a living, breathing beast.

"Feeling any better?" she asked Ted.

"Yeah," he sighed. "The sergeant was right about coming out here in the fresh air. It really helps."

Phoebe still felt woozy herself, especially when she looked down at the gray, storm-whipped water or watched the deck rise and fall. But if she kept her eye on the land and remembered to take deep gulps of the cold, bracing air, she just might be able to make it to Fortress Monroe without turning green like most of the other soldiers on board.

She and Ted had hardly been able to contain their excitement as they'd boarded the *Lady Delaware* and sailed out of the port of Alexandria, Virginia, heading down the Potomac River to Fortress Monroe. The ships that made up the Union fleet seemed to come in every size and shape imaginable: oceangoing vessels with tall masts that stuck up in the air like a forest; river steamers, like the vessel they rode on, with belching smokestacks and thumping paddlewheels; long, flat trains of barges, helped along by wheezing tugboats.

And the equipment they carried! Thousands and thousands of tents, horses, and artillery pieces. Boxes and barrels of food and supplies and ammunition. Wagons and caissons, and pontoons for building bridges. Roll after roll of telegraph wire. The dock had teemed with contrabands working for the army, loading endless tons of equipment. Phoebe and Ted had watched the spectacle in awe.

"Would you look at that?" Ted had repeated every second or two. "And look at that over there!" He had pointed to an almost endless row of cannons, lined up wheel to wheel; to a boatload of army mules; to a pyramid of wooden crates. "Did you ever see anything like this in your life?"

Phoebe had been equally amazed. "No, I sure haven't. And look at all them cannonballs, Ted. I'll bet you can't even count them all."

Sergeant Anderson told them that the campaign had begun two weeks ago, with more than four hundred ships shuttling back and forth to the tip of the York-James Peninsula, ferrying the 120,000-man Army of the Potomac and everything they would need to wage war. When Phoebe and Ted's turn had finally come, they'd boarded this river steamer on a blustery day in March.

Now they were nearing the end of their two-hundred-mile voyage and entering the choppier waters of Chesapeake Bay. They would land at Fortress Monroe that afternoon—which was hardly soon enough for Phoebe. She was half starved because she had decided to stop eating after seeing where everybody else's rations had wound up.

"Do you suppose Johnny Reb knows we're coming?" Ted asked suddenly.

"Sure he knows. It's pretty hard to keep all this a secret." She gestured to the parade of boats on the river and to their own ship's deck, which resembled an arsenal. "This is a pretty dumb way to sneak up on somebody."

"What do you mean?"

"I spent a lot of time in the woods back home, hunting deer and snaring rabbits, and I learned that it's best to sneak up on your prey from downwind. You don't want to let him hear you coming. Or get a whiff of you, either."

"This isn't a deer hunt, Ike," Ted said stiffly. "It's war. And General McClellan knows everything there is to know about war."

Phoebe didn't argue with him. Ted would defend his commanding officer no matter what she said.

She could smell the ocean now, and the waves were growing rougher. She turned around to look toward the east. Beyond the last tip of land, gray clouds met the gray horizon with water as far as she could see. She quickly turned back.

"I sure wouldn't like to cross that ocean," she said. "I'll bet it makes a person feel awful small to be sailing way out there."

"Hey," Ted said a few minutes later. "Maybe the Rebels will see us coming with all of this and figure out it's a lost cause. I know I'd surrender if I saw all these cannons and soldiers and guns, wouldn't you?"

Phoebe thought about the question for a moment before answering. "You know what? If someone came after my land this way, I'd fight like a mother bear protecting her cubs. I mean, what if all these soldiers were marching up to your hometown in Pennsylvania, threatening your ma? Would you give up?"

"Never thought of it that way."

"Don't plan on the Rebels waving any white flags, Ted. I figure they'll fight like wildcats to protect what's theirs."

Late that afternoon, the ship landed at Fortress Monroe in the pouring rain. The water was so choppy that Phoebe thought for sure that she would land in the drink as she teetered down the narrow ramp to the landing. The scene on shore looked the same as the one they'd left in Washington—scores of soldiers and ships, and raggedy, dark-faced contrabands stacking endless piles of supplies and equipment.

Phoebe's regiment marched inland and camped in the woods near the fort. The low flatlands near the river were heavily wooded, the ground where the soldiers pitched their tents damp and teeming with wood ticks and mosquitoes. When camp was made, the men sat waiting for a long, dreary week. For every warm, sunny day there were two cold, wet ones, until Phoebe was sure she would never feel completely dry again. They were waiting, she learned, for the remainder of the army and for General McClellan himself to arrive and direct the invasion.

Every morning and evening she and Ted sat on damp logs near the smoldering campfire and picked off wood ticks, a dozen or so of the bloodthirsty critters every day. Ted kept a tally of how many they'd caught, the way he'd once counted stuff in his uncle's factory. He wasn't a country boy, so wood ticks were new to him. Phoebe taught him how to pry them off.

"You gotta dig down with your fingernails and pinch them off, like this," she said. "They burrow down pretty deep, and you'll only get the top half of them if you don't dig. Then the sore will fester. You can't hardly squash the little beggars, neither, so you better throw them in the fire."

"Ugh! I'll bet these are Rebel ticks," Ted said, digging one off his ankle.

"You got one on your neck that's dug in real deep," she told him. "You must've missed him yesterday. You'll have to hold a match or a firebrand to him and heat him up good. Then he'll come crawling out mighty quick."

"I'll bet the Confederates enlisted these ticks and mosquitoes to fight on their side," Ted said as he pitched a tick into the flames. "They're probably breeding them like horses up there in Richmond."

"Yeah, and I'll tell you what else," she said as it began to drizzle again. "This blasted weather is on their side, too."

On the day they finally broke camp and began the twenty-mile march to Yorktown to confront the Rebel army, the sun was shining, the grass was spring green, and the peach trees were in bloom. Phoebe felt on top of the world. With Ted marching beside her all day and snoring beside her in their pup tent at night, she had never felt happier in her life.

But the next day the rain fell in a downpour. Thousands of tramping feet and horses' hooves and wagon wheels quickly turned the road into a sticky, sucking mudhole, trapping the heavy wagons up to their axles in gumbo. Phoebe and Ted's company marched near the rear of the long column of men, and when they weren't helping the teamsters heave the wagons out of the muck, they were standing in a steady deluge, waiting while the other soldiers took their turns at heaving. They reached Yorktown in the early afternoon and heard the sound of Confederate artillery and rifle fire for the first time. It sobered everyone up right quick. After a wet night sleeping on the marshy ground, Phoebe found out the next day what they were up against.

The Confederates were hunkered down behind earthworks fifteen feet thick, surrounded by ditches ten feet deep and fifteen feet wide. If she was within sight of their fortifications, she figured she was also within range of their cannons.

"We're gonna have a fight on our hands for the next few days—that's for sure," she told Ted. "But I'm ready to go at them, aren't you?"

"I've been ready since I put on this uniform last October," he said. "They've had me toting this heavy gun all over the place; it's about time I had a chance to shoot it."

"The Rebels can't possibly have as many soldiers in there as we've got out here," Phoebe guessed, "or they'd be standing cheek to jowl with no room to move. I figure we'll storm the place, don't you think?"

"Little Mac knows what to do. He's a military genius."

But they soon learned that General McClellan had decided not to attack. He dug earthworks of his own instead, parallel to the enemy's, so he could lay siege to Yorktown. The first work crew went out with their shovels under cover of darkness to begin digging. Laboring in silence all night, they made a trench deep enough to crawl into, piling the dirt in a mound that would be high enough for a daytime crew to hide behind. Phoebe and Ted were part of the next day's crew, crouching behind the new mound of dirt, digging like crazy to make the trench deeper, the rampart higher. As she and the other soldiers continued shoveling for the next week, the Confederates occasionally sent artillery shells whistling over their heads, forcing the workers to hunker down in their ditches until they heard the explosion.

"Good thing their aim isn't too good," Ted said after a missile struck a hundred yards in front of them, showering them with dirt.

"They haven't done a lick of damage."

"They're not really trying to stop us from digging," Phoebe said. "I figure they're just testing their aim to see how far they can shoot. Then when our whole army is lined up out here in these holes, they'll be able to kill a whole bunch of us at once. If you ask me, it's a stupid idea to give them free target practice. We should attack the enemy now, before they get their guns all lined up."

But she and the others continued to dig trenches, day after day, with rain falling two-thirds of the time. The only enemies Phoebe had a chance to attack were armies of insects. She was growing disgusted.

"I joined the army nearly eight months ago," she complained, "and all we done so far is march in circles, pick off ticks, and dig holes. I never thought you could win a war this way, did you?"

But Ted's confidence in his commander never wavered. "Little Mac knows what he's doing. You'll see."

Work in the trenches continued for a month. Phoebe also helped construct ramps and log platforms for gun emplacements, preparing sites for the fourteen batteries of heavy cannon the army's engineers were busy hauling through the knee-deep mud to Yorktown. Some of those guns were so massive it took a team of one hundred horses to haul them.

Around the time Phoebe and Ted grew used to the occasional artillery shell screaming over their heads, the Confederates came up with a new game. They sent out a sharpshooter to watch over the trenches, and he picked off workers one by one, whenever somebody accidentally poked his head up too high. Phoebe needed to be especially careful because she was a good three or four inches taller than the others to start with. And the sharpshooter's favorite target area was right where she and Ted were assigned to work. Two men Phoebe had marched with and drilled with since Harrisburg had already been killed when they forgot to keep their heads down.

"Why don't we go at them and fight like soldiers instead of like moles?" she said after the second man died. "When are we gonna quit digging ditches and fight?"

"Little Mac studied modern warfare over in Europe," Ted insisted. "He even wrote books about it."

Phoebe leaned against her shovel. "Well, I'll tell you what. The Rebels are dug in like gophers over there, and I don't need a book to tell me that you can't catch a gopher by digging a hole across the road from him and sitting in it. That varmint will sit tight right where he's at—or else dig himself a back door and skedaddle when you ain't looking. If you want to catch a gopher, you gotta go down his hole, chase him out of it, and hunt him down."

"That's why we're building these gun emplacements," Ted said. "As soon as we're ready, Little Mac's going to *blast* the Rebels out." Without thinking, he stepped up onto the gun platform they were building to gesture enthusiastically toward the Rebel lines.

"Ted, get down!"

Phoebe dove at him, grabbing him around the knees, knocking him off the platform. But at the same instant that she tackled him, she heard the sharp crack of gunfire. Ted hit the mud in the bottom of the trench, and Phoebe fell on top of him.

"Oh, God," she prayed as she scrambled to her knees. "Oh, God . . . oh, God!" She was scared to death that she'd reacted too slowly, that Ted would have a bullet hole through his head like all of the sharpshooter's other victims.

Ted lay on his back in the mud. Phoebe didn't see any blood. He was stunned and gasping for air after having the wind knocked out of him, but he was alive.

"You okay?" she asked.

"Yeah . . . I think so." He slowly sat up, then reached to retrieve his cap, which lay a few feet away. "Hey, he shot a hole through my hat!"

Phoebe turned away, fighting tears of relief. She was angry for her girlish reaction and furious at the Rebel who'd nearly killed her friend. If Ted had been an inch taller, he'd have been a goner.

"That does it," she said, throwing down her own hat. "I'm gonna get me a job as a Yankee sharpshooter and kill that fella myself!"

Sergeant Anderson overheard her words as he hurried over to check on Ted. "Do you really want to have a go at him, Bigelow?" he asked. "Because if anybody can get him, you can. I've seen you shoot."

"I sure would, sir. If you let me climb up one of those trees over there and see where he's at, I'll shoot him down like a treed raccoon."

"All right. I'm tired of losing men. If you want to volunteer to go after him, you have my permission."

Phoebe knew that if she was going to do this, she needed to do it right now, while anger still pumped through her veins and the memory of Ted's close call was still sharp and clear. She picked up her gun, removed the bayonet, and made sure her rifle was properly loaded. Then she checked her cartridge box for spare ammunition—although, if she missed the sniper on the first shot, she'd be a sitting duck until she had a chance to reload.

"Don't do it, Ike," Ted begged. "It's too dangerous. You'll have no cover while you're out in the open climbing a tree, and if he sees you, he can pick you off before you even take aim. We know what a good shot he is. . . . *Please* don't take a chance."

Phoebe was so moved by Ted's concern that she nearly changed her mind. Then she remembered all the men the sniper had killed and how close he'd come to killing Ted, and she got mad all over again.

"I gotta do this," she said. "I gotta get him before he kills anybody else. You can help me by keeping him distracted while I'm out in the open, okay?"

"How are we supposed to do that without getting ourselves killed?"

"Give Johnny Reb something to shoot at. Stick a hat on the end of your bayonet and raise it up just high enough for him to see. While he's busy shooting it off and reloading, I'll get myself up a tree."

Ted clung to Phoebe's sleeve. "Don't go," he pleaded. "It's too risky."

She pulled Ted's hat off his head and stuck her finger through the bullet hole. "I can get him, Ted. Keep him busy for me."

Crouching low, Phoebe made her way down the trench until she was as close to the grove of trees as she could safely get. She drew a deep breath for courage and signaled for someone to tempt the sharpshooter into firing. As soon as she heard the crack of his rifle, she climbed out of the trench and started crawling across the open ground toward the trees. She knew how dangerous this part was. She had to crawl slowly enough so the sniper wouldn't detect her movements but quickly enough to get to the bushes before he finished reloading. *Keep him busy,* she pleaded silently—then she prayed that there wasn't more than one gunman watching.

She finally reached the woods and felt safer after crouching behind a bush. Even so, the trees were not in full leaf yet, and she knew that her blue uniform would probably stick out like a preacher in a bawdy house if he spotted it. She waited for Ted and the others to give the sniper another target, listened for the gunshot, then started climbing the nearest tree while he reloaded, her own rifle slung over her shoulder by its strap.

Phoebe never had been much good at climbing trees, and it seemed to take forever for her to get high enough. All the while, branches kept snapping and rustling and making an awful racket. One branch broke right off in her hand with a loud *crack,* but luckily for her, the sniper picked the same moment to shoot at another one of Ted's targets. The gunman was very quick at reloading and could fire more than the standard three rounds a minute. Phoebe knew she was a good shot, but she hadn't practiced reloading this rifle often enough to do it as fast as the sniper did. And she'd never reloaded while sitting up in a tree. She'd better not miss the first time.

At last she managed to climb high enough to get a good view. Phoebe spotted her quarry on the roof of a house, half hidden behind the chimney. She lifted her rifle to her shoulder and took aim. Then Phoebe froze.

The Rebel soldier didn't look sinister at all but perfectly ordinary, someone she might pass on the street on a sunny day. He was young and fair-haired, somebody's son or brother or sweetheart. She couldn't pull the trigger.

This had happened to her once before in the woods back home. She had always thought of deer as venison, something she killed for food. But one day as she'd taken aim at a doe, the deer had turned her head and gazed at Phoebe. She'd seen the deer's beautiful tawny coat and dark eyes. And the expression in those eyes was not one of fear but of surprise. Phoebe had hesitated as they'd looked eye to eye and was unable to pull the trigger. Then the doe had turned and sped away, white tail flashing as it disappeared into the woods. Phoebe couldn't bring herself to go hunting for a long time after that.

Now she faced a human target—a kid, really, no older than she and Ted. He was looking down at his rifle, reloading it, and he had no idea that she had him in her sights, that his life was about to end. Time seemed to stop.

Then Phoebe realized that the boy was a killer—her enemy. If he spotted her before she took a shot, or if she missed her first shot, he wouldn't hesitate to shoot her. In fact, if Ted had been an inch taller, he would be lying dead in that trench right now with a bullet through his forehead. Even so, Phoebe looked at the Rebel's youthful face again and moved her aim from his chest to his leg. She fired.

Phoebe saw his expression for a split second before he lost his grip on his rifle and began to fall, tumbling off the roof to the ground. It wasn't pain she saw but surprise.

She shouldered her rifle without reloading and slowly climbed down the tree, sliding down the trunk for the last few feet to the ground. She didn't need to move slowly this time but she couldn't seem to make her leaden limbs go any faster. She heard cheering from her fellow soldiers and jogged across the open space, ducking low, then jumped down into the trench. Sergeant Anderson and all the others gave her a hero's welcome. Ted surprised her with a bear hug, slapping her on the back.

"You got him, Ike! You killed your first Rebel!"

"Yeah, I got him."

"I can't believe you took a chance like that. You're about the bravest man I ever met." He released her and held her at arm's length, gazing up at her. "Boy, am I glad you didn't get yourself shot!"

"Yeah, me too." Someone passed Phoebe a hip flask with liquor in it. She pretended to take a gulp. Then passed it on.

"Wait 'til Little Mac hears what you did," Ted said.

"Boys, we've got ourselves a crack sharpshooter," Sergeant Anderson said, pumping her hand.

Ted was still staring at her. "Hey, why the long face? Come on, Ike, you should be celebrating. You killed him."

"Ain't gonna do a lick of good," she said, shaking her head. "They'll just send somebody else up there tomorrow to take his place."

"Let them try," the sergeant said. "We'll send you right back up there to kill that fella, too."

Phoebe was excused from any more digging for the rest of the day and allowed to return to her tent. But as she lay on the sodden ground, listening to the rain pattering on the canvas roof above her head, two thoughts kept circling around and around in her mind. The first was that something terrible could happen to Ted. It almost had. He'd nearly been killed. And for the first time since she'd enlisted, Phoebe felt heart-wrenching fear at the prospect of going into battle—not for herself, but for him. There was suddenly more at stake in this war than her own life. When had that happened? What did it mean?

The second thought that kept coming back to her was how wonderful it had felt to have Ted's arms wrapped around her, hugging her close. She could march and dig and shoot a gun as good as any man or better, but when Ted had held her in his arms, she'd wished he had known that she was a woman. She had longed, in that moment, to lay her head on Ted's chest and weep with sorrow and relief. And to allow him to comfort her.

As she lay on her back in the leaking tent, Phoebe didn't know what to do with such unfamiliar feelings. Ted didn't return them. Ted thought she was a man.

The siege of Yorktown and the endless digging dragged on for a month. By May 3, the gun emplacements were finally finished and General McClellan's huge cannons had been set in their places. Rumors bounced all around Phoebe's camp that the Union was going to start bombarding Yorktown in two days, on May 5. But late in the afternoon of May 3, the Confederate artillery suddenly began to pour a heavy barrage of shells into the Union camps. There was nothing Phoebe could do but hunker down in one of the trenches beside Ted and wait for it to end. It seemed as though it never would.

As evening fell and the sky darkened, enemy cannon continued to pound their encampment. Phoebe and the others hadn't dared to move for hours, even to get food or a drink of water or to use the latrine. She could see bursts of flame roaring from their heavy guns every time they fired, and she watched the shells arc through the night sky like fireworks. The thunderous noise was deafening. Whenever a missile fell nearby, it sounded to Phoebe like a steam locomotive falling from the sky, and she felt all the blood run right down to her toes as she waited for the explosion. The bombardment continued long after she'd stopped praying for it to end. Then, like a vicious thunderstorm fading into the distance, the barrage gradually tapered off, dying away into silence.

At daybreak, an unnatural stillness hovered over Yorktown.

"If they're going to start pounding us again," Ted said, "I wish they'd start now and get it over with."

"You know what?" Phoebe said. "It's a little too quiet over there. I think they're gone, Ted. I think the Rebels kept us pinned down with all that artillery last night so they could skedaddle."

As the morning wore on with neither a sound nor a sign of movement from the Rebels in Yorktown, it began to look as though Phoebe was right. Her regiment and several others were ordered into formation and told to advance toward the enemy lines, guns loaded, bayonets fixed and ready. After sitting in the relative safety of a trench for the past month, Phoebe felt like an easy target as she started forward across the open ground. Her hands were slippery as they tried to grip her gun, and her mouth felt as though she'd gulped a cup of flour.

"Any minute now they're going to start firing at us," she heard Ted mumble beside her. "And when they do, they're going to mow us down like wheat."

"They're just waiting for us to get close enough," someone else agreed.

Suddenly there was an explosion in the forward ranks. Phoebe had to resist the urge to throw herself flat on the ground, expecting enemy shells to begin raining down on them any minute. The colonel called a halt.

Eventually word spread that the explosion had come from a buried enemy artillery shell, set to go off when stepped on. Angered at the loss of several lives, General McClellan ordered Rebel prisoners-of-war to be sent out to search for more buried mines. When the way was cleared, the regiment started forward again, finally reaching the Rebel fortifications that they'd faced from a distance for the past month.

"Gone!" Ted said in disgust. "Look at that, they left their meat on the spit and their biscuits half-baked."

The only sign of the Rebel army was the garbage they'd left behind—piles of animal bones and oyster shells, abandoned campfires, empty bottles and tin cans.

"General McClellan must've thought these Rebels were stupid," Phoebe said. "Did he really expect them to sit still and wait until he had all his guns lined up? These country boys know when to fight and when to skedaddle, and it seems to me that's exactly what they done. They snuck right on out of here in the middle of the night—while we were all snoring so loud we never even heard them."

"But Little Mac—"

"Listen, Little Mac don't know a thing about Rebels." She could see by Ted's glum expression that his faith in the general was starting to waver.

"I can't believe we wasted a whole month digging holes—for nothing," he said.

Phoebe kicked at the remains of a cold campfire. "I can't believe we're standing around here looking at a deserted town when we could be chasing after them."

By the time General McClellan finally gave the order to pursue the enemy, rain had begun to fall. Phoebe and the others marched north through a steady downpour, catching up to the Rebels later that afternoon outside Williamsburg. The heavens seemed to be on the enemy's side once again. The rain slashed down in torrents as the commanding officers ordered Phoebe forward into battle for the first time.

It was a savage battle, too. The Rebels fought like cornered badgers, holding the Union forces back so the main body of Confederates could retreat to Richmond. Phoebe fired and reloaded and fired again, slogging forward through the mud, tripping over the bodies of dead and wounded soldiers, blinded by rain and smoke. The first disfigured corpse she saw, barely recognizable as human, put her in a state of dazed shock. The only thing that kept her firing her rifle and moving through the hail of bullets was the fear that if she stopped she would wind up dead, too.

Blood and rain pooled together, and both flowed in Williamsburg's streets. As the veteran soldiers would say, Phoebe "saw the elephant," and it was huge and gray and terrifying. The Rebel yell alone was enough to make her blood curdle. As men from her regiment fell wounded alongside her, screaming in pain, she prayed she would go deaf from the din of rifle fire so she wouldn't have to hear their agony. She wanted the terror of battle to end. She wanted desperately to live. She wanted to go home and never fight again. But the battle raged on and on . . . violently, endlessly.

Then it was over. Phoebe was too dazed to understand how or when it had happened. The shooting simply died away as the Rebels retreated, and she was surprised to find that she was still alive and unhurt. The bodies of dead and wounded soldiers lay strewn everywhere. She found Ted, mute with shock but unharmed.

He handed her his rifle as if he never wanted to touch it again, and when she looked it over for him, her stomach made a sickening turn. In the heat of battle, Ted had kept on ripping open the paper cartridges, pouring gunpowder down the barrel, ramming bullets into place the way he'd been taught. But he must have forgotten to put a percussion cap on the lock the last few times he's fired. In the deafening noise of combat, he probably hadn't realized that his weapon wasn't firing, because Phoebe found six bullets rammed down the muzzle of his gun. If he had suddenly remembered the cap, all that gunpowder would have blown Ted's face off.

She would tell him about his mistake tomorrow. They'd both had their fill of horror for one day. They found the remainder of their regiment and camped for the night, too shaken to speak of what they had just endured.

Phoebe couldn't find a dry piece of ground anywhere to lie

down on, much less pitch a tent. She and Ted huddled together in a grove of trees, wrapped in their canvas sheets, and tried to sleep sitting up. But even in the dim light of the campfire, she saw that his eyes remained wide open.

"You all right?" she asked softly.

"I don't think I can kill any more people, Ike," he said after a moment. "Did you see some of those dead bodies today, blown all to pieces? I don't think I can point my gun at somebody and do that to them ever again."

"The Rebels ain't losing any sleep worrying about killing you," she said. "They'll shoot you in cold blood and it won't bother them in the least. That's what you gotta remember. You gotta shoot them before they shoot you."

Ted was sitting close to Phoebe, and she felt a tremor shudder through him. "I admire you for not being scared today, Ike."

"What are you talking about? I was scared out of my wits. Look at my hands, Ted. They're still shaking."

"You didn't seem scared. I watched you. You just kept right on shooting. And when they gave the signal to advance, you went forward like you weren't even afraid."

"Well, I was. But I figured I'd better kill as many Rebels as I could before they got around to killing me."

He shuddered again. "I don't think I'm cut out for war. Maybe I should go back home."

"How you figure on doing that? You signed up for three years, remember? They'll shoot you for desertion if you take off. You want to face a firing squad?"

"That's what it felt like today," he said, hugging himself. "God in heaven, I could hear the bullets flying over my head. I saw Parker get hit, right beside me. His blood splattered all over me, and the bones of his leg were—"

"Stop it, Ted. It don't help to think back on it."

He was quiet for a long moment. "What are we doing here, anyway?" he said. "Why are we fighting?"

"The Rebels started it at Fort Sumter, and—"

"I signed up because I thought it would be fun and exciting to get away from home and see new places. Everybody said the war would be over in ninety days, and I didn't want to miss out. But God help me, I'm so scared," he said in a hushed voice. "I'm afraid I'm going to die—and I don't want to die, Ike. And I don't want to end up like one of those poor souls with their legs blown off—"

"Ted, stop! I'm scared to die, too, but we gotta stop thinking about it."

"I can't," he said softly. "Every time I close my eyes I see all those dead bodies, lying there in the mud."

"I know."

And every time they stopped talking, Phoebe could hear the distant cries and moans of the wounded. She knew exactly how Ted felt because she had been thinking the same thoughts. But unlike Ted, she could walk away from this war anytime without worrying about facing a Union firing squad. All she had to do was tell them that she was a woman.

"I haven't done anything with my life, yet," Ted said. "I want to find out what it's like to really kiss a girl. I want to get married and have a family. What if I die and never get a chance to do that?"

She felt him trembling, rocking in place.

"Those men were all alive this morning," he said. "Parker and all the others. . . . They were walking around, laughing, and now . . . Oh, God! I don't want to die, Ike! Sweet Jesus, I don't want to die!" He began to weep.

Without thinking, Phoebe drew Ted into her arms. They cried together for all that they'd seen on that terrible day and for all they would have to see in the days ahead.

She had no idea how long they stayed that way before Ted suddenly tore himself free and scrambled to his feet. A moment later, she heard him being sick in the bushes. Phoebe pressed the heels of her hands to her eyes to stop her own tears and waited for him to return. It sounded like his insides were falling out.

She had helped her brothers butcher hogs every fall and was no stranger to blood. Skinning deer and gutting fish had never bothered her in the least. But the bloody, mutilated bodies she'd seen today had been living, breathing people a short while ago. The blood that had spilled was the same as hers—and she'd seen way too much of it, along with parts of a person's insides that were never meant to be seen. Men shouldn't have to die this horribly. Even her enemies.

She knew then that her brother Junior had been right—girls weren't supposed to fight in wars. But she also knew that she could never leave. Ted Wilson needed her. And so Phoebe determined she would stay in this war and fight alongside him.

Chapter Ten

Washington City
April 1862

Julia dipped her sponge in the basin of water and wrung it out, then bathed Private Ellis Miller's face and neck. His body shook with chills.

"That water is c-cold, ma'am."

"I'm sorry, Ellis, but we need to bring your fever down. This is the only way." She unbuttoned his nightshirt and sponged his chest the way Mrs. Nichols had instructed her. She had been embarrassed to do it at first, realizing at last why everyone was so opposed to hiring young, unmarried women as nurses. But she'd grown used to such duties in the weeks since the measles epidemic had begun.

"You sure this will make me better?" Ellis asked.

"It's what the doctor ordered." Julia couldn't meet his gaze. Ellis' skin was so hot she wondered why it didn't turn the water into steam. His chest heaved beneath her hand as he labored to breathe. A sponge bath was not going to make him better.

Ellis Miller was nineteen years old, a farm boy from Ohio who had never been away from home before—nor had he been exposed to measles until the army had crammed him into a camp with masses of men from all over the country. He was a polite, gentle boy, and Julia longed to help him get well. Instead, he grew steadily worse. His fever soared and his lungs filled with fluid, until now he drifted in and out of delirium, coughing and fighting for every breath he took.

"S-seems like a waste to die this way, doesn't it?" he said through chattering teeth. "I never fought a single Rebel. It'll all be for n-nothing."

Julia had wrestled with the same question as other innocent young men had died from measles and chicken pox over the last few weeks. But her job was to encourage and cheer her patients, not regale them with her own doubts and fears.

"You mustn't think about dying, Ellis. Think about pleasant things. I'll bet a nice young fellow like you has a girl waiting back home, don't you?"

"No, I don't have one." He covered Julia's hand with his own as she bathed his chest, and held it against his heart. "Will you be my girl, Julia? You're the prettiest lady I ever saw."

"You're sweet, Ellis. If only I'd met you sooner . . . but I'm afraid you're too late. I'm already married." She squeezed his hand and then let go.

"Say, Julia," the soldier in the next bed called out, "you promised to leave your husband and marry me, remember?"

"I did no such thing," she said, smiling.

"She's right," someone else called. "Because she's leaving her husband for me, not you. I was here first."

"Tell me about this husband of yours," a third man said. "I'll bet I'm ten times the man he is."

"I don't know," she said, laughing. "You're only a private and he's a lieutenant." Julia was glad to see that they'd made young Ellis Miller smile, too. She was enjoying the good-natured banter when she suddenly heard Dr. McGrath's stern voice.

"Mrs. Hoffman, may I see you for a moment?"

Julia buttoned Ellis' shirt and pulled the covers up to his chin. Then she stood and followed the doctor out into the upstairs hallway, closing the wardroom door behind her.

The doctor absently combed his fingers through his auburn hair as he waited for her. His face wore its habitual, pain-pinched expression. Julia couldn't understand why anyone would continue to drink alcohol when it made him feel so perpetually miserable. She thought

Dr. McGrath would make a fine exhibit for the temperance movement.

"Private Miller has pneumonia," he said abruptly. He glared at Julia as if it were her fault.

"I feared as much. What I can do?"

"Nothing. He's going to die. Quite soon, I would expect." He continued to stare at Julia. She waited. "Will you be able to handle it professionally when he does, Mrs. Hoffman?"

"What do you mean?"

"I heard you flirting with him in there just now. In fact, you flirt with all the men. They're all falling in love with you, and you're encouraging them."

"I do not flirt! I have no interest in any of my patients other than seeing them get well. Besides, they're only joking. They don't mean anything by it. I thought a little good-natured fun would boost morale."

He didn't reply right away but studied her as if she were a scientific specimen. She resented his scrutiny.

"You're very naïve for a married woman," he finally said. "How long did you enjoy marital bliss before your officer-groom left you? I would guess that it wasn't very long. You have no understanding of how a man reacts to a woman."

Julia was momentarily speechless—and quite certain that her face had turned crimson. "Are we going to start sharing all the details of our marriages with each other?" she managed to say. "Because you once told me that your wife and daughter were none of my business." Her words seemed to roll right off him.

"Perhaps I will have to tell you bluntly how men react—they simply look at someone like you and begin having impure thoughts."

"That's outrageous! I am dressed exactly as Miss Dix specified. Very plainly and modestly!"

"If we put you in a nun's habit it wouldn't stop their thoughts." He made a rude gesture to indicate her bosom, and Julia raised her hand to slap him. He caught her by the wrist, stopping her. "I think you will have to leave, Mrs. Hoffman."

"Why? Because of how I look?" She jerked her wrist free from his grip, and the abrupt motion made several of her hairpins slip loose. Her hair began to fall free around her face. "You can't send me away for that! Ask the matrons about my work. Ask the other nurses if they think I'm doing a good job."

"It would be for your own good. To avoid a bad reputation. Some of these men are going to return to their camps raving about the pretty young nurse they fell in love with. Suppose word gets back to your beloved lieutenant, locked away in his dungeon prison? Will he be gracious and understanding about your behavior?"

Julia was so angry she could barely speak. "If I'm not doing a good job, if I'm a terrible nurse, then go ahead and fire me. But don't give me all this pious nonsense about my reputation. That's none of your business and neither is my 'beloved lieutenant.'"

"If you weren't so stubborn, you'd admit that this work isn't what you thought it would be. I can see right through you, Mrs. Hoffman, and what I see is a spoiled little rich girl out to prove some ridiculous point. You weaseled out of your work in the linen room by hiring servants to do it, and I'm wondering how much longer you'll keep changing sheets and giving sponge baths before you give up on that, too. I don't know what you're trying to prove, but it's time for you to quit. Go home. You don't belong here."

"I will not quit!" Julia's entire body trembled with rage. "You have absolutely no grounds to fire me, so you're taking the coward's way out by intimidating me and bullying me so that I'll fall apart and leave. Well, it won't work. I don't care how miserably you treat me—the only way I'll leave is if you order me to go."

"And if Julia goes, we go, too."

Julia turned at the sound of Mrs. Fowle's voice. The matron stood in the hallway behind Julia with Mrs. Morris and Mrs. Nichols. They couldn't have made a more formidable trio if they'd been armed with a cannon.

"We're tired of losing good nurses to your bad temper, Dr. McGrath," Mrs. Fowle said. "We need Julia's help. She is an excellent nurse."

Dr. McGrath folded his arms across his chest. "I see. Is this how it's going to be? Mutiny at Fairfield Hospital?"

Julia was stunned to see a fleeting look of pain cloud his eyes, as if it had hurt him to find himself standing alone, despised by everyone. Then it vanished, and he was his usual cocky self again. "How much is she paying all of you to stand up for her?"

The accusation was so absurd that the women could only stare at him in disbelief. In the stunned silence, Julia heard the telltale groan of the front door opening. Then, a moment later, a man called, "Hello. . . ? Is anyone here?"

Julia knew that voice. It was Congressman Rhodes. Fear tingled through her. Before any of the others could react, she hurried down the stairs to greet him, knowing that if he talked to anyone, if he asked for "Miss" Hoffman and gave away her lie, Dr. McGrath would fire her on the spot.

"Why, Congressman Rhodes, it *is* you," she said, forcing a smile. "I thought I recognized your voice."

"Julia, my dear. You look . . . quite . . . well." His lie was obvious. He had reacted too slowly to disguise his shock at seeing her. And Julia knew she looked shocking. Her dress was water-spotted, her hair was falling down, and she was certain that her face still bore the unmistakable stain of anger.

"It's so good to see you," she said, rolling down her sleeves and smoothing her hair. "What brings you here?" Although Julia suspected she knew all too well what had brought him—her father.

"Why, I've come to see you, of course. Here you are, all alone in Washington, and you haven't even visited us once. You promised you would, but you haven't. So I came to see you."

He pulled a handkerchief from his pocket as if to blow his nose, but Julia caught a whiff of the cologne that permeated the cloth and knew he was using it to cover the stench of sickness. She watched him glance around the foyer and saw it as he must see it. He would report every shabby detail to her father in Philadelphia. Julia longed to take the congressman someplace else to talk, worrying that Dr. McGrath would come thundering down the stairs any minute. But there was no place to go. The doctor's office was in its usual messy state. Today, even his chairs were stacked with papers.

"This is quite a place," Rhodes said. "I've never been to a military hospital before. I must say, it looks most unpromising from the outside. Perhaps, if you could spare the time, you might give me a tour of the inside?"

Julia glanced at the stairs again. There was still no sign of Dr. McGrath. "I would love to, Congressman, but first I need to know if you've ever had the measles."

"You mean the childhood disease? I really couldn't say."

"Well, we're coping with an epidemic of it at the moment. The army moved all the stricken soldiers out of their camps and sent them to the hospitals in order to stop the spread. I would hate to have you contract it, too. Perhaps you could come back next month and take a tour?"

"Next month? Julia, just how long do you plan on working here?"

"For as long as I'm needed."

He looked dismayed but quickly hid it behind a broad smile. "Listen, my dear. The thing is, I'm going home in two weeks. I promised your father I would see how you were faring and maybe bring you home for a little visit, too. What do you say?"

The mention of home brought a wave of homesickness. The doctor's earlier accusation had struck its mark. Julia was discouraged and disappointed with the menial drudgery of nursing work. Giving sponge baths and fanning patients to cool their fevers had not been very rewarding. She'd found little satisfaction in doing tasks her servants had always done at home, such as changing bed linens. The little joy she had found came from talking with her patients—and that had just earned her a reprimand from Dr. McGrath.

Julia longed to go home to Philadelphia with Congressman Rhodes. But knowing that the doctor would celebrate her departure made her all the more determined to stay. Besides, she couldn't quit now after the other nurses had just risked their own positions to stand up for her.

"Shall I talk to the Acting Surgeon on your behalf?" Rhodes persisted. "See if I can get you some time off?"

"No, no," she said quickly. "Getting time off won't be a problem." Coming back would be. If she left now, the doctor would never let her through the door again. "Give me time to think about it. I'll let you know."

Rhodes opened his mouth as though he might argue with her, then seemed to change his mind. "As you wish, my dear. In the meantime, Mrs. Rhodes insists that you come for dinner on Saturday, and I'm afraid she won't take no for an answer. She is so eager to see you again."

"I'd be very happy to come."

"Splendid. I'll send a carriage to fetch you at six. Your father told me where you're staying."

Her father. Julia's suspicions had been correct. He was the source of this new campaign to pressure her.

"Tell Mrs. Rhodes I look forward to seeing her."

On the evening of the dinner at the congressman's house, Julia dug down to the bottom of her trunk and pulled out the only party gown she'd brought to Washington—and discovered that it was wrinkled beyond wearing. At home she would have given it to the servants to freshen up, but Julia didn't have any servants. She recalled, yet again, Nathaniel Greene's accusation that she couldn't do a thing for herself and hurried downstairs to borrow an iron from the landlady.

The cook was preparing dinner on a blazing hot stove, so Julia worked gingerly, remembering how she had burned a hole in one of the bed sheets with an iron that was too hot. Loretta and Belle had taught her how to test the irons by spitting on her finger and touching it to the metal, and she took care to do this. But the process was long and tedious. The skirt of her gown had yards and yards of fabric in it, and the space she'd been given to work in the hot kitchen was cramped.

When the dress finally looked presentable, Julia raced upstairs again and begged the girl who lived in the room next door for help with her corset laces and hoops. Ironing had taken so long that Julia had to hurry with her hair—and the steamy kitchen had made it so curly it was nearly impossible to tame. Every time she brushed it back to pin into a bun, more loose curls would spring free and fall around her face. There wasn't time to fix it. She heard the congressman's carriage arrive.

Julia glanced in the mirror and saw that she didn't need rouge. Her cheeks were still rosy from working in the hot kitchen. She stuffed her feet into her dainty evening slippers and found they barely fit after spending so much time on her feet at work. She took a deep breath and slowly exhaled to calm herself, then gathered her cloak and purse.

The landlady and all the boardinghouse girls were preparing to sit down for dinner when Julia descended the stairs. They stared at her, openmouthed.

"You look beautiful," one of them said in awe. "Like a princess in a fairy tale."

"Thank you." As the coachman helped Julia with her coat, she saw in the hall mirror that it was the truth. In her gown of pale green silk, which draped flatteringly around her shoulders and bosom, she was a different woman from the prim nurse in the high-collared mud-brown dress.

When she arrived at the congressman's house it was like entering another universe, worlds away from the dismal hospital and boardinghouse. His home was awash in glimmering candlelight and the sweet aroma of fine food and wine. Soft piano music blended with the distant sounds of laughter and tinkling china and the ring of fine crystal and silver.

"You look lovely, my dear. Simply lovely," the congressman said in greeting.

Mrs. Rhodes embraced her and kissed her cheek. "Julia, it's so good to see you again." A liveried butler took her cloak.

Julia wondered if this was how explorers felt when they returned to civilization after spending months in the wilderness. She was immediately drawn back to her familiar world, to the warmth and music and laughter, like a bird to her beloved nest. She didn't care what Mrs. Rhodes' motive was for inviting her, she was simply grateful to be back. Indeed, why had she ever left?

The congressman tucked Julia's hand beneath his arm as he led her toward the party. "Come, my dear. There's someone I'd like you to meet."

She walked with him into the drawing room, exulting in the feel of her billowing hoops and whispering petticoats. There were several other guests in the elegant room, most of them mature couples her parents' age. But Mr. Rhodes led her to a young man in his mid-twenties, lounging against the fireplace. He gaped at Julia as she approached, wearing a look of surprise on his face that surely matched her own. It had never occurred to her that the congressman would conspire to play matchmaker. She was so astonished she nearly laughed out loud.

"Julia Hoffman, I'd like you to meet Hiram Stone."

"I'm delighted," Hiram said, beaming.

"The pleasure is mine."

He was a very attractive man with light brown hair and a neatly groomed mustache. She watched him bend to set his glass on an end table and saw grace and strength in his tall body. Broad shoulders filled his expensive, hand-tailored suit. But what drew Julia to him irresistibly was his easy smile. Laugh lines curved naturally from the corners of his blue eyes as if his cheerful good nature was habitual. After spending the last few months with a scowling, disheveled doctor and desperately ill patients, it was a refreshing change to be with a man who was healthy and happy.

"Hiram is a graduate of Yale, my alma mater," Congressman Rhodes said. "He was a first-rate oarsman on their championship crew team."

"Congratulations," she said. That explained his athletic build.

"Julia is the daughter of a dear friend of mine in Philadelphia—Judge Philip Hoffman. Since you're both new to Washington City, I thought you might have something in common."

Hiram hadn't taken his eyes off Julia since she'd entered the room. She remembered Dr. McGrath's crude words about the effect she had on men and couldn't stop the heat from rushing to her face. But Hiram was a gentleman, unlike the boorish doctor, and she saw only admiration in his eyes. And surprise. When he'd come alone to the dinner party, he'd likely never imagined that his blind date would be so pretty.

"Now, if you'll please excuse me," the congressman said, "there's someone I must see." He patted Julia's hand and hurried away to greet another guest.

"He plays the role of Cupid rather well, wouldn't you say?" Hiram asked with a grin.

Julia couldn't help smiling in return. "All he lacks is a bow and a quiver of arrows."

"They're serving punch over there. Shall we get some?" Hiram took Julia's elbow as they crossed to a table with punch and hors d'oeuvres. She couldn't help brushing against him in the crowded room, and the excitement she felt was new and altogether thrilling—so much so that she struggled to make polite conversation.

"What brings you to Washington, Mr. Stone?"

"It's Hiram. And may I call you Julia?"

"Please do."

"I'm here on business. My family owns a manufacturing firm in Bridgeport, Connecticut, and I've come to negotiate a military contract with the army."

Julia knew she should show interest in his work and inquire about the nature of his factory, but curiosity overruled her manners at the mention of Hiram's home state. Dr. McGrath was from Connecticut, too. If she could learn the truth about his mysterious past, perhaps she could use it as ammunition against him. The doctor would never be able to bully her or intimidate her again.

"I'm working for a physician from Connecticut," she said. "New Haven, in fact. Isn't that where Yale University is? I wonder if you've heard of him by any chance—Dr. James McGrath?"

"Sorry, I can't say that I have. But New Haven is a good-sized city," he said, smiling, "and I've managed to stay healthy enough to avoid doctors. Congressman Rhodes told me earlier that you did nursing work in a military hospital. What made you decide on such an unusual pursuit?"

For a long moment, Julia couldn't recall the reason. Then she thought of Nathaniel Greene and the unflattering words she'd overheard him saying in this very house. "I guess it all started at Bull Run," she finally replied. "My uncle and I rode out to watch the battle with Congressman Rhodes. The preparations that the army had made for all the wounded soldiers proved horribly inadequate . . . and I wanted to help."

"So you're not only lovely, you're kindhearted, as well. I like that."

"Tell me about your work."

Hiram spent the next few minutes explaining how his family's business planned to convert to wartime production once he succeeded in winning the army contract he'd come to negotiate. But Julia found nothing arrogant or boastful in his nature. She thoroughly enjoyed his company and his conversation, and when dinner was finally announced, she was pleased to learn that they'd been placed alongside each other at the dining table. He escorted her to the room and helped with her chair.

To Julia, it seemed as if years had passed since she'd enjoyed such a feast, and she had to remind herself not to bolt down her food the way everyone did at the boardinghouse. She'd learned after her first few meals there that if she didn't reach and grab and gulp the stingy portions the way the other girls did, she would leave the table hungry.

As they dined, Hiram proved adept at lively conversation. He was graciously polite and careful to include the other dinner guests seated near him, but he gave Julia the greatest portion of his attention. Most of the table talk centered on the war—the naval battle last month between the *U.S.S. Monitor* and the Confederate ironclad *Virginia,* near Norfolk, and the horrific battle that had taken place on April 6 at Shiloh, Tennessee. Then the conversation shifted to General McClellan and his current campaign to march up the Virginia peninsula and attack the Confederate capital of Richmond. Hiram was such an attentive companion, Julia found herself confiding in him.

"To be honest, I'm quite worried about what might happen when the army reaches Richmond. My mother was born and raised there, and I still have relatives in the city. My cousin Caroline is my age."

He briefly pressed her hand, his brow furrowed with concern. "How inconsiderate of me to gloat over Richmond's imminent capture. How easily one forgets that our enemies in this cursed war are our own countrymen. Tell me, do you think your family will be able to evacuate safely?"

"I don't know. There's no longer any mail service to the Confederate states. Another cousin of mine is in Richmond, as well. But Robert is a Union lieutenant being held captive in Libby Prison."

"I'm so sorry."

"We're praying for McClellan's success so that Robert will be released soon. But also that the battle will spare the innocent civilians."

"It's no wonder you have such a keen interest in this war. Now you must tell me about your work as a nurse."

Julia tried to make nursing sound glamorous as she described it to Hiram, but she was aware of her own disillusionment and the fact that Dr. McGrath didn't want her there. In truth, she was enjoying this evening so much that she didn't care if she ever went back to the hospital again.

"Nursing helps me feel as though I'm doing something useful for my country and for all our brave soldiers," she finished. "Although I can't honestly say that I've enjoyed working with our hospital's surgeon. He drinks overmuch, and he makes everyone's life quite miserable."

"You say this physician is from Connecticut?"

"Yes. The reason I asked you about him earlier is because there are all sorts of rumors flying around the hospital about how he's running away from a sordid past. One version is that he got drunk and caused the death of a wealthy patient. Some say he even spent time in prison for it."

"Wait a minute . . . what was his name again?"

"McGrath. Dr. James McGrath."

"I'm not sure if he's your man, but there was a big scandal in all the New Haven newspapers about two years ago—the year I graduated from Yale, in fact. It seems to me that it involved a drunken doctor and his very wealthy patient. I wonder if that might be the same incident."

Julia stopped eating. She thought she might burst with curiosity. "What happened?"

"Well, a wealthy financier was shot to death, I believe. His doctor had been drinking with him that evening and was found at the scene with the dead man, holding the gun. They had been overheard arguing. The authorities arrested the doctor for murder."

"So he *did* spend time in prison. One of the nurses heard that he had."

"A friend of mine was reading law at Yale at the time, and he was very interested in attending the trial. Judging from all the news reports, it promised to be sensational. But I graduated and returned to Bridgeport before the case came to trial. I'm sorry to say, I've no idea how it turned out."

Julia had no trouble imagining the ill-tempered James McGrath committing murder. But since he was here in Washington, she wondered how he'd gotten away with it. "If it is the same doctor," she said, "it's no wonder he left town and hasn't gone back. It's a pity that we're stuck with him."

"Yes, I don't suppose he could ever practice medicine in the same city after a scandal such as that. Even if he was never convicted, his reputation would be tarnished. People would always point fingers and wonder, 'Was he really guilty, after all?' And they might be afraid to consult him because the suspicion would always be there. Yes, it makes sense that he would leave town."

"You don't recall his name?"

"No, I'm sorry. It was at least two years ago. I can ask my lawyer friend if you'd like. He might recall the name."

"Yes, thank you. I'd appreciate that."

After dinner, the men retired to the congressman's study for their brandy and cigars. Julia joined the women in the parlor for coffee. When the entire dinner party assembled in the drawing room again, Mrs. Rhodes asked Julia to play a piece on the piano for everyone. She could hardly refuse after enjoying the Rhodes' hospitality, even though Julia hadn't been near a piano in months. Years of lessons and hours of practice came back to her quickly though, and she played a simple piece from memory.

Hiram was at her side the moment she finished. "You are very talented, Julia. That was lovely."

"Thank you, but it was really nothing much."

When another guest played a waltz, Hiram asked Julia to dance with him. "I am completely enamored with you," he said as he held her in his arms. "To be quite honest, after everything I'd heard about you beforehand, I'd formed an entirely different opinion of you. But I'm pleased to discover that you're not at all what I had expected."

The knowledge that she'd been a topic of discussion irritated Julia. But Hiram was such a jovial, charming companion she shrugged her annoyance aside. "What did you expect me to be like?" she asked.

He laughed. "Please don't be angry, but I thought you must be a radical suffragette or a social reformer . . . or else a homely old spinster who couldn't find a man and was trying to prove she didn't need one."

"In that case, you were very brave to agree to have dinner with me."

"I'm so glad I did. You are a beautiful, fascinating woman, Julia. May I ask . . . are you doing this—working as a nurse—to shock your family? Or perhaps to escape a bad situation at home? A love interest gone awry?"

Again she thought of Nathaniel. "Not at all," she said. "I'm here to serve my country, just like thousands of other Americans."

"But surely such menial work should be left to a different class of women, don't you think? You should be presiding over a home such as this one, serving your country through respectable charity work. That's the life you were raised for in Philadelphia, wasn't it?"

"Yes . . . but . . ."

"Then why aren't you there?"

Hiram was holding her closely as they waltzed, his warm, smiling eyes gazing into hers. Julia felt so confused she couldn't reply. Then the music ended, and he released her. Congressman Rhodes bustled over to speak with them.

"It's so nice to see you two young people getting on so well. Say, Hiram, would you be willing to see Julia home? And would that be all right with you, my dear?"

They agreed. Julia felt drawn to Hiram, in spite of her growing uncertainty and confusion. They ate dessert and talked some more, and when the dinner party ended, he escorted her outside to his brougham. It had begun to rain, and the sound of it drumming on the carriage roof and splashing beneath the wheels made Julia feel snug and protected as she nestled beside him. He took her hand.

"I would like to court you, Julia, if you would allow me to. I must admit that I'm absolutely smitten by you. Might you be willing to give up your hospital work and your disagreeable doctor and see me again?"

"Why does seeing you depend on my quitting?"

"Well, it would be very awkward otherwise, don't you see? I have my family's good name and social standing to consider. In spite of your own impeccable background, I cannot undertake a serious relationship with a woman who's engaged in such menial, common work."

Julia slipped her hand from between his, keenly aware of her chapped skin and torn cuticles.

"And then there's the very serious matter of your reputation," Hiram continued. "Surely you realize that it's unseemly for a beautiful, young, unmarried woman like yourself to be exposed to the company of the coarsest sort of men, day after day."

"I would hope that a serious suitor would trust me and would defend my reputation. That he'd know that my moral principles are virtuous and my motives are charitable."

She thought of Nathaniel for a third time and of his admiration for the Nightingales. Were there no other men who felt the same way he did? Was she foolish to pursue nursing in order to impress Nathaniel, while allowing a man like Hiram Stone to slip away from her?

"Dear Julia. I do admire your tender heart and your desire to help others. That's part of the attraction I feel for you. So is your dogged persistence against all that society prescribes. But put yourself in your suitor's place for a moment. No gentleman would want his beloved to do such menial work, especially around so many unsavory men. It's fortunate that your father is so understanding."

"You wouldn't be?"

Even in the dark she saw his disarming smile. "If I were ever so fortunate to win a wife as beautiful and as charming as you, I would never let her do another day's work for the rest of her life. I would pamper her, spoil her, and dress her in finery and jewels. And I would never let her leave my side for a single moment, especially to spend it alone in the company of other men."

Julia knew that he meant to woo her with his words, but he made her feel like a porcelain doll that he wanted to place behind glass doors for safekeeping, taking her down only to show her off. Most girls Julia's age would be thrilled by such a loving declaration from an attractive man. What was wrong with her? Why did Hiram's words make her feel trapped instead?

It was still raining when they reached the boardinghouse. Hiram produced an umbrella and gallantly escorted her inside. "You haven't answered my question, Julia. Would you consider courting me? Won't you give me a chance to woo you away from all this?" He gestured to the dreary foyer. It seemed cold and desolate in the dim lamplight, especially after the sparkle and gaiety of the congressman's home.

But before Julia could reply, her landlady hurried out to the foyer from the sitting room, waving a piece of paper. "This message arrived for you several hours ago, Miss Hoffman. They said it was urgent and that I should give it to you right away."

Julia quickly unfolded the note and saw that it was from Mrs. Nichols at the hospital. "One of my patients is dying," she told Hiram. "He's calling for me and can't seem to be comforted. The matron has asked me to come."

He frowned. "Now? So late at night? How does she expect you to get there?"

"I'm quite capable of getting around Washington City," Julia said. "I've been doing it on my own for three months."

"I cannot allow it. Congressman Rhodes would be furious with me. My driver and I will take you."

Neither of them spoke as they drove through the muddy, rain-soaked streets to the hospital. Julia's thoughts were on Ellis Miller, tragically dying at age nineteen. What should she say to him? How could she possibly comfort him in the face of such a meaningless death? She'd never sat at anyone's bedside as they lay dying, and the prospect frightened her.

And what about her conflicting feelings for Hiram Stone? He was everything most women wanted in a suitor, with none of the arrogance she'd so hated in Arthur Hoyt. Yet the thought of being Hiram's possession, of letting him make all the decisions in her life—

including whether or not she could work as a nurse—frightened her as badly as what she was about to face at the hospital. She was aware that she hadn't answered his question. Would she give up nursing and allow him to court her?

He opened the umbrella again when they reached the hospital and accompanied her to the door. "Thank you. I—" she began.

"May I come inside? I'd like to watch you work, if I may."

"Have you had the measles? There's been an outbreak, and you really shouldn't come any farther unless you've had them."

"I have, in fact." He flashed his disarming smile again. "I recall that I rather enjoyed being peppered with spots like a Dalmatian."

She led him upstairs and into the wardroom and then stopped short. Dr. McGrath sat on Ellis Miller's bed, with one end of his stethoscope pressed to his ear, the other to Ellis' chest. The doctor's clothes were so wrinkled he might have slept in them, his auburn hair was uncombed, his shirtsleeves rolled up to his elbows. Julia could hear Ellis' tortured breathing from across the room. The doctor rested his hand on the boy's forehead, but it seemed more a gesture of tenderness than a medical one. Then he stood.

When Dr. McGrath turned around and saw Julia, he froze. The expression on his face was one she had never seen on him before—vulnerable and utterly defenseless. "Look at you," he said softly.

Julia realized that she still wore her silk evening gown. "I-I'm sorry, Doctor. I didn't have time to change. I got a message saying that Private Miller was asking for me, and I came right away. This is Hiram Stone," she said, gesturing behind her. "He and I were guests of Congressman Rhodes this evening, and Mr. Stone was kind enough to drive me here."

Dr. McGrath crossed the room while Julia spoke. He stopped when he reached the doorway where she stood. "Miller is dying," he said in an angry whisper. "Don't give him false hopes." He pushed past them and descended the creaking stairs.

Hiram waited near the door as Julia went to the boy's bedside. She gazed at his thin, pale face, battling her tears, then sat on his bed as the doctor had. "Private Miller? Ellis, can you hear me?" she asked softly.

His eyes fluttered open, and she saw him trying to focus them.

"Are you . . . an angel?" he whispered.

"No, Ellis, it's me . . . Nurse Hoffman . . . Julia. I heard that you were asking for me—so I came." She took his hand in hers. His skin was oven-hot.

"Will you be my girl now?" He clung to her hand as if she had the power to hold him back from the gates of death.

"I . . . I would love to be your girl." She tenderly brushed his hair off his forehead, just as the doctor had done.

"I'm scared," he whispered. "I wanted to die bravely . . . but . . ."

"You are brave," she said. "I've watched you struggle these last few days when it was so hard for you to breathe. And you never complained, Ellis. You never lost faith. You're the bravest man I've ever met."

"Will you write to my ma? She would want a lock of my hair. Will you. . . ?"

"Of course." Julia instinctively reached out to stroke his hair again, knowing even as she promised that someone else would have to do it. She could never find the courage to cut off a lock of Ellis Miller's silky hair after he was dead.

For the next few hours, Julia stayed by his bedside, murmuring words of comfort as he drifted in and out of consciousness. She begged God to give her the right words, desperately summoning everything she could recall from years of church attendance, reciting the Twenty-third Psalm to him and the Lord's Prayer.

"Do you know Jesus Christ?" she asked when he awoke briefly.

"Yes . . ."

"Then trust Him, Ellis. Hold on to His hand, just like you're holding mine. Jesus said, 'In my Father's house are many mansions . . . I go to prepare a place for you . . . that where I am, there ye may be also.'"

His labored breathing grew more erratic as his life slipped away. He no longer had enough strength to cough. Julia ached for him, prayed for him, promised him that he would wake up in paradise with Jesus, where there would be no more pain or tears.

Hours passed. Ellis Miller closed his eyes a final time. He exhaled a sigh—and he was gone.

Julia held her own breath as a holy silence filled the room, pouring into the space that had been filled with his painful breathing only seconds ago. She bowed her head, overwhelmed—not only by the perfect peace that had settled over Ellis in his final moments, but also by the peace that engulfed her. For the first time in her life, Julia felt God's loving presence surrounding her. He was pleased with her.

". . . Inasmuch as ye have done it unto one of the least of these my brethren," He seemed to say, *"ye have done it unto me . . ."*

Julia finally released Ellis' limp hand. She gently pulled the sheet over his face and then fled the room.

Hiram stood waiting in the darkened hallway, a shadowy figure who opened his arms to her, offering comfort. She went to him and buried her face on his chest, weeping. She felt his arms encircling her. He held her tenderly, never saying a word, his hands warm against her back.

When her grief was exhausted, Julia slowly became aware that Hiram's expensive shirt felt oddly coarse beneath her cheek. His arms felt different, too. His height and his scent were not as she remembered them when they'd danced earlier. She drew back and looked up. Dr. McGrath was holding her.

His arms fell to his sides as he released her. Then he moved past her without a word and went into the wardroom.

Julia found Hiram Stone outside on the front step, smoking a cigarette. The rain had finally stopped. "I'm so sorry," she said. "You needn't have waited."

He tossed the cigarette to the ground and crushed it with his shoe. "I'll take you home."

Tears continued to roll down Julia's face as they drove, and she wiped them away with her fingers. Hiram pulled a clean handkerchief from his pocket and pressed it into her hand.

"It's wrong to put yourself through such a harrowing ordeal, Julia. You're much too tenderhearted for this sort of work. I wish I could spare you . . . protect you. Please, promise me you'll go home to Philadelphia with Congressman Rhodes. I'll travel by steamer from Bridgeport to visit you."

It sounded so tempting—to leave all this suffering behind, to go home and resume the life she'd always known. She'd promised her father she would take courting seriously when she returned, and Hiram Stone was a very tempting suitor.

But the afterglow of God's peace and presence still warmed her, like the coals of a fading fire, and she longed to rekindle those flames, to feel God's benediction once again, more than she longed for home.

"I can't go home, Hiram."

"But what you went through tonight—you should be sheltered from such ugliness."

"It wasn't ugly at all." Yes, it had been difficult and heartrending, yet God's presence had transformed the moment of death into something holy. He had been with her and with Ellis Miller.

For most of her life, Julia had sought to please people—her parents, her social peers, handsome suitors like Nathaniel Greene and Hiram Stone. But for the first time she understood that nothing was as important as pleasing God, feeling His blessing on her life.

"I don't want to go home," she said. "I don't want to be sheltered, and I don't want to quit nursing. Don't you see, Hiram? Tonight, for the first time in my life, I did something that truly mattered."

When Julia arrived at the hospital the following afternoon, Ellis Miller's bed was empty. His knapsack and other meager belongings lay piled on the bare mattress. Mrs. Nichols came to Julia and put her arm around her shoulders.

"That was a lovely thing you did, coming back to stay with him that way until he passed on. Would you be able to write a little note to his mother so we could send it with his things?"

"Of course. Only . . . I promised Ellis that I would send her a lock of his hair."

"I took care of it," she said, pulling an envelope from her pocket. She looked up at Julia's tears and said, "You'll never get used to watching one of your boys die, my dear . . . but it does get easier in time."

They sat down on the bed together and had just begun sorting through Ellis' things when Mrs. Fowle came to the door and motioned them out into the hallway. "I have wonderful news, ladies," she whispered. "We're getting a new doctor."

"It's about time," Mrs. Nichols said with a sigh. "Are they tossing that old drunkard back in jail?"

"No, someone from the Surgeon General's office came this morning and told Dr. McGrath he was needed on the Peninsula as a field surgeon. He's downstairs packing right now."

"Good riddance to him."

"The new doctor is supposed to be arriving later today."

Julia was barely listening. Memories of the Battle of Bull Run flashed through her mind, and with them came an overpowering conviction that she was also needed at the field hospital, not here tending measles. It was no longer a matter of proving herself to Nathaniel Green or escaping the boredom of her high-society life. It was what God commanded in His Word: ". . . Inasmuch as ye have done it unto one of the least of these . . ."

"I need to talk to Dr. McGrath before he leaves," she said, excusing herself. She hurried downstairs to his office and found him packing all his medical instruments into a beautiful wooden case that was open on his desk, placing each item—knives, forceps, scissors, probes, scalpels—into its specially made compartment.

"Dr. McGrath, may I go to the field hospital with you?" she asked.

"What a perfectly ridiculous question," he said without looking up. He packed a knife that he had been using for a letter opener, then picked up the odd trumpetlike instrument that Julia had learned was a stethoscope. "The answer is *no*."

"Why not?"

"The army has no use for a nurse who will faint when the blood starts to flow."

"I'm prepared."

"No, you are *not* prepared, my naïve Mrs. Hoffman. Even I am not prepared for what's about to happen. Treating measles is one thing. The battlefield is hell on earth. You've had your fun playing nurse. We'll be sure to tell the brave Lieutenant Hoffman what a good little nurse his wife was. But now the game is going to get rough. You would not be able to cope."

"How do you know that? What makes you so sure?" Julia had no sooner said the words than she remembered how she had fallen to pieces in the doctor's arms last night. She was offering him the perfect opportunity to humiliate her. But to her enormous surprise and relief, the doctor never mentioned the incident.

"In your daily social rounds back home in Philadelphia," he said, "did you have a lot of experience with blown-off limbs and spilled guts? Did you watch an amputation or two while you sipped your afternoon tea?" He opened a drawer in the wooden case while he spoke and lifted out a stainless steel saw, testing the jagged teeth with his thumb before fitting the instrument back into place.

Julia swallowed. "I witnessed the battle of Bull Run."

"You did nursing work there?"

She didn't answer.

"I thought not. Go home. You've had your fun. The real doctors and nurses will have work to do, and we won't have time to pick you up off the ground every time you faint, or wipe the vomit off your face so you can get back to work."

He fastened the latches and set the case on his chair, then began clearing his desk. As he stacked discharge papers and requisition forms into neat piles, Julia saw the top of his desk for the first time. Then he opened a leather satchel and packed the photograph of his wife and daughter without even glancing at it. He pulled a pile of letters tied with string from a desk drawer and tossed them in, then added another letter, written on identical stationery, which had arrived from New Haven in the morning mail. He hadn't even opened it.

Julia wished she knew if he was the doctor Hiram Stone had described. If she had been certain, she would have said, *"I know what happened in New Haven. I know why you ran away,"* and he would have been forced to let her come with him. But Julia couldn't take that chance. If he wasn't the same doctor, she'd make a fool of herself.

"If you don't think I'm ready for field work," she finally said, "then let me help some other way."

"Women do not belong anywhere near the battlefield, especially women of your social class. The army won't allow it, and neither will I." He stopped working to stare at the top of his desk for a long moment, then turned to Julia. "What I cannot comprehend is why you would even want to go."

Julia didn't know why herself, except that she longed for what she had experienced last night—the joy of being used by God, of doing something that truly mattered. Instead, she said the first lie she could think of.

"Robert . . . my h-husband . . . is in Richmond. When our troops liberate the city, I want to be there to help him and the other prisoners."

Dr. McGrath came around from behind his desk. As he moved toward Julia she instinctively backed away until, without realizing it, she stood in the hallway outside his office.

"Nice try," he told her. "The answer is still *no*."

He closed the door in her face.

Chapter Eleven

The Peninsula
May 1862

"Ain't that the most peculiar thing you ever saw?" Phoebe asked. She stood beside Ted, shading her eyes against the morning sun, watching as Professor Thaddeus Lowe's observation balloon, the *Intrepid,* filled with air.

"Hang on to those lines, boys!" the professor shouted. "Don't let go!"

Phoebe and the other volunteers gripped the guide ropes as two horse-drawn hydrogen generators pumped warm air through the hoses and into the balloon. The giant air-filled bubble swelled into a globe, then lifted up, coming to life before Phoebe's eyes.

"Do you really think it will fly?" she asked Ted.

"Sure. I heard they've been using observation balloons for some time now. They can look right into the Rebels' camps and even count how many soldiers and cannons they have."

"Get in, General. Quick," Professor Lowe shouted, beckoning to General Fitz-John Porter. "It's ready to go." The general climbed into a large basket that was fastened to the balloon with ropes. He clung to the sides of the basket for dear life as it began to bounce along the ground, then finally lifted off. The guide ropes tugged against Phoebe's hands.

"Would you go up in that thing?" she asked Ted as they watched the huge cloth bubble slowly carry the general into the sky.

"Hey, I think it would be fun—as long as I'd still be tied to the ground, like he is. Even after he gets too high for these guide ropes, he's going to be tethered by that long rope over there. He can't go far, and they can always pull him back."

The professor signaled for Phoebe and the others to release their ropes, and the balloon climbed to treetop height, drifting north on the wind.

"Ain't he afraid the Rebels will shoot at him?" Phoebe asked.

"I guess they've tried it a few times already. Good thing they've always missed."

Phoebe tried to imagine what it would be like to soar high in the air like that and look down on the world from above. Her stomach made a little flip at the idea. Even so, she thought she'd like to try it once if she ever got the chance.

The odd contraption continued its slow rise into the sky, the anchoring rope swiftly unraveling like kite string. But when the balloon was about one hundred feet above the ground, the tethering rope suddenly snapped. Phoebe heard a collective gasp. Professor Lowe and all the others watched in horror as General Porter sailed gracefully north toward Richmond, unhindered.

For a long moment, everyone seemed too stunned to speak. Then Ted grabbed Phoebe's arm and towed her toward Professor Lowe. "Hey, my friend Ike is a first-rate sharpshooter. Want him to shoot that thing down for you?"

"No!" One of the general's aides blocked their path as if Ted had suggested she shoot at Porter himself, not at the balloon. "We can't take a chance on him hitting the general."

"But Ike never misses," Ted said. "Besides, the Rebels might start shooting first, you know. And they won't be aiming for the balloon."

"I fear it's already too late," Lowe said, gazing mournfully at the sky. "Surely the general's out of range by now."

Phoebe was glad not to be put on the spot. It was one thing to go after a sniper when she was hopping mad, but it was another thing entirely to fire at a balloon with a Union general on board.

"Ain't there any way to steer that thing?" she asked as it grew smaller and smaller against the sky.

"I'm afraid not," Lowe said. "I only hope the general thinks to pull the valve rope and deflate the balloon."

As they watched, the globe appeared to sag slightly; it started looking less like a globe every second. Then it gradually sank lower as it sailed into the distance.

"Hey, it looks like it's coming down," Ted said, pointing.

"Thank God! General Porter must have opened the valve." Lowe sank down onto a wooden crate, looking as though he had been punched in the gut. The general's aide quickly sent a search party to pick up Porter, and everyone breathed a sigh of relief.

"That's all for today, boys," Lowe said. "You volunteers may as well return to your camps."

The excitement over, Phoebe started back across the field to her tent. "Maybe General Porter was tired of marching through all this mud to get to Richmond," she told Ted. Their shoes were making squishing sounds in the soggy field. "We've been crawling along about as fast as caterpillars for weeks. Maybe he decided he'd fly there, instead."

"Wish we could all fly to Richmond," Ted grumbled.

By the time they reached camp, groundwater was already seeping into Phoebe's shoes, soaking her last pair of dry socks. They arrived in time to hear the news that General McClellan had ordered them to march.

As if the weather took its cue from the general, thick, dark storm clouds began moving in from the west as soon as he gave the marching orders. The morning sun quickly disappeared, the sky lowered, and by the time Phoebe's regiment was packed and ready to leave, it had begun to rain again.

Phoebe pulled her jacket collar up around her neck to keep out the rain. "If God ain't on the Rebels' side, the weather sure is," she said for the hundredth time. She stepped from the field where they'd camped onto the road that headed north—and sank to her ankles into thick Virginia mud.

"I've been drenched for so long," Ted said, "I forget what it feels like to be dry. My toes are as wrinkled as an old man's."

Phoebe's regiment hadn't seen combat since that terrible afternoon in Williamsburg, more than three weeks ago. Neither she nor Ted ever mentioned that day again, nor the paralyzing fear they'd both felt that night. But Phoebe knew they were in for another fight, just like it or worse, in the days ahead. They'd heard reports of skirmishes, and some of the men in the forward ranks who had crossed the Chickahominy River said they were close enough to Richmond to hear the church bells ringing. Phoebe found herself wishing for the long, boring days they'd spent back in Washington, before any of them knew what they were in for. At least then, fear hadn't writhed through her stomach like a snake at the thought of facing that screaming gray line of Rebels again.

As the army continued its slow crawl toward Richmond, the mosquitoes were as thick as fog in the swampy woods. Hundreds of men had already fallen sick with malaria and fevers, and Phoebe worried every day that she would join them. With most of the roads flooded and the surrounding forests too thick with vegetation to pass through, army engineers had to construct miles and miles of corduroy roads to keep the cannons, artillery, and wagon trains of supplies moving. Phoebe and Ted took their turn at road-building—chopping down trees, driving wooden pilings into the sodden ground, attaching a raft of logs to the pilings, then covering the finished roadbed with a layer of mud to smooth it.

The heavy spring rains left every creek, river, and stream flooded well beyond its banks. The Rebels had destroyed all the bridges as they'd withdrawn to Richmond, and the larger, swiftly moving rivers were nearly impossible to ford. Progress halted as work crews labored with engineers to construct new bridges, many of which looked like they just might wash away before everyone was across.

On that wet, dreary afternoon, Phoebe's regiment came to one such bridge spanning a flooded river. As she waited for her turn to cross, she could see the rickety span swaying beneath hundreds of marching feet. The swirling water was so high it sloshed over the roadbed as it rushed past with a roar, piling debris against the sagging logs.

"Do you think that bridge is going to hold?" Ted asked. "I can't swim."

"If you fall into that river, you won't have to worry about swimming," she told him. "You'll be washed away so fast you'll be back at Fortress Monroe before we even hear you holler for help."

"Thanks a lot. I feel much better now."

The sky opened up in a downpour as Phoebe's turn came. She could feel the river tugging at the slippery logs beneath her feet as she started across. She knew she had to watch her step, but the swaying motion and swirling water gave her a queasy feeling whenever she looked down. She kept her eye on Ted instead, who was marching right in front of her.

When they were about five feet from the opposite shore, Phoebe heard a shout, and suddenly she felt the bridge being jerked out from beneath her like a carpet. She lunged toward the riverbank, propelling Ted with her, both of them straining to grab hold of anything they could reach to keep from being washed away. But her hands found nothing to grasp, and she felt the angry river tugging her down, pulling her underwater.

The shock of the icy water forced all the breath from her lungs, and for a terrible moment she couldn't think what to do. The river roared in her ears as she sank beneath the surface. The heavy knapsack and rifle she carried were trying to tug her backward, weighing her down, holding her underwater. She kicked and struggled with every ounce of strength she had, fighting against the extra weight and the river's current, desperate to save herself.

God, help me! she prayed.

At last her head surfaced and she gulped air. She saw hands reaching for her, and she stretched her own out toward them. A moment later, Phoebe felt strong arms grabbing her, pulling her free from the water's grip, hauling her onto the muddy riverbank. They dragged Ted ashore beside her, coughing muddy water from his lungs. They sat together, shivering in the spring air, watching as others were pulled to safety—and as others not as fortunate washed downstream with the remnants of the bridge.

Someone built a fire. Both survivors and rescuers huddled near it, sipping whiskey-laced coffee, trying to warm themselves and dry out. Phoebe wrung water from her bedding and from the extra clothing in her knapsack with trembling hands. She hoped the others wouldn't notice the tears in her eyes, or if they did, they would think the smoky fire caused them.

She had nearly died. So had Ted. She wished now that she hadn't joked about him not being able to swim. He sat huddled beside her, shivering. She wanted to say something, to apologize, but she couldn't make her stiff, shuddering jaws form words.

When everyone had dried out enough to stop shaking, they shouldered their sodden packs and marched on, through woods that were wet and gloomy and jungle-thick. But Phoebe couldn't stop thinking about the cold, dark river that had grabbed her and held her in its grasp, trying to swallow her alive. She had cried out to God for help, and He had saved her. She'd never asked God for anything before, but after reading her little Bible all these weeks, she had done it without thinking. God had saved her. She was alive. And so was Ted.

Late in the afternoon, the rain finally stopped. Phoebe's regiment emerged from the woods and began passing croplands, fenced fields, and the carefully tended grounds of a plantation. When they reached a narrow, tree-lined lane that led to the manor house, Colonel Drake ordered them to leave the main road and proceed toward it, their weapons loaded and ready to fire.

The white two-story home sat on a small rise, shaded by oak and chestnut trees and surrounded by lush, fenced fields and orchards. There was a quiet dignity and stillness about the plantation that made the soldiers hush their voices as they approached, as if they'd come upon a queen seated on her throne.

"If this ain't the most beautiful farm I ever seen," Phoebe murmured.

The front door of the plantation house opened, and a middle-aged man emerged, unarmed, to stand on the portico between its stately pillars. Phoebe thought that President Lincoln himself, standing on the White House steps, couldn't look more noble and proud than this man did. He calmly watched as Colonel Drake and his aides approached.

"I'll thank you to stop right there," the man said when they were within a few yards. "I am William Fletcher, owner of Hilltop Plantation, and you, sir, are trespassing on private property."

Colonel Drake halted at the bottom of the steps. "If you're willing to swear allegiance to the United States of America, Mr. Fletcher, then we'll leave you and your property alone."

"I owe allegiance only to God and to the sovereign state of Virginia," Fletcher replied.

Drake's men moved swiftly then, taking the plantation owner prisoner and confiscating his house for the officers to use as their headquarters. Phoebe and the rest of her regiment were ordered to spread out and search the grounds for any armed resisters before finding a place to make camp for the night.

Phoebe set off to explore the plantation. She was too intrigued by the serene beauty of Hilltop to feel threatened by any lingering Rebels. She and Ted followed the driveway around to the rear of the house, where there was a carefully swept yard and several outbuildings. In one of them, the kitchen, a dozen slaves sat huddled in their quarters upstairs, too frightened to come out. The soldiers let them be.

Phoebe walked the well-tended grounds, passing a weaving shed and a smokehouse, a grove of pear and apple trees, a fenced vegetable garden. She couldn't help thinking of her own family's struggling farm. How many years, how much backbreaking labor had it taken to create a plantation this beautiful, to clear a hundred acres of farmland like this, rid it of weeds, and build such fine fences? She couldn't even imagine.

Beyond the cultivated areas, the dense, green woodlands began. They reminded her of the forests back home, and she longed to shed her pack, her rifle, and her shoes and go exploring, alone.

She and Ted walked back down to the bottom of the hill where there was a weathered wooden barn, a windowless tobacco shed, a corncrib, and a blacksmith shop. Phoebe knew that any remaining feed in that corncrib would soon be used to fatten Yankee horses. Across the road, in a nearby field, the other members of her regiment were already setting up camp, trampling the newly cultivated wheat underfoot, pulling down fence rails to build campfires. She ran across the road, yelling at her fellow soldiers to stop.

"What's the problem, Bigelow?" Sergeant Anderson asked when he heard the commotion.

"Please, sir, tell them to show a little respect for this property. It takes years to build fences like these, and if we destroy them all, then the cattle's going to roam wild, and—"

"Calm down, son. The army gave clear instructions that the men are to take only the top rail."

She thought about that for a moment, then shook her head. "But every rail is the top one once the rail above it's taken down. Pretty soon the whole fence will be gone."

Anderson laughed. "You're pretty smart to figure that out, Bigelow."

Phoebe couldn't bear to watch the destruction. She turned around and walked the other way, following a well-worn road beyond the barn. Ted hurried to catch up with her.

"Hey, come on, Ike. Don't take it so hard. The owner's a Confederate. He deserves what he gets for rebelling against his country. Let's—"

Phoebe and Ted both stopped short when they came upon the twin rows of tumbledown shacks, hidden from the manor house by a clump of trees. She would have thought the ramshackle cabins unfit to live in if she hadn't seen with her own eyes that they were inhabited by the plantation's field slaves. A handful of her fellow soldiers, who had arrived first, were trying to coax the frightened souls out of their cabins.

"It's okay. You can come on out. I don't know what your master told you about us Yankees, but we aren't going to hurt you. We're your friends. We've come to set you free."

Little by little, more than fifty slaves ventured out, cautiously greeting the Yankees, accepting a few treats the soldiers offered as tokens of friendship.

"It true what you saying?" a ragged-looking Negro man asked. "We free now?"

"Yes, you're considered spoils of war. You belong to the victors—that's us."

"You mean we can leave Hilltop?" a woman asked. "And Massa Fletcher can't come after us and whip us for escaping?"

"Yes, you're free to leave."

"Where are they gonna go, Ted?" Phoebe whispered. "You

know how many of them we've seen already in Washington and working on the docks. How are these folks gonna live? Where will they find food to eat?"

"Any life is better than staying here and being slaves," Ted replied.

Phoebe peered into one of the empty cabins, and what she saw made her simple cabin back home seem like a palace. The dirt floor was nearly bare of furnishings, flies buzzed around the few scraps of food near the hearth, and the unchinked logs would keep out neither wind nor rain. She didn't want to believe that people had been forced to live this way.

Once the slaves got over their fear, they began to laugh and cheer, dancing for joy in the littered road as they welcomed their saviors. One old Negro woman with small children clinging to her skirts hobbled around, hugging all the soldiers one by one and saying, "God bless you. God bless you, son."

She took Ted into her arms for a hug, but when she drew back again and looked up at him, she broke into a wide smile, as if she recognized him. "Why, you're a quadroon, ain't you, boy? Or an octoroon?"

"No. Leave me alone." He pried her hands off and wheeled around, striding back up the road the way they had come.

"What did she call you?" Phoebe asked when she caught up with him. "A *cartoon*?"

"I don't know what she was babbling on about."

Phoebe decided to let it go. She was feeling confused and shaken herself. Now that she had seen the way the slaves lived, she no longer felt sorry for the plantation owner or for the destruction of his beautiful property. It had all been accomplished at the slaves' expense. And from the looks of it, they had never enjoyed the fruit of all their hard labor.

"I treat my animals back home better than this," she said aloud. She stopped walking suddenly, pulling Ted to a halt beside her. "You know what? That's why we're fighting—it's for those poor, sorry souls back there. It's not for General McClellan or all them other bigwigs in Washington. It's for the slaves. So they don't have to live like that no more."

Ted simply nodded, gazing blindly into the distance.

As they set up their pup tent in one of the fields, Ted was quieter than Phoebe had ever seen him. She worried that she'd said something wrong to make him mad at her. They built a campfire from pine branches to finish drying out their clothes and to help keep some of the mosquitoes away, then started fixing their dinner rations. Phoebe waited for Ted to sit beside her and eat, like he always did, but when she looked around there was no sign of him.

He finally returned empty-handed after dark. He never said a word about where he'd gone or why he hadn't eaten with her, and Phoebe was afraid to ask. If he was mad at her, she might make things worse.

"Hope it don't rain tomorrow," she said. "Maybe we can finally get dried out."

Ted simply nodded and crawled inside their pup tent for the night. She joined him a few minutes later, but she lay awake for a long time, listening to a chorus of frogs celebrating springtime in a pond close by and thinking of home. Ted tossed restlessly beside her.

"You all right?" she finally asked.

He exhaled. "No. There's something I need to tell you." He propped himself up on one elbow, facing Phoebe, his voice just above a whisper. "I've never told this to a living soul before, but you're my friend and I want to tell you. Promise you won't tell anybody else?"

"Sure. I can keep a secret." She waited, unable to imagine what he might say. The moon was out, and as she lay on her side facing him, she could clearly see his boyish features. His brow was furrowed and his brown eyes looked very dark.

"I have a grandmother who lives here in the South somewhere," he said. "She's a slave."

Phoebe couldn't stop her mouth from dropping open. "You mean she . . . she's . . ."

"A Negro. Yes."

Phoebe had no idea what to say. She had always assumed that Ted's dusky skin was brown from the sun, but she realized suddenly that Ted wasn't a farm boy. He worked inside his uncle's factory all day. And even during all those winter months they'd spent in Washington City, Ted's suntan had never faded. He had the full lips that so many of the Negro contrabands had and thick, curly brown hair. Still, she never would have guessed he was part Negro.

"The plantation's white overseer forced himself on my grandmother," Ted continued. "She had a baby girl—my mother. Ma is a mulatto. She looks mostly white, though. My grandmother found out about some Quaker folks, abolitionists, who offered to smuggle my mother up north, into Pennsylvania. My ma left when she was five years old, pretending to be their white daughter. She remembers being a slave and living in a place like this. But she grew up as a white woman and married my father."

"Did your father know that she—?"

"Yeah, he knew. He didn't care." Ted rolled onto his back again, staring up at the canvas roof. "What that old slave woman called me today . . . a quadroon . . . that's what I am, Ike. It means I've got three white grandparents and one Negro one."

Phoebe rolled over onto her back, too, still unsure what to say. "Why are you telling me this?" she finally asked.

"I've always been too ashamed to let anyone know. Ma warned us never to tell a soul because a lot of people won't give you the time of day if they know you're partly Negro. Ma said no matter what, don't ever let on that you've got African blood in you."

"Makes no difference to me if you're an African or an Indian or an Irishman."

"Thanks, Ike," he said softly. "That means a lot. . . . You know, my mother used to tell stories about how horrible her life as a slave was, and today I saw the truth for myself. That's no way to treat people. Did you see that big fancy house? Did you see how those rich white folks were living up there, high on the hog, while those slaves. . . ? That cow barn is nicer than their huts. They shouldn't be treated like animals!" He paused, exhaling angrily. "That old woman? She could be my grandmother, Ike. I'll bet I have aunts and uncles and cousins who are forced to live just like this. . . . Slaves are *people*! Human beings. We share the same blood."

Even though she knew the truth, Phoebe still had a hard time thinking of Ted as kin to those poor souls on Slave Row or the raggedy dock workers they'd seen. He was so smart and handsome and well educated. She'd seen the town in Pennsylvania where he lived, and it was worlds away from this place.

And that must have been his grandmother's dream, she realized—to see her daughter and grandchildren set free from this life, free to live in a mansion like the master's. But what a hard decision it must have been to give her child away to strangers, knowing she would never see her again. Phoebe wondered what it would be like to be loved so much by someone that they would make such a sacrifice for you. She was quite certain that she would never know.

"Say something, Ike. What are you thinking?" Ted asked.

"Your grandmother must have loved your ma an awful lot to let her go like that, so she could have a better life."

"I suppose so. I never thought about it that way." Ted drew a deep breath, then exhaled. "When we win this war, I'm going to find that plantation. I'm going to see if I can find my grandmother and bring her home to live with us."

"Sounds like a good plan. Do you know where it's at?"

He didn't answer. Instead, he said in a low, calm voice, "We nearly drowned in that river today. If we had, we would have died for nothing. Now I'm not afraid to go into battle anymore, Ike, or to die if I have to. You were right in what you said this afternoon—I know why I'm in this war now. It's for slaves like my grandmother. So they can be free. If I have to fight in order to win their freedom . . . well . . . I'm not afraid to do that anymore."

Ted's words made Phoebe afraid. What if his sympathy for the slaves made him reckless and he started taking stupid chances? He could get himself killed.

"Listen, Ted—"

"Do you remember that outdoor church service we went to back in Washington?" he asked, interrupting. "Do you remember what the chaplain preached about?"

Phoebe had been too nervous to hear a word. The only thing she remembered was talking to the young preacher who'd given her a Bible. "Um . . . not really," she said. "That was a while ago."

"He read a Bible verse that said there's no difference between slaves and free men, that we are all one in the Lord's eyes. We ought to be the same in each other's eyes, too. There should be no such thing as slavery. You're right—we're not fighting this war for General McClellan. We're not giving up our homes and our families to follow him. We're fighting the Lord's battles. And if I'm going to give up everything I want in this life, I'm glad it's for that."

Phoebe lay awake for a long time, thinking about Ted's words. The next morning she saw where most of his rations were going. Ted took his food down to Slave Row and shared it with the old woman and the little children she tended. "We're going to win your freedom," he promised her. "You'll see."

Phoebe left him there and went for a walk in the woods alone, following a well-worn path strewn with pine needles. The lush green forest, fragrant with the scent of mulch and pine and alive with the busy rattle of insects, reminded her of home. She crossed a small creek and came to a pond where frogs and turtles sunned themselves on the grassy banks. Even the trees were the same as home—sassafras, white oak, red cedar.

She followed the path to where it ended in a small clearing in a pine grove. Tree trunks soared above her like pillars; the warm, humid air seemed hushed and reverent. But in the deep stillness that surrounded Phoebe, she suddenly felt as though she wasn't alone, as though someone were whispering to her in the wind. She sat down on a log and took out her little Bible, turning through the water-wrinkled pages to the story the preacher had marked for her. She had already read it over and over, countless times, memorizing the story of the little man whose name she couldn't pronounce, the outcast who had climbed a tree to see Jesus. But she read it through once again.

This time, Phoebe remembered how the bridge beneath her feet had suddenly collapsed and how she had sunk beneath the swirling water and had nearly been swept away. Then, when she'd been certain she was lost, she'd cried out to God, and a hand had reached out for her, pulling her to safety.

She read the last line of the outcast's story again, wishing she understood what it really meant: *"For the Son of Man is come to seek and to save that which was lost."*

Chapter Twelve

White House Landing, Virginia
June 1862

Julia lay in her berth aboard the passenger steamer *Potomac Queen,* listening to the steady thump of the paddlewheel as the ship chugged south, rising and falling on the swells. She tried to prepare herself for what lay ahead. Dr. McGrath had insisted she would not be able to cope with the aftermath of a battle, but she was determined to prove him wrong.

Three days ago she had read an article in the morning paper about the battle that had taken place on the Virginia Peninsula near Fair Oaks, not far from the Confederate capital of Richmond. Alongside that article was another one about the U.S. Sanitary Commission's efforts to outfit four passenger steamers as hospital ships. Volunteer nurses were needed on board to help transport wounded soldiers back to Washington. Julia had immediately gone to the Sanitary Commission's offices to volunteer.

"I'm a nurse at Fairfield Hospital," she'd told them, "working under Dr. James McGrath. I read that there's a need for nurses on your hospital ships, and I've come to volunteer."

"Can Dr. McGrath spare you?" the official asked.

"He's already down on the Peninsula, working as a field surgeon. Fairfield is virtually empty at the moment. If I served on one of your ships, I could accompany the wounded men back to my hospital."

"Excuse me for being blunt, but you look very young, Miss—"

"It's *Mrs.* Hoffman. I'm married." The lie came so easily to her now that she almost believed it herself. "I know I look young, but the matrons at Fairfield will be very happy to provide references if you'd like."

"That won't be necessary. We're grateful for your help, Mrs. Hoffman. The army has established an evacuation hospital at White House Landing on the Pamunkey River. You can help us load the wounded on board and care for them on the return trip to Washington."

Julia felt a thrill of victory, as if she'd just won an important battle. She would be where she'd wanted to be at last—near a battlefield like Bull Run. No more linen rooms, no more measles patients, and no more Dr. McGrath. "Thank you so much," she said.

"No, Mrs. Hoffman—thank you."

The *Potomac Queen* was a small passenger steamer with tall black smokestacks and a sloshing paddlewheel. Food and medical supplies, donated to the Sanitary Commission by various charitable organizations, had been loaded on board in Washington. If Julia had been at home in Philadelphia living her former life, she and her friends would have likely raised funds, scraped lint, rolled bandages, and collected many of the other items the ship carried. She had done that sort of work in the past, but it hadn't provided the deep satisfaction she'd felt the night she had comforted Ellis Miller as he lay dying. For that one brief moment, she'd felt as though her life finally mattered.

Julia had already met some of the other nurses on board the *Potomac Queen,* mostly older women with children her own age. She hadn't made any friends. Also volunteering were four Sisters of Charity, hospitaller nuns from the Mother House in Emmitsburg, Maryland. They seemed mysterious and exotic to Julia with their starched white wimples and winglike headpieces. The nuns and the other nurses had quietly kept to themselves throughout the trip. Julia wondered if they, too, were steeling themselves for what lay ahead.

The journey had been a hot and humid one as the ship steamed down the Potomac River to Chesapeake Bay, then traveled up the winding Pamunkey River to its destination. As they neared White House Landing, Julia emerged from her cabin and stood at the rail beside one of the Sisters of Charity. On shore, the dark blue of countless uniforms came into view, blanketing the ground like a carpet. Row after row of white tents sprouted in the distance, much like the army bases she'd seen all around Washington before the Peninsula Campaign had begun. But even before the ship finished docking, the atmosphere in this camp seemed very different from the camps in Washington. No military bands played rousing tunes here; she saw no waving banners and heard none of the soldiers' usual boisterous shouts—only a vague, mewling sound she couldn't quite identify.

Then she noticed the stench. Over the past few days she'd grown accustomed to the dank, fishy odor of the muddy river and salty air, but this was the fetid scent of rottenness and decay. It was the stench Dr. McGrath had tested her with on her first day at the hospital, and she recalled how he had laughed when she'd told him she would be prepared for it the next time. She certainly wasn't. Julia pulled a scented handkerchief from her sleeve and held it to her nose, but it was a feeble gesture. The stench crawled inside her until she could even taste it on her tongue.

The scene on shore was one of utter chaos, and no one seemed to be in charge. The ground near the landing was covered with blue-uniformed men, thousands and thousands of them, lying beneath the blazing June sun. She saw a line of flatcars with white awnings parked on a side rail and realized that the train bore a cargo of still more wounded men, packed together like freight. Above the squeal of gulls and the noise of the ship's engines came the strange sound she'd heard from a distance, louder now—a heartrending chorus of moans and cries, the sound of grown men weeping, begging for help, for mercy. The sound sent shivers through her. None of the wounded men were receiving help of any kind as they waited for the hospital ships.

"Dear Lord, have mercy on them," the sister standing at the rail beside Julia said. "The Battle of Fair Oaks was four days ago. Those poor souls have been lying here all this time, waiting for help."

Julia was so horrified by the sheer number of wounded men that she couldn't reply. Nor could she move. The paddlewheel had ceased to churn, and sailors had lowered the gangway into place so the passengers could disembark, but she couldn't imagine stepping off the ship and into the nightmare on shore.

"Well, then," the nun said with a sigh, "I guess it's time we went to work." She took Julia's arm as if they were old friends and propelled her forward down the gangway, following the other nuns and nurses.

Julia stepped into the tide of wounded men as if wading into icy water. The soldiers' cries rose to a clamor as they saw help arriving at last. Some reached out to the women, hanging on to the hems of their skirts, begging for help, crying out with pain and thirst. Dr. McGrath had been right—this was not at all like treating measles. Julia didn't know where to begin. The other volunteer nurses looked equally overwhelmed.

Julia looked down at the soldier nearest her feet. His muddy clothes were stiff with blood from a gaping stomach wound that had never been treated. Flies buzzed all around him. His eyes stared sightlessly into the sky. She quickly turned away from the gruesome sight and saw that the soldier on the other side of her was in his death throes, his final gasping breaths rattling in his throat. All around her she saw men with pallid faces, streaked with blood and mud, men with shattered arms and legs.

Julia's entire body began to tremble as she went into shock. She had wanted to offer comfort as she had with Ellis Miller, but this scene was beyond comprehension. How could she comfort three thousand men? She didn't know enough words, didn't possess enough strength to face such enormous need. She turned her back on the suffering men, just as she had at Bull Run, and ran toward the ship. Nothing had changed. She hadn't changed.

She didn't stop running until she was back on the steamer's deck, gulping huge breaths of tainted air, trying desperately not to be sick. Her arms and legs felt shaky and out of control. The world seemed to be spinning dizzily.

Just when she feared she would faint, one of the Sisters of Charity grabbed Julia and forced her to sit down on a deck chair, then shoved her head down between her knees. "Keep your head down until the dizziness passes," she commanded.

"I made a terrible mistake," Julia said, weeping. Her skirt muffled her voice. "I never should have come here."

"That is undoubtedly true. But listen to me. Those poor souls need help, and there's no time to go back to Washington and find another nurse to replace you. You have no choice but to do it."

"I can't! It's too horrible to look at . . . to listen to." She covered her ears to try to block out the pitiful cries, but there was no remedy for the terrible smell. "I can't do this. I can't!"

"None of us can do this on our own. But our Heavenly Father can give us the strength and courage to face hell itself if we ask Him to—and that's what this place is."

"I don't know how to . . . I've never seen such . . ."

"Of course you haven't. Do you think there is anything in my life at the convent in Maryland that prepared me for this? It's horrifying to witness such suffering. But I've been praying for God's strength all the way here. And now I'm praying that those men will see compassion in my eyes, not horror. On my own, I could never cope with this for one moment. But I know that God has called me to be here. Has He called you?"

Julia remembered God's benediction the night Ellis died, the conviction she'd had that He wanted her to serve in His name. "Yes . . . I once believed that He did, but I . . ."

"Good. Then you can do this. Like the Apostle Paul, we can do all things through Christ who strengthens us."

The nun was right. That was how Julia had gotten through the night with Ellis. She had asked God for help, and He'd given it to her. Only her foolish pride had led her to believe she could cope with this on her own. It galled her to realize that Dr. McGrath had known her better than she knew herself.

"I'm Sister Irene," the nun said. "What's your name?"

"Julia Hoffman."

"Do you know Jesus Christ, Julia? Do you know how to pray?"

"Yes, Sister. I-I do."

"Good. Now lift your head. Stand up, slowly. Start praying for strength, and don't stop until this is over. Don't look at how many thousands of them there are. Look at each man as a single suffering soul. Help him. Then help the next one and the next. One at a time."

"I don't know what to say to them."

"A good many of these men are going to die. They don't need to hear beautiful words. They need to see Jesus Christ in you, giving them a cup of cold water in His name, offering His love and compassion."

The nun circled her arm around Julia's waist and led her down the gangway again and onto the shore. "Remember the words of Isaiah: 'They that wait upon the Lord shall renew their strength . . . they shall walk, and not faint.'"

"Thank you," Julia whispered shakily.

She looked around at the horrific scene again, wondering where to begin. One of the Sanitary Commission's doctors had taken charge, dividing up all the work that needed to be done, issuing orders. He frowned as he looked at Julia's face, which she knew must be deathly pale.

"Fill a bucket with water," he told her. "There's a pump outside the train station. These men need something to drink in this hot sun."

The contrabands were already busy unloading crates of medical supplies, food, and empty buckets from the hospital ship's holds. Julia took a dipper and one of the buckets and made her way through the sea of uniformed bodies to the pump. She recited the Lord's Prayer beneath her breath as she walked, trying not to look at the mangled bodies, trying not to gag at the wretched smell of death that surrounded her. A Negro woman standing outside the depot helped her pump water.

Oh, God, help me. Please, she prayed as she lifted the sloshing pail to begin her work.

The first man she came upon had a bloody bandage around his thigh where his leg ended. Sweat poured down his face, his lips were parched, his eyes dazed with pain. She gently lifted his head and gave him a drink of water from the dipper.

"Thank you. Oh, thank you," he murmured. "God bless you."

She continued on to the next man, trying to keep to a pattern so no one would be overlooked, but the men lay everywhere, scattered across the ground. Many of them were already dead, their corpses bloating beneath the hot sun. There was not enough manpower to help the living, much less remove all the dead soldiers and bury them.

She knelt again and again, returning to the pump whenever her bucket ran dry. As she toted the heavy load back and forth, she was grateful for the practice she'd had carrying water for the laundry. All the while, Julia continued her desperate plea for strength and for the courage not to faint. Her own mouth felt as dry as sand.

"I-I think I'm dying," one boy whispered as she lifted his head. "I don't want to die. . . ."

"Don't give up," she urged. "Hang on. Help is here."

Eventually Julia came upon the doctor who had taken charge. He was kneeling on the ground beside one of the untreated soldiers, but he looked up when he saw Julia. "Nurse? Do you have a minute?"

She edged toward him. He had his medical kit open, a surgical probe in his hand, and she prayed that he wouldn't ask her to assist him in treating wounds.

"These men haven't eaten in days," he said, bending over the soldier. "Tell the women to mix up some cornmeal gruel. Add wine or any other stimulants you can find to it. We need to start giving food as well as water."

"Yes, Doctor."

Julia had never cooked gruel, or anything else, but she did that day. She and the other nurses worked without stopping until it was too dark to see. On one of Julia's trips back to the ship for more food, Sister Irene stopped her and made her sit down and eat some bacon and a piece of hardtack. It was Julia's first taste of the soldiers' usual rations, and she was certain all her teeth would break off as she tried to eat the rocklike cracker. Afterward, she continued her work by candlelight until the wax burned away to a stub. Her legs were so weary from crouching beside the men all day that she could barely stand. At last she staggered back to her cabin on board the ship for a few hours of rest.

At dawn she was up with the sun, feeding the men their breakfast. The Sanitary Commission had finally rounded up a Negro work crew to serve as stretcher-bearers, and they began carrying the wounded on board the ships. With little direction and no organization, the workers haphazardly dumped their pitiful cargo wherever they could find space—in the cabins, on all the decks, in the passageways, and even on the stairs. Soldiers screamed in pain as their stretchers bumped against the walls or someone tripped over one of them on the overcrowded deck. By late afternoon, every square inch of the *Potomac Queen* was packed with suffering men, some lying on mattresses, most on beds of straw. The hospital ship was supposed to carry two hundred and fifty men, but many more than that were eventually crammed on board.

Julia now made her way among the wounded with warm water and soap, washing the accumulated mud and sweat and blood from their faces and hands. She offered a few words of kindness and hope along with food or a blanket or a sip of brandy to ease their pain. Their murmurs of gratitude brought tears to her eyes. Malaria and dysentery had already weakened many of the soldiers who'd camped in the swampy lowlands before they'd been wounded. Some were near death and knew it. To them, she offered prayers and urged faith in the promises of Christ.

Julia felt gritty with dust and sweat, the skirt of her dress muddy and bloodstained. Her hair had been pinned and repinned carelessly without the benefit of a mirror. But she kept on working, praying constantly for strength, offering whatever assistance she could for as long as her own strength held out. Volunteers from the Christian Commission were on their way, she was told. They would help with the overwhelming work that still needed to be done.

Late in the afternoon of the second day, Julia was kneeling on the deck, trying to spoon water into a feverish soldier's mouth, when she heard someone call her name.

"Miss Hoffman? Julia Hoffman?"

She looked up, astonished to see Reverend Nathaniel Greene standing over her. His handsome freckled face looked dusty and weary; his fair hair shone golden in the sun. The sight of him brought tears to her eyes.

"It is you," he said as he crouched beside her. "I can't believe my eyes. I never expected to see you here."

"It's good to see you, too," she managed to say.

"I heard you were in Washington City, working at an army hospital. I must say I'm rather surprised to see . . . How did you come to be here?"

"I read in the newspaper that the Sanitary Commission needed volunteer nurses for their evacuation ships. I wanted to help."

He looked around at the overcrowded deck, then gestured to the hundreds of men still waiting on shore. "I'm certain this is beyond what you ever imagined you would see. It must be very hard for you to cope with such suffering. I know it is for me." His eyes met hers again, and she saw his concern, not only for the wounded men, but also for her welfare. She couldn't believe it.

"I acted disgracefully at Bull Run, Reverend, and I've been so sorry ever since—"

"You don't need to apologize, Miss Hoffman."

"Please, won't you call me Julia?" She hoped that no one, including the half-conscious soldier she was tending, had noticed that Nathaniel had addressed her as "Miss."

"You needn't apologize for Bull Run, Julia. We were all so ill prepared that day. But now . . . it appears you have more than made up for it."

His voice had grown very soft. He continued to stare at Julia as if he couldn't tear his eyes away. She wondered, at first, if it might be because she was barely recognizable in her dirty, disheveled condition. But as he continued to stare, Julia was amazed to see that his gaze was one of admiration.

"I've just arrived," he finally said. "Tell me how I can help. What can I do?"

"You can help us feed everyone. And I know that many of the men would appreciate any comfort or prayers you might offer, Reverend."

"You don't need to call me that." He ran his fingers around the neck of his clerical collar self-consciously. "It's Nathaniel. And if you'll tell me where I can find the food, I'll gladly help."

"I'll show you." She gently lowered the wounded man's head.

Julia started to rise but her legs, weak with fatigue, suddenly gave out, and she fell sideways against the injured man. He screamed in pain and lashed out, his flailing arms striking Julia in the face and knocking her to the deck. Nathaniel scrambled to help her.

"Julia! Are you all right?"

She felt stunned. Her cheek throbbed where she'd been struck. But she was more concerned for the soldier she'd harmed. "I'm sorry! Oh, dear God. We have to help him, Nathaniel. The poor man. He needs something for the pain."

"What should I do?"

"Hold him still for me." Julia had never administered chloroform before, but she'd watched the other nurses do it dozens of times over the past two days. She hurried over to the crate of medical supplies and found a bottle of the drug. While Nathaniel held the moaning man down, Julia poured a small amount of chloroform onto a cloth and held it to the soldier's face. By the time he slipped into unconsciousness, Julia felt limp herself.

Nathaniel released the man, then gently laid his hand on Julia's shoulder. "Are you all right? You should have your eye looked after. I'm afraid it's going to swell where he hit you."

She managed a weary smile as she rubbed her cheekbone. "There are much bigger medical needs around here than mine. I'll be all right." She watched the soldier's chest rise and fall in sleep, silently praying that he would be all right.

"Julia . . ."

When Nathaniel didn't say more she looked up at him. The minister was staring at her, speechless. When he finally could talk, he stammered. "Y-you're amazing. That was . . . you were so caring . . . and . . . and competent."

Julia knew she should feel triumphant. She had accomplished what she'd set out to do nearly a year ago, winning the minister's respect and admiration at last. He was looking at her the way she'd long dreamed that he would. But his words of praise didn't give her the satisfaction she thought they would. She had run away from suffering men a second time yesterday, and she knew all too well that the caring, competent nurse he saw was a fraud.

"You're wrong about me," she said. "I could never do this on my own. I've had to pray for strength since the moment I arrived."

Her words seemed to make him even more attracted to her. "And I can see that He has answered those prayers. We serve a marvelous God, don't we, Julia?"

She realized then that it was God's approval she wanted, not Nathaniel's. The thought so astounded her that she didn't answer him—and barely heard his next question.

"When are you going back to Washington?"

"What. . . ? Oh . . . I think the ship is leaving early tomorrow morning."

"I'll be in Washington myself in a few weeks. I'd like to call on you, if I may."

His words stunned her nearly as much as the blow to her face had. "Of course."

"Where can I find you?" he asked. "What's the name of your hospital?"

The minister's sudden interest in her flustered Julia, but she had the presence of mind to give him directions to the boardinghouse instead of the hospital. The last thing she wanted was for Nathaniel Greene to discover that she had lied in order to become a nurse.

"It would be wonderful to see you when you come to Washington," she said, as if in a dream. "I don't know very many people there besides Congressman Rhodes."

While they talked, she steered the minister through the maze of injured men and showed him where to find food for their patients. Then all thoughts of Nathaniel retreated from her mind as she plunged into her job once again. They worked beside each other for a short time, until Nathaniel was called away to pray with a dying man. She didn't see him again after that.

Long after dark, Sister Irene came to where Julia knelt beside a patient and took her arm, helping her to her feet. "Come, dear. You've done enough. It's time you slept for a little while."

"I no longer have a bed, Sister. They needed the space, so I let them put wounded men in my quarters."

"I think there's an empty corner in our room."

Julia's knees felt so watery she could barely walk. She and Sister Irene held on to each other as they staggered belowdeck to the nuns' tiny stateroom. The other three sisters were already there, sound asleep on the floor after having donated their mattresses. Julia took the blanket the sister offered her and curled up beside her on the floor. Sister Irene looked much less formidable—and surprisingly young—without her headpiece.

Exhausted beyond words, Julia thought that the gentle swaying of the boat and the lapping murmur of the waves would quickly lull her to sleep. But she found herself wide awake, staring at the paneled ceiling, every muscle and bone and joint in her body aching.

"Why are you here, Julia?"

Sister Irene's hushed voice came out of the darkness, her question piercing Julia's heart as if God or one of His angels had asked it. She closed her eyes, and for a moment she was back home in her parlor, dressed in satin and lace and hoopskirts, sipping tea with afternoon callers.

"I want my life to matter," she said quietly.

"I bake bread at the convent," Sister Irene said after a moment. "It seemed a meaningless task at first, especially to a woman who wanted to devote her life to God's work. Anyone can make bread, given a little instruction. And of course it gets eaten as quickly as I bake it, then I must do it all over again the next day. But I've learned that any task you do has meaning if it's done unto the Lord and according to His purposes. Your life will matter in His eyes."

"But even baking bread seems more meaningful than dressing up in fancy clothes and attending teas and parties back home."

The nun rolled over to face Julia. "God puts each of us in a different place with a different task to do. But no matter where we find ourselves, God's greatest commandment is that we love—our enemies as well as our neighbors. If we do that, our life will have meaning whether we're at a tea party or on a hospital ship."

"I came here for selfish reasons," Julia found herself confessing. "Someone accused me of being shallow and spoiled—and he was right. I came here to prove him wrong. I wanted to prove that I could be compassionate and caring." And today she had done that. She'd won Nathaniel's admiration at last. So why did the victory seem so hollow? "I wanted to change, Sister Irene. But the only thing that's different is where I am and what I'm doing. I'm still self-centered. I'm still doing all this for selfish reasons, not out of love."

The nun was quiet for a long moment. Julia was aware once again of the pitiful cries and moans outside her cabin that never ceased. Then the sister said, "You can make up your mind and discipline yourself to do any task—kneading bread, caring for the wounded, changing bandages. But we can't simply make up our mind to love others. The only way we can love the way God wants us to is when the Holy Spirit loves through us, when we give up control of our lives to Him. We prayed for strength these past few days, Julia, and God answered our prayer. Now we must pray for love."

"Some people are very difficult to love," Julia said, thinking of James McGrath. "They push everyone away and don't seem to want even a simple friendship."

"I know. I've met people like that, and you know what? They're the ones we must pray for the most. Because they need our love the very most."

Chapter Thirteen

Mechanicsville, Virginia
July 1862

Phoebe rolled her trousers above her knees and waded into Beaver Dam Creek. She had hoped for a few minutes alone to wash her socks and spare shirt in the sluggish water, but she heard laughter and the voices of her fellow soldiers as they came down the path through the woods, and she knew she wouldn't have privacy much longer. As a handful of men from her company emerged into the clearing, Ted's boyish voice carried above the others.

"Hey, everybody. Quiet a minute. Listen . . ."

The rustling branches and tromping feet stopped. Phoebe listened with them. Above the hot summer sounds of buzzing insects and flowing water she heard bells, gently tolling in the distance.

"Hear that?" Ted asked. "Those are Richmond's church bells. That's how close we are."

"Well, what are we waiting for?" one of the men asked. "Let's go burn the place down and hang ol' Jeff Davis from a flagpole!" The others cheered. The joking laughter resumed.

Phoebe quickly finished rinsing her clothes and climbed the riverbank to retrieve her shoes. The men had come to bathe in the creek and were already peeling off their clothes. She didn't want to stick around.

Phoebe envied their freedom. Her wool uniform was so hot and scratchy in the scorching July heat that she felt like she was being burned at the stake. Sweat poured down her face and soaked the armpits of her shirt, in spite of her brief wade into the river. Ted looked cooler already, stripped down to his trousers. She hoped he was having too much fun to notice that she was leaving, but no such luck.

"Hey, where're you going? Aren't you going to cool off?" he asked her.

"I'm done already."

"Well, you didn't get very clean. No offense, Ike, but you still stink. And why are you wearing all those clothes? For pete's sake, take your blasted shirt off, for once."

Phoebe slowly pulled her shirttails out of her pants and undid one button, stalling for time. "How come we haven't attacked Richmond, Ted? We're this close, we got all these men and guns . . . What do you suppose we're waiting for?"

He looked a little puzzled at the sudden change of topic. But then he took the bait—just as she'd hoped he would. "We're waiting for reinforcements. There are too many Rebels, and they're dug in all around Richmond just like they were at Yorktown. We have to get our big guns in place first and bombard the stuffing out of them. Then our troops will move in."

"Didn't General McClellan learn his lesson the last time?" she asked as she slowly backed toward the path. Ted was unbuttoning his trousers and she wanted to run. "Them Rebels know better than to sit still and wait until we have them in our sights."

"Why don't you go tell that to Little Mac, Ike? He'll be very glad for your advice." He wore a peculiar grin, as if he might be plotting something. Phoebe didn't want to wait around and find out what it was.

"I think I'll do that," she said, and she strode off into the woods as if she had every intention of marching right up to the general's tent. She heard muffled laughter behind her and knew she should run, but she was barefooted. When Phoebe stopped to put on her shoes, the men ambushed her.

Ted led the attack, laughing and giving a bloodcurdling imitation of the Rebel yell. She tried to fight back, but there were too many of them and she really didn't want to hurt anybody since they thought it was all in fun. They dragged her to the riverbank, pulling off her shoes and her trousers as they went. But they would have to knock her unconscious before she'd let them take off her shirt and her union suit. She clutched her shirtfront tightly with both hands.

"You're gonna drown me," she yelled, struggling. "I can't swim!"

"That water isn't even over your head." Ted laughed and hooted as they threw her in. A moment later, they all jumped in after her.

"Hey, no hard feelings?" he asked, wading over to her.

"Naw, it feels good." And it did. Without her wool uniform, Phoebe felt cool for the first time since falling into the flooded river last spring.

"You are the oddest fellow I ever met," Ted said. "Imagine, wearing that hot old union suit under your clothes all the time—even in the middle of summer."

In reply, Phoebe grabbed Ted's shoulders and pushed him underwater.

That afternoon they were guarding the trenches they had dug behind Beaver Dam Creek when Union pickets came on the double-quick from Mechanicsville with bad news. "At least five Confederate brigades have crossed the Chickahominy River," they reported. "The Rebels are headed this way. We're in for a fight."

A tense hush fell as Phoebe and the others quickly checked their ammunition supplies and made sure their weapons were properly loaded, their bayonets fixed. Then they waited, hearts pounding, watching for the first sign of the enemy. It was the first fight Phoebe had been in since Williamsburg, and she was scared.

"Told you them Rebels weren't gonna wait around for us to get our big guns ready," she whispered to Ted.

"Guess Little Mac didn't take your advice, did he?" He flashed a quick, nervous grin. Phoebe saw the tension in his wiry body and in his fidgeting hands and knew he was scared, too. She nudged him playfully with her elbow.

"I never got a chance to warn him, remember? Some fool ambushed me."

A cicada suddenly started to drone nearby, and Ted jumped. "Five brigades," he breathed. "Holy smokes!"

The Confederate attack came like a summer storm, with clouds of smoke and a rain of gunfire. Phoebe heard the peculiar singing sound the bullets made as they whizzed above her head like bees. She forced herself to stay calm and to listen for the bugle signals as she loaded, aimed, fired, and reloaded all that long afternoon. Artillery shook the ground, and sometimes the smoke grew so thick she couldn't even see the charging enemy until they were almost upon her. The stench of sulfur filled the air like the breath of hell.

She kept an eye on Ted, worried that he would forget the percussion caps again and overload his rifle. His face was blackened with gunpowder and his hands trembled as he fumbled in his cartridge box for more ammunition, but he fought bravely beside her without flinching.

A few yards away, Phoebe saw a soldier in her company get hit—one of the men who had thrown her into the creek that morning. His rifle fell from his hands as the force of the bullet jerked him backward, and she knew by the way he lay sprawled in a pool of his own blood that he was dead. The Rebels' rippling cry blended with the screams of the wounded, the dying. Then the deafening roar of artillery drowned out all other sounds. Throughout the long afternoon, Phoebe defended the small patch of earth she'd been assigned, resisting the nearly overpowering instinct to flee as wave after wave of Rebels attacked.

At dark the battle ended. Moonlight revealed the dazed look in everyone's eyes. Few people spoke. Phoebe's muscles ached with strain and tension, as if she had done a full day of hard labor. She'd never known such a powerful thirst. As she and Ted cautiously made their way to the creek to refill their canteens, the bodies of Rebel soldiers lay strewn along the riverbank where she and the others had gone swimming that morning. It seemed a lifetime ago.

"We won the battle, Ted," she said to break the awful silence.

"Hey, guess we showed them." His trembling voice showed no enthusiasm.

Their orders came a few minutes later—prepare to withdraw. The exhausted soldiers stared at one another, bewildered. No one believed that it was true. "Why give up the ground we risked our lives all afternoon to hold?" Ted asked.

"It has to be a mistake," Phoebe said.

But it wasn't. Within the hour, Colonel Drake had ordered their regiment into formation to begin a four-mile retreat, marching to Boatswain's Swamp.

The next day seemed like the recurrence of a terrible nightmare. The Rebels caught up to them and attacked them again near Gaines' Mill. Once more, Phoebe looked death square in the eye and thought for sure that it was coming for her. She crouched in the mud and smoke all day, loading and firing and reloading until she was down to the last two cartridges in her ammunition box. As the sun began to set, the Rebels managed to break through the Yankees' lines in a few places, and it seemed as though they were all about to die. But then she heard the trumpet sounding retreat, and she nudged Ted to his feet and fled in the dark with the other Union soldiers across the Chickahominy River to safety.

The battle had been so intense and the losses on both sides so great that Phoebe thought for sure the war would have to end for lack of soldiers. Nearly a third of the men from her own company had been wounded or killed, but she and Ted had come through it unhurt for a second day. A bullet had passed clear through the sleeve of Ted's uniform, leaving a ragged hole but thankfully missing his arm. To have survived two days of savage fighting in a row seemed like a miracle.

Then the incomprehensible orders came once more. They were withdrawing again, to Harrison's Landing, a fortified camp on the James River more than twenty-five miles south of Richmond. Phoebe could scarcely believe it.

"After all the time and trouble it took us to get here?" she said. "We ain't even licked! Why are we going backward?"

Ted shook his head in disbelief. "We were close enough to Richmond to hear their blasted church bells."

The retreat continued, with Phoebe's regiment crossing White Oak Swamp during the night. But the Rebel pursuit continued, as well. They attacked again at Glendale crossroads, the two armies battling each other in another vicious fight that killed several more men that Phoebe had known since training camp. Day after day of relentless combat had left her and Ted badly shaken and resigned to the fact that tomorrow it might be their turn to die. But even though the Union line held at Glendale, the orders came once again to retreat during the night.

"Why are we letting Bobby Lee chase us off like a bunch of scared rabbits?" Phoebe wondered. Ted shook his head, bewildered.

Another long march after another hard fight left Phoebe and everyone else exhausted. She'd suffered from a terrible headache all that day, which she figured was from all the noise of battle. But as she plodded up the rise to Malvern Hill, where they planned to camp for the night, the first terrible wave of illness struck her like a blow. She was suddenly so light-headed and sick to her stomach that she dropped to her knees, bending her head to the ground, unable to climb another step. Ted hurried to her side.

"Hey, don't stop now. We're not to the top yet."

She lifted her head to look at him and felt so dizzy she nearly vomited. "I can't . . . move. . . ."

"What's the matter?" he asked, crouching beside her.

"I don't know . . . I've been feeling poorly all day."

"Let's get you to the top. Then you can rest." Ted helped her to her feet. The dizziness was so overpowering that she had to close her eyes to make it stop. She stumbled the rest of the way up Malvern Hill like a blind woman, leaning on her friend. If she opened her eyes she knew she would faint.

"You're hot as a pig on a spit," Ted told her.

"I know . . ." Sweat drenched Phoebe's clothes as though she had just taken a dip in the river.

The shakes started as she sat watching Ted pitch their tent at the top of the plateau. He untied her bedroll and wrapped a blanket around her, but the terrible shivering didn't stop. As soon as the tent was ready, she crawled inside and passed out. During the night she was out of her mind with fever.

"I'll bet you caught the ague in one of those blasted swamps we marched through," Ted said the next morning. He helped her to the surgeon's tent during sick call, where a whole swarm of fever patients stood waiting. The doctor dosed them all with quinine and sent them back to their companies. He couldn't afford to take up space with malaria patients when there would be gunshot wounds to attend to soon.

The Rebel attack came later that morning. It started with a barrage of Confederate artillery. There was nothing Phoebe and Ted could do but hunker down and wait for it to stop, praying they wouldn't be hit. Then came the assault. As the Rebel infantry charged up the exposed hill, Union cannon opened fire. Waves of canister shot toppled the Rebel soldiers like rows of dominoes.

"You gotta be awful brave to keep charging up the hill like that," she told Ted above the din. Phoebe wanted the carnage to stop. She didn't think she could stand to watch another man die. Besides, she needed to lie down. Sweat poured down her face and stung her eyes, but whether it was from the searing heat or her rising fever, she couldn't tell.

"You don't look so good," Ted said. "You better go back to our tent and take another dose of quinine."

Phoebe didn't want to be sick. She couldn't be sick. If she wound up in the hospital the doctor would find out she was a girl. "I'm okay," she insisted, but she said it through chattering teeth.

Ted took her rifle from her shaking hands. "Come on. Put your arm around my neck. I'll walk you back."

Phoebe slept through the battle of Malvern Hill. The thunder of guns and the moans of the wounded wove in and out of her feverish nightmares until she was no longer sure what was real and what wasn't. Then everything fell silent. The next thing she knew, Ted was lifting her head so she could swallow more quinine. There was just enough light in the tent for her to see his worried face.

"Is the fighting over already?" she asked.

"It's night, Ike. You slept all day. Feel any better?"

"What about the battle?" She threw off the blanket and tried to rise, convinced that she had to go back out there and fight or she would get into trouble. Ted held her down.

"It's all over. The Confederates finally backed off. But Lord, what a price they paid. You should see all of them lying out there on the hill. Some of them are still alive, and it looks like the ground is moving." She saw him shudder. "Hey, are you hungry? Want me to fix some coffee?"

"No thanks. I've tasted your coffee."

He smiled but it didn't quite reach his eyes.

"What's the matter, Ted?"

"You feel good enough to get up? We've got orders to break camp."

"Are we gonna chase after them and finish them off?"

He shook his head. "We're retreating again. Farther south."

"Tonight? But if the Rebels are already half licked, why don't we stay and fight? We got the high ground."

"I don't know why," he said angrily. "I don't know what these blasted generals are doing anymore. But I do know that a lot of good men died this week, and when we leave it will all be for nothing."

Phoebe slowly sat up and looked around the tent in the fading light. If she moved carefully the dizziness wasn't too bad. She could help Ted pack everything up and get ready to go. She only hoped she had enough strength to march through the night.

"You know what makes me angriest of all?" Ted asked. "We told all the Negroes to stay put. We convinced most of them not to follow along after our army, telling them we were going to take Richmond and set them all free. They would be spoils of war after we liberated Virginia."

His face looked dark in the twilight, his Negro features more prominent. She remembered how bravely he'd fought for the past week and realized that all this time he had been thinking of the slaves—like the ones they'd left behind at Hilltop. Like his grandmother.

"They stayed behind, Ike," he said softly. "All those women and children stayed. And now they're slaves again."

Chapter Fourteen

Washington City
July 1862

Julia stumbled up the steps to the boardinghouse, clutching the railing, too tired to lift her feet. As she switched her satchel to her other hand to reach for the doorknob, the door suddenly opened from the inside.

"Miss Hoffman, welcome home," her landlady said.

Julia never would have believed that the shabby boardinghouse or its prim proprietress would look welcoming to her, but after living on the hospital ship for the past week, they seemed inviting indeed. Julia had worn the same clothes day and night for the entire time. She had barely slept or eaten. She couldn't recall the last time that she'd had a free moment to wash her face or comb her hair.

"I heard a carriage pull up and saw that it was you," the woman said. "Poor dear, you look exhausted. Come in, come in."

"Thank you. To tell the truth, I am quite spent."

"Supper isn't for another hour . . . but can I get you anything in the meantime? A cold drink?"

Her landlady's uncharacteristic behavior surprised Julia. She was grateful for the change, but she couldn't help wondering what had brought it about. "Would it be possible to have a hot bath?" Julia asked, scarcely daring to hope.

"Of course, dear. I'll have the kitchen girl start one for you right away."

At home Julia could have ordered a hot bath any time she wanted one, yet she had taken the luxury completely for granted. Now the prospect of immersing herself in steaming water brought tears of gratitude to her eyes. "Thank you so much, ma'am," she said.

"You're very welcome. I've been reading in the newspaper about the wonderful work that all you nurses are doing to help our poor, suffering boys. A warm bath is the very least I can offer you in return. Oh, before I forget, I have something for you." She rummaged through a drawer in the hall table and produced a letter. "This came for you while you were gone."

Julia quickly read the return address and saw that it was from Hiram Stone in Connecticut. Her heart made a little leap of excitement. She smiled without realizing it.

"From an admirer, dear?" the landlady asked, watching her.

"Yes, I guess you could call him that." She thanked the woman again and climbed the stairs to her room.

The windows had remained closed for the past week, and the tiny room felt hotter than a kitchen at dinnertime. The air was stale and smelled of the previous tenant's dirty feet. Julia tried to heave open one of the sashes, but it was too heavy to manage in her weary state. She sank down on the bed to read Hiram's letter, fanning herself with the envelope.

My dear Miss Hoffman,

I hope this letter finds you well. As you'll see from the address, I have returned to my home in Bridgeport once again. I was able to secure the military contract I came to Washington to pursue, so these past weeks have been very busy ones for me.

I haven't been able to stop thinking about you, however, or the lovely evening we spent at Congressman Rhodes' home. I can only hope that your memories of our time together are as warm as my own and that you also think of me from time to time.

As promised, I have inquired into the strange New Haven murder case for you. The name of the man who was shot to death was Eldon Matthews Tyler, age sixty-one, a wealthy banker and financier.

The physician involved was Dr. James Joseph McGrath, age thirty, who had a successful medical practice among New Haven's wealthiest citizens before the tragedy occurred. The doctor was reportedly drunk on the night of the murder and had been heard arguing with Mr. Tyler, yet charges have not been formally filed against him. No one seems to know why not, and he is evidently free on bond for the time being. I couldn't recall the name of the disagreeable doctor you are working for, but I sincerely hope that it is not this murderous fellow. I trust this information will be useful to you.

Please let me know if you ever consider returning to Philadelphia. I would so look forward to seeing you again.

Fondly,
Hiram Stone

It chilled Julia to think that she had indeed worked for "this murderous fellow." The killer had to be the same man she knew—the name was identical, his age was about right, and he was also from New Haven. Not that it mattered anymore. James McGrath was no longer at Fairfield Hospital.

Before she'd volunteered for the evacuation ship, Julia had worked briefly with the physician who had replaced him. Dr. John Whitney was white-haired, absentminded, and so impossibly old-fashioned that Julia wouldn't have been surprised to learn that he still prescribed leeches. Dr. Whitney preferred to use recovering soldiers from the Invalid Corps for his nursing staff and clearly believed that every woman belonged at home, including all of his women nurses. But at least he wasn't a drunkard. Or a murderer.

Julia slid Hiram's letter back into the envelope, wondering what to make of this information—and what to make of Hiram Stone. In the end, she decided she was much too exhausted to think about anything at all. She would take her hot bath, wash away a week's worth of sweat, grime, and weariness, then crawl into bed and sleep for as long as it took to feel human again.

But early the next morning, the landlady awakened Julia with an urgent message from Mrs. Fowle. Fairfield Hospital was overflowing with casualties from the evacuation ships. She begged Julia to come at once and help out. Though groggy and exhausted, this time Julia was wise enough to pray for strength on the carriage ride to the hospital.

"Are we ever glad to see you," Mrs. Fowle said when Julia arrived. "I knew the Commission's ships were back because they've brought us hundreds of patients. I was hoping you were back, too—and that you were still willing to work here."

"I'll work for as long as I'm needed—that is, if Dr. Whitney will have me."

"Oh, he's a harmless old fellow. Just ignore him when he starts grumbling about 'proper women's work.' We've all learned to. His Invalid Corps is handy for many things, but they definitely lack a woman's touch when it comes to nursing."

The matron sent Julia to one of the second-floor wards to do the same work she had done at White House Landing—feeding patients, offering comfort, bathing their faces to cool their fevers. The men suffered from every sort of wound imaginable, along with bloody dysentery, malaria, and other fevers. As the July temperatures soared above ninety degrees, the stifling hospital reeked of excrement and death.

Then, just when things had started to ease, more casualties arrived from the Seven Days' Battles that raged on the Virginia Peninsula. Along with these new patients came a very unwelcome surprise—Dr. McGrath returned. Julia was trying to persuade a feverish soldier to eat the milk toast Dr. Whitney had prescribed when she heard McGrath's gruff voice in the doorway behind her.

"Well, well. Mrs. Hoffman. Don't tell me you're still here?"

Julia nearly groaned aloud when she saw him. He looked as ornery and disheveled as ever—hands on hips, sleeves rolled up, auburn hair unkempt. After what she'd learned about him from Hiram Stone, Julia felt a little afraid of him.

"Yes, I'm still here, Doctor. You seem surprised."

"Frankly, yes. Now that we're treating real battlefield casualties instead of measles and chicken pox, I'm quite surprised. I didn't think you had it in you to face such gruesome stuff."

He was baiting her. Julia knew she should ignore him, but she couldn't stop herself. "Well, you're wrong. After you left I volunteered to serve as a nurse with the Sanitary Commission. I went to the Peninsula and worked on one of their evacuation ships."

"Bravo!" He wore a smirk on his face as he mockingly

applauded her. "I hope you proved what you set out to prove."

"I wasn't trying to prove anything."

"Of course you were." He made certain he had the last word by walking away. She wanted to throw something at him.

"Who was that?" her patient asked.

She exhaled in frustration. "Dr. McGrath. He's in charge of this hospital." *Unfortunately,* she added to herself.

"Do you think he'll make me eat this blasted milk toast, too?"

Julia gave up trying to feed it to him. She dropped the spoon into the pasty mixture and set the bowl on the night table. "No, he's actually quite kind to his patients." *The ones he doesn't murder, that is.* "He'll probably feed you steak and whiskey."

Later that night, dismayed by the doctor's return—and her reaction to him—Julia thought of Sister Irene's words to her on board the hospital ship. God's greatest commandment was to love others. And difficult people like James McGrath needed love the most. Grudgingly, Julia prayed for enough patience to be kind to him. Her first opportunity came the next day. The doctor walked into her ward as she was feeding one of the men his breakfast.

"Put the bowl down, Mrs. Hoffman," he said without a word of greeting. "Someone from the Invalid Corps can feed your patients and perform all those other menial duties. Since you're an experienced nurse now, you should be changing dressings and assisting with surgical procedures."

"Yes, of course." But she continued to feed the last few spoonfuls to her patient, careful not to meet the doctor's gaze. He would surely see how upset she was at the prospect of tending wounds.

Julia was not at all certain she could perform such duties. She had always looked away, unnerved, whenever the other nurses changed a patient's dressing. But pride made her unwilling to admit as much to Dr. McGrath. He was certain to have a sarcastic comment and a knowing laugh at her expense. He might even send her home if she refused. But an even bigger problem was that she had led him to believe she'd gained nursing experience while working on the hospital ship. He was about to discover that she had no idea how to change surgical dressings and care for amputated limbs.

By the time her patient swallowed his last bite, Julia had made up her mind. She had learned to wash linens, build fires, cook gruel, and perform a dozen other distasteful duties that she never would have believed she could do. Now she would just have to bluff her way through these new tasks, too.

"I'm waiting, Mrs. Hoffman," the doctor said. And none too patiently, judging by his scowling face. He stood across the room beside a patient's bed, his arms crossed.

"Sorry, Doctor." She reluctantly joined him at the bedside.

"Now, I have my own way of doing things," he told her, "so if you don't mind, I'd prefer that you forget everything you've learned from the other physicians and let me show you exactly how I want things done."

"That's fine with me." She nearly sighed aloud with relief. She hadn't asked God for help, but He'd sent her a little just the same.

For the next few hours as they went from bed to bed, Dr. McGrath taught her how to care for wounds. He showed her how to cleanse them, how to treat them with iodine or carbolic acid, how to apply poultices and dressings, and which danger signs he wanted her to watch for.

"Did you see how swollen and erythematous that man's skin was?" he asked, pulling her aside after tending a patient. "When you see inflammation like that it could be a sign of pyemia—blood poisoning. The danger is that it will spread through his body to his heart valves or his lungs. It's our job to make certain that he doesn't survive his wounds only to die of complications."

They moved to another patient, newly arrived from the battlefield, and the doctor shook his head in disgust at the condition of the bullet wound in the man's thigh.

"I'm very meticulous about cleanliness, Mrs. Hoffman, so I'd like you to be, too. I believe that any foreign material—fragments of clothing, grass, dirt—that isn't cleansed from these wounds right away can cause complications. And we don't want complications, remember?"

"Yes, from pyemia. I remember."

"Now, this is putrefaction," he told her after removing another patient's dressing. "Healthy tissue dies whenever there is an inadequate blood supply. The procedure I'm about to show you, this process of removing dead tissue, is called debridement."

Julia forced herself to watch, telling herself that it was no different from learning the steps involved in any task, such as a complicated needlepoint stitch or playing a piece on the piano.

"You all right?" he asked after finishing with the ghastly wound.

"I'm fine," she lied. She had been praying that she wouldn't faint. It was close to lunchtime, and if her stomach hadn't been empty she would have surely vomited.

"We'll need to watch that last patient carefully," he said. "Further amputation might be necessary." He showed her how to spot the signs of gangrene and erysipelas, and insisted that such patients be isolated in a separate ward. "Other physicians think these are foolish precautions, but I've learned that they sometimes save lives."

In spite of her squeamishness, Julia found that the things Dr. McGrath explained to her about the body's healing process fascinated her. If she detached herself from the notion that she was seeing blood and bone and ragged wounds and approached her task as a job that needed to be done, like scrubbing laundry, she found the work interesting and oddly satisfying. She might eventually get used to it.

She was also surprised to see a different side of James McGrath. He knew all his patients by name and always spent a moment talking with them, listening attentively as they spoke of their sweethearts and families back home. He fought as hard as any soldier on the battlefield against the diseases that attacked his patients, refusing to give up hope, using every resource available to him. And as she worked alongside him all morning, Julia discovered that he was surprisingly kind and courteous to her, as well.

When they reached the last patient in the ward, Dr. McGrath stood back, motioning for Julia to go first. "And now, Mrs. Hoffman, you will show me what you've learned."

Julia pulled up a chair beside the bed and began removing the old dressing as Dr. McGrath stood behind her, watching. The soldier, no older than she was, had his right arm amputated above his elbow. She had spent time with him the past few days, feeding him, writing a letter home for him, trying to convince him that his girlfriend would still find him handsome in spite of his injury. Julia knew she didn't dare show revulsion now.

At first her hands trembled as she worked, but she found that if she talked to the soldier and focused on him instead of herself, her nervousness subsided. She had to concentrate so hard in order not to forget any important steps that she soon found herself applying the fresh dressing without once feeling ill.

"Excellent," the doctor told her when she finished. "You have a nice gentle touch."

Julia looked up at him in surprise. It was the first compliment he'd ever paid her.

"But you will have to learn to work faster," he added, frowning. "Our wards are filled with patients, so I'll expect you to be efficient."

Julia's new skills were tested to the extreme after the second Battle of Bull Run at the end of August. It was another terrible defeat for the Union, but unlike the first battle, the wounded soldiers received much better care. The army not only had better hospital facilities, but they had organized an ambulance corps to quickly transport the casualties to Washington. Hundreds of them arrived at Fairfield Hospital.

Julia slowly gained respect for Dr. McGrath's considerable skills as a physician as they were forced to work together. He labored hard to save the lives of patients whom the elderly Dr. Whitney and even the doctors on board the hospital ships where she'd worked would have given up as hopeless. She learned to work smoothly with him, as a matched team of horses might pull together, and it sometimes seemed during those long hours beside him on the wards that they had become friends.

But when he wasn't with his patients, James McGrath continued to be rude and ill-tempered, growling at anyone who raised her voice above a whisper. Julia learned to tiptoe past his darkened office when he sat inside doing his paper work. She wished she could ask Sister Irene how to act lovingly toward such a complicated, contradictory man.

As she was leaving the hospital one evening in September, Julia saw James still at work at his desk, buried behind his endless stack of papers, his forehead propped against his fist. A tumbler of amber liquid sat in front of him along with the photograph of his wife and daughter. Julia usually tried to scurry past him without being seen, but tonight he looked pitifully lonely to her, a man whose only friend was a glass of whiskey. She decided to make an effort to be pleasant to him instead of avoiding him, reminding herself that he was the same man she enjoyed working with on the wards. She stopped for a moment in his doorway.

"Good night, Dr. McGrath. I'll see you tomorrow."

He pushed his chair back with a loud scrape as if he was about to rise. "What game are you playing now?" he asked, glaring at her. She was immediately sorry that she had spoken.

"I simply said good night—a common social courtesy, by the way—yet you've managed to take offense. Why do you do that? Why do you insist on pushing everyone away? And why do you always distrust my motives?"

He stood, his arms folded across his chest. "Because you still haven't told me the real reason why you're here, doing this work. Is it because you want to be here or because someone else expects it of you?"

She saw what he was doing—trying to take the focus off himself and his own rude behavior by putting her on the defensive. Even so, the question made her angry and she wanted to answer it. "I'm here because I choose to be here."

"And what does your husband say about it?"

"My husband is none of your business," she said wearily. "And would it really make a difference if I discussed him with you? Would you treat me any kinder?"

"Try me and see. Does your husband have a name?"

She knew she was digging herself into a deep hole with her lies, but she was tired of the doctor's harassment. "His name is Robert. And neither he nor anyone else expects me to be a nurse. It's my own choice."

"Ah. So that means either the good lieutenant is a liberal thinker when it comes to his wife's unconventional activities *or* he doesn't know about them. Since most of the career military men I know are rather conservative fellows, I'm guessing that it's the latter. Poor Robert doesn't know that you're here. Tell me, what do you suppose he'll say when he finds out what you've been up to in his absence?"

Julia thought of the real Robert Hoffman—her cousin. He wouldn't understand her determination to be a nurse any more than the rest of her family did. He would be horrified to learn where she'd been and what she'd seen and all the demeaning work she'd done. Scandalized, in fact. Just as Hiram Stone had been. The only man who seemed to understand and approve of her actions was Nathaniel Greene. Julia decided to picture the minister as her husband when she answered the doctor's questions.

"He will be very proud of me."

The doctor gave a grunt. It might have been disgust or derision or disbelief, Julia couldn't tell which. He unfolded his arms and walked around the desk toward her, absently twisting his wedding ring as he spoke. "Well, there are rumors afoot that the Rebels are on the march again. Looks like our boys are going to have to go stop them. That means there will be more work for us to do very soon. Have you had your fill yet, Mrs. Hoffman? If so, now would be a good time to be a submissive little wife and go home."

Julia had had enough of the man. It was impossible to be kind to him. "I'll do whatever I please," she said coldly. "Good night." She turned to leave and nearly collided with a man who was stepping through the front door. "Oh . . . excuse me."

Then she looked up and saw who it was—Reverend Nathaniel Greene. It was as if she had conjured him out of the blue by thinking about him a moment ago. How had he suddenly materialized in the front foyer of the hospital?

"Julia," he said, smiling broadly. "I see that I *have* come to the right place. From the outside, this building looks as though it should be condemned."

"What are you doing here?" Her words came out in a horrified whisper. Nathaniel didn't seem to notice.

"I arrived in Washington earlier today, and I'm leaving again tomorrow, but I had to see you. I went to your residence, and your landlady directed me here."

This was certain to end in disaster. Nathaniel was going to

expose her lies in front of Dr. McGrath, who had emerged from his office to stand in the foyer, right behind her. She had to be polite and make proper introductions—but she saw a terrible collision coming and felt desperate to avoid it. She had to get these two men apart, quickly.

"Dr. McGrath, I'd like you to meet an old friend of our family, Reverend Nathaniel Greene, pastor of our church in Philadelphia. He's been working with the U.S. Christian Commission for the past several months and is on his way home."

The doctor simply nodded, rudely refusing to say "How do you do" or shake Nathaniel's hand.

"I was just on my way to the boardinghouse," she told Nathaniel. "Quick! Do you think we could stop your carriage from leaving? It's so hard to catch another one at this time of day." She tried to pull him toward the door, but he wouldn't budge.

"Don't worry, I asked the driver to wait in case I didn't find you here. You're very fortunate, Dr. McGrath, to have such a fine nurse as Julia working in your hospital. I ran into her at White House Landing last June, and I saw firsthand what a wonderful job she does. Everyone she worked with had nothing but praise for her."

The doctor gave another one of his ambiguous grunts.

"I can't wait to see her family in Philadelphia and tell them what amazing work she's doing. Correct me if I'm wrong, Julia, but I had the impression that your father wasn't exactly thrilled with the idea of you becoming a nurse."

"Perhaps not in the beginning," she said quickly, "but he supports my decision now." She hoped that neither of them would see how nervous this conversation was making her.

"And speaking of your family," Nathaniel continued, "I could have kicked myself for not asking you about Robert the last time I saw you. Has there been any news of your—?"

"No! None at all. Not a word." Julia could scarcely breathe. "He's still in Libby Prison in Richmond, as far as we know. Well, good night, Doctor." She gave him a hasty wave and turned to Nathaniel, practically shoving him backward through the door, saying, "You're a savior, coming along with a carriage when you did. It's so difficult to find one at this hour."

She shuddered with relief when the door banged shut behind them.

"Your Dr. McGrath is a rather rude fellow, isn't he?" Nathaniel said when they were in the carriage.

"Yes, that's why I wanted to leave quickly. He's a very good physician but a complete boor when it comes to social skills. It would have been quite useless for you to waste any more time trying to engage him in polite conversation."

She debated briefly whether to tell the minister what she'd learned about the doctor from Hiram Stone, then decided not to. She couldn't risk Nathaniel mentioning it to her father. Judge Hoffman would haul her home on the very first train if he learned she was working for a murderer.

"Can I take you someplace for dinner?" Nathaniel asked.

Julia was so surprised by his invitation that it took her a moment to reply. "It's kind of you to offer, but I couldn't possibly go anywhere dressed like this. I've been working all day. I should change my clothes first and freshen up."

Nathaniel gazed at her as if it didn't matter to him if she was wearing rags. "You look quite lovely to me. Besides, I'm afraid there isn't time for you to change and still go to dinner. I have a meeting later this evening that I can't avoid. I'm so sorry. And then my train to Philadelphia leaves early tomorrow morning. I shouldn't have presumed on your time this way, but I wanted to see you again."

"It's good to see you, too, Nathaniel." It was. He looked wonderful, this man she had dreamed of for so long. Julia wished she could write a letter to her cousin Caroline. *At last! At long last, I have my wish!* she would tell her.

"I'm not really hungry," she said. "Maybe we could just take a carriage ride around Washington City until your meeting." She was content to simply sit beside him in the carriage and finally see the admiration in his eyes.

"That sounds good to me." Nathaniel took a moment to instruct his driver, then turned his attention back to Julia. "Ever since I saw you working in Virginia, I couldn't stop thinking about you. I know it's selfish of me, but I wish you were returning to Philadelphia, too.

I wish I could spend more time with you. When do you think you will be coming home?"

Julia longed to say, *I'll go home with you tomorrow.* Doctor McGrath had warned her that there might be another battle soon and that now would be a good time to leave. But then she thought of the hospital wards filled with wounded men and knew that a small part of her didn't want to go home, even if it was with Nathaniel Greene. Her patients depended on her. They looked forward to her smile and a few simple words of comfort to ease their pain.

"The hospital is full right now," she said. "It's so hard to leave—"

"Of course. I'm sure you'll come home as soon as you can."

How different Nathaniel was from Hiram Stone—and from most of the other men in her social circle.

"May I ask . . . a woman as lovely as you are . . . is it too much to hope that you haven't found a beau yet?"

Could he possibly be serious? What miracle had transpired that had finally allowed her to win his heart? She looked at his face, wondering if he was mocking her—or if she was dreaming. He wore the same lovesick expression in his gray-blue eyes that she'd seen in Hiram Stone's.

"I've been much too busy to do any courting," she managed to say.

"Good. Then I'll trust that, if it's the Lord's will, He'll bring us together when the time is right. I've waited a long time to find someone, Julia. And I nearly despaired of ever finding a woman like you—selfless, giving, compassionate. When I think of all the luxuries you've sacrificed in order to work as a nurse . . . well . . . the least I can do is be as unselfish as you are and wait a little longer."

Something in his words struck Julia as wrong. She needed to tell him that the image he had formed of her wasn't right. She was not selfless and giving; she was a fraud who had become a nurse in order to impress him and win his heart. Because if she really had won him, she would have to live up to that false image in order to keep him.

His first assessment of her on the morning after Bull Run had been the truer one—she was shallow and spoiled and unbearably self-absorbed. But as she sat in the carriage with him, holding his hand at last, Julia had no idea how to stop the charade she had set in motion without losing him again.

Chapter Fifteen

Sharpsburg, Maryland
September 1862

Phoebe crawled out of her tent shortly before dawn and made her way through the woods to the creek, alone. Her fever, which had raged all night, had finally broken. She still felt weak from this latest bout of malaria, but at least she had stopped shaking. Poor Ted couldn't have gotten much sleep with her moaning and thrashing beside him in their tent all night. He'd finally fetched her a dose of quinine from the regimental surgeon, and that had done the trick. She couldn't remember if she had thanked him.

Her symptoms had been coming and going ever since she'd marched through White Oak Swamp last July—every few days at first, but now dwindling down to every few weeks. In early September, the regiment had boarded a steamship at Harrison's Landing and sailed up the Potomac River to Washington City. They'd come right back to where they'd started from seven months ago with nothing to show for it. The Union was still split in two. Richmond was still the Rebel capital. The Negroes were still slaves. All that equipment, all that time, all those dead and wounded soldiers—for nothing. The waste of it made Phoebe sick.

The regiment had barely had time to make a proper camp in Washington before they'd learned that the Rebels were on the move, marching north into Maryland. Fearing an attack on Washington or

Baltimore, General McClellan had ordered his army to go after them. Phoebe and Ted had packed their knapsacks again and marched into Maryland with the eighty-five-thousand-man army and a train of three thousand wagons, strung out for miles. There was no mud this time, only billowing clouds of choking dust, kicked up by thousands of horses and tramping feet.

Now, after several days of marching and a long night of fever, Phoebe felt filthy. She had risen early to cool off in Antietam Creek before anyone else was awake. Leaving her uniform on shore, she waded into the chilly water in her union suit, which she never took off. But it had been almost a year since she had wrapped the muslin around her bosom to flatten it, and the filthy cloth had rotted into shreds from dirt and sweat and age. Her fingers poked through it like paper. Phoebe quickly unbuttoned her underwear and stripped off the tattered cloth, letting it float away downstream. Then she took out the bar of soap she had tucked into her sleeve and washed her sweaty skin before buttoning up again.

It felt good to be clean, even if the water was cold enough to make her shiver. She lay back in the creek and wet her hair then scrubbed it clean with the soap, holding her breath and ducking under to rinse it. When she finished, Phoebe rose up out of the water, her wet union suit clinging to her body.

Ted stood on shore.

They stared at each other for a long, horrible moment before Phoebe shrieked and dove behind the bush where her uniform was. But even as she scrambled into her clothes, she knew it was too late. She'd seen Ted's dazed eyes, wide with disbelief, his slack jaw. He had dropped straight to the ground on his backside, as if someone had pulled a chair out from under him.

Phoebe tried to think what to do as she quickly pulled on her trousers and shoved her arms into the sleeves of her jacket. She didn't bother with her shirt. She scooped up her shoes and the rest of her clothes and hurried out to where she'd left him. Ted was gone. She heard him stumbling through the bushes. Phoebe tore off after him, buttoning her jacket as she ran.

"Ted! Ted, wait up!"

She easily caught up with him even though she was barefooted.

Ted was so bewildered with shock that he had strayed from the path and was groping blindly through the brush. He staggered as though he was about to faint. When she grabbed the back of his jacket to stop him, he collapsed to the ground again.

"Get away from me! Get away!" He held his arms outstretched to keep her at bay.

"Stop it, Ted. It's me."

"No . . . no . . . it's your face, but it's on the wrong body!"

She exhaled and passed her hand over her eyes, struggling not to cry. "Why did you have to go and follow me? You know I like my privacy."

"You had a fever all night. I wanted to make sure you weren't sick." But now Ted was the one who looked sick.

Phoebe turned away, wishing she could erase the look of revulsion on his face and replace it with his familiar, friendly grin. Her best friend—her only friend—had seen her as she really was, and he was horrified.

"Don't tell nobody. Please, Ted. You can't tell nobody."

He scrambled to his feet as if he was about to run. "Don't *tell* anybody? Are you *crazy*? No, get away from me," he said when she tried to grab his sleeve to stop him. He took off blindly through the brush again. Phoebe followed, hopping from foot to foot as she put on her shoes.

"What's wrong with you, Ted? Ain't we still friends?"

He whirled around to face her. "How could you do this to me? I've been with you day and night . . . sleeping beside you . . . getting undressed . . . and . . . and everything! I didn't know you were a—"

"Don't say it! I don't want anyone to know."

He sank to the ground again, covering his face with his hands. "This can't be true. I don't believe it."

"Then forget about it. Forget what you saw, and let's just go on like we always were. Nothing's changed."

"Nothing's changed? You're not . . . you're not a *man*! For crying out loud, you beat up the Bailey brothers! You shot a sniper! You do everything like a man—shooting, fighting. . . . How could you do all those things? Girls aren't supposed to kill people, Ike. They—" He stopped short, groaning. "That isn't even your real name, is it?"

"Yes, it is. My brothers always called me Ike. Ted, listen to me, please."

But he wasn't listening. He covered his face again, moaning. "Oh, my God. How could you do this to me?"

She knelt in front of him and grabbed his shoulders, shaking him. "Look at me, Ted. I look like a man. I'm big and I'm tall and I'm ugly. You think anybody's gonna marry me? I got no life at all as a girl. But like you said, I can march and fight and shoot a gun. I made a darn good soldier . . . and a friend. We're best friends, ain't we, Ted? That won't change."

He twisted away from her and stood again. "Friends don't play dirty tricks on each other. They don't lie about who they really are. I told you the truth about my grandmother, and here you've been lying to me all along."

She kept pace with him as he started tromping through the woods again. "Suppose I had told you the truth. What would you have done?"

"I don't know. . . . Probably would've turned you in—like I'm going to do right now. You can't keep pretending."

"See? That's why I didn't tell—"

"You lied to me! I feel like a fool!" He clenched his teeth and his fists, walking faster. "You know, I'd like to beat the tar out of you for this, but I don't hit girls!"

"Besides, you'd lose," Phoebe said, hoping he'd smile. He didn't. "Listen, I'm the same person I was yesterday, ain't I? I'm still *me*."

He stopped walking again, shaking his head in a baffled way as if struggling to comprehend the truth. "No, you're not. . . . You're a girl. For crying out loud, I've been telling all my secrets to a *girl*! You know how scared I was at Williamsburg . . . and I even bawled on your shoulder!"

"Oh, so what?" In her desperation, Phoebe tried making light of it, hoping Ted would get over his shock and laugh it off. "What's the harm in being a girl and saying I was a man? It's a lot better than being a man and making you think I was a girl, ain't it?"

Her attempt at humor fell flat. Ted was growing angrier by the minute. "You have to tell them, Ike. You can't keep lying like this."

"Why not?"

"It isn't right for a girl to fight a war. And I don't feel right being with you anymore . . . sleeping beside you. . . . Oh, Lord! Do you have any idea what the other fellows are going to say about us when they find out you're a girl? I'll be humiliated!"

Tears filled Phoebe's eyes at his words. The others wouldn't envy him for sleeping with her all this time—they would make fun of him for being with such an ugly woman. "You don't have to share a tent with me no more. But please don't tell nobody, okay?"

"Somebody has to tell them. If you don't, I will."

"No! Please don't do that. I got no place to go if I leave the army and nothing to go back to."

"Go home to your family."

"All I have left is three brothers, and they're off fighting the war, too. Our farm's rented out while they're gone. I got no place to go, Ted."

"Well, I can't share a tent with you—and I can't pretend that I don't know the truth. I can't keep quiet knowing what I do. Women don't belong in a war."

"Just give me some time to figure out where to go, okay? Then I promise I'll leave. Please don't tell nobody until then."

"I'll think about it." He started walking blindly again, tree branches whipping against his face.

"Ted, stop!"

"Why should I?"

"Because you're going the wrong way. Camp is that way," she said, pointing. "If you don't turn around soon the Rebel pickets are gonna shoot you."

"Great!" he said, flapping his arms in exasperation. "Thanks for destroying the last few remnants of my pride, Ike."

"I didn't want you to get shot," she said meekly.

"All this time I've been trying to keep up with you," he said, walking toward her again. "To be as brave as you, to shoot as good as you do, to get around in the woods like you do. You even risked your life to save me when I was fool enough to stick my head out of the trench. I looked up to you in every way. I wanted to prove I was a *man*—like you! And now I find out I can't even keep up with a *girl*? That a sniper would have shot me or I would have walked right into the Rebel lines if a blasted *girl* didn't keep saving my neck? Why don't you just shoot me in the head, Ike—or whoever you are—and put me out of my misery?"

He stomped past her, headed in the right direction this time. Phoebe didn't follow him. Instead, she sank down in the woods, alone, and sobbed.

It didn't take more than a day or two for the other men in Phoebe's company to notice that she and Ted weren't speaking to each other.

"You two have a fight?" Sergeant Anderson asked as Phoebe sat eating her dinner all alone.

"Yeah, Ted's pretty sore at me," she said, pushing her food around on her plate.

"You've been friends since way back in Harrisburg. It doesn't seem right not seeing you together."

Phoebe nodded, afraid she would cry if she tried to speak. It was awful having Ted look at her like he hated her guts—or worse, looking right past her. She had no one to share her canvas sheet with, to cook up a mess of beef and hardtack for, or to laugh with over a cup of bitter coffee. She missed Ted. She'd felt unloved and friendless all her life until she met him, but she had never felt lonely. Now that she'd lost her best friend, she thought she just might die of loneliness.

"You want to tell me what happened?" the sergeant asked, crouching beside her. "Maybe I can help patch things up?"

"Aw, it ain't that serious," she lied. "Ted's sore at me because I wouldn't see the doctor when I had a fever. He'll get over it."

"Listen, there's going to be a fight here any day, and we have to all work together as a team. We can't have hard feelings against each other when the real enemy's out there." He pointed to the woods with his thumb.

"I know. Ted's still my best friend, sir."

"It don't seem right you two not bunking together." He shook his head sadly. "You want me to talk to him?"

"Please don't do that," she said quickly. "He'll cool off in another day or two."

She was afraid that Ted would spill her secret if Sergeant Anderson talked to him. She had asked Ted to wait a few days so she could decide where to go, but she still hadn't figured anything out. Truth was, she wanted to stay here. She kept hoping Ted would forgive her and say it didn't matter that she had lied to him, and everything could go back to the way it was. It didn't look like that was going to happen, though.

The sergeant stood again. "Well, you let me know if you want my help, son," he said before moving away.

Early the next day, the battle began. Phoebe's regiment, under General Hooker's command, was ordered to take part in the attack. They would march across a cornfield toward a small whitewashed church without a steeple. The Confederates were waiting out there, but they had their backs to the Potomac River. They wouldn't escape.

Union drums began to pound at dawn, stirring the men's blood and signaling to prepare to march. As Phoebe loaded her rifle and checked her ammunition supply, Ted approached her for the first time in two days. But as he pulled her aside, she could tell by his expression that he was still angry.

"You said you were going to turn yourself in," he said through clenched teeth.

"I got no place to go, Ted."

"I don't care! Tell them you're sick again. Tell them you have to stay behind. There's going to be an awful fight today, and you've got no business going out there!" He hurried away again as if she had something contagious.

Phoebe lagged behind as they fell into formation so that Ted would think she was staying put. But when the troops began to move out, she maneuvered into place right behind him, where she could keep an eye on him. If Ted Wilson got wounded in battle, Phoebe Bigelow would be right beside him to carry him to the field hospital. He would say it was humiliating to be rescued by a girl again, but she didn't care one whit.

The morning mist was just starting to rise, the trees barely showing their fall colors as she marched out of the woods and into a field of corn as tall as her head. She didn't get very far before the rumble of artillery began thundering all around her. She remembered Malvern Hill and how brave the Confederate soldiers had seemed, marching straight into enemy cannon fire. As the ground shook beneath her feet, Phoebe didn't feel brave at all.

She'd been in enough artillery barrages in the past months to recognize the sound of canister shot. The shells, filled with thousands of pieces of metal, acted like a gigantic shotgun blast when they exploded, cutting a bloody path through the ranks and killing dozens of men in one blow. Shells were exploding all around her, but she kept marching forward in formation with the others, down through the rows of corn, just as she'd been trained to do.

Suddenly everyone froze as if on command. One of the shells screaming overhead sounded different. It took Phoebe only a second to realize why—it was coming straight toward them. She dove at Ted, tackling him the way she had the day the sniper had fired at him. She landed on top of him, shielding him with her body. At the same instant she heard a deafening explosion. The shock of it blasted through her body as if her insides were trying to escape through her skin and her head might explode. A powerful blow struck the back of her shoulder. She lay there, stunned.

Then debris began raining down on her, pummeling her, burying her in clods of earth and shredded cornstalks and ears of corn. For a long moment the din of battle died away, as if the war had suddenly stopped. She couldn't hear anything, couldn't see anything through the stinging cloud of dust and smoke. She lay on her stomach on top of Ted, her eyes burning, her ears ringing. The place on her back where she'd been punched felt warm and wet.

Phoebe tried to move, but the hand that had punched her held her down. She saw her rifle a few inches away and tried to reach for it, but her arm wouldn't move. As the tingling shock of a million needles gradually died, the pain began—a white-hot fire that spread out from her shoulder and across her back. It was so agonizing that Phoebe thought she might faint. Someone was moving her, trying to roll her over, and she screamed for them to stop.

It was Ted, crawling out from under her. His hair was dusted with gray and his eyes were very wide, staring at her. She saw his lips moving as he mouthed "Ike! Ike!" over and over again, but his voice sounded muffled.

The sun seemed very bright, and she realized that the corn was gone, sheared away as if it had been harvested. The soldiers who had been marching alongside her a moment ago lay sprawled in the furrows in neat rows, as if they'd suddenly decided to lie down and take a nap. None of them moved. But Ted was all right. He was alive. That was all that mattered.

"I'm sorry," she said, but she wasn't sure if Ted could hear her above the deafening explosions that still thundered all around them. She wasn't even certain she had spoken out loud.

He bent toward her. Tears washed two clean paths down his dusty face. He grabbed her beneath her lifeless arms and started moving her, dragging her across the uneven ground on her stomach. The unseen hand twisted a knife in her back. The pain was excruciating, unlike anything she'd ever known.

Phoebe cried out, and the world went black.

The earthshaking explosions jolted Julia awake. It took her a moment to recall where she was—in a canvas tent provided by the Sanitary Commission, camping in a farmer's field outside Sharpsburg, Maryland. But she recognized the sounds of battle right away from her experience at Bull Run—the thunder of artillery, the scream of falling shells. The sun was barely up, but the battle had already begun. She rubbed the sleep from her eyes and hurried outside to join the other nurses, doctors, and ambulance drivers, all waiting grimly for their work to begin.

When the Union Army began moving into Maryland, the newly formed ambulance corps went along with it. Once again, Dr. McGrath had been called into field service. Julia had gone downstairs to his office as he'd packed up his surgical instruments and volunteered to join him. He had cut off her words before she'd even finished her sentence, waving her away like a fly.

"I don't want to hear it, Mrs. Hoffman. The answer is no."

"Why not?" she asked from the doorway. "You know I'm a good nurse. You trained me yourself."

"Women don't belong near the battlefield—especially women who are as young and naïve as you are."

"That's what you said the last time, remember? And I volunteered on an evacuation ship."

He rested both hands on his desk and leaned toward her. "And do you remember how ugly those sights were? Well, it was a picnic compared to a field hospital. Stay here."

Of course she had ignored his orders. The fact that he had demanded she stay behind had made her even more determined to go. Who did he think he was to order her around? She had gone to the Sanitary Commission's offices that same day and volunteered.

The train of ambulances carrying medical supplies and volunteer surgeons and nurses had followed well to the rear of the army. Julia had seen Dr. McGrath on the first night they'd camped, standing near a fire, sipping from a tin cup. He had seen her, too. He had turned his back and walked away.

But there was no sign of the doctor this morning as Julia stood in the chilly fog, waiting for instructions. By the time they moved several loads of medical supplies up to the barnyard and commandeered the farmhouse for an operating room, the casualties were already streaming in. The field hospital was very close to the battleground in a nearby cornfield, so close that Julia could hear the roar of gunfire and the screams of dying men. On top of a nearby hill, she could see Union artillerymen getting ready to fire their cannons.

What began as a trickle of casualties quickly became a deluge. For the next few hours, Julia saw wave after wave of devastating injuries too horrible to comprehend—arms and legs blown off or shattered by Minie balls; chests and stomachs ripped open; faces mutilated beyond recognition. Bloodied, mangled soldiers flooded the barnyard outside the farmhouse, many of them crying out to God for mercy as they waited.

As she struggled to cope with the devastation all around her, Julia knew that Dr. McGrath had been right once again. There was a world of difference between tending wounded men in the safety of White House Landing and trying to keep her wits about her with shells exploding nearby. She mumbled unending prayers as she tied tourniquets and bandaged wounds and offered medicinal brandy to weeping, dying soldiers. Some of the men grew hysterical when they learned they were about to have amputations, and she wept along with them as she tried to calm them, reassuring them that everything would be all right—though she couldn't imagine the horror of having an arm or a leg sawn off. She gave the men food and water, listening to deathbed confessions and tender last words whispered to wives and sweethearts and children.

All the while, Rebel shells continued to explode nearby, crashing in the cornfield and shaking the ground underfoot. The sheer number of casualties and the horrifying nature of their injuries testified to the appalling violence that raged all around her. Long before noon, a swirling cloud of dust and smoke had blotted out the sun. Then the battle shifted in a different direction, and they enjoyed a brief reprieve from the fearsome noise of bombardment. The screams and cries of the wounded quickly filled the void.

Around four o'clock a barrage of artillery suddenly opened fire nearby. The furor of sound and smoke seemed like the end of the world to Julia. As the earth quaked and debris fell from the sky like hail, all the nurses and as many of the men as possible fled into the barn to escape the holocaust. But there was no escape from the fear. Julia cowered in the straw, trembling, wishing with all her heart that she had listened to Dr. McGrath. She was certain that she was about to die.

A long hour later it finally stopped. The world felt strangely quiet. As she ventured outside again, the yard stank of sulfur and smoke. Some of the farmhouse windows had shattered, and there was a gaping hole in the roof, but a light still shone in the kitchen, where the doctors continued to operate. The ambulance drivers soothed their frightened horses, then quickly returned to their duties.

Julia had worked without stopping, without thinking, all day. Now the sun was setting in the west, staining the sky blood red. She leaned against the doorframe of the barn and looked around as if for the first time, slowly comprehending the enormity of what she was witnessing. It wasn't the horror of the scene that stunned her, as gruesome as it was, but the incomprehensible loss of life—all the vibrant young men who had been alive only this morning, laughing and sipping their coffee, now lying shattered and dead. The waste of it—the terrible waste. She slowly slid down the doorframe to the ground, then buried her face in her folded arms and cried.

"Ike! Ike, where are you?" Ted wove in and out among the wounded men, searching for his friend, calling her name. Hundreds and hundreds of blue-uniformed men blanketed the ground around the barn and the farmhouse, and he searched every face in desperation. Some of the men looked up at him as he called out; others gazed sightlessly into the distance, their bodies already growing stiff.

He made his way into the barn where there were more wounded, searching for a thatch of yellow hair, a pair of oversized feet. He saw nurses bending over their patients, tending them. None of the soldiers was as tall as Ike.

He came out of the barn again, wondering if he had missed her somehow. A soldier reached out a hand to grab Ted's pant leg.

"Please, I need water," the man begged. He had a huge hole in his side. His other hand was barely attached to his arm. Ted crouched beside him and gave him a drink from his canteen.

"I'm trying to find my friend," Ted told him. "He was wounded early this morning. Have you seen a big fellow with yellow hair? Ike saved my life. I-I didn't thank him."

The man sighed gratefully when he'd drunk his fill, then licked his lips. "Maybe the ambulance took him."

Ted hurried over to two stretcher-bearers who were loading a man with one leg into the back of a covered wagon. "Do either of you remember a big, tall fellow with yellow hair? He was wounded this morning. In the shoulder."

One orderly shook his head and turned away. The other mumbled, "Needle in a haystack, pal."

Ted ran from wagon to wagon, asking the same question, getting the same weary responses. None of the men would look Ted in the eye, and he knew they weren't looking too closely at the grisly cargo they carried, either.

"Come on, one of you must remember him," he begged. "Ike is very tall. His feet would have hung off the stretcher."

Ted remembered his frustration earlier that morning when he'd wished he were taller himself so he could carry Ike off the field instead of dragging her. He'd been surprised at how light she felt, how bony her ribs were beneath her wool uniform. She had lost a lot of weight while she was sick with malaria.

He'd been so afraid that he would hurt her, dragging her that way. But then the stretcher-bearers had appeared out of nowhere, hurrying toward him, and he'd let them load Ike onto a litter and carry her away. He had wanted to go with them to make sure she was going to be all right. But he'd wanted revenge even more. Once the orderlies assured him that his friend would be taken care of, Ted had run back to where he'd dropped his rifle and charged forward into battle.

"Where are the ambulances taking them?" he now asked one of the drivers. "Maybe my friend is there already."

"There's a train depot not far from here," the driver said, climbing onto the wagon seat. "They'll go by train to a hospital in Washington or Baltimore."

"Have the trains taken anybody yet? Can I ride along with you and look for him on the platform?"

"Sorry. We need every inch of space to transport the wounded. Why don't you talk to the surgeons? Maybe one of them will remember." He snapped the reins and drove away in a cloud of dust.

Ted found three surgeons inside the farmhouse, covered to their elbows in blood. They were arguing as one of them gave chloroform to a man who was laid out on the kitchen table. "I can save this arm," one of the doctors shouted. "Feel his hand. I'm telling you, there's circulation."

"We don't have time for that kind of surgery, James. There are two hundred more just like him out there. The arm's coming off."

There was blood everywhere; the floor was slippery with it. Ted had to look up at the ceiling to keep from getting sick.

"What are you doing in here?" one of the doctors shouted when he saw Ted. "Get out!"

"I'm looking for my friend Ike—a tall fellow with yellow hair. Have you—"

"We look at wounds, not faces. And we don't ask names."

"He was wounded in the shoulder—"

"Him and a hundred others. Out!" The doctor pointed his bloody finger at the door.

Ted finally wandered around to the rear of the barn where the dead bodies were being stacked. Some of them were so badly shattered and bloated they hardly seemed human. He couldn't take any more. This was too horrible. If Ike was among these pitiful souls, he didn't want to know. He didn't want this to be how he remembered his friend.

He wished he could tell Ike how much he liked her, how lonely he'd felt the past few days without her, how sorry he was that he'd gotten mad at her. When he'd heard that shell whistling toward him today, he'd known it was going to hit him. He remembered thinking that he was about to die. Then Ike had flown at him from behind, tackling him the way he had—the way *she* had—on the day the sniper fired. She had covered his body with her own. Ted would have been the one lying here wounded or dead if Ike hadn't saved his life.

Why had she done it? Why had Ike jumped into the path of a shell that was meant for him? Ike—his funny, odd, faithful friend. All this time, Ike had been a girl. And Ted didn't even know her real name. He sat down behind the woodpile where no one would see him and wept.

"Mrs. Hoffman . . ." Julia looked up. The head nurse was standing over her. "Go back to your tent and rest for an hour."

Julia stood, supporting herself on the doorframe of the barn. "I'm sorry. I'm so sorry—"

"You've been working all day. You're no good to us exhausted. People make mistakes when they're exhausted. Go have a short rest and something to eat. Come back in an hour."

"But I'm fine. . . ."

"Rest, Mrs. Hoffman. That's an order."

It seemed wrong to rest with so much work to be done, but Julia knew that the head nurse was right. She remembered being so tired on board the ship that she'd collapsed on top of a wounded man.

Julia walked down the dusty road past the farmhouse, staying close to the side, out of the path of the rumbling ambulances. The nurses' tents had been pitched in a field a short distance from the house.

Julia lifted the tent flap to duck inside, then stopped. A Union soldier lay asleep on her bed. At first she thought she must have gone to the wrong tent. But no, her comb and brush were beside the bed, her carpetbag and shawl lay nearby. Had the man crept in here by mistake?

She crawled inside for a closer look. The soldier was sound asleep. She saw by the fresh dressings that he had been badly wounded and that the surgeons had already operated. She went outside again and walked up the road to where the stretcher-bearers were loading the ambulances.

"I think someone has made a mistake," she said. "There's a wounded soldier in my tent."

A burly, red-faced orderly stepped forward, mopping his brow with a bandanna. "No, ma'am. One of the doctors told us to put him in there."

"But why? Do you remember which doctor it was?"

He chewed his cheek, thinking. "One of the contract surgeons, I think. He wasn't wearing a uniform. And he had a reddish beard."

James McGrath.

"He told you to put him in *my* tent?"

"Yes, ma'am. I don't know why, but I remember that he asked for you by name. He said, 'Mrs. Hoffman needs to take care of this one,' and he told us to put him in your tent."

She felt her anger boiling up like a kettle of water. "Where is the doctor now?"

"Up at the farmhouse."

"Thank you." Julia turned and began marching up the rise to the house.

"Mrs. Hoffman, wait," the orderly called, hurrying after her. "You don't want to go up there. The doctors are still operating."

"I don't care if Dr. McGrath is operating or napping or sunbathing in his union suit. He has no right to put a wounded soldier in my tent, and I intend to tell him so. This is just like him to play a nasty little trick to get rid of me. I'm very tired of his games." She stormed up to the farmhouse in a temper.

As she entered the yard, she noticed an open window on the side of the house and below it a reddish heap, buzzing with flies. At first it didn't register in Julia's mind what she was seeing, but then the grisly pile slowly slid into focus. She recognized a human hand lying on top, palm up. Then a bloody foot.

Julia whirled around and ran, unheeding, in the opposite direction. She didn't get far before she stumbled to her knees and was sick alongside the road. She knelt, too weak to stand, trembling with shock and anger. How could Dr. McGrath do that all day? How could he saw off parts of living, breathing people so callously and toss them out the window like that?

"Are you all right, ma'am?"

She turned at the sound of the orderly's voice. "Yes. Thank you." He helped her to her feet, and she wiped her mouth on her handkerchief, humiliated that he had seen her. He had tried to warn her. "I-I'll still need to speak to Dr. McGrath," she told him. "Will you please let me know when he's finished?"

"Sure, ma'am."

"I'll be in my tent."

She walked back, knees shaking, longing more than ever to lie down and rest in her tent for an hour. But the wounded soldier was still in her bed. She went inside and knelt beside him. He'd been wounded in the torso, which wasn't good. Damage to a patient's lungs and other internal organs usually meant a slow, certain death. He was already having trouble breathing. He was also filthy with crusted blood and dirt and leaves, but she didn't want to wake him. She made sure his wound wasn't bleeding, then went outside again and sat down on the ground. She drew her knees up to her chin, wrapped her arms around them, then lowered her head and closed her eyes.

"Mrs. Hoffman?"

Julia's head jerked up. The orderly she'd spoken to earlier stood in front of her. The sun was gone and a star shone through the haze of smoke in the east. She hadn't meant to sleep that long.

"I'm sorry, ma'am . . . I didn't know you were asleep."

"That's all right. Did you need me for something?"

"That doctor you wanted to talk to is taking a break. You said to let you know."

"Thank you." Julia rose stiffly to her feet. She took a moment to stretch, to wipe the sleep from her eyes, and to comb her hair back with her hands. The air had turned cool now that the sun had set. She ducked inside her tent to get a shawl and heard the wounded man's ragged breathing. He was still unconscious. Julia pulled her wrap around her shoulders and set off up the road to the farmhouse again.

Dr. McGrath sat alone on the front step, his elbows on his thighs, his face in his hands. His white shirt and the front of his trousers were soaked with blood—most of it stiff and dried, but some still wet, making his shirt stick to his skin. He looked beaten, exhausted, every trace of his usual cockiness gone. She felt a wave of pity for him. This was the kind, dedicated physician she had spent hours working beside at Fairfield Hospital. Now he needed care. She decided she would find him some food, offer him a change of clothes and a basin of warm water to wash with.

But as she started toward him again, he lowered his hands and pulled a silver flask from his pocket. All of her compassion fled as he tilted it to his mouth and took a long drink. She hurried over, knowing she'd better speak to him now before he passed out drunk.

"Excuse me, Doctor, but there's a wounded soldier lying in my tent. The orderly told me that *you* ordered him to be put there."

"That's right, Mrs. Hoffman, I did." He spoke very slowly, as if drained of life.

"Well, if that's your idea of a joke, I'm not laughing. I would like the man removed from my tent immediately."

"It isn't a man."

"What do you mean it isn't a man? I saw him myself, as plain as—"

"Go look again. Carefully. It's a woman."

"There is a *man* in a *uniform* in my tent . . . and he's wounded."

The doctor was shaking his head. She noticed that his eyes looked heavy with fatigue. Blood speckled his forehead like freckles. "It's a woman."

"Are . . . are you *sure*?" she stammered.

"You ask the most ridiculous questions," he said, rubbing his eyes with his thumb and forefinger. "I'm a doctor, Mrs. Hoffman. I've studied anatomy. Would you like a detailed explanation of exactly how I determined that the soldier was a woman?"

Julia felt herself blushing. "No, thank you. That won't be necessary. I—I just don't understand what she is doing . . . how . . . why is she wearing a uniform and fighting in the army if—"

"I didn't have time to interview her. I've been busy." He gestured to his bloody clothing. "Now if you don't mind, I'd like to catch a few minutes' rest before the carnage starts up again." He lifted the flask and took another long drink.

"Do you think it's wise to get drunk," she asked coldly, "if you're expecting more casualties?"

"Go away."

"Our soldiers deserve the very best care we can give them, and that includes a sober doctor."

"My sobriety is none of your business."

"But these patients *are* my business."

"I'm warning you, Mrs. Hoffman. Go away before I—"

"Before you what? Before you get drunk and kill somebody else?"

The moment the words were out of her mouth, Julia was sorry. James McGrath's head jerked back as if she had struck him with her fist instead of her words. She'd seen pain often enough in a wounded man's eyes to recognize it in his. She had hurt him deeply.

"Get out of here," he said hoarsely.

"Dr. McGrath, I'm sorry . . . I didn't mean it."

"Yes, you did. Now get away from me."

Julia turned and fled down the road to her tent.

She heard the soldier moaning as she approached. Julia stood outside for a long moment trying to calm herself, wishing she had held her tongue. Her hands were shaking. She told herself to focus on the soldier. He would need food. And water. She remembered that he—no, *she*—was filthy. Julia quickly gathered together what she needed and went inside.

The soldier was tall, so tall her feet hung off Julia's pallet. Her yellow hair was short like a man's, and though her face was smooth and beardless, there was nothing feminine about her features. She looked like a man to Julia—a very tall man. Even so, she wasn't about to check and see. It wouldn't surprise her one bit if this turned out to be one of the doctor's cruel jokes, intended to embarrass her.

Julia knelt and began washing the soldier's face. Her eyes slowly opened and focused on Julia. She tried to move, then groaned in pain.

"Lie still," Julia soothed. "You've been wounded. This is a field hospital. I'm a nurse."

"Ted. . . ? W-where's—"

"You've been wounded."

"No . . . no . . . Ted . . ."

"Shh . . . I'm going to clean some of this mud and blood off you, all right?" The soldier trembled from head to toe, but whether it was from shock or fear Julia couldn't tell. She offered her a sip of brandy to calm her down. "There . . . just lie still, okay? My name is Julia. Can you tell me your name?"

The soldier ran her tongue around her parched lips, then closed her eyes. "Ike Bigelow."

"I—I mean your real name. The doctor said that . . . I mean, he found out that you—"

Ike's face crumpled and she started to cry—silent, gasping sobs that shook through her.

Julia watched helplessly, unsure what to do. "Are you in pain? Can I do anything for you?"

"Go away and leave me alone," she said through her tears.

"I can't do that. This is my tent. I sleep here. They put you in with me because . . . well, I suppose the doctor didn't think you should be out there with all the men."

Ike looked up at Julia, her face blotchy with tears. "I been sleeping with them all these months, ain't I?"

Julia was taken aback. "That . . . that's really none of my business."

Ike shook her head. "It ain't what you think, lady. Did you get a good look at me? Who would ever want a woman who looks like me?"

"Listen . . . Ike . . . What's your real name?" she asked gently.

She hesitated a long time before answering. "It's Phoebe."

"Do you think you could eat something, Phoebe? Are you hungry?"

"No."

"Well, what can I do for you, then?"

"You can leave me alone and let me die."

Chapter Sixteen

Sharpsburg, Maryland
September 1862

Ted watched the wagon approach, chased by a billowing cloud of dust. He kneaded his forage cap in his hands—the cap with a bullet hole through it—as the wagon drew to a halt. "Any word of Ike?" he asked before Sergeant Anderson had a chance to climb down. He got his answer when the officer shook his head.

"Sorry, son. We'll have to list him as missing."

"He was still alive when the stretcher took him," Ted said, trying for the hundredth time to reason it all out. "I looked everywhere for him at the field hospital and couldn't find him. That means he must have been evacuated before I got there." He followed Anderson around to the back of the wagon, watching as he reached for a mailbag.

"Ike's name wasn't on any wounded list at any hospital," Anderson said. "But it wasn't on any dead list, either. We can take hope from that." Anderson looked truly saddened. Ted knew the sergeant had a lot of respect for Ike. All the men in their company did. When the sergeant spoke again his voice was hushed. "Listen . . . they're saying that the casualties aren't just in the thousands this time . . . they're in the *tens* of thousands. I can't comprehend that, can you? More than ten thousand men, dead, wounded, or missing. That's more people than live in my hometown." He exhaled, then heaved the mailbag out of the wagon and set it on the ground. "Maybe he'll write someday and let us know he's okay. Ike knows where to find us."

"I need to talk to him," Ted said. "I've been mad at him. I need to tell him I'm sorry."

Anderson rested his hand on Ted's shoulder. "I talked to him the night before the battle. He said you were still his best friend."

Ted nodded and cleared his throat. He wouldn't cry. It had been five days since the battle, five days since he'd exhausted his tears behind the woodpile. "What about all of Ike's stuff?" he asked hoarsely.

Ted had already gone through Ike's knapsack, at first embarrassed by what he feared he would find. What he did find surprised him: extra socks and a shirt, the usual eating utensils and toiletries, a little money—and that was all. Everything else that Ike had been lugging around in his pack for the past year, like the frying pan and the bottles of blood tonic, had belonged to Ted. She had not only saved Ted's life—she'd been shouldering his load.

"Do you know where we can find his family?" Sergeant Anderson asked.

"He didn't have one. He said his folks were dead and his brothers were all off fighting." Considering Ike's other secret, Ted couldn't help wondering if that was the truth.

"Well, look through his letters. Maybe you can find an address somewhere."

"Ike never got any letters. He never wrote any, either." Ted knew why.

Should he tell Sergeant Anderson the truth, tell him that the man they called Ike Bigelow had been a woman in disguise? Ted had been close to Ike for more than a year. What if no one believed that he had been fooled all that time? Would he get into trouble for being with her? For not telling when he'd found out the truth?

But Ike had begged Ted not to tell. She had saved his life. The least he could do for his friend was keep her secret.

"Well, you were closest to him, son. Do what you think is best with all his things." The sergeant turned and called gruffly to his men, as if embarrassed to let his emotions show in front of Ted. "All right, let's get this wagon unloaded. There's mail."

The sergeant reached into the wagon again and pulled out a folded newspaper. He handed it to Ted. "Here. Maybe this will cheer you up a little."

Ted unfolded it and read the headline: *Lincoln to Emancipate Slaves.* He stared at the words, astonished. He was no longer aware of the crush of men surrounding him, jostling him as they crowded around the wagon. Nor did he wait for his own mail. He plowed through the swarm and headed back to his tent, reading as he walked. As he read the president's proclamation, a quiet joy welled up inside him for the first time since Ike had disappeared.

> *On the first day of January, in the year of our Lord 1863, all persons held as slaves within any State, or designated part of a State, the people whereof shall then be in rebellion against the United States, shall be then, thenceforth, and forever free.*

It was the costly Union victory at Sharpsburg that had led to Lincoln's decision, Ted read. The sacrifice that Ike and all the others had made would now bring freedom to the slaves. Ted thought of his grandmother and of the slaves he'd befriended at Hilltop Plantation. He remembered how Ike had pulled him aside after seeing Slave Row that day, saying, *"You know what? That's why we're fighting—it's for the slaves. So they don't have to live like that no more."*

Ike's sacrifice had saved the lives of countless others besides Ted. More than ever before, Ted knew he had a reason to fight. A reason to win.

Julia ached all over as she walked up the road to the farmhouse. The stiffness came from sleeping on the ground beside her patient for the past five nights, and she wondered how the soldiers managed to sleep on the cold, hard ground for months at a time. The fall morning was crisp and clear, the air scented with ripening apples. She wished she had time to savor the beautiful Maryland countryside, but the suffering and destruction all around her—including the suffering her tentmate was enduring—had overshadowed any loveliness.

At least two other physicians had been performing surgery in the farmhouse along with Dr. McGrath, and Julia hoped to find one of them. With any luck, James would still be in bed, sleeping off his usual hangover, and she wouldn't run into him. When she spotted one of the army doctors sitting on the front step, blowing on a cup of coffee, she was relieved. But just as she reached the porch, Dr. McGrath came through the door. He didn't look ill, for once, but rested and combed and almost personable. Even so, she ignored him, addressing the man with the coffee.

"I'm sorry to bother you, Doctor, but when you have a moment this morning, would you please look at one of my patients?"

"What's the problem?"

"The wound isn't healing well, and when I was changing the dressing this morning I thought I saw something . . . shiny."

"It could be a piece of shrapnel, but are you certain you weren't seeing bone?"

"I don't know. I'd hoped you would take a look."

"This wouldn't be the patient I put in your tent, would it?" Dr. McGrath asked.

The other doctor swiveled around to look up at him. "In her tent? What are you talking about, James?"

"It was a woman, disguised as a man," he said, moving to stand on the stairs. "I pulled some shrapnel out of her shoulder the other day. Under the circumstances, I thought I shouldn't put her with the men."

"Good heavens!" the doctor exclaimed. "Don't these army recruiters have eyes? How on earth did a woman slip past them? And what would possess her to enlist in the army in the first place?"

"Is she the patient, Mrs. Hoffman?" James asked.

The two doctors looked at Julia. She nodded.

"I'll go," James said. "If it is a piece of shrapnel, I'm the one who missed it. Let me get my bag." He was already rolling up his sleeves as he went inside the house to retrieve it.

Julia didn't wait. She started walking back to her tent without him, dreading the next few minutes. She decided that she wouldn't try to apologize for her remarks to him the other evening. She wouldn't mention the incident at all—and she hoped that he wouldn't, either. She waited for him outside her tent, unwilling to share such close quarters with him. Phoebe had passed out earlier as Julia had swabbed iodine on her wound. She was still unconscious.

"I'm going to need plenty of light," Dr. McGrath said when he arrived. "I don't want to move her, so let's pull out a couple of tent stakes and fold the roof back."

Julia did as she was told, then stood aside, watching from a little distance as he knelt beside the patient. He looked up at Julia after a moment, his usual frown back in place.

"Aren't you going to assist me, Mrs. Hoffman? I need your help."

She drew a deep breath. "What would you like me to do?"

"Come here and show me what you saw."

Julia hated looking at the huge ragged wound in Phoebe's shoulder, but she knelt beside the doctor and gently lifted the dressing she had laid loosely in place. "I was trying to clean away some of the debris and dead tissue. I thought I saw something . . . right around here. . . ."

"Okay. I'm going to have to probe." He opened his medical bag and handed Julia a bottle of chloroform. "Put her out," he said. "And be careful you don't breathe any yourself."

Julia poured a small amount on the cloth.

"I don't like to dig around any more than I have to," he said as he waited for Julia to hold it over Phoebe's face. "If a wound is from a Minie ball or a bullet, I know there will likely be only one pellet to search for—the Rebels don't waste ammunition. But this was canister shot—hundreds of pieces of metal that spew out of one shell. Devastating stuff."

The doctor pulled a slender, curved probe from his bag, and Julia quickly looked away. Several long minutes passed as he worked in silence. "There," he said at last, "I think I feel something. Hand me the forceps, please." She pulled a pair from his bag and placed them in his outstretched hand. "Sponge, please." She gave him one. A few moments later, he was done. "You have good eyes, Mrs. Hoffman. Would you like to keep this little demon for a souvenir?" He held up the bloody forceps, gripping a jagged piece of metal the size of a dime.

"No, thank you."

He tended the wound himself, applying the iodine and a clean dressing. Then he examined Phoebe, checking her pulse and listening to her chest with his stethoscope. When he finished, he sighed. "Well, I don't like the looks of things. There's damage to her scapula and who knows what else. But just continue as you are. You're doing everything that can be done."

He was being pleasant and professional. He hadn't mentioned their last meeting. Julia was so relieved that she summoned the courage to ask him a question. "I can't get her to eat anything, Doctor. It's been several days. She keeps saying she wants to die."

He closed his bag and stood. "Even if she eats, she might get her wish. But if she doesn't eat, I can guarantee she will."

"How can I get her to eat?"

"Hmm. I can see where you might have a problem, Mrs. Hoffman. Usually you simply flirt with your patients to get them to cooperate, don't you?"

She stared at him, afraid to answer. She'd been cruel to him and knew she deserved his cruelty in return. But his next words seemed to come out of nowhere.

"How did you hear that I killed a man?"

His voice was so quiet, so intense, that it sent a shiver down Julia's spine. She could tell that he wasn't going to leave until she answered him.

"I met a man from Connecticut," she managed to say. "He read about it in the newspaper."

"I see." He stared at her for a very long time. "Aren't you afraid to work with a murderer?" he asked in the same hushed voice.

This time she couldn't answer. She was afraid to move, afraid to breathe, as if a predator were watching her, waiting to pounce if she made one wrong move.

"Well," he said after a moment. "I think you've answered my question." He smiled sadly and walked away.

Phoebe opened her eyes and looked around. She was in her tent. It was light outside. Someone was kneeling beside her. "Ted?" she whispered. The name didn't come out right. Her mouth was dry and bitter tasting.

"Good morning, Phoebe. How do you feel?" It was a woman's voice, not Ted's.

She remembered then where she was. The pain in her shoulder was an agonizing reminder. It never stopped. She closed her eyes, hoping the blackness would swallow her again, bringing relief.

"No, don't go to sleep. I brought you some food." The woman set something down beside Phoebe that smelled good. "Please, you have to eat."

"Why?" Phoebe knew she was dying. Why drag it out? Why not simply close her eyes and get it over with?

"Because . . . Do it for . . . for Ted."

"What?" Phoebe's eyes flew open. She stared at the woman in surprise.

"You keep asking for Ted. I thought maybe he was someone special to you. I hoped that you might want to get well for his sake."

"I don't know what you're talking about," Phoebe lied.

"Well, is there someone else we can write a letter to? Someone you'd like to have come and take care of you? Maybe bring you something special from home?"

She shook her head. "Let me die. It don't matter. Nobody will care."

"I don't believe you, Phoebe. There must be somebody."

The nurse was young and very pretty. She made Phoebe feel uglier than ever. Even the woman's name, Julia, was pretty. Phoebe wished she would go away.

"Well, there ain't nobody who cares, and that's the truth." She closed her eyes, longing to die so the terrible pain would stop.

"God cares," Julia said softly. She stroked Phoebe's forehead, brushing back her hair. "God loves you."

Phoebe didn't believe it. If God cared one whit about her, He wouldn't have made her so homely. And He would have given her at least one person in the whole wide world who loved her.

"God don't care about me, either," she told Julia.

The nurse closed her eyes for a moment, biting her lip. When she opened them again she said, "Let me ask you something.

Suppose someone had been willing to die for you? Suppose he had thrown himself between you and that artillery shell and had taken this wound in your place so that you could live—even if it meant he would die. That would prove that the person loved you, wouldn't it?"

That was exactly what Phoebe had done. She had thrown herself on top of Ted, getting wounded in his place so that he would live. That must mean that she loved him. Phoebe Bigelow was in love with Ted Wilson. She admitted the truth for the first time. But then, she'd never loved anyone before and hadn't any idea what it felt like. Was it love when you wanted to be with someone all the time and you felt lost and empty when they weren't by your side? Did it mean savoring the way they moved and laughed and frowned—and staying awake at night just to watch their face while they slept? Was that love? Was it wanting so much for the other person to live that you would gladly suffer and die in their place?

Tears rolled down Phoebe's face. She couldn't wipe them away. Her injured arm wouldn't move, and she was lying on the other one. Julia wiped the tears away for her.

"That's what Jesus did," Julia said. "He gave his life, dying in your place, so you could live."

Phoebe knew the Easter story—how the Son of God had been crucified on a cross. But it had never made sense to her before. She hadn't known what it meant to love someone so much that you would die for him. Maybe this explained the words she had been wondering about: *"For the Son of man is come to seek and to save that which was lost."*

"Jesus isn't the only one who loves you," Julia said. "God allowed His Son to leave heaven and come down to earth. He gave up His only Son so that we could live. That's how much God loves you."

Phoebe thought of Ted's grandmother, how she had loved her daughter so much she had let her go so that future children could be free. Phoebe had wished that someone would love her that much.

"If you died for someone else, Phoebe, wouldn't you want that person to live? Wouldn't you want your sacrifice to have meaning?"

Phoebe closed her eyes and saw Ted's face. He had lived. She had saved him because she had wanted him to live.

"God cares if you die," Julia said. She lifted Phoebe's head a little and held the spoon to her lips. "Please, won't you try to eat some of this food?"

Phoebe finally opened her mouth and ate.

Chapter Seventeen

Washington City
December 1862

Julia tried to ignore the letter on her dresser as she hurriedly pinned up her hair for work, but it nagged at her. It had arrived two days ago, and though she usually answered her mail promptly, she hadn't answered this one yet. Her mother had written most of it, but she had attached pleading notes from Julia's father, her sister, Rosalie, her aunt Eunice, and even Robert's parents. All of them begged her to come home to Philadelphia for Christmas.

The truth was, Julia was desperately homesick when she wasn't working at the hospital. She couldn't bear the thought of spending Christmas alone in the bleak boardinghouse, eating stringy roast beef far away from her family. But she feared going home for two reasons. The first was that her father would probably never allow her to return to Washington. Julia knew that once she was home she would be drawn back to her old way of life as if wading into a powerful current, and she wouldn't be able to—wouldn't want to—escape its pull. Especially if Nathaniel Greene was still interested in courting her. At the same time, she felt guilty because the only reason she had wanted to become a nurse was to win a man's heart—and now that she'd won it she was content to quit. Worse, Nathaniel thought her sacrifice had been selfless. He didn't know her true motives.

The other reason she hesitated to leave was because of her

patient, Phoebe Bigelow. Julia had brought her back from Sharpsburg to convalesce in Fairfield Hospital, and it still wasn't clear if she would live or die. Besides struggling to recover from her wound, Phoebe was also gravely ill with blood poisoning and pneumonia, as were many of the other soldiers wounded in the battle. Dr. McGrath had ordered a partition of curtains made around Phoebe's bed, which had been placed in a corner of the downstairs ward beside the cabinet of medical supplies. She could still have her privacy, yet the doctor hoped it would cheer her to be with other people. Instead, Phoebe barely spoke to anyone. She seemed deeply depressed. The only person who could coax her to eat was Julia. What would happen to Phoebe if Julia went home to Philadelphia?

"I'll answer you tonight," Julia said aloud, patting the letter as if soothing a baby. She would see if Phoebe felt any better—and perhaps convince her to accept Mrs. Fowle's care in her place.

Julia put on her coat and bonnet and hurried down the stairs, always with the same thought at this time of day—how long would she have to stand in the wind and cold this morning before finding a carriage? The winter had been an unusually cold one, and snow had already fallen. But when she opened the door, she saw Congressman Rhodes' carriage waiting by the front walk.

"Good morning, Miss Hoffman," he called. "May I offer you a ride?" The congressman stuck his head out of the carriage window, smiling broadly.

"You're a lifesaver," she said as she climbed in beside him. But she knew why he had come before he said a single word. "You *are* taking me to the hospital, aren't you?" she asked.

"I'll take you wherever you wish to go . . . but I sincerely hope you will let me take you home to Philadelphia at the end of the week. That's when Mrs. Rhodes and I are leaving."

"Let me guess—my parents wrote and asked you to convince me, didn't they?"

"Dear girl, they have buried me in correspondence. I won't be able to face the judge if I come home without you. So I decided I would accompany you to the hospital this morning and plead with your acting surgeon myself to grant you a leave for the holiday."

"Thank you, but that isn't necessary. I know he'll grant me a leave if I ask for one."

"Then I gather that you haven't asked," Rhodes said quietly.

"Not yet. We've been overwhelmed these past months coping with all the soldiers who were wounded at Antietam."

"A dreadful waste," Rhodes said with a sigh. "They're estimating our final toll at more than twelve thousand casualties. Can you imagine that? Still, we drove the Rebels to their knees. Why on earth General McClellan didn't follow up his victory and put an end to Lee is beyond me. Well, it's beyond everyone! Let's hope Ambrose Burnside will get the job done. He's a rather ridiculous-looking fellow with all that absurd facial hair, but he's a better general than McClellan was. At least Burnside has the army marching toward Richmond again. Hopefully this will be the last battle we'll have to fight. I think the war will end very soon, before the year is over. Heaven knows I'm certainly tired of it."

"How far are they from Richmond?" Julia asked, thinking of her cousin Caroline.

"They're in Fredericksburg. It's about halfway between Washington and Richmond. And it looks as though there might be a battle there shortly. The Confederates are marshalling their troops—but we have to cross the Rappahannock River first. The blasted Rebels burned all the bridges, of course. We'll have to construct pontoon bridges. Nasty inconvenience."

Julia allowed the congressman to ramble on about the war as they drove, grateful for the change of topic. But when they finally arrived at the hospital, he quickly returned to his reason for seeing her.

"My dear," he said, taking her hands, "won't you—" He stopped abruptly and looked down. "What *have* you been doing with these hands, Julia? My scrubwoman's hands are softer than these."

"I know." She tried to free herself, but he wouldn't let go. His eyes searched hers.

"If you're doing penance for Bull Run, you've already atoned for—"

"It isn't that," she said quickly. "I enjoy my work, in spite of what my hands look like."

"Promise me you'll come home with us this Friday," he begged. "I'll purchase the tickets today."

Julia didn't see any way out of it. She was afraid he would come inside the hospital and make a scene if she refused. "All right," she said. "I promise." The moment she made the decision, Julia felt immediately relieved. She was going home.

"Oh, and Julia," Rhodes added as she climbed from the carriage, "when you greet your parents, wear gloves."

Julia hurried inside, nearly tripping over a pile of letters that the mailman had deposited inside the front door. She scooped them up and set them on Dr. McGrath's desk while she hung up her coat and bonnet. His office was empty. Most of the letters were for the soldiers, and she took a moment to sort through them, separating the ones for the patients on second floor from the ones downstairs. In the middle of the pile, she found a letter for James.

The stationery was cream vellum. A feminine hand had written in dark ink, *Dr. James J. McGrath*. The return address read *Mrs. James McGrath, Whitney Avenue, New Haven, Connecticut*. Julia laid the letter on his desk.

She carried the rest of the mail into the downstairs ward and saw the doctor standing beside a patient's bed. Just as she entered, James threw back his head and laughed, then rested his hand on the man's shoulder for a moment.

"No, I hadn't heard that one before, Hamilton. That's a good one." His laughter was a very rare sound. The only time she ever heard it was when he joked with his patients. She liked being with him then, making the rounds, working alongside him.

Julia carried the letters over to one of the volunteers. "Good morning, Mrs. Gardner. The morning mail just came. Would you please help me pass it out?"

"I'd be glad to." Mrs. Gardner was one of several women at the hospital who had come to Washington after learning that their loved ones had been wounded. But like all the other mothers and wives and sisters, she helped tend to the needs of all the men, not just her own. Julia gave Mrs. Gardner half the letters to distribute and was about to take the rest upstairs when the doctor called her over. He was going to see Phoebe next.

"Were there any letters for Miss Bigelow?" he asked.

"No. I asked her several times if she wanted me to write to anyone for her, and she said there was no one to write to. She has three brothers in the army, but she doesn't know where they are."

"Find out their names. I'll see what I can do."

He motioned for Julia to follow him as he ducked behind the bed curtains. Phoebe had fallen asleep reading the small, badly wrinkled Bible Julia had found in her uniform pocket. She had offered to give her one in better condition, but Phoebe had refused. She read the book every day as if it were a letter from home.

The doctor bent over the bed and rested his hand on Phoebe's forehead for a moment. Julia had seen him do it countless times with his other patients, and she was always struck by the tenderness of the gesture, as if he longed to impart healing through his touch. She liked this man very much and didn't feel at all afraid of him. But every time he walked out of the ward and returned to his office he became that other, disagreeable man.

He listened with his stethoscope, then exhaled. "I want you to start giving her quinine. I think there may be more than one cause for her fever."

"Yes, Doctor. Should I wake her now and give it to her?"

"Let her sleep."

When he turned to his next patient, Julia hurried upstairs. The men were always overjoyed to receive mail—and she made sure to spend a few extra minutes with the ones who didn't.

Julia daydreamed of home all morning as she worked, planning what she would wear on the journey and which Philadelphia stores she would shop in for Christmas presents. She couldn't help thinking about Nathaniel, wondering if he would ask her to the Music Society's Christmas Ball, dreaming of what it would be like to dance with him. She imagined herself in a new ball gown, whirling around the floor in his arms, gazing up into his handsome face. Maybe on the carriage ride home Nathaniel would lean close to her and steal a kiss and it would be as wonderful as she'd dreamed a kiss would be.

"You sure look happy today, Mrs. Hoffman," one of her patients commented.

"Yes, Private Carter, I guess I am."

At noon she went downstairs to make sure Phoebe ate some lunch. Julia found her propped up in bed, awkwardly eating a bowl of soup with her left hand. Doctor McGrath had immobilized her right arm in a sling while her shoulder healed.

"Are you doing okay, Phoebe?" she asked.

"Thought I'd save you the bother of fussing with me."

"It's no bother." But at least Julia knew Phoebe wouldn't starve if she went home to Philadelphia. And Phoebe seemed a little stronger today. When she finished the soup, Julia gave her some quinine and then coaxed her into talking about her brothers.

"Junior's the oldest," Phoebe began.

"Is that his real name or a nickname?"

"I guess he's called Curtis, after Pa. The other two are named Willard and Jack."

"Do you know where they went to enlist?"

"They said they was going to Cincinnati, but I don't know for sure. Why are you asking about them?"

"Wouldn't you like to write to them and find out how they're doing?"

Phoebe's face went rigid. "Junior will be mad when he finds out I left home."

"Where is home, Phoebe?"

She slowly slid down in bed until she was lying on her side, then closed her eyes. "Ain't none of your business."

The encounter unsettled Julia. Phoebe obviously had her secrets—but then, so did she. All that afternoon, whenever Julia tried to imagine herself with Nathaniel Greene, she now felt a growing sense of unease. Should she allow him to go on thinking she was selfless and compassionate? Or should she tell him the truth about her true motivation and about the lies she'd told in order to become a nurse? By the end of the day, Julia still hadn't decided.

But she had made up her mind to tell Dr. McGrath that she would be returning to Philadelphia at the end of the week. She went to his office in the front hallway to speak with him and met up with a uniformed army officer who was just leaving.

"Very good, James," the man said, shaking the doctor's hand.

"I'll see you in Fredericksburg." He tipped his hat to Julia as he went out the door. "Ma'am . . ."

Dr. McGrath was needed in the field again. That meant they would also need nurses. Julia suddenly decided that she would go to Fredericksburg, too. The congressman had said it would be the last battle of the war. This would probably be the last chance she had to serve on the battlefield before returning to her former life in Philadelphia. She would go, not to impress anyone this time, but out of compassion. She would serve God one last time.

Her mind made up, Julia walked into Dr. McGrath's office. "I'm going to Fredericksburg, too," she told him.

"Why should I care what you do?" He sat behind his desk, shuffling through papers. He didn't look up. "I know better than to try and stop you," he added.

"The Sanitary Commission always needs volunteers," she said. "They'll be happy to have me. But I thought since we're used to working with each other that I would save you the trouble of training a new nurse. I know you have your own way of doing things. And you know how well we work together."

He sighed and leaned back in his chair. "I don't suppose you would like to tell me *why* you're going?"

"For the same reasons that you are. I want to help."

He leaned forward again, studying her carefully. "And you aren't afraid?" he asked quietly.

Julia didn't know which he meant—was she afraid of the battle or of him?

"No," she said. But she was a little afraid . . . of both.

He pulled out his pocket watch and looked at it. "You don't have much time to pack, Mrs. Hoffman. The ship I'm taking to Aquia Landing leaves Alexandria tomorrow morning at five o'clock."

"I'll be there," she said.

Fredericksburg, Virginia
December 1862

Julia and James were among the dozens of doctors and nurses who boarded the *Mary Jane* the next morning to sail forty miles down the Potomac to Aquia Landing. From there it was a much shorter trip by train to Falmouth on the north bank of the Rappahannock. Across the river lay the city of Fredericksburg. Julia saw the city in the fading light that first evening, a sleepy cluster of houses and brick buildings with graceful church steeples pointing to the sky. Stone piers on each bank of the river and one in its center marked the place where a railroad bridge had once stood. Before dawn, Julia was told, army engineers would begin constructing pontoon bridges across the water so the assault could begin.

Julia and the other nurses spent a cold night sleeping on empty pews in one of Falmouth's churches. Tomorrow it would become a hospital. She had spent several hours that evening helping James arrange everything the way he wanted it.

The distant boom of a cannon awakened her the next morning. As the sun burned away the mist that hovered over the river, she could see the partially completed pontoon bridges. She also saw puffs of smoke from the Confederate side and heard the crack of rifles as Rebel sharpshooters opened fire on the laborers and engineers. Wounded bridge workers began arriving at the field hospital a short time later. Julia's job had begun.

She assisted James with wound dressings until early afternoon, when the army decided that too many of their workmen were being injured. They halted construction and brought in one hundred artillery pieces, aiming them at Fredericksburg. Bombarding the city would annihilate Rebel resistance so that the bridges could be completed safely.

The horrific cannon fire lasted for two hours. Even with cotton stuffed in her ears, Julia thought she would go deaf from the noise. She sat on one of the church pews and prayed for the town's citizens—especially the innocent women and children who might be trapped in the holocaust. Long after the violence ended, Julia's knees continued to shake.

When the smoke cleared, the town stood in ruins. Julia didn't see how anyone could have survived such an onslaught. But as soon as the engineers resumed work on the bridges, the Rebel sharpshooters quickly put the hospital back in business.

"All we did was give the Confederates some nice piles of rubble to hide behind," she heard James say as he bent to examine one of the newest shooting victims.

"We wasted our cannonballs for nothing," the soldier breathed.

"We wasted an entire town for nothing," James said.

More wounded men poured into the hospital after the army finally sent squadrons of soldiers across the river in pontoon boats to clear the Rebels out. The skirmishing and the incoming casualties lasted all afternoon. By nightfall the bridges were complete, and most of the men who had been wounded that day were on their way to the evacuation ships. The doctors needed to make room in the hospitals for more casualties tomorrow.

Her work finished for the day, Julia put on her coat and went outside to stand in the smoke-filled air, gazing at the destruction across the river. Flames from the still-burning town lit the night sky, interspersed with bright flashes of Confederate artillery hidden in the hills above it. It was a nightmarish scene, yet she couldn't look away.

A few minutes later the church door opened and James came outside to stand alongside her. They listened to the rumble of distant cannon and watched the flames lick the night sky for several minutes without speaking.

"Why do you suppose something this horrifying is so fascinating?" he finally asked.

"I don't know," she said, shivering. "I've been wondering how I would feel if that were my city—if Confederate guns turned Philadelphia into rubble and flames."

The lights of distant campfires flickered in the night. The evening breeze carried shouts and laughter and the whinnies of horses from far away.

"Do you think anyone who experiences this can ever be the

same?" James asked. His voice was very soft. "Will you be the same, Julia? Will you be able to return to your dinner parties and charity balls and forget this ever happened?"

She tried to imagine herself in a ball gown, whirling in Nathaniel Greene's arms—and couldn't. "Right now I can't imagine that this war will ever end. Or that anyone will be alive when it does," she said.

They fell silent again. Somewhere in the distance a military band played "Hail Columbia." James reached into the breast pocket of his jacket and pulled out his silver flask. Flames reflected off its shiny surface as he unscrewed the cap and tilted it to his lips to drink.

"Don't," Julia whispered.

"Pardon me?"

She'd seen him sick on enough mornings to know that if he got drunk tonight he would wake up feeling miserable tomorrow. Aside from acting rude and ill-tempered, he wouldn't be able to concentrate and his hands would shake—he'd be of little use as a physician. She had gained so much respect for him after watching him with his patients and working alongside him in the field hospital all day, and she didn't want him to degrade himself by getting drunk. She longed to stop him from destroying the better part of himself.

"I don't think getting drunk is the answer," she said.

"Oh, really?" he said acidly. "The answer to what?" When she didn't reply he held up the flask. "I suppose you know why I carry this around?"

She wanted to say, *Yes, it's because of what happened in New Haven.* But she remembered his reaction at the farmhouse in Sharpsburg, the deep pain she'd seen in his eyes. She wouldn't mention the murder again.

"You're a gifted doctor," she said. "It's a mystery to everyone back at Fairfield Hospital why you cause yourself such misery by getting drunk so often."

"Have you ever tried it, Mrs. Hoffman? Would you like a little taste?" He held the flask out to her.

"No, thank you."

"Go ahead, take a drink. I insist. Maybe you'll be the first to unlock the mystery of why I drink." He shoved it in front of her face. "Take a sip."

The metal felt cold as he shoved it roughly against her lips. He tipped it up. She opened her mouth to prevent him from pouring the liquor down her chin—and because she was afraid of angering him. She swallowed, expecting the bitter taste, the burning fire of strong drink. Instead, she tasted nothing at all.

"It's water," she said in surprise.

"Ah! Very good. Now you've solved the mystery of why James McGrath drinks."

She looked up at him.

"Because I'm thirsty, Mrs. Hoffman."

"But . . . it's not always water. I've seen you with a hangover on plenty of mornings. You come to work all rumpled, as if you've slept in your clothes, and you sit in your office with the curtains drawn, telling us not to shout. Everyone knows it's because you got drunk the night before."

"Don't believe everything you hear."

"But I've seen you with a hangover."

"No. You haven't. You've seen me with a migraine headache."

"You have a tumbler on your desk with—"

"Willow bark tea. It seems to help my migraines."

She stared at him in disbelief, struggling to fit what he was telling her with what she'd seen.

"Have you ever had a migraine, Mrs. Hoffman?" he asked. "The pain is incapacitating. It begins behind your eyes, and it feels as though a bright light is shining in your face, even when your eyes are closed. Sometimes the light begins to sparkle, adding to the pain. As the headache builds, the slightest sound, the slightest movement, intensifies the pain tenfold, until you're nauseated with it. You can't help vomiting. All you want to do is curl into a ball in a dark, quiet place and plead with God to make it stop. But of course you can't do that when there's work to be done. Laudanum helps deaden the pain, but I'm no good to anyone drugged, am I?"

"Are you telling me you don't drink?"

"I used to. Perhaps too much at times."

His eyes looked tired and sad as he gazed into the distance. She wondered what he was remembering. According to Hiram Stone, James had killed a man when he was drunk.

"But I don't drink anymore," he said, lifting the flask. "Just water."

"You must know about all the rumors," Julia said. "Everyone at the hospital thinks you're an alcoholic."

He shrugged. "So what?"

"Why do you let them think that? Why don't you tell them the truth?"

"Because I really don't care what everyone thinks." He took another long drink and wiped his mouth with his fist. "Considering the way you've disregarded the opinions and expectations of your own social class, I would think that you, of all people, should understand that."

"I don't," she said. "I don't understand it at all." Julia shook her head, as if to shake away the familiar image of him of as a drunkard and replace it with this new one. The pale, pain-pinched face and trembling hands she'd seen on so many mornings were not the result of his drunkenness but of an affliction that was totally beyond his control. She stared at him, his face lit by the flames of the burning town, and saw a completely different man.

"Well," he said abruptly, "I'm going to bed. Tomorrow will be a very long day for all of us."

Julia watched him disappear into the house and felt like an utter fool.

The next day Union troops crossed the river into Fredericksburg. When they discovered that the Rebels had moved to the heights outside the city, Yankee soldiers went on a rampage through the town, breaking into deserted homes and stores, smashing and destroying and looting.

Later that afternoon, when Julia crossed the river in an ambulance to help set up a field hospital in town, the sight of the ravaged city sickened her. Household goods—feather beds and rocking chairs and smashed teacups—lay trampled and discarded in the streets, while soldiers roamed freely through the ruined homes, stuffing valuables into their pockets and knapsacks. The commanding officers were doing nothing at all to stop the looting. She quickly turned away, disgusted with mankind, and set about her own work.

The doctors selected a large brick warehouse near one of the pontoon bridges for a temporary hospital and operating room. Julia helped James stock it with food and water and medical supplies, preparing for the battle that would begin the next day. She recrossed the river that night to sleep in the church in Falmouth once again.

At eight-thirty the next morning, Union troops began advancing toward the Rebel lines under the cover of fog. When it lifted, the assault began. Julia returned to the warehouse, where she could clearly hear the battle raging all day in the hills behind the city. As thousands of wounded men poured into the hospital, she learned from her patients what was happening.

"The Rebels hold the high ground," one exhausted man told her, "yet our generals keep hurling men at them in wave after wave."

"We're out in the open," another soldier added, "and the Rebels are protected by a stone wall. They're just mowing us down like wheat as we come up the hill."

It seemed like insanity to her. The terrible slaughter lasted all day, with nothing to show for it in the end except casualties. As night fell and the temperature dropped, the men who still streamed into the hospital told Julia that thousands more injured men lay pinned down on the hillside, freezing. They were forced to huddle beneath the dead bodies of their friends for protection, not daring to move—or they'd be shot at.

Julia had labored all day in the hope that General Burnside would be victorious, that this would be the last battle any of them would have to endure. As her strength began to give out, it no longer looked as if victory was possible. She was exhausted, both physically and emotionally. She couldn't help wondering how James was holding up—if the stress had caused one of his migraine headaches to strike at the worst possible time. When she had a free moment, she decided to check on him.

The doctors had set up their operating rooms in the warehouse's offices. As she neared that area, Julia heard James shouting at his fellow physicians.

"Look, the surgery is going too slowly this way. If we all split up and get the nurses to assist us, we can accomplish three times as much."

"It's against the rules, James. The army's medical director specifically ordered field surgeons to work in teams of three."

"Why don't you go explain that to those dying men out there?" James asked. "You go tell a soldier who's been waiting in agony all afternoon, 'Sorry you have to die, but it's against the rules for less than three of us to save your life.'"

"We're just following orders."

"Oh yeah? Well, I'm not."

Julia watched as James began moving office furniture and lanterns around so he could set up another operating table. "Those pitiful souls who are being slaughtered out on those heights are just following orders, too," he said as he worked. "Someone needs to call a halt to it. In the meantime, we need to take responsibility for what's going on in this operating room. The medical director isn't here; we are." He moved his case of surgical instruments within reach of the table. When he looked up to tell the orderlies to bring him a patient, he saw Julia standing outside the door.

"Mrs. Hoffman, will you come here and assist me, please?"

One of the doctors held up his hands. "I can't allow this, James. She's not a physician."

"She's a trained nurse. I taught her myself. If she helps, we'll get twice as much done, save twice as many lives."

"Regulations require at least two surgeons to approve amputations."

"Fine! The two of you can approve the amputations, and I'll do all the other procedures. Okay? Can we begin?" He waited while the other two doctors huddled together, arguing over whether or not they should allow James to go ahead. Minutes passed, until he finally threw up his hands in frustration.

"I don't have time for this. Men are dying while you two gentlemen discuss army regulations. Mrs. Hoffman . . . if you will, please?"

Julia moved forward into the room, too stunned by the speed of events to do otherwise. She had never watched a doctor perform surgery before. She was quite certain she would faint at the sight.

But when James gripped her shoulders, his eyes searching hers, and asked, "Can you stand this, Mrs. Hoffman? Will you help me?" she could only nod.

The orderlies carried in the first patient, a boy with a gunshot wound beneath his collarbone. He couldn't have been more than eighteen years old. James gently rolled him over to search for an exit wound, then began loosening his clothing.

"Am I going to make it, Doc?" the soldier gasped.

James laid his hand on the boy's head. "We'll do our best."

Dread shuddered through Julia when she realized that "we" included her. She now shared the responsibility for trying to save his life. She knew then that she needed to pray for all the strength and courage God would give her. For this boy's sake, she dared not faint or run away.

James showed her how much ether to pour into the copper face cone. "Keep this away from the lamps," he warned. "Ether is highly flammable. Hold the cone firmly over his nose and mouth, like that. . . . Good. That's enough." He turned to his wooden case of surgical instruments and selected a probe. "Keep an eye on him. If he starts to come around before I'm finished, give him more."

Julia nodded, too nervous to speak. She looked away as James maneuvered the probe into the bullet wound. She didn't realize how quiet it was or that she was holding her breath until she heard the delicate click of metal against metal as the probe touched the bullet. James smiled faintly.

"Hand me the forceps. . . . Thank you. Now grab a sponge and mop up some of this blood to give me some exposure. . . . Good."

She glanced at James' face and saw beads of sweat running down his forehead and into his eyes. Julia grabbed a clean towel and wiped his forehead for him.

"Thanks. That's much better." A few moments later, he withdrew the forceps, gripping a bloody chunk of metal. He dropped it into a tin can that was already half full of pellets. "I'll need one of those sutures in a minute," he said as he swabbed the wound with carbolic acid. "The needles . . . with the silk thread. . . . Yes." Then it was over. It seemed as though mere moments had passed. The orderlies carried the boy away and brought in the next patient as James wiped his hands.

Julia gradually began to relax, drawing courage from his confident skill and quietly stated orders. Little by little she found she could watch James work. She forgot that she was looking at blood and shattered bone and ripped muscle as she watched his hands, strong and dexterous—mending, repairing, healing. She learned to anticipate what he needed and had it ready before he asked.

As the hours passed, her legs grew weary and her back ached from standing in one place. She longed to quit and lie down, but James worked tirelessly, long after the other two doctors had sat down to rest.

When the orderlies finally stopped bringing patients, James leaned against the operating table and pulled out his pocket watch. "Twenty past midnight," he sighed. "If the generals could stand in our place for one day, maybe this would end." He shook his head and returned the watch to his pocket, then raised his arms, stretching his back and neck. "I need some fresh air."

A rush of cold wind shivered through Julia as he opened the office door and stepped outside, closing it behind him. Her hair was escaping from its pins, so she pulled out the remaining ones and shook her head to let it fall freely around her shoulders. She was about to leave the office and look for a place to lie down when James suddenly opened the door again. He picked up a discarded uniform jacket he found lying across a chair and handed it to her. "Mrs. Hoffman . . . Julia. Put this on and come outside with me for a moment."

She couldn't imagine why he needed her, but thinking it must be an emergency, she quickly did as she was told. Just outside the door, James stopped her.

"Look," he said, pointing up at the sky. "The northern lights."

Above the river, from one end of the horizon to the other, the sky was alive with shimmering waves of light. Shades of red and green and dazzling white hung above her head like a luminous curtain. She quickly forgot the cold and her aching weariness, lost in the beauty of the heavenly aurora. She had never seen anything this magnificent in her life, nor did she believe she ever would again.

She leaned against the wall beside James and silently marveled at the show.

"God gave the Israelites fire by night," he said quietly, "to keep them from despair. Tonight He gave us this."

She looked up at James, watching his face as he watched the lights perform their flickering dance. And suddenly she no longer believed that he had ever killed a man. James worked much too hard to preserve life. She would never believe he could end one. He hated death. She had seen him locked in combat with it tonight as if it were his enemy. The real James McGrath was this man, the doctor who was gentle and caring with his patients, who fought each of their illnesses as if it were a personal grudge match. The gruff anger and rudeness he often hid behind were a front, designed to keep people at bay for some reason. If he really had shot a man there would be another explanation for it—just as there had been another explanation for his "hangovers."

"You did a remarkable job tonight, Julia," he said, still gazing up at the sky. "Once you caught on, you anticipated what I needed before I asked. I've never worked that smoothly with anyone before, not even other doctors."

"It could have been this way all along," she said. "Back in Washington, too. But from the very first day I arrived, you seemed determined to drive me away—and everyone else, too, for that matter. You'll probably push me away again tomorrow. What I don't understand is why. Why do you work so hard to keep me at a distance?"

He turned his gaze to her, his face somber. Their eyes met. "For the same reason people keep sparks away from gunpowder."

"I-I don't understand." But her heart had begun to beat very fast.

"I think you do, Julia."

He reached out and gently brushed his fingers across her cheek. She froze. Her heart raced so fast she was certain it would burst. Then James slowly leaned toward her and touched his lips to hers. Julia's body went weak and shivery all over, as if she had suddenly taken ill. The kiss lasted only a moment before he pulled back and looked at her again. His breath had quickened, and he stood so close she could feel it on her face. She could smell his scent and taste the lingering flavor of his lips. The kiss had been like a sip of something sweet, and she hungered for more.

As if he had read her thoughts, James suddenly took her face in both his hands and pressed his mouth to hers, kissing her as if he needed to draw life from her. She had been kissed only once before—a stolen kiss that left her feeling angry and cheated. But the way James kissed her now was every bit as wonderful as she had dreamed it would be. He buried his fingers in her hair and kissed her throat, her temple, her forehead. His beard sent shivers through her as it brushed her skin. Then his lips found her mouth again, and he kissed her long and deep.

Julia encircled him with her arms and drew him closer. Their bodies touched as he pressed her back against the wall. The sensations that washed over her as she moved her hands across his shoulders were so powerful, so overwhelming, she felt she might faint from them. She didn't want James to ever stop.

But he did. He released her so suddenly it was as if someone had grabbed his shirt and jerked him backward.

"No . . ." he whispered. "No!" She saw horror in his eyes before he closed them. He bent forward, his hands on his thighs, struggling for breath. "I'm sorry," he said hoarsely. "That shouldn't have happened. Forgive me." Then he turned and fled into the night before Julia could speak.

She felt weak-kneed, shaken, the crush of his mouth still fresh on hers, the caress of his hands still tingling through her hair. She felt incomplete, as if an orchestra had abruptly stopped before the song ended; as if a plate of luscious food had been snatched away, leaving her hungry for more.

"No," she whispered, just as James had done. But she didn't mean it the way he had. She meant, "Don't go . . . come back."

She wanted his hands to caress her again, those strong, capable hands she'd watched earlier that night, working carefully, skillfully, the golden ring glinting on his left hand in the lamplight. And she suddenly realized, with the same horror as James, what they had done. He was married. She had willingly kissed a married man, held another woman's husband, a little girl's father, in her arms.

"Oh, God," she murmured. Her knees gave way, and she slowly

slid down the wall to the ground. "Oh, God, forgive me."

When the sun rose a few hours later, Julia hadn't slept. She had gone back inside the warehouse, found the quiet corner where the other nurses were sleeping, wrapped herself in a blanket, and lain down. But sleep wouldn't come, in spite of her exhaustion. Now the nurses and orderlies had begun to wake up and move around. She heard the injured men moaning. She couldn't force herself to move.

One of the orderlies approached her. "Mrs. Hoffman?"

She sat up. "Yes?"

"We're getting the ambulances ready to take the wounded men to the train depot and Aquia Landing. Dr. McGrath said you volunteered to go with them on one of the evacuation ships."

It took her a moment to comprehend what was happening. James was sending her back to Washington, separating the sparks from the gunpowder. "Y-yes. Yes, I did volunteer," she stammered.

"We'll be out front whenever you're ready."

Julia quickly gathered her meager belongings. She was glad that she was leaving, glad that she didn't have to face James. She couldn't forget how she had responded to him, pulling him closer instead of pushing him away. How could she ever forgive herself for coveting another woman's husband? And James believed that she was married, too, that she, also, had betrayed her wedding vows last night.

In the ambulance, on the hospital train, on board the evacuation ship, Julia spent every minute, every mile of the journey working with the wounded soldiers. It was her punishment, meant to assuage her guilt. It didn't.

By the time she reached Washington, Congressman Rhodes had long since departed for Philadelphia. But Julia would not allow herself to go home for Christmas. Nathaniel Greene was home. She couldn't face him, couldn't face her family, until she'd paid her penance in full.

For the next week, Julia spent all day and most of her spare time at the hospital, helping to decorate the wards with pines, celebrating the holiday with the soldiers, nursing the casualties from

Fredericksburg until she was weak with exhaustion. All the while she dreaded the day that James would return. She held her breath every time a carriage pulled up or the front door opened.

In January, Julia overheard Mrs. Fowle telling one of the soldiers that Dr. McGrath had returned to Connecticut. "How did you hear that?" Julia asked the matron.

"Dr. Whitney told me. Besides, it's been two weeks since a letter arrived from Mrs. McGrath. The prodigal husband finally went home."

Julia turned away as tears unexpectedly filled her eyes. She had no idea at all what they were for.

Chapter Eighteen

Washington City
April 1863

Phoebe stood behind the curtained partition in her little corner of the hospital ward and looked down at the new chemise and underdrawers she had just put on. Unlike the muslin hand-me-downs from Widow Garlock, these were made of fine white cotton and trimmed with eyelet and tiny rows of tucks. "You didn't need to go and make these underthings so frilly," she told Julia. "Ain't nobody gonna see them but me."

"But it's nice to wear pretty things, isn't it?" Julia asked. "I know it always makes me feel good."

Phoebe sat down on the bed and pulled on a pair of new woolen stockings. They felt soft and smooth and had a fancy design knitted into them. She looked up at Julia. "I don't know how I'll ever pay you back for all of these things."

"I told you, I don't want you to pay me," Julia said a little crossly. "They're gifts, Phoebe. It makes me happy to buy them for you. We need to celebrate the fact that you're finally well enough to leave the hospital and go home. For a while there, we didn't know if you were going to live or not."

"But they must've cost a lot of money—"

"Not really. Besides, I have a lot of money. Now stand up so I can lace your corset."

"Do I have to wear that thing? The last time I tried on a corset it felt like I'd fallen out of a tree and had the wind knocked out of me."

Julia smiled. "I won't need to pull it very tight. You've gotten so thin since you've been ill. You have a nice slender figure now. A lot of women will envy you."

Phoebe let her lace it up. Then Julia slipped a new corded petticoat over her head. She had to stand on tiptoe to do it, since Phoebe was so tall.

"Folks in Bone Hollow will say I'm putting on airs when I show up in such fancy clothes. They'll say, 'You can't make a silk purse out of a sow's ear.'" She wished Julia had bought her a plain old shirt and a pair of overalls instead.

"If they say that it's because they're jealous," Julia said, lifting the skirt over Phoebe's head. "I hope I measured you right for this skirt and bodice. If not, the seamstress said you could come back anytime and she would make alterations."

"I'm sure they'll be fine." Phoebe had picked a plain dark blue calico print for the skirt and matching long-sleeved top. It had plain cuffs and a simple row of buttons down the front, but Julia had made the sleeves fashionably full and added three rows of fancy tucks around the hem of the skirt.

"I have one more surprise," Julia said, unwrapping a tissue-paper package. "I bought you a white lace collar and a brooch to wear at the neck when you want to dress up a little. See?"

"But . . . I can't thank you enough." Phoebe bit her lip, determined not to cry. Julia pulled her into her arms and hugged her. Julia felt small and fragile to Phoebe as she hugged her back.

"Please don't try to," Julia said. "It doesn't count as a good deed in heaven if I get something in return—and I need all the good credit I can get." Julia's voice suddenly sounded very sad, but before Phoebe could ask her what she meant, Julia said, "Now sit down on the bed and let me fix your hair."

Phoebe's hair had grown nearly two inches since she'd been wounded in September. It didn't quite touch her shoulders yet, but Julia insisted that it was long enough for her to pin back and cover with a ribbon. She handed Phoebe a mirror so she could watch, but she was almost afraid to look.

"I wish we had a full-length mirror so you could see how lovely you look in your new dress," Julia said as she brushed her hair.

Phoebe didn't feel lovely, even with pretty clothes on and her hair fixed up. She looked at her reflection in the mirror and knew that Ted Wilson would still never want to steal a kiss from her or carry her picture in his pocket. Julia was the kind of girl that all the men wanted for their sweetheart.

"Can I ask you a question?" Julia said when she finished with Phoebe's hair. "I've been curious for a long time. . . . Why did you do it? Why did you pretend that you were a man?"

Phoebe looked down at her lap. "Because I was no good at being a woman. No one's ever going to marry me. I'm too big and tall and ugly." She realized that it was still true. When she arrived home in a few days, her only choice would be to work for Mrs. Haggerty again, or someone just like her. "I figured since I looked like a man and could shoot a gun like a man, I may as well pretend I was one."

"Phoebe, look in the mirror," Julia said gently. "You're tall, but you're not built like a man. You've got a very nice figure." She pointed to the shoulder line of her own dress. "Women have dropped shoulders like these sewn on their dresses on purpose so their shoulders will look as nice and wide as yours."

"This ain't a pretty face."

Julia shook her head. "I know you'll never believe me, but you have a very nice face. And there are other things for a woman to do besides get married. You can lead a full life without a husband. Take Dorothea Dix, for example—"

"Oh, sure," Phoebe said angrily. "You can say that because you're pretty and you're married. You probably had lots of men lining up to ask you, right?"

Julia didn't reply. She couldn't seem to meet Phoebe's gaze.

"You ain't answering because I'm right, ain't I? You never had to worry about finding a husband."

"Phoebe, I came here to be a nurse because I wanted to do more with my life than just find a husband and get married. I wanted to be more than a pretty face. This is just the outside," she said, touching her own cheek. "I wanted to be beautiful on the inside. That's what really counts."

"But you already are a good person on the inside."

"No," Julia said, shaking her head. "I'm not. You don't know me." She sat down on the bed beside Phoebe, toying with the hairbrush. "I once overheard a man say that it didn't matter to him that I was pretty. He had looked at my heart and what he saw was ugly. He was right—I saw it, too. And even though I've tried very hard to change, I've seen even uglier things in my heart since then." She drew a deep breath and exhaled before continuing. "There was another man who was attracted to me because I was pretty, but he didn't want me to be a nurse. He wanted me all to himself, to show me off so everyone would say what a pretty wife he had. But that was all that he loved about me. He didn't know me or care about what I was like on the inside."

Phoebe remembered how the soldiers used to show off their sweethearts' pictures, bragging about how pretty they were. "Which of those two men is your husband?" she asked Julia.

"Neither. I'm going to tell you a secret, Phoebe. I think you'll understand since you had a secret yourself for so long." Julia hesitated, then drew another deep breath. "I'm not married. I lied. I said that I was because no one would let me be a nurse if I was single."

Phoebe stared. "But . . . you told us all about your husband. You said he was in a Rebel prison."

"There is a real Robert Hoffman, and he *is* in Libby Prison. But he's my cousin, not my husband."

Phoebe couldn't reply. She thought she understood a little of Ted's shock and surprise when he had learned her own secret. It was no fun discovering that someone you admired had lied to you. And Phoebe's lie had been even worse than Julia's.

"I feel so bad about lying," Julia said. "I know it was wrong, and I pray that God will forgive me for it—and for all of my other sins. You're my friend, Phoebe, and I . . . I wanted you to know the truth."

"Do you think you'll ever get married, though?" Phoebe finally asked.

"I hope to marry someday. But I want to find a man who loves the real me. Isn't that what you want, too? Wouldn't that be much better than marrying a man who only wants you because you're pretty?"

"I been in love," Phoebe said quietly. "And if I looked like you do, he would have loved me back. And you know what? Even if he only loved me on the outside, that would be a whole heap better than him not loving me at all."

Julia stared down at her hands, looking sadder than Phoebe had ever seen her look. "I'm going to miss you, Phoebe Bigelow."

"Yeah . . . me too," she said hoarsely. She stood, suddenly wanting to get all the good-byes over with and leave before she started to cry. "I hope you find somebody, Julia. You deserve a good life in return for all you done for me. And don't worry—I ain't gonna try and thank you again. I want you to get your reward." She was glad when Julia smiled faintly. "Listen, I'm gonna go say good-bye to the other nurses now and let them see how you tried to fix me up."

"They'll tell you the same thing I did—that you look lovely."

Phoebe nodded. "Since I don't like saying good-bye and all that, I'm going to leave and go on ahead of you to your boardinghouse, okay? We can say good-bye tomorrow morning when you take me to the train station."

"All right. I'll see you later, Phoebe."

The matrons and nurses had been kind to Phoebe, but she hurried through all the farewells, embarrassed by the attention. When she finally managed to tear herself away and get to the front door, she spotted Dr. McGrath working in his office. Phoebe hesitated, aware that he always held himself aloof from everybody—and even more so since he'd returned to the hospital a month ago after his leave of absence. But he had saved her life, and she needed to thank him.

"Dr. McGrath, I guess you know I'm going home today," she said shyly. "I just thought I'd say good-bye. And I wanted to thank you for helping me get better."

He leaned back in his chair and smiled at her. "You look very nice as a woman, Miss Bigelow."

"Oh. Thanks." She felt herself blushing. "I have Julia to thank for this dress and all."

He nodded absently, his smile gone. "I . . . uh . . . I trust you won't be enlisting again any time soon?"

"No, sir. I reckon I'll just go on home."

"Listen, I'll be glad to write up some discharge papers for you under your other name. You fought in some major battles. You deserve to have an honorable discharge listed on the records."

"No thanks. I told a lie, and there ain't nothing honorable about lying."

"Well, you know where to find me if you change your mind."

"Thanks for everything, Dr. McGrath. Good-bye."

"Good-bye, Miss Bigelow. And good luck to you."

As she walked out of Fairfield Hospital that beautiful spring morning, Phoebe wondered what she would do with "good luck." As far as she was concerned, it was bad luck that she was back to being a woman, worse luck that she was going home to Bone Hollow, and the worst luck of all that there wasn't a soul in the world who cared if she lived or died. If God loved her as much as Julia claimed, it seemed to Phoebe that now would be a good time to give her a sign.

James McGrath watched Phoebe leave Fairfield Hospital and wondered what would become of her. She looked so uncomfortable in her new dress that it wouldn't surprise him in the least if she was back in trousers by nightfall. He sighed. Phoebe had thanked him for saving her life, but the truth was that she owed a bigger debt to Julia than to him. She was the one who had spotted the piece of shrapnel, who had cared for Phoebe day after day, who had convinced Phoebe to live when she was ready to give up and die.

He sighed again and rubbed his eyes, wishing he could rub Julia from his mind. He returned to his mail. His weekly letter had arrived that morning from New Haven, and he carefully slit the envelope open with a knife. James felt his chest tighten as he unfolded a childish drawing of water and boats, the tall masts pointing to a bright orange sun. His daughter had scrawled a note to him across the top.

Dear Daddy,

We saw some ships today. I drew a picture of them for you.

Love, Kate

James left the two-page letter, written on cream vellum stationery, inside the envelope, unread. Lost in his thoughts, he was only vaguely aware of the front door groaning open, then banging closed again. A moment later he heard a man's voice speaking from his office doorway. "Excuse me, Doctor . . ."

James looked up to see a tall, dark-haired man in an officer's uniform watching him. The soldier was very thin, as if he might be recovering from an illness or an injury. Yet there was an intensity in his gaze, a predator's alertness in his posture that James found unsettling. He quickly folded his daughter's drawing and stuffed it back inside the envelope as if he were ashamed of it, though he couldn't have said why.

"I'm sorry to disturb you," the stranger said. "I'm Lieutenant Robert Hoffman. I'm looking for my—"

"Julia."

James said the name aloud, finishing the lieutenant's sentence. He heard the longing in his own voice and hoped her husband hadn't.

"Yes, Julia Hoffman. I was told I might find her here." The lieutenant stood rigidly at attention, as if awaiting military inspection. James rose and extended his hand.

"James McGrath. Julia told us you've been held prisoner in . . . Richmond, wasn't it?"

"Yes."

"Then I assume there must have been a prisoner exchange. How fortunate for you."

"There wasn't an exchange," he said without emotion. "I escaped."

"Ah. And Julia doesn't know. She . . . well, I expect she'll be overjoyed to see you." James looked down at the top of his desk, pushing papers around, unable to face the man. He felt absurdly pleased that Robert Hoffman wasn't handsome and was stunned to realize that he was jealous of this man—Julia's husband. James wondered how Lieutenant Hoffman would react if he knew that James had kissed his wife. And that she had kissed him back.

"Is she here?" Hoffman asked. "I've come to take her home to Philadelphia with me."

There was an aloofness in his manner that James found disturbing. Hoffman's gaze was austere, unsmiling. A man who was about to hold his beautiful wife for the first time in a year and a half shouldn't seem this cold and indifferent. James knew how prison could profoundly alter a man, and he felt a ripple of fear for Julia.

"She's upstairs," James said. "If you'd like to wait here, I'll go fetch her."

"Yes. Thank you."

It required a great effort for James to move his feet, as if someone had nailed them to the floor. The stairs seemed steeper than he remembered, and he had to grip the banister as he climbed them. When he got to the wardroom door he stood for a long moment, watching Julia. She sat in a chair beside a patient's bed, writing a letter he was dictating to his family. The soldier saw James first and stopped midsentence.

"What's wrong, Doc?"

James wondered if the terrible pain he felt was visible on his face. Julia looked up, too, then quickly stood.

"What happened?" she asked.

James forced himself to smile as he walked toward her. "Nothing . . . that is . . . I have wonderful news, Mrs. Hoffman. Your husband is here."

"What. . . ?"

Julia swayed, and the paper and pen slid from her hands to the floor. The color leeched from her face as if she'd severed an artery. James gripped her arms to steady her.

"Hang on. I've got you." He cleared the knot from his throat. "It's true . . . your husband is waiting downstairs. And he's fine—all in one piece, I'm happy to say."

"Robert is . . . here?"

"Yes. He has come to take you home." James could feel her body trembling beneath his hands, and he was afraid to let her go for fear she would topple over. "Do you think you can walk, or would you like me to help you?"

"You can let go of me," she said. "I can walk." Her face was very pale.

James released her, then watched as Julia slowly crossed the room like a woman in a dream. He felt relieved that he didn't have to help her. He didn't want to watch as she ran into her husband's waiting arms.

When she reached the door, James suddenly realized that Julia was about to walk out of his life forever. He would never see her again. "Good-bye, Mrs. Hoffman," he called after her. "I . . . I think I speak for everyone when I say . . . it has been a pleasure working with you."

She paused, nodding slightly, then continued her dreamlike walk without answering. His words had sounded cold. They were not at all what he'd wanted to say, what he wished he could say. He heard the stairs creak one by one as she descended them. He realized he was holding his breath. He quickly crossed the room to shut the door behind her, hoping to muffle the sound of their joyous reunion. When he turned around again, he saw all of the soldiers watching him.

"Guess that's a happy ending, right, Doc?" one of them asked quietly.

"Yes. Yes, it is. Mrs. Hoffman's husband has been locked in a Rebel prison. . . . He just told me that he escaped. . . . Remarkable, really . . . escaping." James bent to pick up the pen and paper that Julia had dropped and saw that his hands were trembling. He needed a drink.

"You don't look so good, Doc," the man in the bed beside him said.

James lowered himself onto the chair where Julia had been sitting. The seat still held her warmth. "Just thinking about my own wife," he murmured.

"Yeah," the soldier said. "I know what you mean. It's been a long time since I held my wife in my arms."

James waited until he was sure the Hoffmans were gone before returning to his office downstairs. He rummaged noisily though his desk, opening and slamming drawers and cupboards, desperate for a shot of whiskey. Then he remembered the medicinal brandy he carried in his bag.

The first swig burned all the way to his stomach. He couldn't imagine that he'd ever enjoyed this taste. He sank down in his chair, grimacing as he swallowed a second shot and a third. He remembered quite clearly the last time he'd drunk this much, but he didn't care.

His wife, Ellen, stared at him from across his desk. He picked up the photograph and studied her face. Then his eyes moved to little Kate's face, beside her. Guilt struck him like a blow to the stomach. It was wrong for him to feel what he felt for Julia Hoffman, wrong to remember the power of her kiss that night in Fredericksburg when he couldn't remember what Ellen's kisses were like. He laid the photograph facedown on his desk.

"Thou shalt not covet thy neighbor's wife." Well, here was one more reason for God to condemn him—as if there weren't enough reasons to send him to hell already.

Lieutenant Hoffman had returned to claim his wife. She would go home to Philadelphia with him. James wouldn't need to see her every day and think about her every night or remember how glorious her hair had felt beneath his hands.

He took another drink and set the bottle on his desk. He began twisting his wedding ring, gently at first, but gradually tugging it harder and harder until he managed to yank it all the way off. His hand felt naked without it. But why wear a symbol that no longer had meaning—*unending love . . . until death parted us*?

Now that the ring was off, James didn't know what to do with it. He finally dropped it into the envelope with the unread letter and his daughter's drawing, then stuffed the envelope into the drawer with all the others and closed it. He was staring blankly at the brandy bottle when two of the ward matrons came to his office door.

"Is it true what some of the soldiers are saying?" Mrs. Fowle asked. "Has Mrs. Hoffman's husband really come for her?"

"It's true."

Mrs. Fowle clapped her hands. "Oh, that's wonderful!"

"I wonder why she didn't introduce him to us?" Mrs. Nichols said.

"The man hasn't slept with her in more than a year," James said gruffly. "I'm sure he had plans for the evening that didn't include introductions."

The two women stared at him in shock. Mrs. Fowle's cheeks turned bright pink. "I see that you've been drinking," she said coldly. "Even so, your vulgarity in the presence of women is inexcusable."

"Then go away and let me get drunk in peace."

"'As a dog returneth to his vomit,'" Mrs. Nichols quoted, "'so a fool returneth to his folly.'"

When they were gone, James took a long drink of brandy, then wiped his mouth. He leaned his head back, staring up at the cracked ceiling, waiting for the once-familiar numbness to flow through his body, waiting for it to dull his thoughts and erase his pain.

Julia's elegant traveling suit felt fussy and uncomfortable to her after wearing plain clothes for so long. She looked at her reflection in the boardinghouse mirror as Phoebe fastened the long row of buttons down the back. It hardly seemed possible that she'd helped Phoebe get dressed only this morning. Julia had thought she would be seeing Phoebe off for home; now the tables had turned—and so quickly that Julia was still reeling. With few belongings in the sparsely furnished room, it hadn't taken her long to pack.

"Seems funny, us both going home, don't it?" Phoebe asked.

"I'm as surprised as you are, believe me. But Robert is very eager to leave, and our family doesn't want us to waste another moment."

Phoebe finished closing the last button and sat down on the sagging bed. Julia went to the mirror to tidy her hair. "I'll bet you're excited," Phoebe said.

"Yes . . . and no." Julia's reflection looked wavy and unfocused. She couldn't tell if it was from the mirror or the tears in her eyes.

Her feelings were all jumbled together, the happy ones and the sad ones, as if two orchestras were playing conflicting tunes. Her cousin Robert was alive and safe, and she was overjoyed to see him. But a chapter in her life was ending forever and she felt a terrible loss.

"I didn't even have a chance to say good-bye to everyone at the hospital," Julia said. "I had to leave right away so they wouldn't find out . . . you know . . ."

"That he's your cousin and not your husband."

"Yes. And so Robert wouldn't find out how I've been using his name all this time. I feel terrible for lying. Please, don't tell anyone."

"Don't worry. I don't reckon I'll ever see any of them again. Besides, I know how it feels to have your lies found out. Folks look at you differently, and they feel like fools for believing you."

"At least my lies didn't hurt anyone, as far as I know. And at least I got to be a nurse for a while." She brushed away the tears that rolled down her cheeks.

"What will you do once you're back home?"

"I don't know." And that was the worst part, Julia realized. The future was like a huge empty room with nothing to fill it. After working so hard for so long, she didn't know how she would suddenly face that void. The only glimmer of hope she saw was in her relationship with Nathaniel Greene.

Julia put her hairbrush in the steamer trunk and closed the lid. She had tossed most of her clothing in without folding it properly, and now she had trouble fastening the latches.

"Want me to help you sit on that?" Phoebe asked.

"Yes, I think you'd better." When they finally got it closed and locked, Julia said, "I'm sorry I won't be able to take you to the train station tomorrow."

"That's okay. You know, I been thinking . . . maybe I'll stay an extra day or two and look around Washington City if that's okay. I didn't get to see much of it when I was in the army."

"I'm sure that would be all right. I've paid the rent here for the entire month of April. I just thought . . . aren't you in a hurry to get home?"

"Ain't nobody waiting there for me like they're waiting for you."

"How long has it been since you were home, Phoebe?"

"More than a year and a half. How 'bout you?"

"Just over a year."

"It's funny, ain't it?" Phoebe asked. "After all we've been through, we're both right back where we started. Nothing's changed. Even the war still goes on."

Julia had left Fairfield Hospital just as she'd found it a year ago, with Mrs. Fowle and the other matrons at war with Dr. McGrath—and with James sitting alone in his office, barely speaking a civil word to the nurses. The matrons still believed that he was an alcoholic. Julia had been afraid to tell them the truth, afraid they'd ask too many questions about how she had gotten close enough to him to discover his secret. Her face would surely betray her if she talked about James. The women would surely see her feelings for him—and her guilt. Those feelings were still very strong, too. They'd rekindled all over again when James had held her today in the wardroom. And though she knew it was wrong, she was filled with grief because she would never see him again.

"I'm going to go now, Phoebe," she said quietly.

"You need help with this trunk?"

"Robert and the carriage driver will be up in a moment to fetch it." Her eyes filled with tears as she pulled Phoebe into her arms for one last hug. "Good-bye, then."

"Good-bye."

Julia tried to turn her thoughts toward home and her family as she hurried from the room. But a terrible sense of loss followed her down the stairs like a shadow and settled in the carriage seat beside her.

PART TWO

The path of the righteous is like the first gleam of dawn,

shining ever brighter till the full light of day.

Proverbs 4:18 NIV

Chapter Nineteen

Washington City
April 1863

Phoebe hurried through the crowded streets, wishing she knew what time it was, hoping she wasn't too late for dinner at the boardinghouse. One week after Julia left, Phoebe was still in Washington, still living in her rented room. During the day she wandered the muddy streets, searching the faces of all the soldiers she passed. She hadn't stayed to see the sights as she'd told Julia but rather to try to find news of her old regiment, to learn where Ted was and what he was doing. Since Phoebe didn't know where to go in Washington to find out such information, she spent each day walking through the streets or watching new recruits drill, remembering the year she had spent in the army with Ted.

As she revisited some of the places they'd gone together, Phoebe kept hoping she'd see his boyish grin or hear him shout, "Hey, Ike!" If she could just see him from a distance, one more time, then she would go home happy.

Today's search, like all the others, had proven fruitless. She'd passed thousands of soldiers and had become skilled at scanning each face, but none of them had been Ted's. Then, when she reached the main thoroughfare near the boardinghouse, Phoebe suddenly did spot a familiar face. Dr. McGrath stood out from the crowd with his dark auburn hair and ginger beard. He carried a leather bag and walked with his sturdy shoulders hunched, his head down, as if moving forward into a stiff wind, even though the April evening was mild. Phoebe watched him from across the street, and when she saw him turn off the main street into a narrow lane she knew he was lost. She had taken that wrong turn herself and found out that it led to a dismal part of town where the former slaves lived.

Phoebe quickly crossed the street, threading her way around carriages and teams of horses, lifting her skirts to keep them out of the mud. She pushed through the crowd on the other side and found the alley the doctor had turned down. He was a block ahead of her, almost to the shantytown beneath the railway trestle. She hurried to catch up.

A crowd of Negroes suddenly rushed toward Dr. McGrath when he reached the end of the street, old people and children and women carrying babies. They quickly surrounded him and carried him along like a hero returning from battle. He wasn't lost, after all. Phoebe followed at a distance, wondering what was going on.

Dr. McGrath stopped in front of one of the shacks, took off his coat, and rolled up his sleeves. Then he bent to duck inside with his bag. He stayed in the shanty for ten long minutes, but Phoebe couldn't make herself leave. Drawn to stay for reasons she didn't understand, she slowly edged forward to listen.

When the doctor finally emerged from the shack again, the people flooded around him, clamoring for his help. "Don't worry," he said, holding out his hands. "I'll stay until I've seen everyone." He glanced around at the growing crowd—and suddenly spotted Phoebe. She knew she must look out of place here, a tall white woman in a sea of dark faces. "Miss Bigelow?" he asked in surprise. "What are you doing here?"

It was hard to answer since she really didn't know. "I-I saw you on the street . . . and . . . I'm staying in a boardinghouse near here."

"I thought you went home."

"Not yet. Listen, do you think. . . ? I mean . . . I could help if you want."

He started to shake his head, and she could tell he was about to say no, but then he stopped. He studied her for a long moment, then said, "All right. I could use some help."

For the next several hours, Phoebe worked as the doctor's assistant—holding a candle so he could see to stitch up a cut; handing him the supplies and instruments he needed; holding down a feverish patient to keep him from thrashing. They tended children who were sick with measles and croup, yanked a dock worker's dislocated arm back into its socket, and delivered a baby who was born feet-first. Phoebe had never witnessed a birth before, and tears streamed down her cheeks as the doctor laid the squalling child in his mother's arms. Phoebe thought she understood why Dr. McGrath wanted to do this work—why he needed to do it after witnessing so much destruction and death on the battlefield.

They finished shortly before dawn, just as the sky was growing light. Phoebe had missed a night's sleep, but she didn't feel at all tired. Dr. McGrath looked exhausted, though, his trousers baggy from crouching on the ground, his shirt stained with sweat and soot, his sleeves wrinkled from being rolled up all night. He used to arrive at Fairfield Hospital on many mornings looking all rumpled like this—now Phoebe knew why. She didn't need to ask why he worked alone, in secret. The medicines in the doctor's bag were labeled *U.S. Army*.

"I'll walk you home," he told her as he closed his bag. They finally managed to tear themselves away from the grateful couple whose baby they'd delivered and started walking back up the lane to the main street.

"How often do you do this?" Phoebe asked after a moment.

He shrugged. "Whenever I can."

"Why?"

"That's always the big question, isn't it? Motivation." He sighed. "I could say it's because I have the skill and therefore the duty to use it—to whom much is given, much will be required, and all that. But the plain ugly truth is probably guilt. I suppose this is my way of seeking atonement."

Phoebe wasn't sure what he meant, but she knew that helping him tonight had been one of the most satisfying things she'd ever done. "Next time you come. . . ? Could I help you again?" she asked.

"Now it's my turn to ask why."

"Well, for one thing, I killed people when I was a soldier. It would be nice to . . . you know . . . make up for it. Besides, I got nothing else to do, no place to go."

"I thought you were on your way home?"

"I don't want to go home," she admitted. "That's why I pretended I was a man and joined the army in the first place—to get away from home."

He gave a humorless laugh. "It looks like we have a lot in common, then. We're both seeking atonement, and we're both trying to escape from home. I should warn you, though; it has been my experience that you can never escape your past."

"But wait. Can I ask you something?" They had reached the main thoroughfare. Phoebe stopped beneath one of the gaslights and pulled her little Bible out of the pocket of her skirt. She leafed through it to find the spot she had marked. "It says here, 'Therefore if any man be in Christ, he is a new creature: old things are passed away; behold, all things are become new.' What does that mean?"

"I'm the wrong person to ask." He started walking again. Phoebe hurried to catch up with him.

"Well, do you know a good church where I could go and ask? Because I got a whole bunch of underlined parts in here that I can't figure out. You think maybe a preacher would know?"

"I'm afraid I can't help you." His pace quickened.

"Wait! You didn't answer my other question, about helping you. Will you let me come back to the shantytown with you?"

He stopped walking and turned to her, resting his hand on her shoulder. His eyes searched hers. "Phoebe . . . how were you wounded?" His voice was gentle, not accusing, but she was still afraid to answer, afraid that he wouldn't believe her.

"I know what everybody thinks," she finally said. "I was wounded in the back, so it must mean that I was running away. I heard all the doctors talking about me when I was lying on the stretcher. One of them said to just let me die because I must be a coward, a deserter. But I also heard you arguing with him. And then you operated on me anyway. I never thanked you for it."

"No need. I thought it should be left to judges and juries to decide guilt or innocence, not doctors. It isn't my place to convict you without a fair trial or to play God and allow you to die. But when I discovered that you were a woman, I knew you weren't a coward. You were hit in the back because you were shielding someone, weren't you?"

She nodded, wondering how he'd guessed.

"I thought so. Men are known for displaying great courage in battle. But I've seen women show the same courage protecting the people they love." The doctor was quiet for a moment, then asked, "Did he live? Your friend?"

"Yeah. He made it."

"Does he know that you lived?"

Phoebe shook her head.

"You might want to write and tell him."

"I can't. He doesn't know . . ." She let her voice trail off, unable to say the words out loud. She tilted her head up to the morning sky so her tears wouldn't fall.

"He doesn't know you're a woman?"

"No, he knows that. He found out by accident two days before I got wounded. We were together for a whole year, and I don't think he'll ever forgive me for lying to him all that time. What I meant was, he doesn't know how I feel . . . about him."

"You saved his life, Phoebe. I think you told him pretty clearly how you feel."

"Oh. I reckon I did." But she wondered if Ted would see it as an act of love or if he would be mad because a girl had saved him—again.

"Listen, thanks for your help tonight," Dr. McGrath said. "I'd be happy to let you work with me at the shantytown again, but I'm not coming back for a while. I'm being reassigned to a field hospital—" He stopped, his face brightening as if he'd suddenly had an idea. "Phoebe . . . would you like to come with me and work as a nurse?"

"You'd let me do that?"

"I think you'd make a wonderful nurse. You've been on a battlefield and probably won't be squeamish about what you'll see. And I imagine you know exactly how those wounded soldiers feel. You're already used to army life and living under primitive conditions. . . .

I'd be happy to have you work with me as a nurse."

"Really? When? Where are we going?"

He smiled faintly. "Back to Fredericksburg. The Union is going to pursue Lee's Army of Northern Virginia again now that the roads are drying out. I'm leaving tomorrow."

Phoebe was pretty sure that Ted and the rest of her regiment were already down in that area—probably in General Hooker's winter camp in Falmouth. She might get her wish to see him again. Best of all, she wouldn't have to go home and work for Mrs. Haggerty.

"I'll go with you," she said.

"Good. Show me where you're staying, and I'll come by with a carriage tomorrow morning to pick you up."

"How . . . how can I ever thank you?"

"No need. But that verse you read . . . about being a new man? If you ever find out what it means, let me know."

Philadelphia
April 1863

Julia sat at her bedroom dressing table, staring at herself in the mirror. Her mother hovered behind her, offering advice as if Julia were a small child instead of a twenty-year-old woman. "Try putting a little more rouge on your cheeks, dear. You look so pale."

Julia did as she was told, but she doubted it would help. The problem wasn't how thin and pale she'd grown from working herself to exhaustion in the past year. The problem had something to do with her eyes, as if they were reservoirs, filled with all she'd seen and experienced. Her cousin Robert had the same look in his eyes. They'd both witnessed suffering and death and couldn't forget.

"Here, put this ribbon in her hair, Inga," Julia's mother ordered. "Maybe that will brighten her face up a bit."

Julia's scalp tingled as her maid raked the brush through her thick hair. It reminded her of how it felt to have James' fingers caress her hair. Tears filled her eyes.

Her mother saw them, reflected in the mirror. "What's wrong? Is Inga brushing too hard?"

"A little," Julia lied. She wondered what her mother would say if she told her the truth—that she was remembering being kissed by a married man. That they were tears of guilt and regret. And loss.

"I don't believe you," her mother said softly. "But never mind. If you smile, people will think they're tears of joy. That you're happy to be home again."

"I am happy to be home, Mother."

It was wonderful at first, lingering in a hot bath, sleeping in a soft bed, eating rich food, and being pampered by everyone. Her beautiful dresses were always pressed and ready to wear, a carriage was waiting when she needed one, the fire in her room was always lit, her laundry fresh and clean. If nothing else, Julia had a new appreciation for the hard work that her servants did. But every time she heard news of another battle, she couldn't help thinking of the work that needed to be done, the lives that needed to be saved.

Mrs. Hoffman gently rubbed Julia's shoulder. "I wish I knew what makes you so sad."

"I wish I knew, too." A tear escaped and rolled down her cheek.

"Oh dear. Please don't start that. Your eyes will be all puffy, and we're already late."

Julia dabbed her eyes and stood. "Let's go." Her father would be waiting for them downstairs in his study, waiting to walk down the street together on this beautiful April evening to the reception being given for Robert at his parents' home. But Julia's mother shooed the maid out of the bedroom first, then stopped Julia before she could follow her through the door.

"Wait, dear. There's something more I need to say—in private." Mrs. Hoffman smoothed her skirt and tugged nervously at a sleeve, as if trying to decide how to begin. "For the past year there have been many people who haven't quite believed your father and me when we've told them where you've been and what you've been doing. It's hard for them to understand why a beautiful young woman with the best possible marriage prospects would want to lower herself in such a way. There were rumors that you'd had a breakdown and were in seclusion. And I could only thank God that you weren't in a serious relationship with anyone or there probably would have been rumors about a child."

"I'm sorry. I-I didn't realize . . ."

"Of course the congressman and his wife have vouched for your reputation, and Reverend Greene gave a glowing report on you when he returned. But please, for your reputation's sake—for your family's sake—try to behave appropriately tonight."

"What do you mean?"

"You know, dear . . . Don't go in to gory details about all your experiences, and don't try to shock everyone. The fact that you've lowered yourself to do this sort of work in the first place is shocking enough."

"But what if someone asks me what I've been doing all this time?"

"Try to describe it in . . . in a *nice* way."

Julia knew there was no nice way to describe her work. She would try, though, for her parents' sake. She would leave out the torn limbs and gaping stomach wounds and describe the compassion she tried to show, the encouragement she tried to give.

"The first patient I ever lost was Ellis Miller," she said quietly. "He was nineteen, far from home, with no mother or sister to hold him or comfort him or bathe his fever. So I took their places, holding his hand and praying with him until he passed away."

"No, no, no," Mother said, her hands fluttering. "Don't you see? It's that sort of *intimacy* that's so shocking for a single girl—bathing and hand-holding. People won't understand."

"Then I promise I won't talk about any of it."

"Well, don't be secretive. It will look as though you're hiding something if you're too close-mouthed."

"I don't know what you want from me," Julia said, exasperated. "Maybe I should stay home."

"Then the gossip will really fly! Just be yourself, Julia—your old self, the happy, good-natured Julia we all knew before the war. Remember when Caroline still lived with us? All the fun you used to have?"

Julia remembered James turning to her the night Fredericksburg was in flames and asking, *"Do you think anyone who experiences this can ever be the same?"* She wasn't the same person she'd been before the war. She could never be that person again.

"It's bad enough that poor Robert is so morose," Mother continued. "But at least people understand that he was in prison. There's a reason for it. If you love your cousin, you might try to be cheerful for his sake if not for ours."

Julia forced the picture of James from her mind and replaced it with a different one. She was on board the ship at White House Landing, listening to Sister Irene's soft voice in the darkness. *"If we obey His command to love others, our life will have meaning whether we're at a tea party or on a hospital ship."*

"You're right, Mother," Julia said, forcing a smile. "This is a wonderful occasion, and I promise I'll be the perfect daughter."

The moment she arrived at Robert's house, Julia pushed all of her disquieting thoughts aside and mingled with the other guests. She flirted and flattered and played the role of beautiful socialite perfectly, as if she had never seen a battlefield or watched men die in agony. Robert was home. She would celebrate this moment, forgetting the past, not worrying about her future. She circulated through the crowd, careful not to talk to any one person for very long, forestalling the inevitable questions about her year in Washington.

Then Julia spotted Nathaniel Greene across the room, leaning casually against a chair, a contented expression on his handsome face. The shadow of loss that had been trailing her slipped away as her long-held feelings for Nathaniel rekindled. He looked up and saw Julia watching him. And to her utter amazement, he excused himself from the conversation he was holding and hurried over to her side.

"Julia! I heard you were back. Welcome home."

"Thank you. It's good to be home."

"It seems like ages since I've seen you," he said, his eyes holding hers. "I'm still quite disappointed that we couldn't have dinner together the last time I was in Washington City. My time was so short."

"I enjoyed our carriage ride, Nathaniel. And I don't recall missing dinner at all."

"You're kind. I hope you'll let me make it up to you. Will you be staying in Philadelphia long?"

"I . . . Yes. That is . . . I won't be returning to Washington City." She felt her smile falter for the first time. Her father had taken her into his study two nights ago and made it clear that her nursing career was over. She'd had her own way for a year, he'd been indulgent, but now Julia would be expected to take courtship seriously, as she'd promised him she would. At age twenty, it was high time she was married and settled down. She wondered how Nathaniel would take this news, if he would think less of her for abandoning her nursing duties before the war ended.

"That's wonderful news," he said. "I'm glad you aren't going back." When he smiled broadly, she was astonished. "I'm well-known for being blunt, Julia. I need to say what's on my mind. Now that you're back to stay, I fear there will be a long line of gentlemen waiting to court you. May I push my way to the front of it?"

She smiled in return, and for the first time that evening it was genuine. "Nothing would please me more, Nathaniel."

Chancellorsville, Virginia
May 1863

The thunder of heavy guns shook the ground. Phoebe knelt beside the soldier and felt for his heartbeat the way that Dr. McGrath had shown her. It pulsed weakly beneath her fingers. She was all out of army-issue tourniquets, so she tied a piece of torn-up bed sheet around the man's leg, as tightly as she could, to stop the bleeding. She gave him a drink of water and some morphine for the pain.

"I'm real sorry, but you'll have to wait in line for surgery," she told him. "It might be a while. Can you stand it?" He could only moan in reply.

Phoebe looked up. The stretcher-bearers were hurrying toward her, bringing more casualties. "Hang on," she told him. "Don't give up hope."

It was different being on this side of the war. It sounded just the same—the rumble of cannon, the rattle of gunfire, the blood-chilling Rebel scream. And the smoke and the moans and the heart-pounding rush of fear were all the same. But now Phoebe was stopping blood, not shedding it. She never wanted to kill a man again.

Phoebe and the other nurses and doctors had followed at the rear of General Hooker's troops as they'd marched west from their winter quarters at Falmouth. They'd crossed the river a few miles upstream, then circled back to attack the Rebels on their side of the river. The battles had been fierce for the past few days, her own work unending. Yet for all the vicious fighting, she had just heard the upsetting news that the Union troops were pulling back, giving up in defeat. It was what they'd done when she'd fought on the Peninsula with Ted.

Phoebe braced herself as the orderlies ran toward her with another stretcher. Her old regiment was fighting out there, and some of these soldiers might be men she knew. She always scanned the wounded men's faces, but she knew before they even got close that the man they were bringing to her was too tall to be Ted. His feet hung off the end of the stretcher.

"Set him down right here," she said. "I'll tend him." She crouched beside the man and dipped her cloth into the bucket of water to wash his wounds. But when she saw his familiar face and wiry yellow hair, the shock was so great she lost her balance and toppled to one side, nearly upsetting the bucket.

"Willard!"

Panic and fear swept through Phoebe at the sight of her brother's ashen face. She quickly scrambled to her knees and bent over him, gently slapping his cheeks and calling his name. "Willard . . . Willard, can you hear me? Come on, say something!"

He groaned and began to cough, bringing up blood. She felt for his pulse, her hands trembling, then looked him over and saw that he had a chest wound. His uniform jacket was drenched with blood. *God! Oh, God!*

"Hang on, Willard," she said, struggling to her feet. "I'll be right back."

The doctors were operating outside on a table made from a plank and four flour barrels. Phoebe stood back and waited anxiously, not daring to look as they finished amputating a man's arm.

Then she hurried over before they had a chance to call for another patient.

"Dr. McGrath, I need you to come!" she begged, tugging his sleeve. "It's my brother Willard."

"He'll have to wait his turn," one of the army doctors said. "No favoritism."

James ignored the man. "Where is he, Phoebe? Show me."

He followed her back to where Willard lay and knelt beside him, feeling for his pulse. When Dr. McGrath gently unbuttoned Willard's jacket and shirt and peeled them back, Phoebe saw for herself how terrible his wound was. The hole beneath his breastbone was the size of a fist. His abdomen looked large and swollen. James pressed on it lightly, then let go, and Willard startled with pain.

"Help me roll him over a little," James said. Willard cried out when they moved him. James lifted the back of Willard's jacket to look, then laid him flat again. "Do you have any morphine?" he asked Phoebe.

She handed him a container of powder, and James sprinkled it into the wound. He stood, motioning for Phoebe to walk with him.

"I'm sorry, Phoebe. Whatever hit him went all the way through. There's major damage to his liver, signs of peritonitis. I don't know how he's still alive." He stopped walking and turned to face her, resting his hands on her shoulders. "I know how difficult it is when it's your own family and there's nothing you can do. . . ." He looked away for a moment, then met her gaze again. "Are you going to be all right?"

She nodded. "I knew it wasn't good. He was coughing blood. I just needed to make sure." She sounded much braver than she felt.

"Give him as much morphine as he needs." The doctor squeezed her shoulders, then hurried back to the operating table.

Phoebe sat down beside her brother again and carefully lifted his head into her lap. He was sweating and pale. She bathed his face and neck with water, calling his name. "Come on, Willard, don't be ornery now. Wake up and say something. It's me . . . your sister, Ike."

He slowly opened his eyes. "Ike?"

"Yeah, you remember me, don't you? The sister you left behind?" She tried to smile.

" 'Course I do. But you ain't supposed to be here. . . . Thought I was seeing things."

"No, it's really me. I'm a nurse, Will. I'm working for the army, just like you."

He shook his head from side to side, his face angry. "Not supposed to be here. Supposed to be home with Miz Haggerty. Can't you ever do what you're told?"

"Not unless you and Junior sit on me and make me. Besides, the army pays me more than Mrs. Haggerty ever would of. They give me food and a place to stay, too."

He closed his eyes, his anger gone. "Well, I guess that's okay, then. You're earning your keep."

"Want some water?" She held the dipper to his lips and offered him another drink. He coughed most of it back up along with more blood. She wiped his face again. It was as white as flour. "You hear anything about Junior and Jack?" she asked.

"Jack got hit in the leg last year. Took him to some hospital. Junior's okay."

"I'll be glad when this war ends and we can get our farm back from Jeb, won't you? I hope he ain't made a mess of it by now or worked those sorry horses of ours half to death. It'll be nice being all together again, won't it?"

Willard nodded. "You look different . . . wearing a dress. Remind me of Ma. . . ." His breathing was becoming more ragged. He needed to gulp air between every few words. Phoebe knew he was slipping away, but she wanted to keep him talking, keep him with her for just a little longer.

"I can't remember our ma at all, can you, Will?"

"She was pretty, like you. . . . Used to sit . . . on my bed . . . stroke my hair . . . like you're doing . . . until I fell asleep. You have her name."

"Her name was Phoebe?"

"Yeah. Didn't you know?"

"Nobody ever told me. You all never talked about her much."

"Pa took to calling you Ike . . . after she died."

When he started to close his eyes, Phoebe said, "Hey, did you hear the news? They're gonna make us a brand-new state next month. They say that the whole western part of Virginia decided not to rebel, so they're making it into a new state. Bone Hollow is still in the Union. Ain't that good news, Will? Maybe you or Junior can run for governor."

"I'm not gonna make it, am I? That's why they ain't operating."

"Sure you are. You got to wait your turn is all."

"You're lying, Ike. I always knew . . . when you was lying."

"Am not."

He groped for her hand and gripped it in his own. "Who's gonna take care of you . . . if none of us . . . make it back?"

"I reckon I can take care of myself," she said, biting her lip.

He smiled faintly. "Yeah, you always could. Don't you know . . . a man likes to take care of a woman?"

The tears she'd been holding back finally started to fall as she thought of Ted. "No, Willard, I didn't know that. Nobody ever told me."

"Phoebe. . . ?" he said weakly. "I'm sorry we ran off . . . and left you all alone."

"That's okay. I forgive you."

But as her tears fell on his pale, still face, she didn't know if her brother had heard her or not.

Chapter Twenty

Philadelphia,
June 1863

Julia stood alone in the vast exhibition hall and gazed at the tattered remnants of the Christian Commission's fair. The crowds that had filled the building for the past three days had all gone home, the patriotic bunting drooped from the rafters, and a lone worker swept the littered floor with a broom. It was late. The fair was over. It was past time for Julia to go home. They'd collected tons of food and clothing for the comfort and relief of soldiers, and thousands of dollars in donations to purchase Bibles, religious tracts, and medical supplies for the Commission to distribute. She'd worked hard to make the fair a success, and it had filled the void in her life for the past month. But what would she do now that the fair was over?

"Julia?" Nathaniel's voice echoed in the deserted hall. "Don't tell me you're still here? Do you need a ride home?" He jogged up the long aisle toward her, looking as fresh and buoyant as if it were morning, not late at night on the last day of the fair. She marveled at how Nathaniel's "causes" always seemed to energize him, not deplete him.

"No, my coach is outside," she said. "I was just leaving. Why are you still here?"

"We were counting the donations. You won't believe it—more than twelve thousand dollars so far! What an enormous success!"

Nathaniel was beaming. "And we owe it all to you, Julia."

"I hardly think that's true. There were hundreds of people involved."

"But you organized all this. And you're the one who convinced some very wealthy donors to make contributions. None of the Christian Commission's other fairs have been as successful as this one."

"That's wonderful news. I'm glad it went so well."

"And I'm glad we had a chance to work together for these past few weeks." His voice grew softer. He stood very close to her. "Julia, this is how I long imagined it would be, having a partner and a helpmeet who would aid me in my work."

She felt a prickle of irritation, like a stone in her shoe. "I consider this *my* work, too."

"I know," he said, smiling. "That's what's so wonderful about it. You're willing to make my causes your very own."

He still wasn't getting it. Julia opened her mouth to explain to him that she would have worked just as hard for the Christian Commission if he hadn't been involved, but before she could speak, he did.

"You worked so tirelessly for me on this fair. And you were always so willing to do any task I gave you. You truly went the extra mile—even now, staying around to help until the very end. You're so hardworking and generous and selfless—"

"Please stop. I am not all those things."

"Did I mention modest, too?" he asked, grinning. Nathaniel's charm and natural charisma added to his enormous attractiveness. He was a godly man, a passionate preacher. Julia did not feel worthy of his flattery.

"I'm human, Nathaniel. I make mistakes like everyone else. I sometimes need forgiveness."

"Of course. We all do." He was flying high on the fair's success and doing his best to lift her up with him. But the loss that had shadowed her for so long seemed to drape across her shoulders, weighing her down. "Julia, what's wrong?" he asked.

"It's hard to live up to your opinion of me. I can't spend my life on a pedestal. One wrong move and I'll fall, and then you'll see me as I truly am."

"I have seen you as you truly are, on that hospital ship. And I never saw a kinder, lovelier woman. You're so different from all the other young ladies at church. None of them would ever be willing to make all the sacrifices you've made to become a nurse—to work so selflessly amidst such horror and despair. You are a beautiful person, Julia. I don't understand why it upsets you to hear that."

"I miss working at the hospital." The simple truth surprised her. "Charity work just isn't the same." She remembered the night she had helped James operate, the many hours they'd spent together on the wards, battling to save lives. Her eyes filled with tears.

Nathaniel studied her for a long moment, his eyes more gray than blue in the dim light. "Will you marry me, Julia?" he said suddenly. "We could spend our lifetime working together this way. I know we haven't courted for very long, but I've found the woman I want to marry, and I don't want to lose you. Please say you will."

Julia imagined herself working alongside Nathaniel as she had worked beside James and said, "Yes. I'll marry you."

Two years ago, after her behavior at Bull Run, she never would have believed that Nathaniel would ask. And now he had. Her life with him would have purpose and meaning. She would be more than the porcelain doll on a shelf that Hiram Stone had described. She would be able to forget James, pushing all her memories of him into the past.

Nathaniel smiled broadly at her reply, then sobered. He was going to kiss her. Julia held her breath, her heart racing as she looked up into his handsome face. He rested his hands lightly on her arms and closed his eyes as he leaned toward her. His lips pressed against hers for a few seconds, then he pulled back to look at her.

The kiss had been prim and stiff, as if Nathaniel were pressing a brass stamp into soft wax to seal a letter. It seemed more a sign of ownership than passion. Julia remembered James' kiss and felt a loss. She longed to put her hands in Nathaniel's fair hair and pull him toward her, to feel the warmth of his face against hers, his arms surrounding her, holding her close. But he took a step back.

"I'll need to ask your father's permission before we can make it official," he said. "And I want to buy you a ring."

He reached for her hand and held it stiffly, as if holding a china teacup. His fingers were cool. Again she thought of James, of the tender gesture she'd seen so many times as he rested his hand on a patient's brow. James had held her face in his hands with that same tenderness the night he'd kissed her. His hands had been warm.

"And I would like to arrange for my father to meet you," Nathaniel continued.

Julia shook herself. She had just accepted a proposal of marriage from Nathaniel, the man she had loved for all these years. Why on earth was she thinking of another man's kiss, another man's touch? A married man.

"I can only afford two or three servants on my minister's salary," Nathaniel said. "I'm afraid ours will be a much simpler life than what you're accustomed to. But I think I know you well enough to know that an extravagant lifestyle doesn't matter to you."

"It doesn't," she replied, dazed.

"I'll make an appointment to talk with your father as soon as possible . . . if that's okay?"

"Of course."

"I hope you don't want a long engagement, Julia. I believe that once you find the person who's right for you, there's no sense in waiting. And I think ours is a partnership made in heaven, don't you?"

She opened her mouth to speak but nothing came out. She couldn't comprehend that the man she'd long dreamed of had just asked her to marry him.

"Julia, you're speechless. I hope it's with happiness?"

"Yes," she whispered. "It is."

She wanted him to kiss her again, to erase forever the memory of James' kiss with a memorable one of his own. Instead, Nathaniel took her arm and led her toward the door.

"You must be exhausted from working these last three days. I know I am. I want you to go home now, dear, and get some rest. Let's find your coachman."

Alone in her carriage, Julia realized that Nathaniel had never once said, "I love you."

"General Lee and his Rebels have crossed the border into Pennsylvania," Julia's father told her the next morning.

"Pennsylvania! They're *here*?"

"I'm afraid so." He sat at the breakfast table, frowning as he read the morning newspaper. His food sat untouched in front of him. Julia had picked up an empty plate to fill with food from the silver chargers on the buffet, but she set it down again.

"How close are they?"

"The paper says near Chambersburg. That's about one hundred and fifty miles from here. Apparently the Rebels are pillaging the countryside for food as they go. Disgraceful behavior!"

"Our Union soldiers are no better, Daddy. I saw what they did to Fredericksburg, Virginia, with my own eyes. It wasn't even for food. They were just looting and destroying for the fun of it." Julia also remembered the vicious cannonading that the town had endured and how she had pictured her own city being bombarded that way. "Do you think the Rebels will come as far as Philadelphia?"

"No one knows where they're headed, but it does look as though there will be fighting on Union soil soon. They're not too far from Harrisburg." He folded the paper and laid it beside his plate, then stood. "God help us. General Meade had better do a better job of stopping Lee than Hooker or Burnside or McClellan did."

All thoughts of her engagement to Nathaniel took second place in Julia's mind for the next few days as the citizens of Philadelphia held their breath, waiting for news of the Confederate invasion. Nor did Nathaniel have time to approach Julia's father and make his proposal official as he and his Commission volunteers prepared to ship the goods they had just collected to needy Union soldiers.

On the morning of July 3, Julia and her father read news of a horrific series of battles that had taken place near the little-known Pennsylvania town of Gettysburg. Alongside the reports, the paper printed an urgent plea for volunteer physicians and nurses to help cope with the enormous casualties, estimated to be in the tens of thousands.

Julia didn't ask her father for permission to go. As soon as he left for work, she hurried down to the Christian Commission's offices to find Nathaniel. He would likely answer the plea for volunteers and deliver the badly needed supplies to Gettysburg himself. She found him hard at work, his sleeves rolled up like a laborer, loading crates, barrels, and the Commission's tenting equipment onto a hired dray to transport them to the railroad station.

"I'm glad you've come," Nathaniel said when he saw her. He set the box he carried onto the back of the wagon and dusted his hands on his trousers. "I was afraid I'd have to write you a note. I'm leaving shortly for Gettysburg."

"I thought you might be. I'm going, too."

He glanced around as if fearing someone might have overheard, then pulled Julia inside to his office. "I can't let you do that. It isn't proper. If we were already married it would be appropriate to have you come along and help me, but we're not even officially engaged."

"I'm not going to help *you*," she said impatiently. "I'm trained as a nurse. They're calling for volunteers. I'm going to help care for the wounded."

"No. I can't allow it."

Julia stared at him, dumbstruck by his refusal. Why was he forbidding her to do the very thing he'd once claimed to admire? And what right did he have to forbid her to go in the first place?

"You are not my husband yet," she said, barely controlling her temper. "It isn't up to you to grant me permission. I'm going to Gettysburg, Nathaniel. My question is, may I travel with the Commission's female volunteers, or should I look for another way to get there?"

He took a long moment to answer, and she knew he was battling his anger, too. "All of the Commission's female volunteers are either married or widowed. You're single."

Ever since Nathaniel had proposed, Julia wondered if she should confess her original motives to him and admit that she had lied about being married in order to become a nurse. Seeing his reaction now and his puzzling opposition, she knew that confessing would be a mistake. She wanted to go and couldn't risk him stopping her.

"I know I'm single," she replied. "I was single when I worked on the battlefields at Antietam and Fredericksburg, and I was single when you and I worked together on the hospital ship on the Peninsula. How is this any different?"

"Because you're going to be my wife. I feel protective of you and your reputation."

"Are you sure you don't mean *your* reputation?"

She could tell by Nathaniel's reaction that her outspokenness had stunned him. She wondered if he would change his mind about marrying her. She thought it ironic that she had become a nurse to win his admiration and now her commitment to nursing might cause her to lose him. She pushed aside her anger to plead with him.

"Listen, I feel called to go. My work is important to me, just as your work is important to you. The fact that I am single, with no husband or children to bind me, is what gives me the freedom to serve those in need. Please, Nathaniel, let's not argue about it. May I travel with the Commission, or should I look for another means of getting there?"

He looked away, his face cold. "Since you've reminded me that I'm not yet in a position to dictate to you, then I must ask if you have your father's permission."

"He knows you're a trustworthy man. And the Christian Commission's reputation is well-known. There's no question of impropriety."

"Then I guess I have no choice," he said stiffly. "Our train to Hanover leaves in about three hours. Now please excuse me. I have a lot of work to do." He turned to leave, but she held his arm, stopping him.

"Are you angry with me?"

"A little," he said, not meeting her gaze. "But I'll get over it."

Gettysburg
July 1863

Phoebe lifted the soldier's head and held the tin cup of wine to his lips. "Here you go, see if you can swallow a little bit of this. I know you're hurting, and I wish we had something stronger, but this is all we got for now."

"Thanks," he whispered.

"You want a little more? Is there anything else I can do for you?" When he shook his head, Phoebe laid him down again and moved to her next patient. "How you doing? Can you swallow a little wine? I know it ain't much of a breakfast, but it might ease your pain a little."

"Breakfast? Is it morning?" he asked.

"Sure is. Sun's just about to peek above that hill over there. See how pretty the sky looks?" It was the third sunrise Phoebe had watched with very little sleep in between. She didn't know how long she could keep on working like this, but with nursing help in short supply, she knew she had to try.

"Lift me up so I can see," the man begged.

"You sure?" she asked. "I don't want to hurt you none."

"Don't worry," he said, grimacing in pain. "I know I'm dying. It's probably the last sunrise I'll ever see."

"You can't lose hope," she said as she helped him sit. "We're doing everything we can to see that you make it."

But helping him and the thousands of others just like him was an overwhelming task. Phoebe and the other nurses and doctors had arrived at the battlefield outside Gettysburg after the fighting had already begun. There had been no time to set up a proper field hospital or operating facilities, nor were there enough medical supplies to meet the enormous need. As General Meade marched his army north to chase Lee's, he had ordered the wagon trains to carry ammunition and military equipment instead of medical supplies. The wounded soldiers had started to arrive before Phoebe and the other nurses had time to unpack what little they had. And with no tents for a field hospital, they'd been forced to care for the wounded in the open, outside the farmhouse where Dr. McGrath and the other surgeons were operating.

Phoebe left the soldier to enjoy what might well be his last sunrise and moved to the next man. When she saw that he was a Rebel soldier, she hesitated. All the wounded men had been mixed together, both Rebels and Yankees, but they were too badly injured to fight each other. Phoebe couldn't forget that a Rebel shell had killed her brother. Another one had wounded her. She could still feel the ache in her shoulder as she knelt and lifted the Rebel's head.

"You want a little sip of wine?"

He nodded and drank a few gulps. "We lost the battle yesterday, didn't we?" he asked as she laid him down again. "I'm a prisoner."

She'd been told that the Rebels had retreated across the Potomac during the night after yesterday's battle. Three days of terrible fighting had left thousands of men on both sides wounded and slaughtered. The Confederate soldiers who were too badly injured to travel had been left behind. Many Confederate surgeons had stayed behind with them to care for their men.

"This here is a field hospital," she told him. "I'm a nurse, not a prison guard. And don't ask me nothing about any battles. I'm too busy taking care of folks to keep score."

She moved to her next patient, also a Rebel. As she worked, she was gradually aware that one of the Confederate doctors was watching her. He was an unusually tall, gangly young fellow with a drooping mustache and several days' stubble on his chin. She'd seen him moving among the men, working day and night like all the other doctors, never looking to see what uniform a man wore. He was sitting beneath a tree just a few yards away from her.

She glanced up at him and their eyes met. Hers narrowed. "You checking up on me?" she asked. "Making sure I don't poison them or something?"

He laughed, and the sound was as loose and free as his long-limbed body. "No, ma'am. You don't look like the sort of lady who'd do a thing like that. But I *was* watching you, I confess. And I reckon I owe you an explanation why."

"You don't owe me nothing," she said, looking away. As she started to move to the next patient, the doctor held out a tin cup.

"Mind if I have a little drop of that? I'd prefer coffee this time of day, but I'll take whatever I can get."

Phoebe walked down the row to where he sat and poured from the bottle she carried. She'd been told it was communion wine taken from a nearby church.

"Whoa! That's plenty. Can't be getting drunk, now, can I? . . .

Wait," he said when she started to move away. "I was listening to you talk to the men. You sound just like the folks back home. I confess I was feeling a little homesick, especially for a woman's voice, so that's why I was watching you. Just wanted to think about home a little."

"I ain't a Confederate like you," she said coldly. But she had noticed his familiar drawl. After living amongst northerners for nearly two years, she'd grown used to the funny way they talked. This doctor's voice reminded her of home.

"No, ma'am. I knew you weren't a Confederate," he said. "Where are you from, if you don't mind my asking?"

"I do mind."

He laughed again. "That's okay, I don't blame you. This war has us all suspicious of each other, I reckon. I'm from Berkeley County, Virginia—not all that far from here, truth be told. Just across the Pennsylvania border. You probably never heard of my little hamlet, but the closest town of any size is Martinsburg."

He lived in the next county over from Phoebe, not far from Bone Hollow. "Berkeley County ain't part of Virginia no more," she told him. "They just made a whole chunk of Virginia into a new state."

"That's what I heard. But I haven't been home since the war started."

"You joined the Confederacy," she said bluntly.

"Well, yes, ma'am, I guess I did. But it wasn't so much a matter of me joining them as them conscripting me. I'd just finished studying medicine in Charlottesville, and I was apprenticed to a doctor there. They needed doctors when the war started, so they grabbed me. How about you? How'd you get here? Followed your husband, I suppose?"

"I ain't married."

"Now, ma'am, I have a hard time believing that. Pretty gal like you?"

"Are you making fun of me?"

He looked truly surprised. "No, ma'am! I'm real partial to yellow hair, and yours is about the prettiest color yellow I've ever seen. Reminds me of corn tassels. You're a strong gal and a fine nurse.

I've watched you working. These southern belles who like to faint at the drop of a hat leave me cold. . . . Ma'am?" he said when she started to move away again. "Won't you please tell me your name, so I don't have to keep calling you ma'am?"

She hesitated. "It's Phoebe."

"Mine's Daniel . . . Daniel Morrison." He stuck out his hand to shake hers. Phoebe found herself warming to him against her will.

"You got a wife and children waiting for you, Dr. Morrison?"

"No, the gals back home never did see much to like about me," he said, laughing. "They said I looked like a bag of bones all strung together every which way. Got no social graces to speak of, either, because I always had my nose in a book. And a country doctor from Berkeley County can't offer a gal much in the way of finery and things."

"You think you'll go back home when the war's over?" she asked.

He sighed. "Sometimes it's hard to imagine that this war ever will be over, isn't it? But, yeah, I'd like to go back to Berkeley County and be a doctor. That's all I ever wanted. How about you?"

"I haven't had much time to think about it," she said, shrugging. "I guess I won't have much choice except to go home."

He smiled. "Well, when you get there, I'll bet some lucky fella's gonna snap you up for his wife right quick."

Phoebe stared hard at him to see if he was poking fun, but she saw only admiration in his eyes. He was looking at her the way a man looks at a woman—something she'd never experienced before. He smiled shyly as she continued to study him, then slowly rose to his feet.

"Thanks for the wine. I sure did enjoy talking with you, Phoebe. You take care, now."

The first thing Julia noticed when the Christian Commission arrived in Gettysburg was the stench. The dead couldn't be buried fast enough, and the corpses of fallen army horses lay strewn on the ground, as well, bloating in the sun. Volunteers scattered chloride of lime everywhere, but it was a feeble gesture in the heat of summer.

The smell of death and decay permeated every breath of air Julia took.

Improvised field hospitals had been set up wherever there was a need and a space—in houses, barns, and churches, even beneath covered bridges. Julia's task was to drive around in the hired wagon with the other female volunteers and distribute food and medical supplies where they were needed. But she had prepared a satchel for herself with clean bandages and iodine and medicinal brandy, and she was prepared to leave the group and stay to help wherever extra nurses were needed.

One of the first farms they came upon on the outskirts of Gettysburg presented a now-familiar sight. Hundreds of badly injured men spilled from every shed and farm building, lying scattered across the yard beneath the trees. As her wagon pulled to a stop, the farmer's wife came forward to tell them that the biggest need was for food and for help feeding all the men. Julia set to work with the others, preparing to distribute the soup and bread they'd brought.

She hadn't worked for very long when an army doctor suddenly emerged from the farmhouse shouting, "I need a nurse! Quickly!"

"I'm a trained nurse," Julia said. "I've just arrived. How can I help?"

"Come inside. Bring your things and some food if you have it."

Julia grabbed her satchel and followed him inside, her heart pounding with both readiness and fear.

"One of our surgeons has collapsed," he told her as they walked through an enclosed back porch leading to the kitchen. "We carried him into the parlor, and we need someone to attend him while we continue our work."

He pointed to an open door off the kitchen, which led to a small sitting room. But first Julia would have to walk through the kitchen, which was being used as an operating room. The orderlies had carried in an injured soldier ahead of her, and he cried out in pain as they transferred him to the makeshift operating table. Julia looked away to avoid seeing his mutilated leg. Remnants of clothing and severed limbs lay piled in a corner near the hearth. There was blood everywhere. The wooden floor was slick with it. She closed her eyes, pausing for a moment.

"Are you all right?" the doctor asked.

"Yes . . . Do you know what's wrong with this surgeon? Why he collapsed?"

"Exhaustion. He's been working for three days without stopping. I don't believe he's eaten anything or slept in all that time. He collapsed a few moments ago, probably from fatigue and hunger."

Julia got as far as the parlor doorway and froze. The doctor lay on the sofa, unconscious. He had one arm slung across his eyes as if shielding them, but even with most of his face covered, she recognized him immediately—James McGrath. She wanted to back away, to run from the farmhouse.

"Shouldn't you just let him sleep?" she asked.

"Of course. But you must get him to eat something first. He's one of our best surgeons. We need to get him back on his feet soon, or countless men will die." The doctor left Julia and returned to his work.

She stared at James for a long moment, unable to move. There were thousands of wounded soldiers she could be helping, lying in homes and churches and barns all around Gettysburg. And there must be hundreds and hundreds of doctors and volunteer nurses, as well. What strange twist of fate had thrown her and James McGrath together again?

Julia knew that she shouldn't stay here alone with him. One of the married volunteers could just as easily feed him. She should go back outside and get someone else to do this. But before she could leave, there was a commotion in the kitchen as the wounded soldier began screaming. Something crashed to the floor. James moaned at the sound and tried to bury his face in the sofa. She knew about his headaches, knew how light and sound intensified his pain—and she knew she was meant to be here.

Julia immediately closed the door to the kitchen behind her, then crossed the room to close all the curtains. When the room was as dark as she could make it, she pulled a wad of bandages from her satchel, dampened it with cold water from her canteen, then lifted James' arm away from his face and covered his eyes with the cloth. She wet a second cloth and laid it across his forehead and used cotton lint to help plug his ears. Then she knelt beside the sofa to decide what to do next.

He was filthy from having collapsed onto the kitchen floor. She soaked another cloth, rubbed it with the bar of soap she carried, and cleaned the blood and filth off his hair and face. She found a fresh bruise where he'd bumped his head when he'd fallen, and she dabbed the cut with iodine. When his face was clean, she tied a strip of cloth around his head to hold the thick compress in place over his eyes in case he rolled over.

His shirt had to go next. It was disgusting—stiff in some places, sticky in others, and soaked through to his skin with three days' worth of blood. James remained asleep as she gently rolled him over and stripped off his ruined shirt. It surprised her to discover that beneath his disheveled, ill-fitting clothes he was lean and well-built, with a strong torso and muscled arms. The hair on his chest was ginger-colored like his beard.

Julia had cleaned the blood off other wounded men countless times, but she slowly became aware of the impropriety of what she was doing as she worked on James McGrath. An unmarried woman simply shouldn't be performing such duties. It was what everyone—her father, Dorothea Dix, Nathaniel—had been telling her all along. She hadn't worried much about her reputation when she was in Washington pretending to be married to Robert, but she was no longer pretending. The other Commission volunteers knew she was single. If one of them were to walk into the darkened sitting room right now and see her alone with a half-naked man, Julia's reputation would be ruined. So would her future as a minister's wife.

And there was something more. She was no longer able to deny the strong attraction she felt toward James McGrath, an attraction that was very wrong.

Julia was suddenly in a hurry to finish. She quickly washed his bloodstained hands. She noticed that they were bare, but it took a moment for the truth to register—James wasn't wearing his wedding ring. She dropped his left hand in shock.

What did it mean? Had he removed the ring so he could operate? But Julia had assisted him with surgery in Fredericksburg and he hadn't removed it then. She scrambled to her feet. She felt close to panic and didn't know why. She needed to leave. But she hadn't fed him yet, and that was what the other doctor had specifically asked her to do.

Unwilling to go through the kitchen again, Julia found the front door to the farmhouse and hurried around to where her fellow volunteers were distributing soup. She silently took a tin bowl and spoon and was about to go back inside when one of the other ladies stopped her.

"You look quite pale, Julia. Are you all right? Is it horribly gruesome in there?"

She grasped the excuse like a lifeline. "Yes. They're performing surgery. Please warn everyone to stay outside."

"What about you? Can you stand it?"

"I'm nearly finished."

Julia returned through the front door and latched it from the inside. She set the bowl on a table near the sofa and then lifted James' head, propping him up with pillows. "Dr. McGrath . . ." she murmured, shaking his shoulder to wake him. "Doctor, you need to eat something."

It took several minutes to stir him into consciousness. He moaned and groped with one hand to feel the compress covering his eyes.

"Leave it there," she said, pulling his hand away. "Your hands are trembling. I'll feed you." She breathed a sigh of relief when he didn't argue. Neither of them spoke while she spooned soup into his mouth. "Would you like more?" she asked when it was gone.

"No," he said with a weary groan. "I have to go back to work. Bring me some strong coffee."

"All right," she said, removing the cushions from behind his head. "I'll be right back with some. Rest for another minute."

But James quickly passed out from exhaustion again, as she suspected he would. Julia removed his shoes and socks, then gently brushed his hair off his forehead.

"If you're seeking atonement, James McGrath, you've paid for it," she murmured. "You've been to hell."

For the next two hours, Julia helped the other women distribute soup to the wounded men outside. When everyone had their fill, they loaded the wagon to move on to the next field hospital. Extra nurses were needed here, but Julia knew this was not the place where she should stay and work.

As they drove past the farmhouse, she caught a glimpse of Dr. McGrath standing on the back porch, calling for another patient. His clean shirt was already splattered with blood.

Phoebe stood outside the farmhouse, eating a slice of bread that the lady volunteers had left behind for the doctors and nurses. The sun was going down, and she couldn't remember eating much all day. It tasted like a bite of heaven.

"Phoebe?"

She turned and saw Dr. McGrath leaning against the back door.

"Is there more of that bread somewhere?" he asked.

"Here," she said, handing him a fresh loaf. "They left a whole bunch. Help yourself."

"Thanks." He tore off a piece and chewed slowly, gazing into the distance at the farmer's trampled wheat field and the low hills beyond. Phoebe thought she'd never seen a man look so weary and still be standing.

"We're leaving tomorrow," he said after swallowing. "Our orders just came. General Meade is going to pursue Lee's army, and since he's expecting a fight, he has decided to take most of the army's surgeons along. Only about a hundred or so will stay behind."

"That's not very many doctors for all these men."

"No. It's not. They're saying there might be as many as twenty thousand casualties here."

Phoebe shook her head, unable to comprehend such a number. She knew that her old regiment had taken part in the fighting at Gettysburg, and she longed to search among the dead and wounded for Ted. But with so many thousands, it was like searching for a needle in a haystack. It had been nearly a year since she'd last seen Ted. She wondered if she would ever see him again.

"I'll leave it up to you to decide if you want to come with me tomorrow or stay here to help," Dr. McGrath said. "Once the rail lines are restored, the injured will be evacuated to Baltimore and

Washington. You can work at Fairfield Hospital if you'd like."

Phoebe thought about it for a moment. She was afraid that the other doctors would never let an uneducated backwoods gal like her be their nurse. "No, I'll go with you, Dr. McGrath."

He nodded absently and tore off another piece of bread.

"Some Confederate doctors stayed behind with their men," Phoebe said after a moment. "What will happen to them? Are they prisoners now?"

"I don't know." He shrugged, then went back inside.

The summer sky seemed to stay light a long time after sunset as Phoebe stood in the yard, thinking about Dr. Daniel Morrison from Berkeley County. There were a lot of things in her little Bible that she still didn't understand, but there was no mistaking the Lord's command to love your enemies. She sighed and picked up one of the loaves of bread, knowing where she was most likely to find the Rebel doctor.

"Dr. Morrison?"

He had been kneeling beside a patient, but he quickly stood at the sound of her voice and swept off his hat. "Evening, ma'am."

She had to look up to see his face. "I thought you might like some bread before it was all gone."

"Thank you kindly. Will you have some with me?"

"No, go ahead. I already ate mine." She fidgeted awkwardly, staring down at her shoes. "I'm leaving tomorrow," she finally said. "I've come to say good-bye . . . and to tell you that I'm sorry I wasn't very friendly yesterday. It's just that . . . the Rebels killed my brother Willard. I know it wasn't your fault. I got no right to hate you for it."

"That's okay, Phoebe. I understand."

She exhaled in relief. "I was also wondering what was gonna happen to you. Are the Yankees gonna let you go when you're finished here, or will you have to go to prison?"

He shrugged. "They haven't told me yet. I hear there are several thousand wounded Rebel prisoners here in Gettysburg besides my own men. Guess if I have a choice, I'll stay with them."

"Well, I wish you luck, Doctor."

"Thanks. It has been a pleasure making your acquaintance." He stuck out his hand to shake hers. "If you're ever in Berkeley County when this war's over, you come see me, okay?"

She nodded and then looked up at him again. "My last name's Bigelow. I'm from Bone Hollow. It's right next door in Morgan County."

He smiled broadly. "It sure is. Maybe our paths will cross again, Phoebe Bigelow—God willing."

Julia walked down the long path between the rows of tents, searching for Nathaniel. The July afternoon was sweltering, and she unfastened the top button of her dress as she walked, then rolled up the long sleeves. Her mother would scold her for exposing her fair skin to the sun, but it was impossible to carry a parasol while nursing sick patients. Better to let her skin darken than to faint from the heat.

She finally found Nathaniel crouched beside the last tent, pounding in a stake. She paused to watch him. His bare forearms were tanned from the summer sun and dappled with freckles; his golden hair was bleached a shade lighter than usual. He stood and grabbed the tent pole in his fist, shaking it slightly to test it. He was a fine-looking man.

"Nathaniel!" she called.

He looked up and smiled when he saw her. She had scarcely talked to him in the three weeks they'd been in Gettysburg. The Commission's male and female volunteers had been housed at separate tent sites, and she and Nathaniel had worked at different tasks during the day. When the badly needed medical tents had finally arrived, he and the other men labored for a week to set them up. The new field hospital had six rows of tents with four hundred tents in each row. Each tent could hold twelve patients.

The wounded had been collected from temporary hospitals all over Gettysburg, including the church where Julia had been nursing. The line of stretchers was a mile and a half long as volunteers transported the soldiers to the new hospital.

"I got your message," she said. "You wanted to see me?"

"We're finished here," he said, gesturing to the tent. "Our group is returning to Philadelphia tomorrow. Can you help me spread the word among all the ladies so everyone will be ready to leave?"

Julia had already accepted an assignment at the new hospital, caring for two dozen gravely ill men. She had been dreading the day she would have to tell Nathaniel, unsure of his reaction. "I'm not going with you," she said quietly.

He folded his arms across his chest, his face turned to stone. "Don't do this to me, Julia."

"I need to stay. There is still a terrible shortage of doctors and nurses. I can help save lives. I know how to dress wounds and which warning signs to watch for. There are so few experienced nurses. I'm needed here."

"You came with the Commission. It's my responsibility to see you safely home."

"And what will I do once I'm there? Did you ever stop and think about that? How can I sit around sipping afternoon tea when people are dying?"

"Your father entrusted you to my care. What am I supposed to tell him?"

"The truth—that I defied both of you and stayed behind. I'll write him a note if you'd like."

He ran his fingers through his thick hair and exhaled angrily. "You're making a mistake. Scripture clearly says that we are to honor our father and mother—"

"Stop it, Nathaniel. You know as well as I do that the Lord's greatest commandments are to love God and love our neighbor. I'd be committing a much greater sin if I turned my back on men in need so that I could sit in a comfortable church pew in Philadelphia."

Nathaniel paced angrily in front of the empty tent. He looked as though he wanted to smash something. "You force me to have such conflicting feelings, Julia. I admire you so much. I don't know how you do this work. I can barely stand to see these pitiful souls. And the smell . . . What you do is remarkable." He stopped pacing and turned to her, pleading with her. "But you're going to be my wife. Can you understand that I feel protective of you? That I want you to be safe and sheltered?"

"Yes, of course I do." She rested her hand on his arm to soothe him. "But I'm quite safe here. There are other Christian Commission volunteers from other cities who are staying longer—"

"That's not the point," he said, shrugging her hand away. "I know that our engagement isn't official. I have no right to demand that you return to Philadelphia with me. I understand why you want to stay. . . ."

"Then why are you so angry with me?"

He began pacing again. "This isn't easy to say . . . without sounding like I'm . . ." He exhaled angrily.

Julia had heard his blunt opinion of her two years ago after Bull Run. Anything he said now couldn't possibly be as devastating as that had been. "Just tell me," she said.

He hesitated. "You are a very strong-willed woman, Julia."

She almost smiled. It felt like a compliment. "These times call for strength," she said quietly. "I've talked to some of the women in this community, and I've learned that the war has forced them to do all manner of things in their husbands' absences—plow fields, run their shops and businesses . . ."

"Yes, and ever since the war began, you've been given an extraordinary amount of freedom for a woman of your social standing. But when we're married . . . Scripture commands the husband to be the head of the household. The wife is commanded to submit to him. I need to know if you believe that. Or if you intend to defy me the way you're defying your father. Because my home will be run according to God's law."

"*Our* home," she whispered.

"Pardon?"

"Nothing." This was the way marriage was for every couple Julia knew. She had been raised to expect nothing different. She loved Nathaniel. He was a godly man, not a tyrant. The war would end, and nurses would no longer be needed. Things would go back to the way they'd been since Adam and Eve. Nathaniel would no longer need to feel threatened by her strong will.

"Of course that's the way our home will be," she said. "I won't defy you. In our marriage vows, won't I be promising before God to obey you?"

"And a husband vows to protect his wife," he said. "That's all I'm trying to do."

"I know. But neither of us has taken those vows yet. I'm serving God here. We can trust Him to look after me, can't we?"

He nodded reluctantly. Julia saw some of the tension in his body ease. Neither of them spoke for a long moment. Then Julia said, "Please don't be angry with me. We may not see each other for a while."

He sighed. "I'm not angry." Some of the warmth returned to his eyes, but his face was somber.

Julia wanted him to hold her, to reassure her. She longed to know what it felt like to have his strong arms surrounding her and to rest her head against his shoulder. They were relatively alone, sheltered behind the last tent in the row. She moved a step closer.

"Will I see you again before you leave?" she asked, gazing up at him.

"Probably not."

She wanted him to kiss her. Instead, he took her hand and pressed it.

"Good-bye, Julia."

Chapter Twenty-one

Philadelphia
September 1863

Julia stared out of the window as the train slowed. The familiar sights of Philadelphia were all sliding past, but she felt no joy in returning home. With her work in Gettysburg finished, the heavy sadness that had weighed on her when she first came home from Washington settled over her once again. Her growing relationship with Nathaniel had helped lift the shadow for a while, but now she was quite certain that she had lost him.

Nathaniel hadn't answered any of the letters she'd sent from Gettysburg. She knew he'd been angry with her for going there in the first place and angry with her all over again for staying behind. He had surely changed his mind about marrying her after learning how outspoken and strong-willed she was. And he obviously hadn't believed her when she'd promised to be a submissive wife. Convinced she had lost him, Julia had spent the long journey wondering what she would do with herself once she was home.

But when her train finally pulled into the station late that afternoon, Julia saw Nathaniel standing on the platform. Her heart squeezed at the sight of him. The gloomy train station was filled with people, but he stood out in the noisy, jostling mob as if lit by a beam of sunlight. She quickly looked around for her parents, thinking Nathaniel must be meeting someone else, but her parents weren't there. As the conductor helped Julia off the train, Nathaniel spotted her and a broad smile lit up his handsome face. He pushed his way toward her and lightly kissed her cheek in greeting. She was afraid she might cry.

"Do you have any baggage?" he shouted above the clamor of hissing steam and excited voices.

"No, I came with only these two." She showed him the two satchels she carried, one in each hand. He took the bags from her.

"Take my arm so we won't get separated," he said. She linked her arm through his as they plowed through the crowd to the street outside. She was surprised to see her family's coachman waiting at the curb. Nathaniel had come in her father's carriage.

"There is so much to tell you," Nathaniel said after they'd settled inside. "I hardly know where to begin."

"I've missed you," she said. "Did you get my letters?"

"Yes, I got them." But he offered no explanation for not answering them as his words poured out in a rush of excitement. "Julia, I've spoken to your father. He has given me his permission to marry you. We have his blessing." He seemed nervous suddenly, the first time she'd ever seen him that way. He dug in one pocket, then the next, then finally looked relieved when he found what he was searching for in the inside pocket of his jacket. His fingers shook slightly as he opened the small box and removed a ring. He took her hand. "Will you marry me, Julia?"

"Yes, yes, yes!"

She could scarcely contain her joy. She watched his face as he looked down to slide the ring onto her finger and saw that he was blushing. She wanted so badly to throw her arms around his neck and kiss him, but she waited. He finally looked up at her again. They were alone in the enclosed carriage. They were going to be man and wife. Nathaniel leaned toward Julia and briefly pressed his lips to hers. Then he settled back in his seat once more.

Was that all? Julia struggled to hide her disappointment. They had been apart for two months, he had just asked her to marry him, and all Nathaniel had to offer her was a quick, chaste kiss? She didn't want to remember the passion of James' kiss, didn't want to think about him ever again, but Nathaniel was making it very difficult to forget.

"Your parents would like to announce our engagement at a formal party that will be held in your home," he said. "I believe your mother has already begun making the arrangements. I've asked my father and mother to come from New York for the event so that everyone can get acquainted. We will also be announcing our engagement to my congregation with a small reception." Nathaniel recited these plans as if organizing some mundane event, not their engagement. Julia could barely restrain her excitement.

"How soon will we be married?" she asked.

He frowned slightly. "Well, that's something we need to discuss. I suppose you've heard about the Federal draft call that was issued this summer?"

"Yes, of course. When I was in Gettysburg, I read in the newspaper about the awful riots in New York." All men between the ages of twenty and forty-five had been enrolled in the military draft, and when the first names had been selected in New York City, bloody rioting had broken out. Rosalie's husband had paid a three hundred dollar commutation fee to be excused from military service, but the average man couldn't afford such a high price. Julia felt a tremor of fear. "What does the draft have to do with us?"

"I've decided not to wait to be drafted. I'm going to enlist."

"*No!*" she cried. "Nathaniel, you *can't*!" All of the horrors that Julia had witnessed on the battlefield, all of the bloodied, suffering, dying men, came back to her in an instant. The mutilated bodies all had Nathaniel's face. She couldn't breathe. The carriage seemed to spin in circles until she was certain she was going to be sick.

"Wait, Julia . . . listen. I'm sorry; I should have explained it better. I'll be an army chaplain, not a soldier. Listen . . ." He gripped her shoulders, shaking her slightly. "Don't faint on me. You're quite pale. Are you all right?"

"You won't be fighting?"

"I'll be assigned to a regiment, and I'll be marching and camping in the field with the men but not as a combatant."

Julia had been to enough battlefields to know that enemy artillery shells could strike the men in the rear as easily as those on the front lines. "Please don't do this," she begged. "My father will pay for your substitute if you're drafted. Please . . ."

"It's too late. I've already arranged to enlist. I want to go, Julia."

She closed her eyes, struggling for control. "How soon are you leaving?"

"Not for a few months. Are you all right?"

She nodded weakly. "We'll be married before you go, won't we?"

He hesitated for a long moment. "No. That wouldn't be fair to you. How can I be a proper husband to you when I'm hundreds of miles away? And my army pay will be even worse than my minister's salary."

"I don't care. Other married men have left their wives to go to war. Besides, I'm sure my father will provide for me—"

"No. I won't marry you until I can provide for you myself." The sharpness in his voice silenced her. She longed to plead with him not to make her wait. She didn't care about money. She wanted their new life to begin now. But Nathaniel had already made it clear that he would make all their decisions. Arguing with him would only make him angry.

"So we'll have to wait until your enlistment is up?" she asked.

"Yes, three years from now. Unless the war ends sooner."

She drew a deep breath. "I'll feel so useless waiting here all alone while you're away. Would it be all right with you if I went back to Washington and worked in the hospital in the meantime?"

He shook his head. "I talked with your father about that when I asked for your hand. He and I agreed that you've done more than your share of work for the war effort. Neither of us wants you to return to nursing."

A tear escaped and rolled down her cheek. She quickly wiped it away. "I wouldn't be nursing for 'the war effort.' On the night that my first patient died, I felt God's blessing on my work. I felt Him say that what I did 'for the least of these' I was doing for Him."

"And Jesus also said that even a cup of cold water given in His name is enough. He is just as pleased with the charity work you do here."

"There's an army hospital here in Philadelphia," she said hopefully. "I could volunteer—"

"No. Our engagement will be announced soon. It's out of the question for you to spend so much time in the company of so many men. Especially here in Philadelphia, where you would be seen by people we know."

"But you said you admired me for being a nurse, for being caring and compassionate. If that's what you loved about me, why are you forbidding me to be those very things?"

"Because my parishioners have clear expectations about their minister's wife. You've attended this church your entire life, Julia. You move in the same social circles as these men and women. And you know very well that they don't approve of your work as a nurse. I want to return here after the war, to this church, and it's very important that my congregation accepts you. Besides, there are ways for you to be the compassionate, caring woman I admire and still remain within the boundaries of your role as my wife."

"The people at church don't understand what nurses do—"

"I know, and we're not going to change their minds. There are other duties for women that have long been accepted by our society. They involve the home and the family, respectable charities, helping the poor, the work you've done for the Commission. You can serve God by doing those things."

She gazed down at her hand, still in his, and at the new ring he'd just placed on her finger. When she didn't reply, he lifted her chin to make her look at him.

"I'm sorry there are so many restrictions. A minister's life is lived under constant scrutiny. I must be above reproach, without even a glimmer of impropriety in anything I do or say. You're not only giving up a large measure of your wealth but also a large measure of your privacy if you marry me. And I'm asking you to wait three more years, besides. I won't blame you if you change your mind about marrying me, Julia. I'll be disappointed, but I'll understand. Do you still want to accept my proposal?"

"I haven't changed my mind. I still want to marry you." But she also knew from what he'd just said about living under scrutiny and being above reproach that she would have to wait three more years before he held her or kissed her the way she longed for him to do. He was more virtuous and self-disciplined than she was, willing to "separate the sparks from the gunpowder." That knowledge only made her feel guiltier for what she still felt for James.

Nathaniel smiled. She saw relief and love in his eyes. "I'm so blessed to have a wife who wants to serve God," he said. "We'll have the rest of our lives to minister together once this war is over. I promise."

Philadelphia
January 1864

It was cold inside the church, colder still outside in the snow-covered city. The gray, drab day matched the raw, desolate feeling in Julia's heart as she sat in the Hoffman family pew between her parents. The organ droned the processional, and the senior pastor entered with Nathaniel and the young ministerial candidate who would replace him. Nathaniel wore his new army uniform, decorated with the chaplain's insignia, instead of his clerical robes. This morning he would preach his last sermon before entering the military. He was leaving early tomorrow morning.

Throughout the first part of the service, Julia's mind felt as numb as her cold hands and feet. If she prayed night and day for the next three years, would it be enough to protect Nathaniel from the danger he was about to face? She thought of the thousands of soldiers she had tended, of the thousands of loved ones they'd left behind, and for the first time she understood the anxiety those families felt. She fingered her wadded handkerchief and tried to remember all the assurances Nathaniel had given her over the past few weeks. "The safest place to be," he'd told her, "is in the will of God."

When the time came for Nathaniel to step up to the pulpit she felt a thrill of excitement—the pride of ownership. She'd been drawn to this dynamic man ever since she'd first heard him preach more than five years ago. Now he was going to be her husband. Her parents had hosted an official engagement party with more than one hundred guests. Julia had met Nathaniel's mother and his father, who was also a preacher. They'd seemed dour, humorless, and plain—and Julia wondered if it was the result of living their lives in the ministry under constant observation.

Nathaniel's announcement to the church congregation of their marriage had also been well received. Julia's mother had been all aflutter ever since, eager to begin planning the wedding, Julia's trousseau, her bridal reception. Julia had little enthusiasm for an event three long years in the future. The past few months since she'd returned from Gettysburg had flown by too swiftly. Between Nathaniel's church duties and his Commission work, he had barely had time to see Julia.

Now the congregation fell silent as he climbed into the pulpit for the last time. He was well-known for his blunt, impassioned preaching, and they expected nothing less on this final morning.

"For nearly three years now," he began, "our nation has been embroiled in a savage war that seems unending. It's hard for us to comprehend the vast destruction that has left cities and communities in flaming ruins, or the horror of so many thousands of young lives lost. The architect of all this hatred and devastation has left his unmistakable signature on his work. It has been Satan's goal since the beginning of time to destroy God's world, to bring about the death of His crowning creation, mankind—which was made in His image, instilled with the breath of His life. We see evil in our world and we ask, 'Why doesn't God do something? Where is the kingdom Christ promised?'

"This past summer the war was brought to our own soil. Young men from this congregation have been wounded, others have been imprisoned, still others have perished. It's easy to have faith when the battles are fought far away, easy to go about our daily lives when the people we love are safe. But when the war affects us, when it hits home, it shows us what we are made of and reveals the truth about our faith. We can retreat to a place of fear and isolation, justifying our hatred toward our enemies. Or we can pray Christ's great prayer, 'Thy kingdom come,' and then answer His call, knowing that the kingdom of God is within *you*.

"The believer should not despair in times of war, when hatred and death and destruction are unleashed. Nor should we ask, 'Where is God in all of this?' God is in *us,* His body. Satan is hard at work, and it's time for Christ's body to get to work, as well. Jesus asks us to take up our cross and follow Him, to display His kingdom to the world through individual acts of sacrifice and love. Ours is a God of history. He has placed us in *this* time and place for a reason. We should ask, 'What would He have me do for Him now, in this hour?' Then go forward in His strength and do it.

"This is not a war between two differing peoples but a war against evil and injustice. God desires to fight against those forces through us, through our daily acts of love and sacrifice. The sorrow and suffering we face is meant to change us so that our lives reflect His love. That's how we tell the Gospel story over and over again. We show it afresh through the way we live and love. And it's in these daily sacrifices, as we overcome hatred and injustice, that our lives will find meaning and purpose. We live or die not for ourselves but for His kingdom.

"How would God have us live in the times He has appointed for us? The Israelites followed the pillar of fire by night, when it was so dark they couldn't see. Jesus said, 'I am the light of the world: he that followeth me shall not walk in darkness, but shall have the light of life.' Our nation has been plunged into the darkness of war and hatred. But if we follow Christ's example of love and sacrifice, we'll know we are walking in His light. And God's kingdom *will* triumph—not Satan's—if we, His body, follow where Christ leads.

"I leave you with these words from the book of Romans: 'I beseech you therefore, brethren, by the mercies of God, that ye present your bodies a living sacrifice, holy, acceptable unto God, which is your reasonable service.' Amen."

A long moment of silence echoed through the church when Nathaniel finished. Julia sat in her pew in stunned silence, as well. She had all but forgotten that it was Nathaniel speaking. It seemed that God himself had spoken to her heart, calling her to serve in His name. It was true that she had become a nurse for selfish reasons, but God had transformed her through all that she'd experienced into an instrument He could use. Now her heart longed to answer His call.

As Nathaniel took his seat and the worship service continued, Julia became aware of him once again. And she wondered how he could preach those words with such passion and conviction, how he could call his congregation to sacrifice in Christ's name, and then tell her to stay home where it was safe. Was this congregation's opinion of her really more important than what God was calling her to do?

She stood for the closing hymn, "A Mighty Fortress Is Our God," feeling confused and disillusioned. The words she sang seemed to confirm what Nathaniel had preached from the pulpit, not what he said to her in private: "*. . . For still our ancient foe doth seek to work us woe; his craft and power are great, and armed with cruel hate, on earth is not his equal.*" Satan was the enemy, not her fellow countrymen. This war wasn't against the Southern states but against the hatred and lies that had turned brother against brother.

"*. . . Did we in our own strength confide, our striving would be losing. . . .*" Julia thought of how Sister Irene had urged her to pray for strength to work in His name. And God had answered her prayer, enabling her to do what would have been impossible on her own. "*. . . Let goods and kindred go . . . His kingdom is forever.*" How could she refuse to answer God's call?

When the service ended, Julia couldn't even approach Nathaniel through the throng of well-wishers. But he came to her house later that afternoon to say good-bye.

"I don't want to prolong this," he said when they were finally alone in the parlor. "It's too hard on both of us. I'll write to you as soon as I know my address, and we can speak our hearts in our letters."

"Wait . . . Before you go, Nathaniel, there's something I must ask you." She chose her words carefully, unwilling to make him angry or spoil their parting. "In your sermon this morning, I felt as if every word was meant for me. I want to answer God's call. I want to work for His kingdom."

"That's wonderful," he said, smiling.

"But I feel that my calling is to be a nurse."

His smile faded. "We've discussed this before. I thought the matter was settled."

"Listen, you know the truth about the work I do as a nurse. You know the enormous need. And you know my motives are pure. Yet you seem to care more about what your congregation thinks than what God is calling me to do. It's all about appearances. God enabled me to become a nurse in spite of huge obstacles. He's calling me to do that work now, using your own voice, your own sermon. And I'm willing to go. Why are you standing in my way?"

He looked at her for a long time without answering. Julia could scarcely breathe. "I'm not standing in your way," he finally said. "The choice is yours, Julia. It always has been. If you choose to marry me, then you must accept your role as my helpmate. The work you are called to do in our marriage will be to help me with my ministry. And that means earning my congregation's acceptance. But if you feel that God is calling you to be something else—to be a nurse—then perhaps He's asking you to remain single, like Miss Dix."

"I wouldn't have to choose between the two if we were married. It's perfectly acceptable for married women to work in hospitals. And I could afford to support myself on my army pay."

"It is not acceptable to me. How can I vow before God to protect and support you one day, then walk away from you and leave you alone in a strange city with no support the next? I take my vows as a husband very seriously." His eyes searched hers, and she saw the deep sorrow she was causing him. "Do you want to call it off, Julia?" he asked.

"No. I love you."

"I love you, too," he said for the first time. "I pray that you'll have peace in your heart concerning what your role will be." In the silence that fell between them, the clock in the front hallway suddenly struck the hour. It seemed prophetic to Julia, but she didn't know how or why.

"I'm sorry to leave you this way," Nathaniel said, "but it's late. I need to go. I promise I'll write."

The tears she'd been holding back began to fall at his words.

"Please don't cry," he said. "It only makes it harder to say goodbye. I'll be safe in God's hands."

Without thinking, Julia threw her arms around him, clinging

tightly to him. He seemed startled at first and hesitated for a moment, then his arms encircled her and held her in return.

"Julia . . . Julia . . ." he whispered. She heard the emotion in his breaking voice. "As soon as I come home, we'll be married. I promise." Then he pulled back and lifted her chin to look into her eyes. His were moist. He kissed her gently, tenderly, but it was over much too quickly. He wiped her tears. "God speed the day when we're together again."

Brandy Station, Virginia
May 1864

Phoebe scanned all the faces of the men who had gathered at the outdoor worship service, searching for Ted's. More than a year and a half had passed since she'd last seen him. She'd learned that her old regiment had spent the winter down here, but thousands of tents and the ramshackle huts the troops had built were spread out over a wide area, and the odds of finding Ted seemed pretty slim. It was hard to believe that Ted's three-year enlistment would be up this fall—if he made it through alive and uninjured, that is.

Phoebe had spent the winter working at the hospital in Washington City with Dr. McGrath, going with him sometimes to the shantytown to take care of the former slaves. Now the army had a new commander, General Ulysses S. Grant, and it was clear that he was preparing for battle as soon as the spring weather arrived. The train that had carried Phoebe and the other medical staff south from Washington to Brandy Station had also carried mountains of equipment and supplies for waging war. Thousands of troops and cannons and canvas-topped supply wagons were massing here, waiting to cross the Rapidan River and engage the Confederates who were camped on the other side. Finding Ted wouldn't be easy, but this Sunday church service seemed like a good place to start.

As the chaplain stood to begin his sermon, Phoebe recognized the handsome preacher immediately. He was the same man who had given her the Bible in Washington City more than two years ago.

Ted had coaxed her to go to church with him on that long-ago morning, but she hadn't heard a word of the sermon. She was only half-listening now as she continued to search the crowd for him.

"As you go forward into battle," the minister was saying, "you've been trained to listen for the sound of the trumpet. You respond to that call, obeying your officers' commands. But the Bible says that one day the last trumpet will sound and Christ will return for His people. Will you recognize His call? Will you hear it and respond to our Lord's command? He will return in judgment and with fire, and the apostle Paul writes in Corinthians that 'the fire shall try every man's work of what sort it is.'"

It was a stirring sermon, and the men seemed to receive it with enthusiasm. But when it ended and the crowd melted away again to return to their camps, Phoebe was keenly disappointed that she'd seen no sign of Ted. She was about to leave when the young preacher strode right up to her and tipped his hat.

"Good morning, ma'am. I'm Reverend Nathaniel Greene. Can I help you with something? You look a bit lost."

"Phoebe Bigelow," she said. "I'm a nurse over at the field hospital." She remembered how kind this minister had seemed the last time that they'd met, how he'd given her the Bible and had shown her the story of the little man who'd wanted to see Jesus. She summoned her courage.

"There's some places I've underlined in my Bible," she said. "Do you think maybe you could explain them to me sometime when you get a—?"

Before she could finish, a soldier pushed his way between them, interrupting. "I need to speak to you, Reverend. It's important." He seemed very agitated.

"Can it wait a moment?" the minister asked. "Miss Bigelow was just—"

"Never mind," Phoebe said quickly. "We can talk another time. I need to get on back to the hospital."

"Are you a nurse?" the soldier asked, stopping her. "Then you'd better hear this, too."

"What is this about?" Nathaniel asked. "Tell me your name."

"It's Noah Murdock. Make the lady stay, Reverend. She needs to hear this, too."

"Are you sure you don't want to speak to me in private?" he asked.

"No, I want everyone to know. The man should be hanged!"

"All right, Murdock. Take a minute to calm down, and then you can tell me what's troubling you. Would you mind staying, Miss Bigelow?"

"I guess not," she said, shrugging. But she felt very uncomfortable, unable to imagine what Murdock was babbling about. What did her being a nurse have to do with hanging a man?

"I've been feeling poorly lately," the soldier began, "so I went to see a doctor this morning. Turns out I know the man. His name is McGrath. And he's a cold-blooded murderer."

A chill went through Phoebe at his words.

"Hold on," the minister said. "That's a very serious accusation. You'd better explain yourself."

The man exhaled angrily. "Before the war, I worked up in Connecticut as a coachman for a rich banker named Tyler. McGrath was Mr. Tyler's doctor and long-time friend. He used to come to the house every week and sometimes I drove them places, so I know it's him. It's the same man!"

"All right, I believe you," Nathaniel said calmly. "Go on."

"One night when I was having dinner with the other servants in the kitchen, Mr. Tyler's butler came running out saying there was a loud argument going on between the two men in the study. They'd been drinking heavily, and the butler wanted me to help throw the doctor out of the house since he was a good-sized man and poor Mr. Tyler was old and ill. I followed the butler into the main part of the house, and I could hear Mr. Tyler shouting as soon as we entered the hallway. He was saying, 'Help me! Help me!' But we were too late. All of a sudden we heard a gunshot. When we burst into the room, Mr. Tyler was dead, shot in the head, point-blank. The doctor still held the pistol in his hand, and he was covered all over in Mr. Tyler's blood. He was saying, 'I'm sorry, Eldon. I'm sorry,' over and over.

"We wrestled the gun out of his hand and held him down until the police arrived. It's the same man, Reverend. He's a murderer, and I don't want him taking care of my friends and me. He should hang for his crime!"

"Why didn't he?" Reverend Greene asked. "Wasn't there a trial? If there were witnesses and the man confessed . . ."

"I don't know why he didn't. He was in prison the last I knew. But I had to find another job after Mr. Tyler was murdered. A friend got me work in Pennsylvania."

"How long ago was this? Is it possible the doctor already served his prison sentence?"

"No, sir. He murdered Mr. Tyler in the spring of 1860—barely four years ago. That's not enough time for a murderer to stay behind bars."

"Do you think he might be a fugitive?"

"I don't know," Murdock replied. "He's using his own name—that's how brazen the man is. If he got away with murder once, don't you think he'll do it again?"

"All right. I'll look into the affair," Nathaniel said. "If the doctor is wanted for murder in Connecticut, then he should be relieved of duty immediately."

"I'll take you to him," Murdock said. "Between the two of us, we can grab him, Reverend."

"Hold on. I think you'd better stay here and let me talk to him alone first."

"What good will talking do? I should have gone to the provost marshal, not you." Murdock turned away in disgust.

The minister planted a hand on Murdock's shoulder and swung him around to stop him. "Listen, Dr. McGrath can't go anywhere. There are one hundred thousand troops here in Brandy Station. I understand why you're upset, but let's not get carried away and turn this into a lynching."

The thought of her friend being strung up by an angry mob sent another shiver of fear through Phoebe. She had an overwhelming urge to run ahead and warn Dr. McGrath to flee, but the minister was right—there was no place for him to go.

"The doctor deserves to have his say," Nathaniel said. "Let me talk to him, and then we can decide what to do next. Do you know this doctor, Miss Bigelow?" he asked, turning to Phoebe. Her heart sped up.

"Yes, sir. I do."

"Do you know if he ever lived in Connecticut?"

She shrugged. Phoebe didn't know for certain. But she had seen some of the letters that arrived from the doctor's wife every week. The return address was a city in Connecticut.

"I think you'd better wait here," Nathaniel told the soldier. "Miss Bigelow will take me to him. I'll let you know what he has to say."

Phoebe felt like a traitor as she walked across the campground to the field hospital with the minister. She didn't want to believe that Dr. McGrath had murdered somebody. But she remembered the first night she'd ever worked with him and how he'd told her he had come to Washington to escape, just as she'd run away from home. *"I should warn you,"* he'd said that night, *"it has been my experience that you can never escape your past."*

"I assume that you knew nothing of this man's past when you began working with him?" the minister asked, interrupting her thoughts.

"No, sir. I didn't think it mattered when there were wounded soldiers to take care of." Phoebe knew that the other nurses at Fairfield Hospital didn't get along too well with Dr. McGrath, but she liked him in spite of his gruffness. "He doesn't kill people," she added. "He would never harm the soldiers under his care. He saved my life."

"Your life? How so?"

Now she would have to explain about all her lies, and Phoebe didn't want to do that. "I was sick and nearly died," she said instead. "He was my doctor. I'm alive because of him. Listen, I'll show you where his tent is, but I don't want any part of this."

"No, wait. You just heard a very serious accusation being leveled against the doctor. It's only fair that you stay and hear his side of it. Especially since you have to work with him every day. You shouldn't be left with doubt and suspicion."

It was true. Phoebe would always wonder if Dr. McGrath was truly capable of killing someone in cold blood. "That's him over there," she finally said, nodding her head. The doctor stood behind the cluster of hospital tents, sipping from his silver pocket flask and gazing into the distant woods. "He's the fellow with the reddish beard."

The minister's brows raised in surprise. "Really? I've met that man before, in Washington. Come with me, Miss Bigelow. Please."

She followed reluctantly as the minister strode over to Dr. McGrath and extended his hand. "Good morning. I'm Nathaniel Greene, the regimental chaplain. This is an amazing coincidence, but we've met once before, in Washington. You were at a hospital there, weren't you?"

"Yes." Dr. McGrath seemed wary and not at all friendly. But Phoebe knew it was his usual manner.

"You probably don't remember me. It was more than a year and a half ago. I came to the hospital to visit one of your nurses, Julia Hoffman."

His words startled Phoebe. "You know Julia?" she asked. When he didn't answer, she looked from the minister to the doctor and thought she saw a flicker of fear cross Dr. McGrath's face.

"What about her?" he asked.

"This has nothing to do with Julia. It's somewhat of a private matter," he said, glancing around the noisy camp. "Perhaps you'd like to go somewhere—"

"Just get to the point."

"All right." Nathaniel drew a quick breath. "A man named Noah Murdock came to see me. He says he once knew you in Connecticut. He told a rather gruesome story about a murder in which he claims you killed a man. Since your nurse, Miss Bigelow, happened to hear his accusation, I thought she should stay and hear your side of it, as well. Murdock claims you shot his employer, Mr. Tyler, in cold blood."

Dr. McGrath crossed his arms. He remained silent, his face as hard as stone.

Phoebe felt embarrassed for the doctor. She wished she hadn't come.

The minister cleared his throat. "I told Murdock I would try to clear things up with you. He's concerned because you're responsible for the welfare of his regiment. He also seems to think you might be a fugitive." He paused, and Phoebe could tell that he was trying to be cautious in what he said. "I'm not accusing you, Doctor. If you have an explanation in your defense this would be a good time to give it. If Murdock is mistaken, I wish you'd tell me and I'll gladly apologize for bothering you."

"Are you through?" the doctor asked coldly.

"I'm simply trying to be fair and hear both sides of this story."

"I don't owe you or anyone else an explanation," Dr. McGrath said. He turned and walked away, ducking into his tent at the end of the row.

The minister seemed bewildered. He stared at the row of tents for a long moment as if unsure what to do next. "Well," he finally said, "Julia warned me that he was a difficult man to converse with."

Phoebe's mind stirred from its state of numbed shock when he mentioned her friend a second time. She wanted desperately to ease the tension, to replace the suspicion and ugliness with something pleasant. "I know Julia Hoffman, too," she said. "We worked at the same hospital."

"She's my fiancée," the minister said offhandedly, his mind obviously still on the doctor. "We were engaged to be married this past fall."

Phoebe remembered how Julia had longed to find a man who loved her for herself, not for her beauty. Reverend Greene was very handsome. They would make quite a couple. And surely a minister would look at the good in a person and love Julia for all the right reasons, wouldn't he?

"When you write to her," Phoebe said, "tell her I'm real happy for her. She's an awful good nurse, you know. She did a lot of good and saved a lot of lives."

He frowned. "Yes, I know." Something Phoebe had said made him uncomfortable, but she didn't know what. "I had no idea Julia was working with a doctor with such an unsavory past," the minister said. "Thank God she's no longer with him."

"You believe that soldier's story?" Phoebe said in surprise. "You think the doctor really murdered somebody?"

"Well, if there was any other explanation, I see no reason why Dr. McGrath wasn't willing to tell us and clear his name."

A sick feeling of dread for the doctor slowly crawled through her. Surely the minister wouldn't allow a lynching. "What are you going to do about all of this?" she asked.

"Well, I'll have to contact the authorities in Connecticut and see if he's a fugitive. If so, it will be up to the provost marshal to take care of it, not me."

"I don't believe it," Phoebe said. "I don't believe he would shoot someone like that. Or if he did do it, he's changed an awful lot since then. I ain't afraid of him, and the men don't need to be afraid, either. God can change people, Reverend. I read where Peter was running scared and saying he didn't even know Jesus, but afterwards Jesus forgave him and gave him another chance. Can't people give Dr. McGrath another chance, too? He's already saved thousands of lives, and he'll save a lot more if you don't lock him up in prison. Ain't we supposed to forgive people?"

"Are you preaching to me, Miss Bigelow?" He smiled faintly, but it didn't quite reach his eyes. "At any rate, it isn't up to me. It's up to a judge and jury to decide."

Dr. McGrath had said the same thing to Phoebe when she'd asked why he'd saved her life. He hadn't believed that she was a coward. He hadn't judged her, and she didn't want to judge him, either. After the minister left, she slowly walked down the long row to the doctor's tent.

"Dr. McGrath?" she called. "It's me, Phoebe Bigelow. Can I talk to you?"

"Come in." He sat alone inside the tent on a campstool, rubbing his eyes. "If you have any doubts about me, Phoebe," he said quietly, "if you're afraid to work with me now, I'll understand."

"No, sir. I ain't afraid. I just come to say I don't believe it. I don't believe you'd ever kill anybody." He nodded slightly and closed his eyes. But not before Phoebe saw the look of pain in them. "That's all. So I reckon I'll just go check on our patients now."

As she ducked through the door again, she thought she heard him say, "Thank you."

Chapter Twenty-two

Brandy Station, Virginia
May 1864

The battle in the Virginia Wilderness began just a few days later, giving Phoebe little time to worry about what would happen to Dr. McGrath. Their field division hospital crossed the Rapidan River, following the advancing army, and they were quickly overwhelmed with wounded men to treat. From everything those poor souls told her, it appeared that the fierce fighting taking place in the dense woods was a living nightmare of horror and confusion.

The battle was with the thick, tangled undergrowth as much as with the Rebels. There was no clear path, few places to take cover, and no distinct battle lines. The confused, disorganized men fought desperately, heroically, sometimes hand-to-hand, using bayonets or the butts of their rifles. Even seasoned veterans told Phoebe that it was the most horrifying battle they'd ever fought. And it went on and on, without a victory.

Late in the afternoon, Phoebe crouched to help a man who'd had part of his hand shot off and immediately recognized him. It was her old friend Sergeant Anderson. For a long moment she couldn't speak, afraid he would recognize her, afraid she was going to be in terrible trouble. Then her concern for his suffering took over.

"It's good that the bleeding stopped," she told him, "but it's gonna be a while before the surgeons can take a look at you. I can give you some whiskey in the meantime, or there's morphine if the pain's too bad."

He was sweating and white with shock, but he said, "Whiskey's okay. Save the strong stuff for those who really need it."

She put the cup in his good hand and helped him take a drink. He was studying her. "You look familiar," he said between swallows. "Do I know you, ma'am?"

Phoebe decided to lie. It was easier that way. She asked him which company he was in, and when he told her she said, "You must know my brother, Ike Bigelow."

"Yeah, maybe that's it. I do see a family resemblance. You twins or something?"

She nodded vaguely.

"I'm sorry about Ike going missing, ma'am. I don't know if you ever heard about it or not, but he was a good man and a brave soldier. Best marksman I ever met."

Phoebe's heart pounded with fear and dread as she prepared to ask the sergeant her next question. She needed to know the answer, but she was terrified to ask, terrified to hear his reply. "Um . . . Ike always used to write and tell me about his friend Ted Wilson. How's he doing these days?"

"Wilson turned out to be a real good soldier, too. He tried very hard to find out what happened to your brother. Wouldn't give up looking for him for the longest time. He was pretty broken up over his disappearance."

"Is Ted still alive? Is he all right?" She held her breath. Her heart seemed to stop beating as she waited for his reply.

"I had coffee with him this morning, right before this mess started."

Phoebe rose to her feet and fled, unable to utter a word. When she reached the supply wagon, she sank down behind it and wept. Ted was alive, grinning his boyish smile, drinking the awful coffee he always made. She cried with happiness and longing until she had no tears left.

A few hours later, Phoebe overheard two stretcher-bearers explaining to Dr. McGrath how the wounded soldier they'd just brought in had been badly burned. "The rifle fire was so heavy it set the woods on fire. We got this fella out, but most of the injured men who were laying in there couldn't escape in time, and they burned to death."

"It was terrible, Doc. We could hear them screaming for help, but we couldn't get to them."

"Are there more in there now?" the doctor asked.

"Yeah, but we can't find them all because they're scattered all over the woods."

"We know where there's a whole bunch of wounded men from a Pennsylvania regiment, but we can't get to them."

"Why not?" Dr. McGrath asked.

"The Rebels shoot at everything that moves. There's a captain and about thirty of our wounded boys pinned down, and the Rebels fire at us whenever we try to go in after them."

"Is it possible to take me to them? Could I treat them where they are?" he asked.

"The Rebels won't care if you're a doctor. They'll shoot you for trying."

"Wait here," the doctor said. "I'll get my bag."

Phoebe trailed behind him as Dr. McGrath went to the medical supply wagon and quickly filled his bag with chloroform, morphine, bandages, and surgical instruments. "I want to go with you," she told him.

"Not where there's fighting, Phoebe," he said without looking up. "This is as close to the battle lines as I ever want my nurses to get."

"It's my old regiment," she said quietly. "Ted might be one of those wounded men."

He looked up. "Is he the man whose life you saved once before?"

She nodded.

"You would risk your life to save him a second time?"

"I'd do it a hundred times. If you don't let me go with you, I'll go in there by myself."

He didn't reply. Instead, he closed his bag and walked back to the waiting men. Phoebe simply followed.

The ambulance drove them as close as it could get, then the stretcher-bearers took them as far into the woods as they dared. Dr. McGrath walked in front of Phoebe for the rest of the way, ducking low and following the sound of moaning men as Rebel bullets whistled overhead and thudded into tree trunks. Curiously, Phoebe didn't feel at all afraid.

They found the injured men lying in a hollow in a grove of trees. Ted was not among them. Several of the soldiers had already died, but Phoebe and Dr. McGrath quickly set to work helping the living. She gave them chloroform while he operated to remove any bullets. She passed around water and gave morphine, calmed and fed and comforted them as best she could. When it grew dark and the risk of sniper-fire lessened, she and Dr. McGrath walked back through the woods to fetch the stretcher-bearers.

As the two of them sat alone beside the road, waiting for the ambulance to return, Phoebe summoned the courage to ask him the question she'd been wondering all afternoon. "Why'd you take a chance like that, Dr. McGrath? You could've been killed. In fact, I almost think that's what you were trying to do."

"Perhaps I was," he said quietly.

"Why?"

He sighed. "It takes less courage to end your life in a burst of glory than to face the mistakes you've made and start over."

"But you can start over no matter how many mistakes you made," she said. "I did."

He shook his head.

"Remember that first night I helped you at the shantytown," Phoebe asked, "and I read a Bible verse to you about being a new person? Remember that? You said to let you know if I ever found out what it meant. Well, I think I'm starting to figure it out." She paused, and the soft hooting of an owl and the call of a whippoorwill seemed out of place after all the carnage that she'd seen that day.

"We all tell lies and hurt people and do awful things," she said. "I was never very nice to anybody, and I used to beat kids up at school and treat my brothers mean. Later on I even killed people when I was pretending to be a man. The first one was a young fellow sitting on a rooftop in Yorktown. He was a sniper, and I aimed for his leg, but the fall might've killed him. And I killed a lot of others after him. But the worst thing I ever done was to live my life without God. I never once asked Him which way to go or what I should do. I deserve to die for all that. There's a bullet with my name on it heading toward me, and God is right to kill me. I made myself His enemy. But Jesus came in between that bullet and me. He covered me with His own body when I deserved to die, and He died in my place. I guess He done that for everybody, not just me."

Dr. McGrath shook his head. "I've seen the worst in mankind, Phoebe. You have, too. Why would Christ do that? Why not just give us the punishment we deserve?"

"Same reason I saved Ted. Jesus saw someone He loved in trouble, and He just had to do it. I loved Ted, and I never even thought twice about saving him. But the best part is that now God lets me start all over again. It's like all the things I've done don't matter no more. Sure, there's still people in Bone Hollow who knew me before and know what I done. But what they think don't matter. It's what God says that counts, and He says I'm brand-new, like that little baby we delivered in the shantytown—all fresh and new with a whole life ahead of me."

"So you've found the atonement you sought by working as a nurse," the doctor said.

"I'm not sure I know what that means."

"It means you're getting a chance to make up for all the things you've done wrong by working here, going through this hell on earth."

"No, that ain't it. I could work as a nurse for a hundred years and it still wouldn't make things right in God's eyes. Jesus already did that for me. I work as a nurse because I want to share His love with others. I never knew anything about love before the war started. Isn't it funny that it took something this awful, with all the killing and suffering, for me to find out what love is?"

"What is love, Phoebe?" he asked quietly.

"It's a gift. It's never something you work for. Ted didn't do a single thing to make me love him. He was just Ted. God loves me the same way, and He says I'm supposed to share that love with others, whether they deserve it or not. It was hard, at first, to help the Rebels. But I know I'm supposed to forgive them the way God forgave me, so I'm trying."

"You've found forgiveness?" he murmured, almost to himself.

"Yes."

They sat in the darkness for several minutes. Phoebe was aware of how the gentle evening sounds of crickets and frogs blended with the distant crack of a rifle or a man's moan, how the fresh scents of earth and pine mingled with the bitter smell of smoke and gunpowder. Strangely, she felt at peace, even though she sat in the middle of a horrible battleground.

Dr. McGrath scooped up a twig and slowly began breaking it into pieces. As he did, he began to talk, his voice hoarse and filled with pain. "Eldon Tyler had been my patient for several years. He was a wealthy financier with everything a man could ask for in this life—except his health. I saw him regularly, at least once a week, and he always shared a glass of his imported Scotch whiskey with me. The cause of his symptoms eluded me for a while until he hinted one night that he had a fondness for . . . how shall I say this? For a certain type of disreputable woman. I realized then, as he had suspected all along, that he had syphilis. And I immediately knew that the disease was now in the third and final stage.

"The last night I saw Eldon . . ." The doctor paused, drawing a breath as if for strength.

"You don't need to tell me this," Phoebe said.

"I know. But I want to. On that last night, when I listened to Eldon's heart, I heard valve damage. He was experiencing some loss of sensation in his legs, which meant the disease was already affecting his brain.

" 'Will I go insane?' he asked me. I didn't want to answer him.

" 'There's no way to tell for sure.' I hedged.

" 'Is there anything you can do?' He spoke calmly, as if asking me if I thought it would rain.

" 'There is no cure, Eldon. I'm sorry.'

" 'Sit down, James,' he said. 'Have a drink with me.'

"I was upset. I allowed him to fill and refill my glass. I confess that I drank more that night than I usually did, but he kept pouring and pouring, and it seemed to cheer him to see me drink. I wanted to dull my thoughts. My pride couldn't handle the fact that I couldn't cure Eldon Tyler.

"'I want to show you something,' he said after a while. He opened his desk drawer and took out a set of dueling pistols. He offered me one, asked me what I thought of it, and when I stood to take it, I felt the effects of the whiskey. I had to sit again to stop the dizziness. And then he began saying the most terrible things about Ellen—my wife. I won't repeat them because they were so shocking. And the language he used . . . I'd never known him to speak so coarsely. I thought he must have already begun losing his mind.

"'Eldon, I must go,' I said when he wouldn't stop. He began to shout.

"'What kind of man are you? Won't you even defend your wife's honor?' He started waving the second pistol and calling me terrible names. I realized that he was trying to draw me into a duel—although I couldn't think why he would do that at the time. I was too shocked by the change in him to think very clearly. And I felt responsible. I was his physician and his friend. I was angry with myself because I couldn't help him. He would go insane and die very horribly, and there was nothing I could do. I was already grieving his dissolution and was not thinking straight from all the Scotch. I stood again.

"'Would you like some laudanum?' I asked, hoping it would calm him.

"'No! I want you to help me!'

"'There's nothing I can do. I'm sorry.'

"'You can end my suffering and let me die honorably in a duel, before my sons have to chain me up in the basement as a madman. You can put a bullet through my head, James! For God's sake, help me! Help me!'

"'I can't do that.' I laid the pistol down. I needed to take the other gun away from him, to sedate him and get him into bed. He'd drunk a great deal of Scotch, too. I started around the desk toward him. I was tipsy, moving too slowly. Before I could get to him, he suddenly put the pistol to his own head—and fired."

James closed his eyes. He grew very still, as if reliving the horror.

"I wanted the clock to turn back," he said hoarsely. "I wanted a second chance to get to him in time. I'd been trained to heal, and in my horror and shock I tried to . . . to gather the pieces of him and put them back together, to fix him. I didn't really know what I was doing, but the servants found me that way, covered with Eldon's blood and brain matter, trying futilely to piece him back together and undo the damage that the pistol had done. I was weeping and saying over and over, 'I'm sorry, Eldon. I'm so sorry.' The gun that had dropped from his hand was somehow in my own.

"The servants called the authorities. They'd heard Eldon shouting, arguing with me. I was too incoherent with grief and shock—and too much Scotch—to explain what had happened. They arrested me for murder.

"I spent a month in prison. The prosecutors felt they had enough evidence against me to go to trial. Everyone believed that I'd murdered him. In fact, most people still believe it—like the fellow you met the other day. But eventually Eldon's attorney found the suicide note he'd written, detailing his plans, saying that if I couldn't cure him, he would end his own life. The note had somehow been overlooked for all that time . . . I'm not sure how. They weren't expecting to find one, I guess. Eldon told about his incurable disease and his plans to kill himself. Someone finally believed me when I said I hadn't pulled the trigger.

"But Eldon had ordered his attorney to spare no expense in keeping the details out of the newspapers, and the Tyler family has enough wealth and political connections to do just that. To save the family from scandal, Eldon's true medical condition was never made known, nor was the fact of his suicide. The authorities quietly released me from jail, all charges dropped. Your minister friend will find that out when he investigates. But no public explanation was ever given. Most people believe I'm guilty. My reputation, my medical practice—my life—were ruined over a murder I didn't commit."

He fell silent again. Phoebe could hear the rumble of the returning ambulance in the distance and the sound of the stretcher-bearers coming through the woods behind her with some of the wounded men. She rose to her feet, straightening her cramped legs. "You should fight back, Dr. McGrath. Make it clear to everybody what happened. It ain't fair."

He slowly rose to stand beside her, shaking his head. "Perhaps it isn't fair, but it is justice," he said softly. "I am a murderer, Phoebe. I didn't kill Eldon Tyler . . . but I did kill someone else."

Philadelphia
May 1864

Julia sat at the breakfast table with her father, watching his face as he read the morning newspaper. He usually read articles aloud to her and her mother, sometimes denouncing the secretary of war or various army generals for the decisions they'd made. But this morning he was unusually quiet. Julia feared she knew why—Nathaniel's regiment must have gone into battle.

"What's in the news this morning?" she finally asked.

"More of the same." He folded the paper closed. "The fighting has shifted to a place called Spotsylvania Court House."

"More casualties?" Julia asked, almost in a whisper. She pictured James bent over a makeshift operating table and wished she was working alongside him.

"General Grant is getting the job done," the judge replied. "He isn't going to retreat like all the other generals before him. Of course, there will be a high price to pay."

"How many, Daddy?"

"I won't discuss it," he said, rising. "It's a morbid way to begin the day. You and I both have work to do." He left the table, his food barely touched, his coffee cup still full. The judge usually left his newspaper lying on the table when he was finished, but this morning he took it with him.

"Is that what you're wearing to the church guild meeting?" Julia's mother asked as she swept into the room a few minutes later. "Where's your father? He hasn't left already, has he? What time is it? Why didn't he tell me he was leaving early?"

Julia didn't know which question to answer first. "Daddy is finished eating. I think there was something in the paper that upset him, but he wouldn't say what. And yes, this is what I'm wearing to the meeting. Why?"

"You're deliberately undermining your natural beauty, Julia. I do hope you're not going to end up like Nathaniel Greene's mother, so drab and plain. A minister's wife needn't be an ugly old crow, you know."

"And what do you suppose the ladies' guild would say if I flounced into the meeting in silk and jewels?"

"There is such a thing as a happy medium. And you are still our daughter, not Nathaniel's wife. There are expectations within our social circle, as well."

"I know," Julia said. "I can scarcely keep track of them all." And she wondered, on top of everything else, if God was pleased with her.

Later, as Julia stood in the front hallway, waiting for the coachman to bring the carriage around, she spotted her father's newspaper, lying on the desk in his study. She went into his room. When she unfolded the paper she saw right away why her father had hidden it from her. A headline on the front page read, *More Work Than There Are Hands to Do*.

Wounded soldiers had been evacuated to Fredericksburg, the article explained, but the army had made no hospital preparations there ahead of time. *There were stretchers and ambulances at the front, trains and boats at the rear, but no personnel or equipment in the middle,* she read, *and the delay caused untold suffering*. Men lay unattended for days, without proper food or shelter. A handful of surgeons and nurses were unable to cope with the nearly eight thousand casualties that poured in. The need for medical supplies and for volunteer nurses and doctors was enormous. The article ended with a frantic appeal for help; more battles were expected in the coming days as the armies of Grant and Lee clashed. There was "more work than there were hands to do."

"Why are you here, Julia?" her mother asked from the doorway.

Julia remembered the night on board the hospital ship when Sister Irene's voice had come out of the darkness, asking her the same question.

"I don't know. . . ." Julia murmured. "I should be in Fredericksburg."

"Where? What is the matter with you this morning? You're supposed to be at a meeting at the church in a few minutes. If you don't hurry, you'll be late—and that will make a worse impression on Nathaniel's congregation than the clothes you wear."

"All right, Mother," she sighed. "I'm going."

Julia was the last to arrive at the meeting. She was well aware of a few disapproving frowns. She sat quietly, demurely, listening as the president of the ladies' guild droned through the items on their agenda. There was a long discussion over whether or not they should participate in an interfaith memorial service at a local cemetery, since there were denominational differences between the various churches. The ladies decided they would not attend. Another item concerned the seating at an upcoming tea; two parishioners, locked in a long-standing feud, would both be attending and must be tactfully kept apart. Then there was the question of whether donors' names should be listed alphabetically or according to the amount of money they contributed to the memorial fund. But the longest and most heated debate concerned which color to paint the vestry—white, ivory, or pale yellow.

Above the sound of cultured voices and tinkling teacups, Julia thought she could hear the anguished cries and moans of suffering men, the unending wail she sometimes heard in her dreams. Why was she here?

"What do you think, Julia?"

She came out of her reverie to find all the ladies watching her.

"After all," the guild president said, "your future husband will be using the vestry regularly. Which color do you think your reverend Greene would prefer?"

Julia stared at her. "What a perfectly ridiculous question," she replied. She thought of Dr. McGrath, remembering how often he had said the same words to her. Unlike Nathaniel, James had never cared what people thought of him. She set her teacup on the table beside her chair and stood, trembling with emotion.

"An entire race of people lives in poverty and slavery in this country. Our nation is being swallowed alive in hatred and war and death. And we're arguing over what color to paint the vestry?"

She saw shock and surprise on every woman's face, but Julia couldn't stop herself. "Satan is the enemy—not the South, not other churches, not each other. We pray the Lord's Prayer every week, saying 'Thy kingdom come,' then we sit around waiting for it to magically float down from heaven on a silver platter. Didn't you hear what Nathaniel preached in his last sermon? The kingdom is within *us*. The only way it's going to come is if we fight for it. And how can we fight Satan if we're busy with trivial things—or worse still, busy fighting each other?"

Julia was aware that she was burning her bridges behind her, just as the Rebels had done in Fredericksburg, leaving only the stone piers behind. She knew the enormous effort it had required to rebuild those bridges, the terrible cost. But she also knew that withdrawing from conflict only prolonged it, allowing the enemy to fight another day. The words of the hymn they'd sung on Nathaniel's last Sunday echoed through her mind: *Let goods and kindred go . . . His kingdom is forever.*

"You know, women are part of His kingdom, too," she told the astonished ladies. "Every single one of us should get down on our knees and ask God what He wants us to do for Him. Then maybe we'll stop building our own comfortable little realms and get about our Father's business."

Julia walked out, knowing she had made her choice and that it was the right one. She told her coachman to take her to the Christian Commission offices, and when she learned that several members of the group were leaving that afternoon to take food and medical supplies to Fredericksburg, she went straight home to pack. Thankfully, her mother wasn't at home. She wrote a note to her father, explaining that she was leaving to be a nurse again, and left it in his study beside the newspaper article. She ended the note with these words: *I'm sorry that I had to disobey your wishes. But "Whether it be right in the sight of God to hearken unto you more than unto God, judge ye."*

The hardest part was letting Nathaniel go. But Julia knew she'd broken her engagement to him the moment she had stood and admonished the women at the guild meeting. She would have to write and tell him about the choice she'd made, but she sat on the train with a blank piece of writing paper in front of her, not knowing what to say.

She loved him. That hadn't changed. She wanted to be his wife more than anything . . . no, not more than anything. She wanted to obey God more, and she felt Him calling her to be a nurse. What good was the congregation's approval or Nathaniel's approval if she turned her back on God? Jesus had said that the two greatest commandments were to love God and love her neighbor. He'd told a parable about helping the wounded man lying on the side of the road. He'd said, "Go, and do thou likewise." But how could she explain that to Nathaniel? She'd tried once before and he'd said the choice was hers to make. He wouldn't stand in her way if she chose to be a nurse. But in doing so, she would be choosing not to be his wife.

It was the most difficult decision she had ever made in her life. But the fact that Julia was riding south on a train told her that she'd already made it. Now if only her heart could accept it.

Julia's notepaper was still blank when she reached Washington City. She and the other Christian Commission volunteers spent several hectic hours booking passage on a steamship that would carry them and their supplies down the Potomac. She tried once more to write a letter to Nathaniel after she was on board the ship. She pleaded with him to understand her decision and forgive her. She begged him to say that he still loved her, that he still wanted to marry her. But before the ship landed in Virginia, she tore the letter into tiny pieces and threw them overboard.

It was pouring rain when Julia's ship docked. The Confederates had destroyed the rail line to Fredericksburg, so the group would have to travel by wagon the rest of the way. But when she climbed up from the wharf and looked down the road, she saw hundreds and hundreds of ambulances lined up as far as she could see. They were sunk to their hubs in mud. Several Commission workers from New York State had arrived the day before and were waiting in their tents for the roads to dry; Julia asked them about the ambulances.

"They're filled with wounded men from the battle that took place in Spotsylvania a few days ago," a clergyman told her.

"A few days ago! Have they had medical treatment?"

"No, ma'am. They were brought to Fredericksburg first, but there was no room for them there. The city is overflowing with casualties as it is. So they brought them all here to wait for the evacuation ships. When it started to rain, the wagons got stuck in the mud."

"Has anyone here been tending the soldiers? Do they at least have food and water?"

One of the female volunteers shrugged helplessly. "There's no way to get down the road to them through all this mud."

Julia stared at her. "Couldn't we walk down?"

"The mud is knee-deep!" one of the ladies said.

Julia drew a deep breath. "If you would be so kind as to help me fill some baskets with food, I'm willing to wade through the mud."

Four days later, Julia finally arrived in Fredericksburg. Reminders of James were everywhere, and she couldn't help thinking of him—even though she knew her feelings for him were very wrong. As night fell, she stood on the hill overlooking the river, remembering how the northern lights had blazed in the sky on that December night more than a year ago. James had said the lights were heaven-sent, to keep the world from despair. The despair and suffering she found in this city were greater than any she had ever seen.

Julia still hadn't written to Nathaniel, but she knew that she couldn't put it off any longer. In the end, as painful as it was, she decided that what she had to say was really very simple:

Dear Nathaniel,

I am in Fredericksburg, Virginia, working as a nurse. I'm sorry.

Julia

Chapter Twenty-three

Cold Harbor, Virginia
May 1864

The soldier groaned in pain as Phoebe tore open the sleeve of his uniform to examine his wound. One look at the raw flesh and shattered elbow told her that he would need surgery. She poured powdered morphine into the wound, then carefully removed some of his gear and sponged his face to make him more comfortable while he waited his turn. The temporary field hospital had been set up outside a small whitewashed church near a crossroads called Cold Harbor—mere miles from Richmond. As the battle raged nearby, the church had quickly filled with hundreds of casualties until the yard was overflowing with them, too. Dr. McGrath and the other surgeons couldn't keep up.

"Would you like a sip of brandy?" she asked the soldier.

He nodded. She could tell by his new uniform and youthful face that he was a fresh recruit—as she once had been. She lifted his head to help him drink and brushed against a piece of paper fastened to the back of his uniform. "What's this?" she asked.

"My name and address. We knew it would be a bloodbath today. The Rebels got here first and dug in behind breastworks. That meant we had to charge across the open field. So last night some of us wrote our names and addresses on paper and pinned it to our coats so they'd know where to send our bodies." He swallowed another sip and looked up at Phoebe. Fear filled his eyes. "Am I going to make it? I-I'm afraid to die."

She remembered how scared she and Ted had been the first time they'd gone into battle at Williamsburg, how terrified they'd both been of dying. She knew exactly how he felt. "We're gonna do our best to see that you live," she told him. "Don't you worry none. Is there anything else I can do for you before I help this next fella?"

"Pray for me. Pray for God to have mercy on my soul."

Phoebe had seen Reverend Greene earlier that morning, moving between the church pews, comforting some of the men. "You know what?" she said, slowly rising to her feet. "I haven't had much practice at praying, but there's a minister here who does it a whole lot better than me. I'll go fetch him for you."

She wove between the sprawled bodies, searching for the minister, wishing she could muffle the pitiful sounds of men moaning and weeping and crying out in pain every time they were moved. The doctors would do their best for them here, but after surgery they would have to endure a long, jolting ambulance ride to the evacuation hospital at White House Landing.

Phoebe found the minister inside the church, kneeling beside a soldier who had just died. Reverend Greene's eyes were closed, and she saw the deep emotion written on his face. She waited quietly until he finished his prayer. "Excuse me, Reverend," she said when he stood again. "There's a soldier over yonder who's asking for somebody to pray with him. Can you spare a moment?"

"Certainly, Miss Bigelow. Lead the way." He followed her in silence. Phoebe knew from her own experience that sometimes the best way to grieve the loss of one patient was to help another.

"This here is Chaplain Greene," she told the soldier. "He'll be glad to pray with you."

"Thanks," he murmured.

She moved on to the next soldier and the next, but she noticed that the minister was still talking with the boy a while later when the orderlies finally carried him to Dr. McGrath for surgery. Phoebe hurried over to join them, remembering the last meeting between the two men and worrying that they might clash again. But the doctor ignored the minister completely as he crouched to examine his patient. And Reverend Greene continued preaching to the boy as if the doctor wasn't even there.

"Those who know Christ have the promise of eternal life," Greene was saying. "Do you have that assurance?"

"Do you have any sensation at all in this hand?" Dr. McGrath asked. The soldier looked from one man to the other as if unsure which one to answer.

"We don't need to fear death, knowing that He has prepared a place for those He loves," Greene continued.

"I'm going to lift your wrist to take your pulse. Tell me if you can feel my fingers."

"Salvation is a free gift. . . ."

Finally the doctor had had enough. "Would you please shut up!" he yelled. "I'm trying to save this man's life."

Reverend Greene frowned. "There is little use in saving his life if his soul is lost." Dr. McGrath stood, motioning for the minister to step aside with him. "Kindly go do your hocus-pocus someplace else. You're scaring my patients. They hear you babbling about heaven and they think they're going to die."

"You know very well that some of them *are* going to die. I'm simply preparing them to meet God."

"They'll meet Him a lot sooner if you don't get out of my way and let me work!" He returned to his patient, signaling to the orderlies to take him into the church for surgery.

The boy's eyes went wide with fear. "No, wait! Where are you taking me? What are you going to do? Come with me, Reverend. I'm scared!"

"There's no room for the chaplain in there," Dr. McGrath said. "He'll be waiting right out here when you come out of surgery."

"You're going to cut my arm off, aren't you? Please don't let him cut it off, Reverend!"

The doctor rested his hand on the boy's head. "A team of three doctors, including myself, will decide what needs to be done. I never amputate without a patient's permission. However, in your case I believe that amputation is necessary."

"No! No! I don't want to lose my arm!"

"It's not possible to repair the massive damage to your elbow. If you won't let us amputate, you may as well stay out here. The chaplain can get you ready to die."

"There's no need to be so cold about it," Reverend Greene said.

"I'm being honest. There's a very good chance he'll live if we amputate. But if he keeps this mess it will putrefy and he'll die of blood poisoning. It's his choice."

"I don't want to die!"

"Let me have a moment to speak with him, please," the minister said.

Dr. McGrath turned to Phoebe. "Who's next, then? Let's go."

A different patient was taken into surgery, and Phoebe watched from a distance as Reverend Greene continued talking to the boy, praying with him. A half hour later Dr. McGrath emerged from the church again.

"He's ready now," the minister told him. "Do what needs to be done."

Phoebe and Reverend Greene were both waiting when the orderlies brought the unconscious boy out of surgery. His elbow ended with a bandaged stump. The minister blanched and quickly looked away. Phoebe didn't blame him one bit. Even after all this time, she still hadn't grown used to the horror of amputation. She gave Reverend Greene a moment to recover before instructing him what to do next.

"It's important to watch for bleeding, Reverend. If you can't stay with him, then wake him up so he can tell somebody else if he starts to bleed."

He nodded, dazed.

"It's also a good idea to keep his arm covered up, at first. Don't let him see . . . what's left . . . until he's prepared for the shock of it."

"How will he see that it's bleeding if he's covered up?"

Phoebe recalled the warm, wet sensation of her own wound and shuddered. "Trust me, he'll know. Come get me if he needs something for the pain." She paused a moment, then added, "And please don't let him give up and die, even if heaven is a pretty nice place."

Phoebe's work seemed unending, the slaughter that was taking place at Cold Harbor unimaginable. A wounded officer told her that he'd seen more than six thousand Union soldiers fall in the first half hour of battle. The medical team fought hard to save every man they could, but there were many who were too severely wounded to survive. All Phoebe could do for those patients was to keep them soothed and comfortable until they died.

At last there was a pause in the battle. The two armies reached a stalemate as they glared at each other across the battlefield—the Rebels defending their land, the Union unwilling to sacrifice any more men by hurling them at the Confederate breastworks. But neither side would call an official ceasefire so that the wounded men, lying in the field between the two armies, could be tended to.

For another long day, Phoebe worked with the ambulance crews to evacuate as many of the previously injured men as they could to White House Landing in order to make room for more casualties. Late in the afternoon she saw Reverend Greene searching for someone among the waiting men.

"You looking for anyone in particular?" she asked as she walked over to talk with him.

"The boy with the amputated arm. The one I prayed with the other day."

"He's doing pretty good. They already took him to White House Landing. Listen, I know it was a terrible thing, but Dr. McGrath was right. Taking that soldier's arm off was the only way to save his life."

The minister glanced around as if expecting the doctor to appear suddenly. "I understand that McGrath is your friend, Miss Bigelow, but I can't pretend to like him. I want you to know that I've sent inquiries to the authorities in Connecticut. I'm awaiting their answer."

"Dr. McGrath told me the whole story. He didn't kill that rich man, the man killed himself. The police found a suicide note. That's why they let the doctor go."

"And you believe his story?"

"Yes, sir. I do. I'm sure the police will tell you the same thing when they write back."

"We'll see. The report has likely been delayed seeing as the army has been on the move all month. The letter probably hasn't caught up with me yet. Even so, the doctor is still a very disagreeable man. I don't know how Julia could stand to work with him for as long as she did."

"If you don't mind me asking . . . how is Julia?"

The minister quickly looked away, but not before Phoebe saw him battle a storm of emotions. She wondered if something terrible had happened to Julia. "She broke off our engagement," he finally managed to say.

"I'm sorry."

He struggled for control. When he turned to Phoebe again, she was surprised to see that the emotion that had won out was anger. "She's down here in Virginia," he said. "She wrote to me from Fredericksburg. She's working there, as a nurse."

"That's not far at all. Maybe you could ride along in one of the ambulances and go talk to her. Find out why she broke it off."

"I know why. She decided she would rather be a nurse than my wife."

"Can't she be both?"

Her question made him angrier still. "No, Miss Bigelow. She cannot."

"Listen, I know this is none of my business," Phoebe said, "but can I tell you something?"

"What."

From the way he said it, Phoebe knew that Reverend Greene did not like people telling him what to do. Even so, she spoke her mind.

"If the man I loved asked me to marry him, I'd be so happy I wouldn't let anything stand in our way. For sure I'd find a way to get to Fredericksburg and talk things over with him."

"Would you give up nursing if he asked you to?"

"That's a dumb question. Why on earth would he ask me to stop helping people?"

His face grew so red and angry looking that all of a sudden Phoebe understood. "That's what happened, isn't it?" she said. "Julia came back to be a nurse, and you didn't want her to."

"I don't want her to be in any danger. Not only is there a risk from bullets and shells, but there are thousands of men in these camps, far away from their homes and wives. A good many of them are unsavory characters, capable of anything. It isn't proper for an unmarried woman to do this sort of work."

"So what I'm doing ain't proper?" she asked. He didn't reply. "You know, that's why I never went to church back home. They were always ticking off all the rules and telling me how I fell short of them all. I was at the hospital with Julia for more than half a year, and she never once did anything improper with any of those men. They respected her. Everyone could tell she came from a high-class family, but she gave up all her servants and money and things so she could help people. Didn't Jesus tell the rich man to sell all he had and give to the poor so he would have treasures in heaven? You ought to be right proud of her."

He seemed taken aback by her words. "I-I was proud of her. It's the people in my church back home that won't understand. They'll never accept her as their minister's wife if she keeps defying convention and scorning proper society."

"So it wasn't Julia who broke it off, then. It was the folks in your church. Seems like you were willing to let them tell you what to do and Julia wasn't."

"She knew how I felt about it," he replied bitterly. "I made my wishes very clear to her. And she went to Fredericksburg anyway."

"Do you love her, Reverend Greene? Or are you content to spend the rest of your life without her? Because it seems to me that if you don't bend a little, that's exactly what you're gonna be doing."

He started to turn away, and Phoebe was sure he was about to storm off. But then they heard Dr. McGrath, of all people, calling to him. "Chaplain . . . Chaplain Greene, wait! I need your help."

Greene paused, turning back. "Yes, what is it?" he asked coldly.

"I can't get any of the military staff to listen to me. I can't even get near them. Maybe they'll listen to you."

Phoebe could tell how upset Dr. McGrath was by the way he ran his fingers through his hair and tugged on his beard. He couldn't seem to stand still.

"For mercy's sake, Chaplain, we've got to convince them to call a truce so we can help the wounded. It's been two days now, and injured soldiers are still lying out there in that field between the two armies. Both sides are too stubborn to call a halt so we can bring them in for treatment. The generals won't even stop to bury their dead."

"Of course I'll help," the minister said. "I'm on good terms with at least one brigadier general. We can start there."

Phoebe watched in amazement as the two men strode off together as if there had never been any hard feelings between them at all. But it wasn't until a third day had come and gone that the opposing generals finally called a temporary cease-fire. When they did, Phoebe prepared to go to work with a host of doctors, nurses, and stretcher-bearers, collecting the wounded and bringing them to the field hospital.

The battle had been spread out over five or six acres—and every inch of the battlefield was strewn with bodies, as thickly as if the men had decided to lie down side by side. Phoebe waded into the midst of the carnage, looking for a survivor to help, gazing at each face, searching for Ted's. But the first dozen soldiers she bent to help were all dead, their bodies already stiff and bloating in the sun. The stench after three days was nauseating. But it wasn't the smell that drove her from the battlefield and back to her tent. It was the vastness of it all, the sheer number of vibrant young men like the ones she had served with, fallen—for nothing. Not one inch of territory had been gained, nor was the war any closer to an end. The senselessness of it left her numb with grief.

She stayed in her tent, weeping, until her tears were finally exhausted. Later, she went back to the church to help. But she didn't find the flurry of activity there that she had expected. One of the nurses told her that Dr. McGrath had returned to his tent, and Phoebe decided to go apologize to him for not helping. He sat inside on a campstool, his head in his hands.

"Doctor McGrath. . . ? I just come to say I'm sorry that I didn't help—"

"It doesn't matter, Phoebe," he said hoarsely. "We were too late."

"What do you mean?"

He lifted his head to look at her, his eyes red with grief. "Do you know how many men we found alive out there?"

She shook her head.

"Two. Only two. Dear God, what a waste. . . ."

City Point, Virginia
July 1864

Julia stood at the steamship's rail with the other Sanitary Commission workers as they docked at City Point, their new hospital base at the junction of the James and Appomattox Rivers. This was the third time the evacuation hospital had been moved since May as they followed Grant's army farther into Virginia. The first move had taken them down the Rappahannock River from Fredericksburg to a new base in Port Royal. In June they'd moved up the Pamunkey River to White House Landing, where Julia had served on the hospital ship with Sister Irene two years ago. Now they had been transferred to Depot Hospital at City Point near Petersburg.

After Cold Harbor, Grant's army had slipped away from the battlefield by night to advance toward Petersburg, crossing the James River on a huge pontoon bridge. Union engineers built the 2,100-foot span in only eight hours, and it had taken the massive army days to finish crossing it. But the four-day battle to take Petersburg, where the Rebels were entrenched, had failed, and now that city was under siege. Julia and the other medical workers had followed Grant's army by ship.

She gazed at her new surroundings as the steamship finished docking. City Point's cluster of homes and church steeples sat on a high bluff overlooking the two rivers. White-roofed army tents far outnumbered the houses, stretching from the village in both directions as far as she could see. Newly built warehouses and workshops clustered along the shore below. She saw so many canvas-covered army wagons lined up near the wharves that she couldn't even begin to count them all.

"This was just a sleepy little village on the river before the war," she heard one of the Commission nurses say. "Now it looks like a major seaport."

Ships' masts filled the harbor like trees in a forest, surrounded by steamboats, barges, rowboats, and skiffs. Julia counted eight wharves spread out along a mile of riverfront, crawling with blue-coated soldiers and Negro dock workers. Barges carried mountains of barrels and crates, and bales of hay for the army's livestock. A row of new caissons and limbers for the field artillery lined one long wharf from the dock to the shore. A seagoing steamer, moored beside her own, unloaded two companies of fresh troops along with dozens of horses. On another wharf, she was amazed to see a barge unloading a steam locomotive onto the railroad tracks that snaked along the foot of the bluff. With all this manpower and equipment, surely victory would come soon.

Julia stepped down the gangplank with the four other Commission nurses and was met by a row of mule-drawn freight wagons. "You the folks from the Sanitary Commission?" one of the teamsters asked.

"Yes, we are," the nursing director replied.

"Otis Whitney," the man said. "I've got orders to haul you and your goods out to Agency Row."

Julia waited on shore while a crew of contrabands loaded the Commission's supplies onto the freight wagons. Above the whistles and shouts of the workmen, she could hear the sound of water lapping against the piers, the braying of mules, the distant whine of a sawmill. The blistering July sun shone bright and hot, reflecting off the river like bronze. There was scarcely a breeze, and the air tasted like hot metal.

When the work was nearly finished, Otis Whitney sidled up to where the women stood waiting. He was a powerfully built man in his mid-thirties with long, greasy black hair and an ill-kempt beard. Julia thought he looked like an outlaw or an escaped convict. He removed his hat to wipe the sweat off his forehead, then jammed it onto his head again. He stood very close to Julia. "You nurses just keep getting prettier and prettier," he said, brushing against her. "What's your name?"

She was so astounded to be addressed in such a familiar fashion by a common teamster that she couldn't reply.

"My name's Otis," he said. "Me and my brother own this freight-hauling business. Also own a little eating establishment where we sell oysters and such to the soldiers. Sell liquor, too, when the provost marshal ain't looking." He winked and nudged her with his elbow. "Doing right well for ourselves since the war started. Reckon we'll be rich by the time it ends. We're moving up in society."

She breathed a sigh of relief when he walked away again to oversee the final loading. But as the wagons were leaving, she was dismayed to learn that Otis Whitney had arranged for the other nurses to ride in three of the wagons, leaving Julia alone with him. "You're gonna ride right up there next to me, darling," he said, patting the seat.

Julia wanted to protest, but it was too late. The other freight wagons were already rolling up the road, and his was the only one left. He kicked a box into place for her to use as a step, then took her hand to help her up onto the wagon seat. He left no space between the two of them when he climbed up beside her. She could only hope that it wasn't a long ride.

"How far away are the Commission's headquarters?" she asked. She shifted her legs and straightened her skirts as an excuse to move away from him, but her efforts were in vain. He leaned against her as he drove his mule team up the hill, brushing shoulders with her again. He smelled of sweat and horses and whiskey.

"Just outside the city a little ways, darling. No more than a mile. It's right across the road from Depot Hospital. We call it Agency Row because there's a whole bunch of relief agencies camped there. They stay in tents. Pretty gal like you ought to be in a house, though. You tell that Commission of yours to grab yourselves a decent Rebel house like some of the army officers did. Be out of the elements that way. 'Course, you're welcome to come stay at my house." He nudged her with his elbow again.

"I'm quite used to a tent, thank you."

The mules snorted and puffed as they climbed up the steep road from the river, passing a grim pyramid of pine coffins waiting to be filled. Julia also saw workers carrying two closed coffins down the wharf to a waiting ship.

"This your first visit to City Point?" Otis asked.

"Yes. I had no idea it was such a busy place."

"I'm told there's some two hundred ships coming and going every day. Made me a rich man. I hear that pretty gals like you are partial to rich men." He winked at her as if they were old friends.

"Is that bread I smell?" she asked, desperate to change the subject.

"Yep. The army has a huge bakery over yonder. They make more than a hundred thousand loaves a day. It's still warm when the men get it in the trenches."

They passed a row of stores and eating houses where sutlers sold nonration food and drink to the soldiers. "That's my establishment," Otis said, pointing to one of the shanties. "How about I treat you to dinner there tonight?"

"Thank you, but my nursing work keeps me much too busy for a social life. I've heard that Depot Hospital is very large."

"More than a thousand tents, all told. Plus there's a separate hospital for the Negroes. They're using colored soldiers now, did you hear? Got a whole bunch of them down here. Can't say as I'll ever get used to the idea of colored fellas toting guns. Ought to stay separate if you ask me. I won't let any of them in my establishment."

Julia saw row after row of hospital tents ahead and the other three freight wagons pulling to a halt. She was relieved that she'd finally arrived. Otis leaped down first and reached up to help Julia. She didn't want him touching her, but it was too far to jump down by herself, and he hadn't put the box in place for a step. She was revolted when he grabbed her waist to lift her down.

"Sure you won't change your mind about dinner?" he asked, his hands lingering a little too long. She twisted away.

"No, thank you. I have too much work to do."

"You're an awful pretty little thing. I told you my name, but you never told me yours."

Julia hesitated, appalled by his coarseness. She considered lying again and telling him she was married, but she was afraid that the other Commission workers would overhear. "It's Hoffman . . . Nurse Hoffman."

"You must have a first name."

"Julia," she said reluctantly.

"Ever had oysters, Julia? I could bring you a mess of them."

"I have, and I don't care much for them. Thanks just the same." She hurried to join the other ladies and settle into her new home. But Otis Whitney continued to hang around as the Commission's goods were unloaded, watching Julia from a distance as she was assigned to a tent. When he was ready to leave, he went out of his way to find her and speak to her one last time.

"I never did see a gal as pretty as you, Julia. I'll bet you and me could have a real good time together. All the single gals I've met around here are in business for themselves, if you know what I mean."

For as long as she'd been a nurse, Julia had never felt afraid of any of the men she'd worked with. Otis Whitney was the first. He was exactly the sort of man that Nathaniel had been worried about—and the main reason why he hadn't wanted her to return to nursing.

"I am not that kind of woman, Mr. Whitney," she said in a shaking voice. "I'm here to take care of the wounded men, nothing else. Now, if you'll please excuse me, I have a great deal of work to do."

Julia was eager to begin work, and she wasted no time unpacking her things. Depot Hospital's location on a high bluff overlooking the Appomattox River was peaceful and serene in spite of the grievous nature of her work. There were plenty of shade trees around, and in the evening a cool breeze often drifted up from the river. She learned that the doctors treated the wounded men at field-dressing stations near the trenches first, then sent them by ambulance train on specially constructed tracks to Depot Hospital. The hospital had its own dock where recuperating patients could be loaded onto ships and sent to hospitals up north.

Most of the patients she tended suffered from gunshot and shrapnel wounds. The opposing armies now lobbed shells and bullets at each other from their networks of trenches as the siege of Petersburg continued.

"When you wake up each morning, you never know if you'll be alive when the sun goes down at night," one soldier told her.

"We're so used to hearing Minie balls whistling over our heads that we don't even duck anymore."

"Is that what happened to you, Captain?" she asked as she carefully removed the dressing on his shoulder. "Did you forget to duck?"

"No, ma'am. A piece of shell hit me. You can see those coming, but there's no place to hide."

Julia checked the wound for signs of pyemia and gangrene as Dr. McGrath had taught her, then doused it with carbolic acid and replaced the bandage. "Did you see this shell coming?" she asked.

The captain nodded. "With shells, the first thing you see is a puff of smoke behind enemy lines. Couple of seconds later, you hear the *boom* and see a dark speck climbing up in the sky. Ever hear a shell screaming through the air, ma'am?"

"Yes, I have. One landed quite close to me at Bull Run."

He gritted his teeth as she worked. "Terrible sound, isn't it? By the time you figure out it's coming right at you, it's too late."

Julia finished dressing his wound and moved to the next patient. "I don't see any wounds at all on you," she said, looking him over.

"Sun got to me," he said. "There's no shade down in those trenches. I was digging away when all of a sudden I felt dizzy and couldn't walk straight. The sergeant thought I was drunk until I fell down and took a fit."

"Can I get you anything?" Julia asked.

"You can do us all a favor and douse him for 'graybacks,'" the captain in the next bed said. "He's lousy with them."

"Won't do any good," the man replied. "They'll be crawling all over me again as soon as I go back. You know what they say, ma'am—we got 'graycoats' in front of us and 'graybacks' on our rear."

Julia couldn't help laughing. Her next patient was smiling, too, even though he looked quite ill. She knew right away from his swollen legs, discolored skin, and puffy mouth that he suffered from a severe case of scurvy. "I just arrived with the Sanitary Commission a few days ago," she told him. "We brought some fresh supplies. What would taste good to you?"

"Anything except those awful desecrated vegetables the army gives us."

Julia smiled. "I think you mean 'desiccated' vegetables."

"No, ma'am, by the time the army's through with them they're desecrated. The doctor's been feeding me potatoes in vinegar, pickles in vinegar, and kraut in vinegar, but I can't say as I care for all that vinegar."

"Let me go see what else I can find," Julia said. "I'll be back shortly."

She left them and started across the hospital grounds, weaving among the rows. Suddenly a familiar figure emerged from a nearby tent. There was no mistaking a woman that tall with hair that yellow. She wore the same dark blue calico dress that Julia had bought for her in Washington.

"Phoebe Bigelow!" Julia said in surprise. She rushed forward to embrace her friend. "What on earth are you doing here? I thought you went home a year ago."

"I never did make it home," Phoebe replied a bit sheepishly. "I was still hanging around Washington City when Dr. McGrath asked me to work with him as a nurse."

"He *asked* you?"

"Yeah. He was going back to Fredericksburg as a field surgeon, and he asked me to come with him."

"He told me women didn't belong on the battlefield."

"They don't. But he knew I already been to the battlefield as a soldier. Tell you the truth, I reckon he was afraid I'd enlist again, so he figured he might as well take me along so he wouldn't have to carve any more shrapnel out of me."

"Would you have enlisted again?" Julia asked.

Phoebe shrugged. "I didn't know what else to do with myself, to tell you the truth. But I like being a nurse real fine."

Julia was almost afraid to ask the next question. "Is Dr. McGrath here at Depot Hospital?"

"Yeah. I can take you to see him if—"

"No, no. I really don't care to see him at all. In fact, I'd just as soon avoid him if I can. Good thing it's a big hospital."

Phoebe studied her curiously for a long moment then said, "I heard you was in Fredericksburg."

"How did you hear that?"

"Your friend Reverend Greene told me. He explained all about your engagement and said that you broke it off."

"Oh, no. Don't tell me Nathaniel is here, too?" Julia glanced around in dread as if he might suddenly appear out of nowhere, as Phoebe had.

"I'm not sure where he's at. I ain't seen him since Cold Harbor. I told him he should go up to Fredericksburg and patch things up with you, but I reckon he's pretty stubborn."

"Nathaniel never answered my last letter. I wasn't even sure he got it. But if he told you our engagement is cancelled . . ." Tears came to Julia's eyes, and she couldn't finish. Phoebe rested her hand on Julia's arm.

"He got mad when he told me about it. He said it was because he didn't want you to be a nurse no more and you wanted to be one. I'm real sorry, Julia. I know how hard it is to lose someone you love."

She could only nod. She was still standing beside Phoebe, trying to pull herself together so she could return to her work, when she heard someone calling her name. She looked up—and was dismayed to see Otis Whitney striding toward her, carrying a small wooden crate.

"Oh no," she moaned.

"Howdy, Julia. I brought you another present."

He held out the box to her. It contained a dozen lemons. Otis looked as though he had recently washed his hair, but it hadn't improved his sinister appearance.

"I'll bet your patients could use these, huh?"

"Yes, they could. Thank you, Mr. Whitney."

He grinned. His eyeteeth were pointed, like a wolf's. "Didn't I ask you to call me Otis?"

"Thank you, Otis. I know a soldier who could use these right away. Good day." Julia hurried away. She was grateful when Phoebe decided to follow her—and Otis didn't.

"He's a mighty rough-looking fella," Phoebe said. "Who is he?"

"He owns the freight-hauling company that brings the Commission all their supplies. He's been showing up nearly every day, bringing me presents. I don't like him hanging around, but the nursing director begged me to be nice to him. She's afraid to make him angry for fear he'll raise our prices—or cut off our supplies altogether." Julia paused when she reached the end of the row. "Otis Whitney makes me nervous, Phoebe. I'm afraid of him."

"I don't blame you one bit. Maybe you should tell him you're married—like you used to tell folks in Washington."

"It's too late. He knows I'm single. I was tired of lying—but now I wish that I had."

Chapter Twenty-four

City Point, Virginia
July 1864

A rumbling, muffled explosion woke Julia from a sound sleep. The ground beneath her trembled like an earthquake. She had been close to the battlefield before, but this was unlike any sound she had ever heard. The sun hadn't risen yet, so she lit a candle and quickly pulled on her clothes. By the time she was dressed, she could hear the distant *boom* of mortar fire. Several other Commission nurses emerged from their tents at the same time she did.

"What was that explosion?" one of them asked.

"I'm not sure, but now they're firing mortars," Julia said. "That means the casualties will start to pour in soon. I'm going over to meet the ambulance train."

For the next hour, Julia worked in the medical supply tent with the other nurses, making sure they had plenty of tourniquets, bandages, morphine, and iodine, along with buckets of water and sponges. She heard the deep murmur of men's voices in the surgical tents as the physicians prepared to operate, making sure all their instruments and supplies of ether and chloroform were ready. In the distance, the sounds of battle grew louder and more intense. There was little Julia could do once everything was unpacked except brace herself for what she was about to face. She stood outside near the railroad tracks, watching as the distant pall of smoke turned the dawning sun fire-red.

"Hello, Mrs. Hoffman."

Julia recognized the sound of James McGrath's voice before she turned to face him. He had stepped up beside her as she'd watched the sunrise. His auburn hair was sleep-tousled, and he was rolling up the sleeves of his shirt in preparation. Julia's heart sped up as she recalled his touch. His kiss was still a vivid memory after all this time. It had been a year since she'd last seen him in Gettysburg, but the strength of her reaction to him surprised her. She quickly looked away, ashamed once again. She should not have such feelings for a married man.

"Hello, Doctor," she said softly.

"You're the last person in the world I ever expected to see working here."

"I know. I'm surprised to be here myself. I kept reading in the papers how there was such a great need for nurses, and I . . . I couldn't seem to stay away." He stood close to her. Her heart continued to race.

"Look at that sky," he said after a moment. He pointed to the horizon, where it appeared that the sun had set the clouds aflame. Julia thought of the night he had shown her the sky in Fredericksburg, and she shivered.

"Have you ever read the book of Revelation, Mrs. Hoffman? These past few months I've wondered if the Apocalypse has finally come—the terrible fury of the wrath of God, unleashed." He exhaled, and when he spoke again his voice was husky with emotion. "I've watched General Grant sacrifice fifty thousand men since spring. Fifty thousand! That's half as many as the entire Union army lost in the prior three years. I'm not sure I can watch it much longer."

"I know. The newspapers are calling Grant a butcher," Julia said.

"And they're calling me a butcher for sending so many men home with missing arms and legs—as if I enjoyed this work."

She was alarmed to hear how depressed and discouraged he sounded—and today's work hadn't even begun. She could hear the ambulance train approaching, bringing in the day's first casualties, and she knew that James would have to begin his grueling task of amputating limbs very soon.

"How long has it been since you've been home?" she asked softly. "Maybe you should take a leave of absence and go be with your family for a little while."

He didn't reply. Instead, he said, "I know why you came back. It's because this war has changed us. We're no longer the same people we were before it began. It's as if we're forever drawn toward death—trying to stop it, trying to change the outcome somehow. . . . Only we can't."

The despair in his voice alarmed her. She groped for words, desperate to say something to comfort him. "James, listen. Death is in God's hands, not yours. It's up to Him to decide who will die today and who will live. But life is in our hands. It's His gift to us. He wants us to enjoy it, celebrate it, treat it as a treasured gift for as long as we have it and never ever take it for granted. You're right, the war has changed me. It's taught me that I must live as gratefully and as unselfishly as I can until the day I die. That's why you should go home and live as—"

"You're here for unselfish reasons?" he asked. "Is that why you decided to become a nurse?"

"No, not at first," she said, remembering. "Your original opinion of me was quite accurate, I'm sorry to say. I was a spoiled rich girl trying to prove something when I first came to Washington. But I've learned a lot since then. At Gettysburg—"

"You were there?"

"Yes." Julia recalled the afternoon she had taken care of him, and for a moment the memory left her shaken. James hadn't been wearing his wedding ring. She instinctively glanced at his hands, looking for it now, but he had his arms folded across his chest, his hands hidden.

"Until Gettysburg," she continued, "I was working for the wrong reasons. At first it was to prove myself worthy in someone's eyes. Later it was out of guilt, trying to find atonement in God's eyes. But atonement is free, never earned. And I've learned that the only person I need to please with my life is God."

She could no longer be heard above the clamoring locomotive

as it rumbled up to the hospital's siding in a cloud of steam. As soon as it halted, the orderlies rushed forward to empty the flatcars, which were loaded with blue-uniformed bodies. Neither Julia nor James moved.

"Maybe this is the Apocalypse," she said, and James bent slightly closer to hear her above the noise. "But as my . . . my minister said, we need to ask God how He wants us to live in the times He has appointed for us. If we work with Him, using the gifts and the strength He provides, then we'll help build His kingdom, for His glory, here on earth. And that's really the only thing that matters."

James was quiet for a long moment. "Julia," he finally said, "does your husband know you're down here?"

She looked up at him. Their eyes met for the first time. "I need to tell you the truth, James," she said, her heart racing faster. "I'm not married. I lied when I came to Washington because it was the only way anyone would ever hire me as a nurse."

He stared speechlessly, a thousand questions in his eyes.

"Robert Hoffman is my cousin," she said. "It was convenient to use his name. After I returned home, I became engaged to a man who I've known for several years, but he wanted me to give up nursing . . . and our engagement ended when I came back here to work."

James gripped her shoulders with both hands as if he needed to steady himself. "You aren't married?"

"Dr. McGrath!" someone shouted, interrupting. "Over here! Hurry!"

"No, I'm not," Julia said. "I'm sorry that I lied to you. Please forgive me."

She watched him carefully for his reaction, but his features showed only shock as he continued to stare at her. His grip hurt her arms.

"Dr. McGrath!" the man shouted a second time. "Please!"

Without another word, James released her and hurried away to attend his first patient.

As Phoebe talked to the steady stream of patients who poured into the hospital, she gradually learned the story of what had caused the thunderous explosion she'd heard early that morning. Union soldiers had dug a five-hundred-foot tunnel beneath Rebel lines and packed it with tons of gunpowder, trying to blast through a Confederate stronghold. When the fuse was lit, it tore a huge hole in the earth, leaving a crater more than two hundred feet long, sixty feet wide, and thirty feet deep. Union troops had rushed forward into the breach, but with no way to scale the wall on the other side they became easy targets for the Rebels. Thousands more Yankees fell as they tried to rescue their comrades.

Phoebe worked all day, meeting trainload after trainload of wounded men. Late that afternoon as the orderlies lifted one more stretcher from the flatcar and laid yet another dying soldier on the ground in front of her, Phoebe suddenly confronted the horror she had long feared. She stared down at the face she had searched thousands of faces to find. The bloody, badly injured man was Ted.

"No . . . Oh, please, God . . ." she begged as she sank to the ground beside him. "Not Ted. . . . Please . . . not him." This was just a terrible dream, and she would soon wake up. Better never to see Ted's face again than to see him like this. But she wasn't dreaming.

Ted was groggy and only half conscious, moaning with pain. Shock had turned his face ash gray. Phoebe ripped his torn pant leg and saw that a shell had shattered his right leg, severing it nearly in half. She could barely see through her tears as she tightened the tourniquet on his thigh and poured powdered morphine onto the raw wound.

"Come on, Ted. Hang in there," she begged as she bathed his face with cool water. "Stay with me . . . stay awake. Come on, you ain't gonna die on me now." His eyes fluttered open and she saw him struggling to stay conscious, to focus on her. He was studying her. "You ain't seeing things, Ted. It's me."

"Ike? What are you. . . ? I thought you . . ."

She took his hand, squeezing it. "No, I'm alive. I'm a nurse now. I'm gonna get you all fixed up. There's this doctor I know, the one who saved my life. I'm gonna get him to help you, Ted. You're gonna make it."

"I know it's bad. I saw my leg. . . ." His entire body started to tremble even though sweat poured off him. His tawny brown skin was as pale as a corpse's.

"You're gonna live!" she shouted. "Hang it all, Ted, listen to me!"

"Hey, don't cry."

"I'm a *girl*!" she sobbed. "And girls can cry all they want to!" She released his hand and leaped up, running blindly toward the surgical tent to find Dr. McGrath. Her body shook nearly as badly as Ted's, making her movements clumsy and awkward.

The surgeons were operating outside on trestle tables. Phoebe didn't care how gory the scene was or whether she was interrupting the doctor or not as she called out to him.

"Dr. McGrath! Please, you gotta come help my friend Ted. He needs help right away, and I want *you* to operate. *Please!*"

He glanced up at her and nodded, then bent over his patient again, tying a suture. "You can finish with this," James told the other doctor. "I'll be right back."

"What? Wait!" the man sputtered. "James, you can't leave! Come back!"

James ignored him. "Show me where he is, Phoebe." He hurried to keep up with her as they jogged back to where she'd left Ted.

"Don't let him die," she begged when they reached his side. "I know you couldn't help my brother Willard, but you got to save Ted! You got to!" She started to kneel beside Ted again, but Dr. McGrath stopped her.

"Is this the man you're in love with?" he asked softly. She nodded. The doctor looked away for a long moment, his eyes closed. "Dear God," he sighed. Then he crouched beside Ted to look at his leg. He gently removed Ted's shoe to feel his toes and checked a spot near his ankle for a pulse. "How are you doing, son?" he asked as he worked.

"Not so good. . . ." Ted shuddered. "You can't save my leg, can you."

The doctor met Ted's gaze. "No. I'm sorry."

"Then don't waste your time on me. Go help someone else. I

don't want to go home without a leg."

"Ted, no!" Phoebe cried.

"I'd rather die than be crippled. I don't want everyone's pity."

"That's a very stupid choice," Dr. McGrath said quietly. "And a very selfish one. What about all the people who love you? They don't care how many legs you have. You should think about them, not yourself."

"Just tell me the truth," Ted said. "Am I gonna die even if you take my leg off?"

The doctor hesitated. "If you let me amputate there's a chance you will recover."

"A *chance*?"

"Yes. But if you don't give me permission, you will die."

"Please listen to him, Ted," Phoebe begged. "He's the best doctor there is."

Doctor McGrath reached out to feel Ted's forehead, his hand resting there for a moment. "Someone reminded me just this morning that life is a gift from God," James said. "You've lived it well so far, fighting for what you believe in. Don't throw it away now. Don't commit suicide."

Ted closed his eyes. He was shivering uncontrollably. "All right. Just get it over with."

James stood and signaled to the orderlies. "This man is next."

Phoebe followed Dr. McGrath as he strode back toward the outdoor operating area, struggling to control her fear. "I want to help you work on him," she said. "I want to make sure everything goes okay."

"I can't allow it, Phoebe. You're too closely involved. Besides, you're shaking like a leaf." He glanced around the crowded rail yard and spotted Julia. "Mrs. Hoffman, come here, please," he called. When Julia hurried over he said, "Stay with Phoebe while I operate on her friend. Keep her away from here."

Phoebe heard Ted cry out, "Oh, God! Oh, God!" as they moved him onto the operating table, his injured leg dangling. She broke down completely in Julia's arms, sobbing.

"He's in good hands," Julia soothed. "James is an excellent surgeon. Come on. You don't want to watch."

But Phoebe couldn't help looking over her shoulder at Ted one last time as Julia led her away. One of the doctors held the ether cone over Ted's face. Dr. McGrath reached into his case of surgical instruments and pulled out a saw. Then the earth tilted, and Phoebe knew she was going to faint.

"Don't look!" Julia said. She pushed Phoebe inside the nearest tent and sat her down on an upturned barrel. She forced Phoebe's head between her knees. "Keep it down until the dizziness passes," she ordered.

Gradually, the blood returned to Phoebe's head and she could lift it. But she couldn't stop her tears from falling or loosen the fear that gripped her heart like a fist.

"Is that soldier someone special to you?" Julia asked as she gently rubbed Phoebe's shoulders.

"Yes. It's Ted," she said. "I . . . I love him."

Julia had tears in her eyes as she knelt in front of Phoebe and wrapped her in her arms. "It's okay," she murmured. "It's okay. I understand."

Depot Hospital
August 1864

Phoebe watched as Dr. McGrath examined Ted's leg. More than a week had passed since Ted had been wounded, and he was gravely ill, lapsing in and out of delirium. When the doctor finished, he gently covered his leg with a sheet, then drew Phoebe aside.

"He has a long way to go, as you well know," he told her. "Right now he's too ill to be evacuated. The movement would kill him. We'll do what we can here to keep his fever down and fight the blood poisoning."

"I'll take real good care of him," she said.

"I know you will."

As soon as the doctor left, Phoebe returned to Ted's bedside. She dipped a sponge in water and began bathing his face to cool his fever. His eyes flickered open.

"Hey, Ike, I'm starting to get used to you being a girl . . . wearing a dress . . . long hair."

"I hate fussing with it every day. I wish it was still short."

He shook his head. "It's nice. It looks like the tassles from an ear of corn."

She tried to smile but tears filled her eyes. "That's what all the fellas tell me."

He reached for her hand as she bathed his chest, covering it with his own. "Phoebe . . . you're the best friend I ever had. Will you promise me something?"

She nodded.

"If anything happens to me, I want you to go see my ma. Take my things to her."

"You're gonna make it, Ted. You're a fighter, I know you are, and you're gonna lick this fever just like you licked the Bailey brothers. Remember?"

"You did most of the work." He smiled and Phoebe's heart squeezed painfully. How she'd missed that grin.

"We licked them together, Ted. And we can fight this fever together, too."

"Take her my things. Swear?"

Phoebe didn't want to think about him dying, didn't want to imagine doing what he was asking her to do. She quickly pictured a different scene instead. "When you're all better and this war's over, we're gonna go to that plantation and find your grandmother, right? She's a free woman now. You fought to win her freedom."

"It was worth losing a leg for that," he said quietly. "Or even a life—if it comes to that."

"Please don't talk that way."

"They have Negro regiments now," Ted said. "Have you heard? They fought right alongside me the other day—and for the first time in my life I felt real proud of who I am and where I came from. I'm not going to hide it anymore. I don't know if you heard, but after the battle at Antietam, where you were wounded, President Lincoln announced that when we win this war, my grandmother and all the other slaves would be set free. I know I joined up for all the wrong reasons, thinking it would be a great adventure and I'd come home a big hero. But the Lord had a much greater purpose for my life than that."

"I know," Phoebe said. "I joined up because I was running away from home. But it seems like I'm doing something good now that I'm here."

Ted nodded. His face looked very pale. She could tell by his eyes that he was in a lot of pain. "Your leg hurting you?" she asked.

"I don't understand why it hurts so much if it's gone."

"You need some more medicine?"

"Not yet. Listen, I want to tell you something. . . . Death comes for all of us, one way or another. In the meantime, Phoebe, you have to live knowing that each day counts. And serving God each day is what makes it count. Live for His glory—whether you understand what He's doing or not. Be faithful to Him."

Phoebe couldn't speak. She looked at the man she loved through a film of tears and dreaded the thought of ever losing him again. "Please don't die," she whispered.

"It isn't up to me. But what I'm trying to tell you is . . . it's all right if I do. I'll be okay . . . and you will be, too."

He was making her face something she didn't want to face. She looked away.

"Do me a favor," Ted said after a moment. "You know that other nurse—the one who's your friend?"

"You mean Julia?"

"Ask her to come here. I need to talk to her for a minute."

"Okay." Phoebe was afraid to ask why. She hurried from the tent, wanting to hide her tears from Ted, and went to find Julia.

As soon as she neared the Sanitary Commission's headquarters, Phoebe saw Otis Whitney's freight wagon and mule team parked outside. Her fists clenched. There was something very frightening about that man. Phoebe didn't like him hanging around her friend all the time, scaring her. High prices or not, the Commission needed to tell him to get lost. As Phoebe walked around the rear of the wagon, she heard Julia's panicked voice.

"Let go of me!"

"You owe me, you little flirt," Otis yelled.

"I have never flirted with you! Let go!"

Phoebe ran behind the tent toward the sound of their voices and saw Otis gripping Julia by the arm, half dragging her away from the hospital.

"You've been accepting my favors and presents all these weeks," he said, "and now you owe me. I'm gonna take what's coming to me."

"Let go of her!" Phoebe shouted.

Otis turned, startled, and Julia broke free. "Who are you?" he demanded as Phoebe strode right up to him. His breath smelled of alcohol.

"I'm her friend. Go home, you lousy drunk. And if you ever lay a hand on her again, Otis Whitney, it will be the last thing you ever do in this life."

"I ain't afraid of you," he slurred.

"You should be." She planted her hand in the center of his chest and pushed him as hard as she could. He staggered backward and nearly fell. Before he had time to recover, Phoebe grabbed Julia's hand and hurried away with her, weaving between the tents until they were out of his sight.

"I was so scared," Julia said, trying not to weep.

"Listen, we got to go report him to somebody. He can't keep coming around like this. He's dangerous."

"I think he was drunk. I'm glad you came when you did."

"Me too. I was looking for you 'cause my friend Ted wants to talk to you. I guess it can wait until another time, though."

Julia drew a shaky breath. "No, I think I'll get over this faster if I do something to take my mind off that horrible man."

"You sure?"

Julia nodded.

"That's Ted's tent over yonder. I reckon he wants to talk to you alone."

"All right."

Phoebe watched as Julia ducked inside, then she looked all around to see if Otis Whitney had followed them. She needed to tell someone about what had just happened, but she didn't know whom to tell. She finally decided on Dr. McGrath and hurried away to find him.

Julia paused just inside the tent and took another deep breath. She was trembling and badly shaken, but she hadn't wanted to worry her friend. Phoebe was right, Otis Whitney should never be allowed near this camp again.

Julia slowly exhaled to calm herself as she walked over to Ted Wilson's bedside. His eyes were closed. His breathing sounded labored. He looked as white as the sheet that was draped over his mutilated leg. Julia closed her eyes as she whispered a prayer for him.

"Thanks for coming so soon."

She opened them at the sound of Ted's voice. "How are you feeling?"

"Not so good. Listen, I know there's a good chance I'm going to die. Would you write a letter home for me?"

"Of course. Let me get some paper." But she wondered, as she rummaged in the supply chest for the writing materials the Commission furnished, why he hadn't asked Phoebe to write it for him. "Okay, go ahead," she said when she was ready.

"It's to my mother," he told her and gave the address. Ted kept his eyes closed as he dictated as if too weak to keep them open. Julia wrote down his words.

Dear Ma,

One of the nurses is writing this because I don't have the strength to write it myself. I need to tell you about a good friend of mine named Ike—I mean, Phoebe—Bigelow. She's a girl, but she's the best friend I ever had. She saved my life twice, and she would save me this time, too, if she could.

I asked Phoebe to bring all of my things to you if I don't make it home. But I'm asking you to take her in and be a mother to her when she does. She needs you, Ma. She never knew her own mother, and she doesn't have any family to go home to. Take care of her for me. She's my best friend.

With love, your son,
Ted

Julia laid the paper on his lap and put the pen in his hand. "Here, you sign it," she said. He scrawled his name, then laid back and closed his eyes again.

"Will you mail it for me?"

"Yes, of course."

"Thanks."

By the time Julia stepped outside the tent again, she felt drained. She looked around for Phoebe, hoping she would be waiting to walk back to her quarters with her, but there was no sign of her. There was no sign of Otis Whitney, either. Julia chided herself for being afraid and set off across the hospital grounds alone.

It seemed to take Phoebe forever to find Dr. McGrath as she searched tent after tent in the sprawling hospital complex. When she finally did, the incident with Otis Whitney alarmed him. "We need to contact the provost marshal right away," he said. "If Whitney threatened her, he should be arrested. Where's Julia now?"

"I left her with Ted."

"Go stay with her, Phoebe. Don't leave her alone for one second."

Phoebe jogged back to Ted's tent as fast as she could, her heart pounding. Julia was gone. "Did you see which way she went?" she asked Ted. He shook his head.

She raced back across the hospital grounds to the Commission headquarters. When Phoebe saw that Otis Whitney's wagon was still parked outside, she felt sick with dread. She quickly searched all of the Commission's tents, one after the other, including Julia's. They were all empty. No one was around.

Phoebe started to panic. What should she do? Where should she go? Was it better to go get help or would that waste too much time? Why, oh why had she left Julia alone? *Dear God,* she prayed, *tell me what to do!*

Two ideas came to her. The first was to run back inside one of the tents she had just searched and grab the rifle she'd seen lying there. She discovered that it wasn't loaded, but there was a cartridge box nearby with everything she needed. Her hands shook so badly, she could scarcely ram a bullet into the barrel and put a firing cap in place. Then she snatched up the box with the extra ammunition, slung the strap over her shoulder, and ran out of the tent again.

The second thought was to go back to where she'd found Otis

with Julia earlier. He had been trying to drag her away somewhere the first time. Maybe he was too drunk to think of a different place this time. Phoebe hurried through the camp to the same spot.

The rows of tents ended here. Beyond them was a narrow field of tall grass, then the strip of woods that ran along the top of the bluff. The railroad tracks and river were at the bottom of the steep cliff. Phoebe watched the wind sweep across the field—and suddenly saw the path of trampled grass. If those were their tracks, Julia was fighting hard. He'd had to drag her.

Phoebe sprinted across the field, following the trail. It ended in the woods. The lush green undergrowth wasn't as dry as the grass and had sprung back into place, erasing their steps. She knew there was a footpath somewhere in the woods that led down to the river, but she had never taken it herself. Nor did she know if Otis had taken it.

Back home, Phoebe used to track wild game through the forest all the time, but she was so panicked now, she couldn't seem to think clearly. Forgetting everything she knew, she plunged blindly through the trees toward the river, praying that she would be able to see Otis from the top of the cliff. She peered over the edge in both directions when she got there, but she saw no movement below. Thinking the footpath was to her left, she jogged along the top of the bluff in that direction, scanning all around her, stopping every dozen yards or so to listen. Nothing.

She kept going, the heavy rifle slippery in her sweating hands, her skirts snagging in the thick brush, the cartridge box banging against her hip. Her lungs felt as if they might burst. When she couldn't run any farther she stopped again, leaning against a tree. She needed air, but she held her breath for a second and listened.

Phoebe heard the muffled scream.

It had come from below, down near the tracks, farther along in the direction she had been running. *Please don't let me be too late,* she prayed. Summoning one last reserve of energy, she ran forward again, scanning the bushes below.

A sudden motion caught her eye—Otis' gingham shirt and dark trousers, moving in the bushes. He was down at the bottom of the cliff in a clump of low brush. Julia was on the ground beneath him, struggling to fight him off as he tried to cover her mouth and hold her down at the same time.

Phoebe knew she would never be able to get down the cliff in time. It would take too long to find the path that Otis had taken. She moved along the rim until she could get a clear aim, then lifted the gun to her shoulder.

"Otis! Let her go or I'll shoot," she shouted. "I got you in my sights."

Otis froze. Then his head jerked up, and he scanned the top of the bluff until he spotted her. "Go away and leave us alone," he called back. "The lady's here willingly."

"You're lying. Let my friend go right now. I don't want to have to shoot you."

He scrambled to his feet, pulling Julia with him. He held her in front of himself as a shield. Phoebe saw the glinting metal of his knife.

"Put the gun down and leave us alone," he shouted, "or I'll slit her pretty little throat."

Phoebe didn't want to kill him. She never wanted to kill another person as long as she lived. She had hoped to aim for his arm or his leg if he forced her to shoot. But he held Julia in front of himself, her long skirts shielding his legs, his arms wrapped around her. He was a foot taller than Julia was. The only thing Phoebe could get a clear shot of was his head.

"Please, Otis. I don't want to kill you. Just let her go and walk away, and we can forget this whole thing ever happened."

"You can't kill me without killing her, too. Now be a good girl and leave us alone. This here is none of your business."

Phoebe hadn't fired a gun in nearly two years. She was scared to death that Otis was right, that she would kill Julia if she tried to kill him. She would have only one chance to hit him, too. If she missed, he could slit Julia's throat by the time Phoebe reloaded. Her shoulder felt weaker since her injury, and she was already having trouble holding the gun steady.

"I'm a crackerjack shot, mister," she said, her voice shaking.

"Sure you are, darling," he taunted. "I hear that all the nurses are." He started slowly backing away, dragging Julia with him.

Phoebe saw him glance over his shoulder to see how far he was from the pile of railroad ties that stood beside the tracks. If she didn't shoot him now, he would soon take cover behind it.

"This is your last warning," she called desperately. "I don't want to kill you, but you have to let Julia go . . . now!"

Her hands were trembling. If her aim was just a fraction too low, Julia would die. Phoebe whispered a prayer—not that she would kill Otis Whitney, but that she wouldn't kill Julia.

"Go ahead and shoot me if you're such a hotshot," he shouted. He had reached the pile of ties. Phoebe was out of time.

She fired.

Above the loud *boom* of the rifle, she thought she heard Julia scream. For a long, terrible moment Phoebe couldn't see anything through the smoke. Then it cleared, and she saw both Julia and Otis sprawled on the ground. Neither of them was moving.

Phoebe slid down the bank toward the tracks, tripping, stumbling, her blasted skirts and petticoats snagging on branches and getting in her way. All the while she kept praying, *Please, God . . . Please, God* . . . as if that might somehow change the outcome.

When she reached the tracks, she saw blood splattered all over both Otis and Julia. It was hard to tell where it had all come from. Phoebe knelt beside them. Through her tears, she saw the bullet hole in Otis Whitney's forehead. He stared sightlessly at the sky. She quickly felt Julia's throat for a pulse.

She found one. Her friend had fainted.

But Phoebe had killed a man. She had killed him. She covered her face with her hands and sobbed.

"It's all over, Julia. Come on, wake up . . . it's over. . . ."

The voice and the pungent odor of smelling salts jerked Julia awake. She opened her eyes and tried to focus on the person who was talking to her. James McGrath held her head in his lap. He was gazing down at her, gently stroking her cheek.

Then Julia remembered Otis Whitney and what he had tried to do to her, and she cried out, her entire body recoiling with horror.

"It's okay," James soothed. "He's gone, Julia. He can't hurt you anymore."

"Where is he?" she whispered.

"Dead."

She reached up to feel her throat, remembering how Otis had pressed his knife to it, how she'd believed she was going to die. Her neck still burned.

"He nicked you a little bit," James said, "but you'll be all right. I've sent for an ambulance to take you up to the hospital. It should be here soon."

"How . . . how did you get here? How did you know where to come?"

"Phoebe told me about the earlier incident, so I went for the provost marshal. We were searching Whitney's wagon when we heard the gunshot."

"Phoebe saved my life," Julia murmured, remembering. "Where is she?" She struggled to sit up and saw her friend huddled a few feet away, her face streaked with gunpowder and tears. Someone had draped a uniform jacket around Phoebe's shoulders, but she still trembled as if the air were freezing cold. Julia crawled toward her and gathered her in her arms.

"I killed him," Phoebe wept. "I didn't want to kill him. . . ."

From the corner of her eye, Julia saw Otis Whitney's boots and sprawled legs. She turned Phoebe away from them. "I know, I know. But he would have killed me, Phoebe. He would have. You had no choice."

"I took a life. . . ."

"No. You saved one."

They held each other, weeping, until the ambulance arrived.

The news spread quickly from one end of City Point to another—a civilian teamster had tried to rape one of the Sanitary Commission nurses, and another nurse had shot him dead. After the ambulance brought Julia back to her tent, she and Phoebe were visited by dozens of Commission personnel and army officials asking to hear their story, questioning them about the sequence of events.

Late in the afternoon when Julia was resting alone, she looked up to see James standing in her doorway, gripping his medical bag.

"I'm not disturbing you, am I?" he asked. "I just came by to see how you and Phoebe are doing."

Julia sat up, her heart racing at the sight of him. "I'm all right. So is Phoebe. She finally stopped shaking a little while ago and went to be with Ted."

"That's good. I brought my bag," he said, raising it slightly. "I . . . um . . . I thought you might need some laudanum to help you sleep tonight." He was frowning, as if a bright light were shining inside the tent. She wondered if he had a migraine headache.

"Thank you, but I think I'll be all right," she replied.

James exhaled. "Julia, I know this is none of my business, and I have no right to tell you what to do . . . but I think you should go home."

She saw the deep concern in his eyes and the same tenderness that she had seen in them this afternoon when she'd first awakened and found him holding her. She remembered how he'd warned her to go home a long time ago when they were still in Washington. How he'd tried to explain the way in which men like Otis Whitney might react to her. He had been right, and she was ashamed for not listening to him sooner.

"I know I should go," she said, looking away. "The other nurses . . . the Commission director . . . they're all telling me the same thing."

"So . . . you're leaving?" he asked softly.

She nodded.

Neither of them spoke for a long moment, and in the silence she heard a wagon rumbling up the road between the tents, stopping out front.

"Julia, I . . . there's so much I want to tell you," James said. "I don't know how to say this . . . where to begin . . ."

She looked up at him and felt her heart constrict. James was in love with her. She could read it on his face, see it in his eyes. And she loved him. She had never meant for that to happen. James was a married man, a father. He had tried so hard to push her away, but she had stubbornly returned to work with him, time after time, tempting him. This was all her fault.

"No, James. Don't say it," she begged—even as another part of her longed to hold him in her arms again, to let herself love him in return.

She heard voices outside, horses. Then another, taller figure appeared in the doorway behind James. The setting sun lit a halo of golden hair. Nathaniel.

"Julia?" he called. "May I come in?" He pushed past James and ducked inside the tent without waiting for her to reply. "Julia," he whispered. "Oh, thank God, thank God! You're okay. You're all right!" He pulled her to her feet and into his arms, holding her, crushing her to himself. She felt his tears in her hair.

"I'm so sorry, Nathaniel. I should have listened to you. I shouldn't have come. I—"

"Shh . . . shh. It doesn't matter now. As long as you're all right."

"Otis didn't hurt me."

"Thank God," he breathed.

"I'm going home," she told him. "As soon as all the arrangements can be made."

"I'm so glad." His arms tightened around her. Then he released her and held her away from himself, gazing down at her. "Julia, it took this tragedy to bring me to my senses. I don't want to lose you. And I still want very much to marry you . . . if you're willing."

She couldn't see past him to see if James was still standing in the doorway, but she knew somehow that he wasn't. She could scarcely believe that it was true—that Nathaniel still loved her, still wanted to marry her.

"Of course," she said. "Of course I'm willing." Julia leaned against him and cried, but not all of her tears were tears of joy.

"You did what you had to do," Ted said when Phoebe finished telling him the story. "You warned him, offered him a way out, but he left you no choice."

"I seen a lot of dead men these past few years," she said with a shudder. "But I never stood next to one that I killed myself."

"Ike," he said quietly. "Let it go. Forgive yourself . . . and let it go." The words rattled hoarsely in his throat. Phoebe hadn't wanted to admit the truth before, but she could no longer ignore the fact that Ted's lungs were filling with fluid. She'd seen it with countless other soldiers. He was coming down with pneumonia. She felt his brow—it was burning hot.

"I'm going to go get some cold water," she said, standing. "I need to bring your fever down."

He caught her wrist, stopping her. "Let me sleep awhile."

"No, you got to fight this, Ted . . . please!"

He nodded and tried to grin. "Okay . . . I'll fight . . . after I sleep."

Suddenly Phoebe heard running footsteps. They stopped outside. She looked up. Otis Whitney stood in the doorway of the tent—except it couldn't be Otis. He was dead. She had seen his lifeless body with her own two eyes.

The man took a step toward her. He held a pistol in his grip. As if in a dream, Phoebe watched him slowly raise it and aim it at her.

"You killed my brother!"

She heard Ted cry, "Look out!" and he sprang up from his bed somehow, his arms encircling Phoebe as he dove sideways, knocking her to the ground. At the same instant she heard a gunshot.

Phoebe lay on the ground, dazed, for a long moment. She was vaguely aware of a scuffle taking place, of someone shouting, "Grab him! Grab that man!"

Ted's body felt oddly heavy on top of hers—a dead weight. He was trying to draw a breath in a long, painful gasp. She wrapped her arms around him. His back was wet and slippery with warm blood.

"No!" she cried. "No, please. . . ."

Slowly, carefully, she sat up, gently rolling Ted sideways to cradle him in her arms. She caressed his face, his curly hair, her hands stained with his blood.

"Why, Ted? Why'd you have to go and get yourself shot?"

He looked up at her for the last time and whispered, "You're my best friend, Ike. . . ."

Chapter Twenty-five

Philadelphia
October 1864

Phoebe gazed out of Julia's bedroom window, watching the carriages roll by in the street below. The trees that lined the boulevard blazed with color, but to Phoebe there was something very sad about them. Their leaves would soon fall to the ground and blow away on the wind, leaving them stark and bare. And deep inside she longed to drift away on the wind along with the leaves.

"Are you ready to go?" Julia asked, moving to stand beside her.

"Would you be mad at me if I stayed here instead of going to the tea?"

"Why? What's wrong?"

"Nothing. It's just that . . ." Phoebe sighed. "I don't want to hurt your feelings, Julia. You been so good to me these past three months, buying me pretty dresses, opening your home to me, taking me places. . . . But I don't belong here. This ain't my life, and I'm never gonna fit in."

Julia moved away and sat down at her little dressing table, her back to the mirror. "I don't think I belong here, either. This feels like such a vain, meaningless life to me."

"That ain't what I meant. You and your family do a lot of good things for people, and you're very generous with your money. But I didn't grow up rich, living in a fancy house like this, and I ain't never gonna fit in. I don't talk proper, I'm scared to death to move around in these hoop skirts for fear I'll knock something over and break it. And I just can't get used to people doing stuff for me that I can do for myself—helping me get dressed, combing my hair, making my bed. Your servants do just about everything but feed me. I ain't an invalid."

"I know. I don't like it, either. I wish . . ." Julia sighed. "I don't even know what I wish for anymore."

Phoebe felt sorry for her friend. Most people would see Julia's fancy life and envy her. Phoebe might have envied her, too, in the past. But now she understood why Julia felt so unhappy, why she longed to do something useful.

"Are you girls ready?" Mrs. Hoffman asked, sweeping into the room. "Our carriage is out front."

"We've decided not to go," Julia said. "Please give Mrs. Rogers our regrets."

"You can't do that. She's expecting you—both of you. Now please hurry. We're already running late."

"Neither of us feels up to this ordeal," Julia said.

"It isn't an 'ordeal,' it's a tea, for goodness' sake. Besides, Mrs. Rogers is a very influential member of our church. You'll need her good will, for Nathaniel's sake."

"But I don't feel like going."

Mrs. Hoffman waved impatiently. "It doesn't matter if you feel like it or not. Nathaniel's career and his best interests always take priority over your own wishes. You're a reflection of him."

"No, I'm not. I'm *me*!"

Mrs. Hoffman stared at her daughter as if she'd lost her mind. "You'd better get over that ridiculous notion before he puts his wedding ring on your finger or you'll ruin his chances for a decent career in the ministry. You're not allowed to be Julia Hoffman once you become Mrs. Nathaniel Greene. Why do you think you give up your name and take your husband's? It's more than a symbol—it's a fact of life."

"I don't want to have this discussion right now," Julia said.

"Good. Then get your coat and let's go." She swept from the room again, an army commander leading her troops into battle.

"The invitation to tea included your name, Phoebe," Julia said after a moment. "They want you to come."

"Yeah, so they can stare. I see the way everybody looks at me, like I'm odd—because I am. Even your folks don't know what to make of me. Your ma's been real good to me, but I think she's a little scared of me, to tell you the truth—like she's worried I'll put a bullet between someone else's eyes if I get riled up."

"She's very grateful to you for saving my life."

"I know. She's told me a hundred times. But none of the other ladies who'll be at the tea this afternoon ever killed a man. They never even met a killer face-to-face before. They all look at me like they can't forget the killing part, even if it was to save you."

"I understand, believe me. For the rest of my life I'll always be 'the girl who was nearly raped.' Most people secretly believe I deserved it for running off to be a nurse in the first place."

"Maybe they think that now, but their tongues will stop wagging sooner or later. Especially after you marry Reverend Greene. You're one of them, you belong here—I don't. You know that it's true, Julia. I think it's time I moved on."

"I know that you're my friend. And that I'll miss you terribly if you leave."

"I'll miss you, too. But I have to go. There's something I got to do. I promised Ted I'd bring all his things to his mother, after . . ." Grief welled up inside Phoebe, as forcefully as if Ted had died that morning. She sank down on the edge of her bed and picked up his knapsack, which she always kept nearby. She lifted it onto her lap, hugging it, resting her cheek against it.

"I been wanting to hang on to all his things because . . . because they remind me of him. I look at his frypan or his silly old bottles of tonic, and I remember—" She couldn't finish. She wiped her tears as they fell. "His shirts still smell like him."

"Then you're not ready yet, Phoebe. It isn't time to give his things away."

She looked up at Julia. "Is it wrong to remember a man who isn't yours and never was, a man you'll never see again?"

An odd look crossed Julia's face. Her eyes filled with tears. "I'm the wrong person to ask that question. We can't stop our memories any more than we can stop falling in love with someone. . . . But Ted did love you, Phoebe. He gave his life for you."

"He told me to make each day count. And I ain't living like that." She swiped impatiently at her tears. "I have to stop remembering and move on, but I don't think I'll ever be able to as long as I keep hanging on to his stuff. I need to give it all back, Julia. And I need to go see where he's buried. Otherwise I'll just be stuck in the same rut in the road all my life. It's time I went to see Ted's mother to give her these things—like I promised."

"I'll go with you."

"Thanks for offering, but I don't think you should run away again."

"I'm not running away, I just want to keep you company so you won't have to travel alone."

"No . . . you're unhappy here, and this would be a good excuse for you to run off again. I been traveling alone most of my life. Ain't nothing new for me. But this is your home. You don't feel like you fit in yet because you haven't been home long enough to get used to this life again. But you will—if you don't keep running away from it. You were born into this."

"I wish I hadn't been."

"Don't you want to marry Reverend Greene and settle down here with him?"

A look of panic crossed Julia's face. She shivered like a cornered rabbit. "I don't know, Phoebe. I don't know if I want to marry him or not. It scares me to think of him swallowing up my life the way Mother just described. Nathaniel knows exactly how he wants his wife to act and what she should say and do every moment, and I don't know if I can live up to his standards. Or if I even want to anymore. I don't know if I love him or not."

Phoebe felt another wave of pity for her friend. "You'll figure it out, in time. Just like it took me a while to figure out what I got to do next."

Julia's maid suddenly appeared in the bedroom doorway. "Mrs. Hoffman says to see what's taking you so long. She's about to lose her temper, she says."

"Tell her we'll be there in a minute." Julia sat very still for a moment as if composing herself, then turned to Phoebe again. "What will you do after you see Ted's mother? Where will you go?"

"I don't know. I ain't thought that far ahead."

"Promise me that you'll write to me and tell me where you are and what you're doing. Even if it's just a short note."

"Why?"

"Because the war isn't over yet—the one inside of us, I mean. You're the only person I can talk to about what it was like to be on those battlefields, to see all those wounded men. And until we get over it, neither one of us is going to be able to figure out who we are or what we want. Am I making any sense?"

"Yeah. I reckon we're as different from each other as a porcupine is from a polecat. But we been to the same place, and it made us the same inside, in our hearts."

"Which one am I?" Julia said, smiling through her tears, "the porcupine or the polecat?"

Phoebe grinned. "I'll be hanged if I know. Let's flip a coin."

Western Pennsylvania
October 1864

Ted's hometown was very much as Phoebe remembered it, even after three years of war. *Three years*. The number startled her. On that warm October day in 1861, she and Ted had both signed up to fight for three years. Their enlistment would have expired this very month. Ted should be the one returning home alive and well, not her.

As the train pulled into the station, Phoebe felt like she was walking backward through time. She remembered sitting alone on the train the last time, too, watching the tearful farewells outside on the platform. Ted's mother had clung to him, weeping, begging him not to go. She'd been so afraid she would lose him, and she had. Ted had returned to her in a coffin. Phoebe felt bad for coming back and poking at a wound that probably hadn't healed yet. But she didn't suppose a mother would ever get over the loss of her only son.

Phoebe stepped off the train and looked around. The hotel where she and all the other soldiers had stayed was down the street a little ways. She had already decided to take a room there for the night after she went to see Ted's mother. Phoebe was still unsure where she would go tomorrow. Or the next day.

She walked slowly into town and turned down the main street. She realized that she was doing it again—searching all the faces she passed, looking for Ted's. She'd done it back in Philadelphia and in Washington and on all the battlefields she'd been to. She'd done it all the way here, too. How long would it take to break the habit, to accept the fact that Ted was dead?

Phoebe paused in front of the store that had been used for a recruiting office. It was where she had met him for the first time, where he'd been given the knapsack she was now carrying. She remembered how funny he'd looked wearing his enormous uniform coat, grinning up at her and saying, *"Hey there . . . want to trade?"*

Cut it out, she told herself. *You can't walk around town bawling or they'll put you in an asylum.*

Two old men sat on the narrow porch in front of the general store, spitting tobacco. She asked them for directions to Cherry Street, the return address on the letters from Ted's mother. They told her it wasn't far, but Phoebe walked there slowly, as if she had miles and miles to go, clutching the pack in front of her with one hand, the valise Julia had given her for her own belongings in the other.

Number fifteen Cherry Street was a small, plain-looking house, worlds away from Julia's enormous mansion in Philadelphia—and worlds away from Phoebe's own rustic cabin back in West Virginia. It was the sort of place she always pictured when she heard the word *home*—a snug, one-story clapboard house surrounded by a fence that needed paint. She was about to go up the front walk and knock on the door when she noticed a string of laundry flapping in the breeze on a clothesline behind the house. She walked around to the backyard and saw Ted's mother, reaching, bending, reaching again as she unpinned the linens and piled them in a wicker basket. Phoebe watched her for several minutes.

She looked so much like Ted with her small stature, tawny skin, and curly brown hair that Phoebe wondered what Ted's father had contributed to his son's appearance. Mrs. Wilson didn't see Phoebe at first. But when she suddenly looked up, she gasped and dropped the sheet she was holding.

"I'm sorry," Phoebe said, hurrying forward to pick it up. "I wasn't trying to sneak up on you, Mrs. Wilson. My name's Phoebe Bigelow, and I came—"

"Phoebe . . ." she repeated, studying her. "Oh, yes. You're Ted's friend . . . Ike."

"H-how did you know?"

She pointed to his knapsack, her eyes filling with tears. "You brought his things home. Ted told me you would come."

"He did?"

"I still have the letter that one of the nurses wrote for him. It was his last one."

Phoebe swallowed the lump of grief that stuck in her throat. Julia must have written it for him. That was why he'd asked Julia to come that last day—that terrible last day.

"You must come inside," Mrs. Wilson said, reaching to take Phoebe's arm. "I'll make tea. We have so much to talk about."

Phoebe stayed the night. She slept in Ted's old bed, even though it was so short her feet hung off the bottom edge. His mother hadn't changed anything in his room since the day he left it three years ago. The next day Mrs. Wilson took Phoebe to the cemetery and showed her Ted's grave beside his father's.

"Please stay, just a little longer," she begged every time Phoebe mentioned that it was time for her to go. And so she stayed, allowing her grief to heal as she shared her sorrow with Ted's mother.

One week turned into two, then three. The presidential election was held in November, and the two women celebrated when they learned that President Lincoln had defeated the other candidate, General George McClellan. "Ted thought the world of General McClellan at first," Phoebe said, remembering. "But he got pretty disgusted with him after he hightailed it off of the Peninsula without a decent fight. Ted would have voted for Mr. Lincoln for sure because he promised to free all the slaves."

Phoebe was still living with Ted's mother when the news came that General Sherman had burned the city of Atlanta. She was there at the end of November when President Lincoln proclaimed a National Day of Thanksgiving. Mrs. Wilson prepared a chicken dinner for the two of them, teaching Phoebe how to make cornbread stuffing and apple pie. Together they read in the newspapers how Union cooks had served more than one hundred thousand Thanksgiving dinners to Grant's army in the trenches at Petersburg. And together the women followed the progress of Sherman's march to the sea and read how he'd presented the city of Savannah, Georgia, to President Lincoln as a Christmas present.

On January 31, 1865, Congress passed the Thirteenth Amendment, abolishing slavery. Phoebe and Ma Wilson wept and hugged and wept some more. "Ted told me your story, Ma," Phoebe said. "It was his dream to find that plantation where you used to live and bring his grandmother home to you after the war."

Ma passed the long winter nights teaching Phoebe how to sew and knit, and telling stories of everything she remembered about her childhood as a slave. She had become the mother Phoebe had never known. As the two women read about the path of destruction General Sherman left across Georgia and South Carolina, Phoebe wondered what would become of the thousands and thousands of former slaves who'd been left homeless and hungry.

"The first time I ever worked as a nurse," she told Ma, "was the night I helped Dr. McGrath take care of some former slaves living in a shantytown." She wondered who was taking care of them now.

In early March, President Lincoln was sworn in for a second term. Phoebe read the words of his inauguration speech aloud to Ma: " 'Fondly do we hope—fervently do we pray—that this mighty scourge of war may speedily pass away. Yet if God wills that it continue until all the wealth piled by the bondsman's two hundred and fifty years of unrequited toil shall be sunk, and until every drop of blood drawn with the lash shall be paid by another drawn with the sword . . . so still must be said, "the judgments of the Lord are true and righteous altogether." ' "

Later that afternoon Phoebe stood at Ted's grave, her arm linked through his mother's. The long, cold winter was nearly over; spring was struggling to break through. And Phoebe knew that her own dark winter was drawing to an end. The time had come for new life to begin—in the countryside all around her and in her own life, as well.

"I have to go, Ma," she said quietly. "The war is gonna start up again soon, and I need to go back and help take care of the soldiers."

"No, stay here, Phoebe," she begged. "Let me take care of you."

Part of Phoebe longed to stay. The pull of her comfortable surroundings was strong, secured by the ties of love that had been knit between the two women. But in another part of Phoebe's heart, she knew she had to go. Before the war started she would have jumped at the chance to stay in a home like this, where she was loved. But things were different now. Phoebe wasn't the same person she was before the war.

"I ain't leaving forever," she said. "I'll come back and see you again when the war ends."

"Why do you have to go?"

"Because . . . because love ain't meant to be kept to ourselves, Ma. It's meant to be shared."

"But it's dangerous near those battlefields. I'm afraid for you. What if something happens to you, too?"

Phoebe looked down at Ted's tombstone for a long moment, studying his name deeply etched into the stone marker. "Ted wasn't afraid to die. He knew what he was living for. Seems like if you know why you're living, you can face death a whole lot better. One of the last things Ted told me was that I should serve the Lord. He said it was the only thing that mattered. That's what I aim to do."

Mrs. Wilson wrapped her arms around Phoebe and hugged her. The tiny woman's head didn't even reach Phoebe's chin. "I love you, honey. Promise me you'll come back and see me again?"

Phoebe remembered the tearful farewells on the train platform three years ago and how she'd wished for a mother like Ted's. Now she had one, and it broke her heart to leave her. "I'll be back," she said through her tears. "I promise."

Philadelphia
April 1865

"Honestly, Julia! Is it really necessary to read three newspapers every morning?" Julia looked up from her reading to find her mother standing beside the breakfast table, her hands on her hips. "You're getting worse than your father."

Julia glanced at the mess she'd made, strewing papers all over the table and even onto the floor. "I'm sorry," she said, bending to gather them. "But Nathaniel is in Petersburg, and I need to find out what's going on there. Things are happening so fast it's hard to keep up."

"Well, what's the latest news?" Mrs. Hoffman asked as she sat down to drink her coffee.

"The Rebels are all but defeated. I think the war is going to end soon."

"Thank God," her mother sighed. "Maybe we can all get back to normal around here."

Julia buried her nose in the paper again. She couldn't seem to get enough information as the war swiftly drew to a close. But each time she read about the latest battles that were taking place, she couldn't help but wish she were there, working beside James again, caring for all the wounded soldiers. She hated observing events from far away through a newspaper, and she felt as though her own life was passing by as she watched other people live theirs. Something huge and important seemed to be missing.

"The city of Richmond fell," Julia read to her mother a few days later. "It says that the Rebels burned everything as they fled. Much of the downtown area is in ruins."

Mrs. Hoffman had to sit down as she absorbed the news. "I pray that your cousin Caroline made it out safely. Maybe our letters will finally get through to her again, and we can find out how she's doing."

"She's probably all right. It says here that most of the residential areas of the city were spared," Julia continued. "President Lincoln paid a visit to Richmond the day after it fell and was met by mobs of cheering slaves."

"I wonder what will become of them all now that they're free," her mother said.

Julia thought of Loretta and Belle and the desperate condition they and their children had been in before she'd hired them to work in the laundry. "I wonder, too," she said. She didn't share with her mother the fact that Union troops had found Richmond's citizens close to starvation. Here in Philadelphia, their family had never gone hungry for a single day during the past four years. Nathaniel had remained safe as a noncombatant, and Rosalie's husband had paid a substitute to serve in his place. Julia couldn't help wondering what life had been like for Caroline in Richmond all these years and if her fiancé had survived the war as a Confederate soldier.

Then one morning Julia read of General Lee's surrender at Appomattox Court House, and she rested her forehead on the table and wept. It was over—the war was truly over. No more young men would have to die, and she wouldn't have to wrestle with her longings to be a nurse anymore. She could, as her mother said, get back to normal life. But what was "normal"?

She read how the Confederate soldiers had been spread so thinly across miles and miles of battlefront that they hadn't stood a chance against hundreds of thousands of Yankees. Many of the men who died in the Rebel trenches had been as old as Julia's father; many others had been mere teenagers. They'd spent the winter without uniforms or shoes or food, starving, while Union soldiers had eaten fresh bread every day, still warm from the bakery in City Point. Now the army hospitals were filling with Union soldiers who had been held captive on Belle Isle and Libby Prison and in other Rebel prison camps. They would need medical attention and nursing care in order to get well. As she read about their desperate condition, Julia longed to care for them herself.

"I guess this means your Nathaniel will be mustered out of service soon," her mother said when victory was announced. "We should start preparing for your wedding."

Julia tried to feel enthused as they visited a dressmaker to look at patterns and fabric samples for her gown. Her future stretched ahead of her, filled with exciting new changes. Why did she still feel so uneasy about starting a new life as Nathaniel's wife?

"It's perfectly normal to feel jittery when you're about to become a bride," her mother told her. "We'll go visit your sister tomorrow. She can tell you that she once felt the same way. She adjusted to her husband."

Julia had learned to do all sorts of things she had never imagined she could do—washing laundry, dressing wounds, working near a battlefield with shells exploding around her, assisting with surgery. She would learn this new role, too. She would adjust to becoming Nathaniel's wife, allowing him to order her life.

As she was preparing to visit Rosalie the next day, Julia heard the worst news of all—President Abraham Lincoln had been assassinated. It was one final blow after four years of death and sorrow, and it shook her to her core. The world had gone insane. Who could ever imagine that someone would kill the president?

"Such a tragedy," Judge Hoffman said, "for that man to have led us through a long, terrible war, only to be killed barely a week after it ends."

The nation came to a standstill to mourn. When the funeral train passed through Philadelphia and Lincoln's coffin lay in Independence Hall, Julia joined the three-mile-long line of mourners to pay her last respects.

The war was over, the guns silenced at last. But she knew that the hatred that had divided a nation for four years, enslaving millions of people and leading to the murder of a president, was far from healed. Nathaniel could preach against that hatred from his pulpit—Julia would serve tea to his parishioners. She remembered how God's presence had surrounded her the night her first patient died: *"Inasmuch as ye have done it unto one of the least of these . . ."* The "least" hardly described Julia's wealthy church. Sister Irene had told her that any task would have meaning if she did it for the Lord, even baking bread—or serving tea.

But as Julia helped her mother draw up a long list of guests for her wedding reception, she couldn't help wondering if this was really the life she was meant to live.

Chapter Twenty-six

Washington City
May 1865

Julia gazed at the throngs of people jamming the sidewalks on both sides of Pennsylvania Avenue. The flag-waving crowd stretched for miles in both directions. "I've never seen this many people in my life!" she told her father. One hundred and fifty thousand soldiers with military bands and cavalry units paraded up the avenue for the Grand Review. Julia had traveled to Washington with her parents to attend the victory parade of the Grand Armies of the Republic as guests of Congressman Rhodes. They had seats close to the reviewing stand where General Grant and President Andrew Johnson surveyed the troops, along with the secretary of war and Generals Sherman and Meade.

Bands played "The Star-Spangled Banner" and "Hail Columbia" as they marched past. The flag of the newly restored Union flew at full mast again for the first time since President Lincoln had died. Regiments proudly displayed their own flags, bearing the names of the battles in which they'd fought. Tears came to Julia's eyes as she read the familiar names, recalling the places where she, too, had served. There was Antietam, where James had brought Phoebe to her tent. Fredericksburg, where she and James had kissed. Gettysburg, where she had nursed James back onto his feet. And Petersburg, where her career as a nurse had ended and she'd seen

James for the last time. All of those battlefields seemed to evoke memories of him and the work they'd done together—but none was as overpowering as her memory of the night the sky had blazed in Fredericksburg.

Julia shook herself to clear her thoughts. She was here to see Nathaniel. She gazed up the street toward the Capitol, where the parade had begun and saw that the new dome, which had been under construction when she'd lived in Washington, was finally finished. A bronze Statue of Freedom was now perched on top, the ugly scaffolding removed. The procession of troops would take two full days to pass, but Julia was only interested in watching on the first day. That was when the Grand Army of the Potomac—Nathaniel's army—would parade past. She searched for him as row after row of men marched by, but the soldiers all looked alike beneath their blue forage caps. She saw his regimental flag but couldn't find him among the many hundreds of men.

Late in the afternoon, she returned to the congressman's house to wait for Nathaniel. Julia hadn't seen him since leaving City Point with Phoebe ten months ago, and she paced the hallway, watching for his carriage. As soon as he stepped through the front door, she rushed toward him, eager to hold him in her arms. But Nathaniel reached to take her hands instead. "Julia! How wonderful to see you!" he said. He kissed her cheek.

She felt cheated, even though she knew how reluctant Nathaniel had always been to show his affection in front of other people. "I've missed you so much," she said.

"Yes," he murmured, then he turned his attention to their host and Julia's father, who were also waiting to greet him. She had to be content to sit near Nathaniel and gaze silently at him for most of the evening as he shared his experiences as an army chaplain with the rest of the guests. At least his handsome face and shining golden hair were pleasant to gaze at.

During dinner her mind spun back to the first time she had ever seen Nathaniel. He'd been fresh out of seminary, arriving in Philadelphia when she was only fifteen to preach in her home church. He'd turned the congregation upside down with his blunt, passionate preaching, and Julia had fallen in love with the handsome, dynamic man at first sight. She hadn't thought of another man since—*except James,* a nagging voice reminded her.

Julia remembered how she used to hug her pillow in bed at night, pretending it was Nathaniel. And she smiled to herself when she recalled all the abolition meetings she'd attended with him in her efforts to win his affection. But all of his passion during those years had been directed toward the cause of abolition, not her.

"What will you do now, Nathaniel?"

Julia didn't realize that she had spoken the question out loud until the dinner conversation suddenly stopped. Everyone stared at her.

"What do you mean?" he asked.

"I was just thinking about all the energy you used to pour into trying to abolish slavery—and now the slaves are free. You've won. I wondered which cause would replace that one in your life."

"Whichever cause the Lord gives me," he said. "My mission in life hasn't changed. It has always been, as the apostle Paul wrote to Timothy, to show myself 'approved unto God, a workman that needeth not to be ashamed.'"

"Is that why you've worked so hard? To win God's approval?"

"Yes, of course. Each one of us will be asked to give an account of our lives on Judgment Day, and I would certainly hate to be found lacking."

"But what about those of us who don't work?" Julia asked. "And what about the thousands of helpless, crippled soldiers who may never live productive lives again? I thought God's love was unconditional. I thought we were accepted as His children because of what Christ has done, not because of what we do."

For the briefest of moments, Nathaniel's eyes sparked with anger. She couldn't imagine why. Then he hid his displeasure behind an indulgent smile and patronizing tone. "Julia, this is hardly the place or the occasion for a theological discussion of grace and good works." He was covering his anger well, but she saw it there just the same, simmering beneath the smooth surface of his words. "Besides, you're changing the subject, dear. Congressman Rhodes and Judge Hoffman were discussing the trials of the assassination conspirators."

Julia leaned back in her seat again. The conversation returned to

Lincoln's assassination. As she puzzled over the reason for Nathaniel's anger, she realized how little she really knew about him. The love she'd felt for him all these years had been based on his handsome appearance and dynamic preaching, and she barely knew the private man beneath the public surface. She had wanted to be loved for who she really was, not because she was pretty—yet she had done the same thing, pursuing Nathaniel for what she'd seen on the outside. She didn't know him at all.

A wave of panic rocked through her. It felt much too overwhelming to be the usual "bride's jitters." She suddenly pushed her chair back and stood.

"Julia? What's wrong?" her father asked.

"It's very warm in here," she said. "I'm going outside for some air."

She made her way through the rooms to the front door and rushed outside to stand on the steps. The night was warm and clear, with millions of stars shining in the sky. But her feelings of panic had followed her outside. So had Nathaniel.

"I'm sorry if I said something to hurt your feelings," he said. "I didn't mean to sound abrupt."

"Why did you fall in love with me?" she asked. "How . . . when did you know that you wanted to marry me?"

"I knew the moment I saw you working on that hospital ship. The conditions were horrifying, yet you were so compassionate and giving, so willing to sacrifice for the sake of others. A minister's wife must have all of those qualities. And I knew you were the wife I'd been searching for."

Julia wouldn't look at him. She wanted to hear what he had to say without being swayed by his good looks and charm. "Should I be the woman you want me to be or the woman God wants me to be?"

"They are the same thing, Julia. God gave you to me to be my helpmate, to support me and my ministry."

"What about my own work? Will I have something else to do besides helping you?"

"Of course. There are numerous charitable causes and mission projects for you to become involved with. The Christian Commission's most successful fund-raisers were the ones you organized. Your upbringing trained you to be exactly what I need in a wife. You're comfortable moving in all the right social circles, you understand church politics—"

"I meant my nursing work. I've been trained for that, too."

He exhaled. She could tell that he was making an effort to be patient with her. "I think it was very clear after what happened at City Point that you're finished with nursing. Besides, now that the war is over, nurses are no longer needed."

"I miss it," she said softly. "It was hard work, and I never would have believed I could do all those things, but part of me still misses it. I felt as though I was useful to God. I could show His love and compassion to people, like those men on that hospital ship."

"I understand. There are things I will always miss about my work as a chaplain, too. But life brings change, Julia. It's time for us to move on to new challenges."

They were both silent for a time. Julia was still reluctant to look up at him.

"What are your plans for tomorrow?" he finally asked. "Are you going back to watch more of the parade?"

"No. I want to go to Fairfield Hospital and see my friend Phoebe. She wrote and told me that she's working there again. But she said the hospital is scheduled to close as soon as the last soldiers are well enough to go home."

"I'll go with you."

"You don't have to do that," she said quickly. How could she confess all her doubts to Phoebe or talk about all the changes in their lives now that the war was over if Nathaniel was there? "It would be very boring for you, listening to two old friends talk. I know how to get around Washington on my own."

"I want to take you," he insisted. "I don't mind waiting while you visit."

Julia knew better than to argue with him. She looked up at him at last, trying to read his thoughts. He smiled at her, his expression tender and loving. They were alone outside and the May evening was warm, but he made no move to embrace her.

"Why won't you kiss me?" she asked.

"Right here? Someone might—"

"We're engaged, Nathaniel. And we're alone."

If someone as saintly as Nathaniel could shed his self-control for a moment, perhaps Julia could finally forgive herself for her moment of weakness with James. But Nathaniel shook his head.

"A minister must live above reproach," he said. He took her arm. "I think we should go back inside."

The following afternoon, Nathaniel borrowed the congressman's carriage to drive Julia to Fairfield Hospital. She had resigned herself to having him tag along; she wouldn't be free to share her heart with Phoebe. But when they pulled up in front of the tumbledown building, he surprised her by saying, "I'll wait here."

"Outside? In the carriage? But . . . but Phoebe and I have a lot to talk about."

"No need to hurry. Take as long as you'd like. I brought two newspapers to read." He held them up to show her.

"I think you're afraid I'll start taking care of patients again," she said, only half teasing.

"Would you?" His expression was dead serious. This was the real reason he had come.

Julia reached for the door handle. "I won't be long."

She climbed out of the carriage and started up the walk, then halted halfway up the hospital steps with one hand on the rickety railing. She pictured James inside at his desk, sifting through endless piles of papers as he'd been doing on the first day she came to Fairfield Hospital. She also recalled the tender expression on his face the last time she'd seen him in her tent at City Point. He had never finished what he'd come to say. A moment later, Nathaniel had pushed past him to say that he still wanted to marry her. She hadn't seen James since.

Suddenly Julia knew that it was very wrong to see him now, to stir up feelings inside both of them that they had no business feeling. She glanced back at the carriage. Nathaniel's face was hidden behind his newspaper. She hurried down the steps again and walked around the building to the rear entrance.

Julia found Phoebe in the downstairs ward just off the kitchen. Her friend had her back turned away from Julia, and she was seated on a chair beside a patient's bed, coaxing him to eat. The soldier's face had been burned and horribly disfigured. As Julia watched and listened from a distance, she realized that the man was blind.

"If you don't eat you'll die, it's as simple as that," Phoebe told him.

"I don't want to live. I'm no good to my family if I can't see."

"Listen, it ain't up to you when you're gonna die any more than it was up to you when you was gonna be born. Those things are up to God, and you ain't Him."

"God should have let me die," he said bitterly. "I can't go home this way."

"The man I loved was killed," Phoebe said, her voice turning soft. "I ain't never gonna see him again in this life. If the only thing that had happened to him was that he'd gone blind, I'd take him that way in a Yankee minute. I'll bet the people who love you feel the same way. You ought to think about them."

She set the bowl of food down on the table beside his bed and stood. "I'll come back a little later, and when I do, I expect you to make up your mind to eat." She turned around to leave and saw Julia.

"What are you doing here?" she cried as they rushed to embrace each other.

"I came to see you. I'm visiting Washington City with my family."

"My, it's good to see you. But why're you sneaking up on me? Did you come in the *back* door?"

"Yes . . . I-I wanted to see if Belle and Loretta still worked here. Their children certainly have grown big, haven't they?"

"They sure have." The skeptical look on Phoebe's face made Julia feel ashamed.

"That's not the whole truth," she said quietly. "I promised myself I wouldn't lie anymore, and I'm already doing it." She drew a deep breath, then sighed. "I didn't want to run into Dr. McGrath. Is he working here, too?"

"Yeah, ever since last winter. He decided not to go back and be a field surgeon anymore. He said he never wanted to saw off another leg as long as he lived."

Julia took Phoebe's arm. "Let's go into the kitchen and talk."

She had to spend a few minutes greeting all the cooks she knew and explaining where she'd been all this time and what she'd been doing. Then she and Phoebe settled down to talk at the small kitchen table. Julia remembered sitting there with Mrs. Fowle and the other matrons on her very first morning at work.

"Why don't you want to see Dr. McGrath?" Phoebe finally asked. "You know all them rumors about him killing a man? They ain't true. He told me the whole story when we were at Cold Harbor. That rich man killed himself."

"I know he isn't a murderer, Phoebe. I saw how hard he works to save lives—as if he has a personal grudge against death. I don't believe he's capable of ending someone's life."

"I know he can be mean to people sometimes," Phoebe said. "I hear him barking at the nurses, and I know he must have barked at you, too. It ain't right for him to act that way, but I think he's hurting inside. The folks back where he comes from still think he killed somebody. He told me that the scandal ruined his life. Your preacher friend accused him of being a murderer, too."

"Nathaniel?"

"Yeah. Someone from Dr. McGrath's hometown came to see Reverend Greene and told him that the doctor had killed a man. I happened to be there and overheard the whole thing. It must be awful to walk around with everybody thinking terrible things about you."

Julia looked away, remembering how she and everyone else had falsely accused James of being an alcoholic.

"But there's more to Dr. McGrath than what everybody sees on the outside," Phoebe continued. "You know how the doctor comes to work all mussed up sometimes? I found out why. He goes to the shantytown and helps all the sick folks who live there, even though they can't even pay him for it. I worked all night with him once. He don't want anybody to know because he takes the medicine and stuff he needs from here."

Julia wasn't surprised to discover yet another piece of the puzzle that was James McGrath.

"He really cares about his patients, too," Phoebe said. "Even when he has to be tough on them in order for them to get better. They can tell how much he cares, and they all love him for it."

"Phoebe, I know that what you're saying is true. I saw glimpses of the real man when I worked with him. I don't know why he pushes people away and builds walls around himself. But I don't think he's really like that, deep inside."

"Then why don't you want to see him again?"

Julia stared down at the scarred tabletop. "Does he still get letters from his wife every week?"

"Yeah, one came in the mail this morning."

"That's why," Julia said, looking up again. "Because he's a married man. I have feelings for him that I shouldn't have. And I think he was starting to feel the same way about me. Otis Whitney accused me of being a flirt and of leading him on, even though I had no intention of doing so. I don't want to play with fire again. I didn't mean to do anything to encourage James that way—" She stopped, remembering how she had responded to his kiss. "I-I have to avoid him, Phoebe."

"You once told me that we can't help falling in love with someone," Phoebe said quietly. "Remember?"

"Yes . . . I know I can't always control what I feel. But I can control how I act." Julia reached across the table to squeeze Phoebe's hand. "Tell me what happened when you went to see Ted's mother."

"We grieved together for a good long while. I reckon I needed that. Then I was able to let go. One of the last things Ted told me was to go on living, knowing that each day counts. That's what I aim to do."

"What will you do after the hospital closes?"

"Well, first I'm going back home to see if my brothers, Jack and Junior, made it through the war. After that . . . I don't know. But I reckon God will show me. What about you? Are you still gonna marry Reverend Greene?"

"Yes. He's waiting outside in the carriage, in fact."

"Why's he waiting out there?"

Julia gave a humorless laugh. "I ran away to be a nurse twice before against his wishes—once to Gettysburg and again to Fredericksburg. I think he wants to make sure I don't do it again."

"I know he was awful mad at you for it. He said you could either be his wife or a nurse but not both. Why did you go back to Fredericksburg if it meant losing the man you love?"

"Because I was convinced that God wanted me to go. That's what I don't understand about marriage, Phoebe. Nathaniel says he'll be the head of our household and he'll make all the decisions. But aren't women allowed to hear from God? Are only our fathers or our husbands qualified to tell us what God wants? I thought I'd heard God speaking to me—but when it came to being a nurse, what Nathaniel said was very different from what God said. Society tells me I must stay in my place and obey my husband. So should I try to become the person he wants me to be or the person God wants me to be?"

"I don't think they should be telling you two different things."

Julia looked at her friend and smiled. Phoebe had more wisdom than most of the other women Julia knew. "You're right. They shouldn't be. You know, when I was growing up I used to think that all I needed in order to have an ideal life was to find the perfect husband. He would give my life meaning and purpose. And, of course, Nathaniel was perfect—hardworking, devout, committed to God . . ."

"Handsome," Phoebe added.

"Yes, handsome, too," she said uneasily. "But sometimes I get the feeling that he's marrying me to complete himself, to fill the part of 'wife' in his life. I wish I knew if he loved me for myself, as someone who is whole and unique, not as an accessory to himself."

"I don't know much about marriages," Phoebe said, "because I ain't seen too many of them. Tell you the truth, I doubt if anyone will ever marry me."

"Maybe I shouldn't marry, either. My mother and most of the other women in my social class don't seem to mind being accessories to their husbands. If I want to be my own person, maybe I should stay single, like Dorothea Dix."

But Julia knew that wasn't the answer, either. She thought about the deep scar on Phoebe's back, how she had been wounded trying to protect the man she loved. How he had died protecting her. That was the kind of love she longed for. "I always thought love was about me," Julia said. "Someone loving *me*. But it isn't about possessing someone or being 'theirs,' is it? It's about loving others, giving yourself to them and for them . . . the way you and Ted loved each other."

Phoebe nodded silently.

"I had no idea who I was before the war," Julia continued, "or what I was really like deep inside. How could I give myself to anybody in love if I didn't know who I was? I used to think I was a pretty good person. Then God used the war and all the hardships He brought me through to break me and change me and shape me into someone He could finally use."

"Seems like we never see the truth about ourselves," Phoebe said, "as long as everything's going pretty good in our lives. But when everything starts falling apart, then we're ready to hear what God has to say. I used to think I was no good—and I wasn't. God used the war to show me that He loved me anyway, and then He helped me learn to love other people."

"So what do we do now?" Julia asked. "I found out who I was while working on the battlefields and in the hospitals. So did you. Now we can give that gift to others. But Nathaniel has his own ideas of who I am and what he thinks I should do. I'm so confused."

"I don't know what to tell you, Julia. I'm just as confused as you are, but in a different way. I used to live all on my own, figuring I didn't need nothing from nobody. Then the war forced me to work together with all kinds of people—rich and poor, men and women—and I found out how much we all need each other. I think God wants people to work together, to take care of each other. But when I leave here, I'll be living all alone again."

"I wish you and I could stay together," Julia said. "I wish we weren't as different as a polecat and a porcupine."

"I know what you mean. But we are different. We have two different lives to live. But even if we can't see exactly where we're going, I reckon God will show us the way. I found this verse that I really like. . . ."

Phoebe pulled out the battered, water-stained Bible Julia had often seen her reading and opened it. "It says, 'The path of the just is as the shining light, that shineth more and more unto the perfect day.'"

"Yes . . ." Julia murmured, "I like that."

They both knew it was time to part and that it was going to be very difficult. When one of the nurses came into the kitchen suddenly, to tell Phoebe that Dr. McGrath was looking for her, they had an excuse to do it quickly. Phoebe and Julia hugged good-bye, promising each other that they would write. Then Phoebe hurried away.

Julia waited a moment, drying her tears, then walked through the ward toward the back door. As she passed the blind soldier's bed, he called out to her.

"Nurse Bigelow? Phoebe, is that you?"

"No, I'm her friend Julia. Can I get you something?"

"I just wanted to tell her I'll eat now."

Julia knew how upset Nathaniel would be if he came inside and found her feeding a patient. But the urge to help the man, to comfort and soothe him, proved too strong to resist. She walked over to his bedside. "I'll help you with your dinner if that's okay."

"Sure."

She sat down and picked up the bowl, then took the soldier's hand. "Here, you hold on to it yourself. It's vegetable soup."

"I can't. I'll spill it."

"No, you won't. Here's the spoon. If you hold the bowl close to your mouth it will be much easier." She guided his hands for the first few mouthfuls until he got used to doing it himself.

"Tell me something . . ." he said between swallows. "I been wondering what Phoebe looks like."

"Well, she's very tall."

"I knew that. I can tell she's tall because her voice comes from farther away than all the other nurses when she stands beside the bed. What color hair does she have?"

"It's blond . . . a very pretty color blond. And her eyes are blue."

"But what does she look like? She won't tell me the truth. She keeps saying she's as homely as a hound dog, but I think she's lying."

"What do you think she looks like?" Julia asked quietly.

"I think she must be very beautiful. I once saw a picture of angels in a Bible and they had blond hair, too. I think she looks as beautiful as them."

Julia was glad the man couldn't see the tears that came to her eyes. No one with natural sight would ever call Phoebe Bigelow beautiful. But the true beauty of Christ's love shone through her life.

"You're right," Julia said. "Phoebe is one of the most beautiful women I've ever met."

"Were you looking for me, Dr. McGrath?" Phoebe found him in the supply room, rummaging through boxes and bottles and piles of bandages, searching for something.

"I can't find the calomel," he said. "Are we all out of it?"

"No, I don't think so."

He had his battered medical bag with him, the one he took whenever he went to the shantytown to work.

"Loretta and Belle told me that all the folks in shantytown are real sick," Phoebe said. "If you're going there tonight, I'd like to go with you."

"No. You can't come this time, Phoebe. From the way they've described the symptoms, I suspect it might be typhoid fever."

"I ain't afraid—"

"I said *no*!" he yelled. "I won't kill you, too! Stay away from there!"

Phoebe stepped back, stunned by the force of his anger. He had never yelled at her before. A moment later he caught himself. He closed his eyes.

"I'm sorry. I shouldn't have spoken to you that way. Please forgive me."

"Of course. It's okay." She touched his arm briefly, then bent to fetch the calomel from a lower cabinet.

His angry words seemed odd to Phoebe: *"I won't kill you, too."* She remembered his confession at Cold Harbor, how he'd admitted that he had murdered someone. And also his emotional reaction when her brother Willard lay dying: *"I know how difficult it is when it's your own family and there's nothing you can do."* It seemed to Phoebe that Dr. McGrath was all bent over beneath a very heavy load, as if carrying a knapsack stuffed full of guilt. He was suffering, and Phoebe wanted to help him, the way she'd helped Ted when his pack was too heavy. She stood again and handed him the lump of calomel.

"Did someone you love die of typhoid?" she asked softly.

At first she didn't think he was going to answer. When he finally looked up at her, his eyes were filled with pain.

"My wife, Ellen."

An enormous silence filled the room. The longer it lasted, the more heavily it seemed to weigh on both of them. "How long ago?" Phoebe finally asked.

"Four years."

"I'm sorry," she whispered.

He closed his eyes again. "It was my fault," he said hoarsely. "I killed her."

"But you just said she died of typhoid."

"I made her go with me to help with an epidemic, like this one. She didn't want to, but I made her. It was right after Eldon Tyler killed himself, and I was still trying to prove to the world that I wasn't a murderer. My medical practice was ruined, and none of my former patients consulted me anymore, so I started working with poor people from the shipyards and the factory tenements. Ellen was afraid to go to such disease-ridden places, but I was driven to prove myself, to win my reputation back. It was all about me . . . and I ignored her fears. When she got sick, I couldn't save her. And she died."

Phoebe swallowed. "It's an awful, helpless feeling when you can't save the person you love."

"Yes. It is." He paused, drawing a breath. "I took a job with the army as a contract surgeon and came here to get away. I was still grieving, and I know I took it out on everyone who worked with me. I still do at times, and I'm sorry. I shouldn't have yelled at you that way."

"What about all the letters from New Haven?" she asked, suddenly remembering them.

"The what? Oh. My mother is taking care of Kate . . . my daughter." He looked down at the calomel in his hands as if he had no idea where it had come from. Then he looked up at Phoebe again and nodded. "Thanks for finding this. I don't want to keep you from your patients."

She didn't move. "After Ted died, I wanted to push everybody away, too. It seemed safer than getting close to people and getting hurt all over again. But it isn't. We were meant to love people, and we need to accept their love in return. Otherwise, we ain't really living."

"I suppose you're right," he said quietly. "I know I was hard on all the nurses, but I had to know what motivated them—if they were doing this work because they wanted to or if it was only to please their husbands, as Ellen had done. I know I was especially hard on Julia Hoffman because I was certain that she was working here to please someone, not because she wanted to be here. Why else would someone as wealthy and as privileged as she is come here to—"

"Julia's here in Washington," Phoebe said, interrupting. "She came to see me today."

"What? Julia's . . . here?"

He was in love with her. Phoebe read it in his eyes and saw it written all over his face. Dr. McGrath had always been good at hiding his feelings, but for once he hadn't been able to. Opening his heart to Phoebe and confessing his grief had made him vulnerable. It was as if she could look straight inside him. "You're in love with Julia, aren't you?" she said.

He quickly closed down again, turning away. "It doesn't really matter how I feel about her. She's going to marry that preacher . . . what's-his-name."

"She doesn't love him. And he ain't right for her. You are."

"Well . . . it's too late now." He shoved the blue lump of calomel into his bag and snapped it shut. He started walking back toward his office. Phoebe followed.

"You know what a wonderful nurse Julia is, but Reverend Greene won't let her be one. He wants to make her into what he wants her to be. She shouldn't marry him."

When the doctor reached his office, Phoebe followed him inside. He looked cornered, as if he wanted to run but had no place to go. "Don't you have work to do?" he asked.

"Julia cares for you, Dr. McGrath. She told me she did."

He stared at her. "When did she tell you that?"

"When she came to see me today. But she's been hiding the way she feels all this time because she thinks you're married." Phoebe gestured to the photograph on his desk. "Everybody thought you were. And we thought all those letters were from your wife."

For a long moment she saw hope flicker in his eyes, as if he could almost believe he might be happy again. Then it passed, replaced by pain. "I killed my wife, Phoebe. I won't marry again."

"You didn't kill your wife. You were trying to help people, to save lives. The same as when I had to kill that man to save Julia's life. You didn't want your wife to die any more than I wanted Otis Whitney to die. Neither one of us set out to do it on purpose. It just happened. I had to ask God to forgive me, and then I had to forgive myself. So do you."

"Asking forgiveness won't change the past."

"No, but you're letting the past ruin today and tomorrow. None of us are the same people we were before the war. God can make us into new people if we ask Him to. Remember?"

"I'm sure God never intended salvation for the likes of me," he said, dropping into his chair. "I certainly don't deserve it."

"You're wrong. If everybody in that shantytown was healthy, you'd have no reason to go there, would you? Jesus said it wasn't the good, healthy people who needed a physician but the sick ones."

He didn't look up. Phoebe was about to go out the door and leave him alone when she suddenly turned back. "If you love Julia, fight for her, Dr. McGrath."

"How?" he asked hoarsely.

"She's staying at that congressman's house. You should go talk to her. Don't let her make a mistake and marry the preacher."

"It's her life. I have no right to interfere."

"You don't have to interfere, just tell her the truth. Tell her that your wife died four years ago. Tell her that you love her. Then let her make up her own mind."

Chapter Twenty-seven

Washington City
May 1865

On Julia's last night in Washington, Congressman Rhodes hosted a dinner party for her and her family. It was a beautiful, elegant affair, with music and fine food and plenty of laughter—as if joy had finally returned to everyone's life now that the war had ended. It reminded Julia of the party she'd attended here three years ago, the night she'd met Hiram Stone—except that tonight her escort was Nathaniel. She saw the love and admiration in his eyes when she descended the stairs in her beautiful new ball gown. And when he seemed reluctant to leave her side for a single moment, her doubts about their upcoming marriage slowly began to evaporate like melting snow.

Late in the evening, as she sat at the dinner table finishing a seven-course meal, the congressman's servant tiptoed into the dining room and tapped Julia on the shoulder. "Excuse me, Miss Hoffman. There is a gentleman at the door asking to speak with you."

"Did he give his name?" Nathaniel asked before Julia could reply.

"Yes, sir. James McGrath."

Julia rose to her feet in alarm. "I hope nothing has happened to Phoebe!" Nathaniel followed her as she hurried to the front hallway.

James stood alone in the foyer where the servant had left him.

His auburn hair was neatly combed, his clothes pressed and tidy for once, as if he'd come to attend the dinner, too. Something inside Julia stirred at the sight of him, and she felt an ache that she didn't understand. She moved closer to Nathaniel, fighting the urge to run to James. She didn't trust herself to speak.

"What can we do for you, Doctor?" Nathaniel asked.

James hesitated. "I'd like a word with Julia, if I may."

"Miss Hoffman and I are engaged to be married," he said pleasantly. "Anything you have to say to her can be said in front of me."

"I'd prefer to speak to her in private." James gestured to the congressman's study.

"Your manners are sorely lacking, Doctor. In polite society, young ladies don't speak to gentlemen behind closed doors. And gentlemen don't barge into private homes unannounced and uninvited at dinnertime. Is this an emergency?"

"No, but—"

"Has something happened to Miss Bigelow?"

"No."

"Then kindly be brief. You're interrupting Julia's dinner."

"All right," he sighed. "But I'm not entirely sure whom I should address." He looked from Nathaniel to Julia and back again. "I once took my daughter to see a puppet show, and while it appeared that the characters were having their say, in reality the puppet master was doing all the talking for them."

"I beg your pardon," Nathaniel said.

"You do Julia a huge disservice by speaking for her, Reverend. Believe me, she does very well speaking for herself. She has told me exactly what she thinks on several occasions."

"I find your attitude and your conversation extremely insulting. Please leave." Nathaniel gestured to the door, but James didn't move.

"The war is over, Greene. Times have changed. Women have conquered new territory and have found new roles for themselves—besides as our 'helpmeet.' They've led the abolition movement, raised thousands of dollars for relief agencies, worked as nurses, run their families' farms and businesses. Several women even became successful spies because men were too dense to believe a woman could pull the wool over their eyes. And I know at least one brave woman who put on a uniform and fought as a soldier. The war changed these women. They proved that they are more than pretty faces. How can they be content to let us order them around again?"

"Are you finished?"

"No. Let me ask you this—have you given any thought to what Julia's role will be after she becomes your wife?"

"Of course I have, and so has Julia. We've discussed the duties that a minister's wife is expected to perform, and—"

"What if she doesn't want to perform those duties? What if there are other things she'd rather do?"

"Don't be absurd. What more could she possibly want? The war is over; there is no longer any need for nurses."

Julia heard Nathaniel speaking for her, putting words in her mouth as James had accused him of doing, but she was too confused and shaken to think clearly.

"I had expectations for my wife, too," James said. "She was to fill the role of a doctor's wife. But Ellen was very unhappy playing that part. She wasn't cut out for helping me treat patients. She did it, of course, because I expected her to. Our marriage vows demanded that she obey me . . . and my expectations caused her death."

His words rocked through Julia like a bomb blast. "Your wife is dead?" she breathed.

"Yes. She helped me treat typhoid patients during an outbreak. She became ill herself and died." James had been speaking calmly, matter-of-factly, until now. For the first time, his voice faltered. "Ellen didn't want to help me. She was always afraid that she would become ill, especially after Kate was born. But I made her do it. After all, the husband is the head of the household, isn't he, Reverend? The wife must submit to his authority, isn't that right?"

"I'm very sorry for your loss," Nathaniel said stiffly. "But I hardly think a minister's wife will be exposed to the same risks—"

"You're not nearly as sorry as I am," James said quietly. "You know what the worst part is? I never bothered to ask Ellen what she wanted to do. I saw her the same way you and every other man sees his wife—as an extension of himself. We believe that women couldn't possibly want anything more than to be married to us, to live in our homes, to take care of us and support our careers. Sound familiar, Reverend? Before you ask Julia to give up all of her own desires to fit into your life, why don't you ask her what she really wants to do?"

Nathaniel didn't reply. He seemed too angry to speak—or perhaps too afraid of losing control. As Julia had listened to James, she felt as if she were running several yards behind him, trying to catch up. She still hadn't absorbed the truth that he had been a widower all this time. The feelings she'd had toward him hadn't been shameful at all.

"I thought I loved my wife," James said, "but it was a very selfish kind of love, based solely on what she could give me. That's what you have for Julia. You want to make her into what you want her to be, then keep her all to yourself, possessing her as your very own, using her to complete yourself. But believe it or not, I know Scripture, too—it says that husbands should love their wives in the same way that Christ loved the church and gave himself up for her. You're not giving up anything for her. Julia is making all the sacrifices—and you'll end up killing her."

Nathaniel seemed to vibrate with the anger he was struggling to control. "I would never harm a hair on her head—"

"Maybe not physically, like I did, but you'll destroy that wonderful stubborn spirit that's uniquely hers. She's strong-willed, outspoken, obstinate at times—hardly ideal qualities for a minister's wife, wouldn't you say? So rather than seeing these as good qualities, you'll try to control them and snuff them out, the way you're silencing her right now."

James took a step closer to Nathaniel, challenging him. "I wish you could have seen Julia scrubbing laundry with her head held high. Or helping me perform surgery, seeing bone and muscle and blood, but never flinching because she knew that lives depended on her. That's the strength of character she has. And that's exactly what you want to destroy in her. I'd hate for that to happen."

Nathaniel finally seemed to have reached his limit. He planted his hand in the middle of James' chest and shoved him backward. "What gives you the right to barge in here and interfere in our private affairs? What makes you think Julia's marriage is any of your business?" He shoved him again.

"Because I'm in love with her."

"How dare you!" Nathaniel shouted. Julia was too stunned to speak.

"That's what I came here to tell her—in private. But you insisted on hearing it, too. It's because I love her that I want what's best for her. If she decides you're the best husband for her—fine, so be it. But you'd better make sure you treat her right, Greene. She deserves it. She is one of the strongest, most unselfish women I've ever met."

Tears came to Julia's eyes as she remembered standing in this very hallway and hearing Nathaniel describe her as shallow, spoiled, and unbearably self-absorbed. She wanted desperately to say something to James, but Nathaniel was so furious with him that she was afraid they would come to blows if this went on much longer.

Nathaniel shoved James backward once again. "Leave!" he shouted. "And don't you dare come near Julia again!"

James' eyes met hers. "Is that what you want, Julia?"

She didn't have time to answer him. Nathaniel grabbed James by the arm, yanked open the door, and shoved him through it. "Julia is in love with me. She wants what I want, and I want you to get out!" He slammed the door closed behind him.

The commotion drew the congressman, Julia's father, and two of the other men into the foyer. "Is everything all right?" Rhodes asked. "What in heaven's name is going on out here?"

"Nothing," Nathaniel said. "Everything's fine, the caller is gone. He was an obnoxious fellow, and I'm afraid I had to be a bit forceful in order to get rid of him. Please assure the women that everything is all right. We'll join you in a moment."

Julia had never seen Nathaniel so angry. She stared at him as if he were a stranger. "I'm glad you're going home tomorrow," he finally said. "That man is dangerous. The safest thing to do is to stay far away from him."

Julia couldn't erase the image of Nathaniel shoving James backward, throwing him out the door, and she wondered which man was more dangerous. "You didn't have to treat him so badly. He wasn't trying to hurt me."

"I treated *him* badly? Did you hear the accusations he was making?"

"James would never hurt me."

Something in Nathaniel's attitude seemed to shift. He looked at Julia as if he'd suddenly decided that she was the enemy. "Did you know he felt this way about you?"

"He . . . he has never declared his feelings before tonight," she said. But that wasn't the whole truth. She'd known exactly how James felt about her since the night he'd kissed her. She couldn't meet Nathaniel's gaze. He noticed.

"Look at me, Julia," he said, lifting her chin. "How does it happen that he has these feelings for you? A man doesn't fall in love without a reason."

"Are you accusing me—?"

"You must have done something to make him think he's in love with you."

"What are you saying?"

"This isn't the first time, remember? There was that coarse fellow in City Point who wanted you, too. Whether you realize it or not, you are doing something to attract a very unsavory type of man."

"James is not unsavory. He—"

"Perhaps you aren't aware of his past, but that man is a suspect in a murder case."

Julia opened her mouth to defend James but knew that if she did, her feelings for him would spill out into the open. Nathaniel was glaring at her, accusing her. If she stayed with him a moment longer she would end up saying things she was sorry for, things she hadn't finished thinking through yet.

"I don't care at all for the way you're speaking to me," she said, her voice trembling. "Please give my apologies to Mrs. Rhodes. I don't feel well. I'm going to bed."

"Julia! We are not finished!"

"Yes, we are. Good night, Nathaniel."

It took Julia a long time to stop shaking. When her mother came upstairs to check on her, Julia told her she had a headache.

She allowed the servants to help her take off her party gown and unpin her hair. Mrs. Rhodes offered her some laudanum to help her sleep. Julia accepted the pills just to get rid of her, but she didn't swallow them.

She lay on her bed in the dark for a long time, listening to the sounds of the party below and thinking about everything that James had said. She understood now why he no longer wore his wedding ring. He was free to tell her that he loved her. She remembered the tender expression on his face when he'd spoken the words tonight, and she knew that he'd been about to tell her the same thing in City Point last summer before she'd stopped him.

He had called her strong-willed, outspoken, obstinate. She was all of those things. And in the end, those words touched Julia's heart more than James' declaration of love. He didn't want to change her, the way Nathaniel did. James saw her for what she was, and he loved her regardless.

Julia climbed out of bed and put on one of her plainer dresses, without hoops. She heaped pillows beneath her covers to make it appear that she was asleep, then took the servants' stairs down to the back entrance. She hurried outside to the stable in the dark to find the Rhodes' coachman.

"I need to go to Fairfield Hospital right away," she told him. "Kindly get a carriage ready for me." Her voice and her demeanor carried authority. The man never questioned the unusual request or the lateness of the hour.

The hospital looked dark and deserted when she arrived. "Wait here," she told the driver. "I'll be right back." Julia didn't expect to find James at the hospital. She had no idea where he lived, but she assumed that someone had to know where to find him in case of an emergency. The front door had been locked for the night. Julia pounded on it as hard as she could and was very surprised when Phoebe opened the door.

"What are you doing here?" Julia asked.

"I live here. Dr. McGrath fixed me a room because there wasn't no place to rent in the whole city. What are *you* doing here?"

"I need to talk to Dr. McGrath."

"He ain't here. He's probably at the shantytown, where Belle and Loretta used to live."

"Thanks." Julia turned to hurry away, but Phoebe grabbed her arm to stop her.

"Whoa! Hold on! He's fighting a typhoid fever epidemic. He don't want me helping him for fear I'll catch it—and he sure as shooting won't want you there. You'd better come back tomorrow."

Julia knew she could never wait until morning. She had let Nathaniel throw James out of the house without saying a word to stop him. James had no idea how she felt about him. "Okay, Phoebe. I'll come back tomorrow," she said. But she hurried down the steps to the carriage and gave the coachman directions to the shantytown.

The driver hesitated. "That's a pretty rough part of town, miss."

"I'll be perfectly safe. I've visited there before. Kindly stop arguing and drive."

The jumbled cluster of shacks and lean-tos had tripled in size since Julia had last seen them. In the dim light of a few flickering campfires, the piles of wreckage that served as houses looked like a vision from a nightmare. The stench of death hit her as soon as she stepped from the carriage.

"You may return home," she told the driver. James would have no choice but to let her stay and work.

"Miss, I never should have brought you here in the first place," the coachman said. "Please, get back in and let me take you home. I'll lose my job for sure."

"Go home, put the carriage in the stable, and go to bed. No one will know I'm missing until morning—and I won't tell a soul that you drove me here." She turned and strode toward the camp.

The first people she stumbled upon were three young Negro men hunched around a smoky fire, sharing a bottle of whiskey. They eyed her from head to toe, then one of them stood. "Lady, you must be lost for sure!" She knew by the way they laughed that they were all drunk.

For a terrible moment, Julia felt the same paralyzing fear that had seized her when Otis Whitney had grabbed her from behind and clamped his hand over her mouth. She had been helpless, unable to fight him off as he'd dragged her down into the bushes and tried to rape her. This time there were three men, all much stronger than she was. She had been a fool to come here.

"I'm not lost," she somehow managed to say. "I'm a nurse. I'm looking for Dr. McGrath. I've come to help him."

The stranger stared at her as if she had spoken a foreign language and he was struggling to translate it. Then he pointed to a nearby shack built from packing crates. It was lit from inside by a lantern. "He's in there, taking care of Ida and her little ones."

"Thank you." She walked toward the shack on rubbery legs.

Inside, a half dozen feverish children lay sprawled on the floor beside their mother. James knelt in the dirt with a limp toddler in his arms, pounding the child's back to break up the phlegm in her lungs. He looked up and saw Julia.

"Don't come in here!" he yelled. "Get out! Get out!"

Still shaken from her memories of Otis, Julia lashed back. "What gives you the right to order me around? This isn't your hospital. I have as much right to work here as you do."

"Please, Julia, it's too dangerous. This is a typhoid epidemic."

"It's my life," she said quietly. "I have as much right to risk it as you do to risk yours." They stared at each other without speaking. But Julia knew that they'd reached an understanding, just the same. "Tell me what to do," she said.

They worked side by side all night. James showed her how he diagnosed typhoid by the characteristic red skin lesions on the patient's chest and abdomen. She helped him dispense calomel to help stop the diarrhea, and potassium nitrate and Dover's powders to induce sweating and bring down their fevers. In some cases, the typhoid had developed into bronchitis and pneumonia. Julia helped him hold feverish children over pans of steaming water to ease their breathing. Neither of them mentioned Nathaniel Greene or spoke of what had happened earlier that evening. It seemed like a lifetime ago.

At dawn, James lifted a sleeping infant from Julia's arms and helped her to her feet. "Come on," he said gently. "We've done all we can. It's time to go home."

Neither of them spoke as they picked their way through the

debris of shantytown. As she walked down the alley toward the main street beside James, Julia felt as if she was returning to another world. The smell and the despair still clung to her, and she longed for a hot bath and several hours' sleep. James looked just as weary. He had opened his heart to her at the congressman's house, but now his carefully constructed walls were back in place again. She knew it was up to her to help him dismantle them.

"What are your plans now that the war is over, James?"

He took a moment to reply. "I've accepted a staff position at another army hospital here in Washington. There are a lot of soldiers who still face a long rehabilitation. And the prisoners of war are in terrible condition, too. Then there are the former slaves. . . . I'll still be needed here for a while."

"Will your hospital need nurses, by any chance?"

He stopped walking. "Why?"

She smiled slightly. "It seems I've just broken my engagement—again. And my father will probably disown me, too, when he learns that I stayed out all night. I could use a job."

"Why would you stay here in Washington? Your home is in Philadelphia."

"The doctor I'm in love with is here in Washington."

He closed his eyes for a long moment, then started walking again. "You came to my hospital in Washington with your chin held high, so stubborn, so determined to be a nurse. I did a cruel thing to you, using that patient with gangrene. Yet you stayed, even though I did my best to get rid of you. I think I knew I would fall in love with you if you stayed. And that's exactly what happened. The night your first patient died and you gave up your elegant evening to come and sit with him . . . I watched you from the hallway. You looked so beautiful, spoke so tenderly to the boy. . . . Then you flew into my arms, and I held you close, and I was sure my heart would break from loving you."

"You did a very good job of pushing me away."

"Sparks and gunpowder, *Mrs.* Hoffman. I believed you were a married woman."

"Would you have hired me if I'd told you the truth?"

"Never."

"That's why I lied."

He stopped walking when they reached the corner and looked down at her. "I have very little to offer you, Julia. I inherited a modest sum of money from Eldon Tyler—compensation, I suppose, for ruining my life. But other than that . . . I know I'm not as good-looking as your minister, and I've been told that I'm rude and disagreeable and mean-tempered. I have a shady past and an uncertain future as I try to start all over again and build a new practice. I also have a seven-year-old daughter I barely know, who's a little frightened of me, I'm sorry to say. I was not a very good husband the first time—"

"Does that mean there might be a second time?" she asked.

"Only if you'll say yes."

"Yes."

He set his medical bag down on the sidewalk and pulled her into his arms, drawing her close. He didn't seem to care that they were on a Washington street at dawn or that a handful of people and carriages were scurrying past.

"That night in Fredericksburg," James said, "when the sky was on fire and we kissed . . . I believed you were married, and I wanted to die of shame afterward."

"I thought you were, too."

He gently caressed her face as she looked up at him. "But there's no need to feel guilty this time, is there?"

"None at all," she whispered.

Bone Hollow, West Virginia
July 1865

Phoebe walked all the way down the long, dusty road from Bone Hollow to her family's cabin, wondering what she would find. Nobody in town had paid her any mind, so she'd walked straight on through it and headed home, hoping that at least one of her brothers would be there. When she got within sight of the place and saw Jack sitting on the front steps, her eyes filled with tears. She was so happy to see him that she wanted to run, but the sun was hot and Phoebe was tired from the long walk home. She lifted her hand and waved instead.

Jack stared at her as if he were seeing a ghost, then grabbed his crutches and scrambled to stand up, hobbling down the road to meet her. His left pant leg was empty below his knee. "Can that be my baby sister . . . Ike. . . ?"

"Yeah, it's me, Jack. How you doing?" They hugged each other awkwardly, Jack's crutches getting in the way. It was the first time she could ever recall having her arms around him when they weren't wrestling or fighting with each other.

"We thought you fell off the edge of the world." Jack's voice sounded husky.

"What do you mean 'we'? Is Junior here, too?"

"Yeah, he's out plowing. He came home from the war all in one piece, which is more than I can say for myself. Hey, are you crying, Ike?"

"So what?" she said, wiping her fist across her face. "I'm a girl, in case you ain't noticed. And girls can cry if they've a mind to."

"I can't believe you're really home," Jack murmured. "Wait 'til Junior sees you. He won't believe his eyes. You're all grown up . . . and you're a girl!"

"What'd you think I was?"

Jack shrugged. "One of us."

Junior seemed tickled to see Phoebe when he came in at noon for his lunch. He grinned from ear to ear at her and gave her a sweaty hug. They sat down to the lunch Jack had fixed, and Phoebe told them where she'd been for the last few years and what she'd been up to. They all grew quiet when she told them about Willard and how she'd been with him when he died at Chancellorsville.

"The doctor couldn't do nothing for him," she said. "But at least he didn't have to die all alone."

They ate in silence for several minutes, then Junior said, "Speaking of doctors, one of them come by a couple times looking for you."

"For *me*?" Phoebe asked in surprise.

"Yeah. What was his name again, Jack?"

"I don't know . . . Morgan . . . Morris. . . ?"

Phoebe nearly dropped her fork. "Daniel Morrison?"

"That's him. Nice fella. Only I gotta say, he looks like somebody built him out of spare parts and kindling wood."

Phoege remembered the gangly Rebel doctor she had met in Gettysburg. But he couldn't have been wearing his Confederate uniform or her brothers would have run him off with the shotgun. Why on earth had he come here to see her? She could feel the heat rushing to her face and hoped her brothers didn't notice. They would tease her from now until next Christmas.

"What did he want?" she finally asked.

"I dunno," Jack said. "But he said he'd be back. Said he's gonna see about getting me a leg made out of cork. Can you picture that?"

"I've seen stranger things," Phoebe said.

By the end of the week, Phoebe was feeling restless again. She'd promised Ma Wilson that she'd come back for a visit, and now that she knew her brothers were okay, she was eager to be on the move. Jack was fixing to drive into Bone Hollow later that day, so she packed her things and got ready to hitch a ride with him.

She was standing on the cabin steps with her satchel in her hand when Dr. Daniel Morrison drove right up to her cabin in his own horse and buggy.

"Good morning, Miss Bigelow," he said, sweeping off his hat. "Are you coming or going?"

"I'm fixing to go. I promised someone up in Pennsylvania I'd go see them."

He jumped down from his rig and stood in front of her, his hands on his hips. "Well, how am I gonna court you if you go running off again?"

"You come here to court me?"

"I sure ain't here to court your ornery brothers."

Phoebe knew that she was blushing, but she couldn't seem to do anything about it. "There're plenty of other girls in Morgan County to court," she said. "Berkeley County, too, for that matter."

"I told you, I'm partial to pretty gals with yellow hair."

Phoebe couldn't speak. He had called her pretty. Her heart began to pound just like it used to do sometimes when she was with Ted. She wished Dr. McGrath was here so she could ask him what was wrong with her, find out if she had something fatal. She looked up at Daniel Morrison and remembered that he was a doctor, too. But the thought of asking him made her heart beat faster still.

"Tell me something," Dr. Morrison said, interrupting her thoughts. "Did you like being a nurse, or are you all through with that now that the war's over?"

"I liked it real fine. I don't know what I'm gonna do with myself now."

"Well, I watched you at Gettysburg, and you were real good at it. I think we'd make a good team, me being a country doctor and all. I could use a good nurse. And I think I'd probably grow on you once you decide to forgive me for being a Rebel and give me half a chance."

Phoebe looked away, gazing into the woods beyond her cabin for a long moment. "I fell in love with a fella during the war," she finally said. "He got killed."

"I'm sorry . . . I really am," he said softly. "Does that mean you're never going to fall in love again?"

"I don't know. He would want me to. Ted would tell me to live my life and be happy."

"Well, do you think I could ever measure up to him?"

Phoebe glanced up at Dr. Morrison and couldn't help smiling when she pictured Ted standing alongside him. "You already got him beat by about twenty inches."

Daniel hitched himself up straight so he would stand even taller. "That's real good news for me, then, isn't it?"

She wanted to smile, to let down her guard, but she was afraid. She frowned and gestured to her satchel. "Listen, I promised Ted's mother I would come back and see her, let her know I was okay. And then I was planning to go look up his grandmother who lives on a plantation down south. It might be a couple of weeks before I get back."

"Want some company?"

"You want to come with me? You don't even know where I'm going."

"Don't matter. Maybe we can get to know each other better along the way."

Phoebe felt afraid. It was safer being alone, safer not to risk falling in love with someone and losing him again. "I been taking care of myself for a long time, you know. I'm used to traveling alone."

"Well, I can see that plain as day. But that isn't why I want to tag along."

"How come, then?"

"The war showed me how short life is. I just wasted four years of it, and I don't aim to waste any more. I aim to live." He grinned, and his smile was so warm and friendly that something inside her melted a little. She thought of Ted's grin.

Then she thought of Dr. McGrath and knew she was wrong to close herself off to people the way he had after his wife died. He had finally found love again with Julia. Maybe she could find it, too.

"You know, you're like a tick on a dog," she told Daniel. "Awful hard to shake off."

"That's the nicest thing a gal ever said to me," he teased.

"If you want to tag along, I don't reckon I can stop you," she said, trying to sound gruff.

"You keep sweet-talking that way, Phoebe Bigelow, I'll be falling in love with you before we cross the state line."

He made her smile again, in spite of all her efforts not to. "You ain't half bad for a Rebel," she told him.

Dr. Daniel Morrison started to laugh—and he laughed so joyously that Phoebe just couldn't help laughing along with him.